"One of the contemporary romance genre's most popular authors!"
—*Rave Reviews*

TWO UNFORGETTABLE ROMANCES IN ONE LOW-COST VOLUME!

OUT OF CONTROL
A WINNING COMBINATION
LORI COPELAND

Author of More Than Six Million Books in Print!

OUT OF CONTROL

"Just what did you tell Nathan you'd like to do to me?"

Price stopped Erin with a masterful kiss. When she was finally able to catch her breath, Erin asked again, "What did you tell him?"

"Promise you won't get mad?" Price grinned cockily.

"I won't get mad."

He leaned over and pulled her close, rubbing against her suggestively as he whispered in her ear.

"Good heavens, Price! You are unbelievable!"

A WINNING COMBINATION

"I really wish we didn't have to face a long drawn-out battle over the baby, Nicholas," Kayla replied firmly.

"We don't. All you have to do is be reasonable."

"Reasonable? What you mean is, all I have to do is give up my baby."

"No, I didn't say that. There are other alternatives."

"Marriage?"

"That was one." The stubborn muscle of Nick's jaw was working as he stared past her. "But you've ruled that out!"

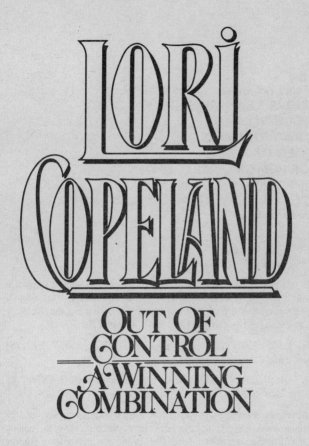

LORI COPELAND

OUT OF CONTROL
A WINNING COMBINATION

LOVE SPELL NEW YORK CITY

LOVE SPELL®

May 1994

Published by

Dorchester Publishing Co., Inc.
276 Fifth Avenue
New York, NY 10001

Printed in the United States of America.

OUT OF CONTROL

To my editor, Lydia E. Paglio, for her marvelous patience and understanding with a new writer.

CHAPTER ONE

"Huntwey fwushed that ball down the toilet again!" Holly Daniels crossed her dainty five-year-old arms in an irritated stance and glared at her honorary aunt.

"Oh, Holly! Not again. Couldn't you have stopped him?" Erin closed her eyes in weary frustration, her headache growing steadily worse. Since she had arrived yesterday to baby-sit with the twins while her best friend, Brenda, and her husband fled gratefully on a well-earned vacation, Huntley had done his best to upset the normal routine of the household. If what Holly said was true, this would be the second time today that the monstrous other half of the adorable little girl standing before her had flushed a ball down the commode, then stood back in calm fascination to watch the water seep nastily over the white porcelain rim.

"*I* told him that plumwers don't come cheap now days," Holly said in a very adult miffed tone, only her lisping speech marring her image, "but he only *defied* me again!"

Erin put down the potato she was peeling for their dinner and tramped agitatedly down the hall to the twins' bedroom. The distinct sound of water overflowing in the small bath reached her ears as she stepped into the room. Huntley looked up from his perch in the middle of the bed, a Captain Marvel comic book clutched in his small chubby hand, and smiled serenely up at her.

"I'm afraid this is one of my bad days, Aunt Erin! The ball fell out of my hand and dropped in there again." He pointed toward the sound of dribbling water, his round brown eyes peeping earnestly back at her from behind the large black horn-rim glasses.

With a mute appeal to heaven for self-control, Erin glowered at him and said in a strident voice, "Are you *sure* it slipped, Huntley, or was it perhaps *thrown* in there again?" Her wide gray eyes pinned him to the bed uncomfortably.

"Nope! It slipped, I'm sure." His eyes dropped self-consciously back to his comic book, trying to ignore her penetrating gaze.

"You know, if you were my little boy, I'm afraid I'd have to paddle you for telling stories," Erin told him ominously as she walked past his bed and on into the bathroom. She flinched as her feet sloshed through the deepening puddle of water on the carpeted floor. The one failing that Brenda and Nathan Daniels had, in her opinion, was that they had not disciplined the twins in any way. Brenda had always been a softhearted person, the mere thought of violence sending her into a tizzy. Nathan, on the other hand, had started out to be firm with the children, but it would upset Brenda to the point of hysteria if he threatened to take action with either of them, so he had stopped putting forth the effort. The result sat in the middle of the bed, calmly chewing on a wad of bubble gum that would choke a horse, while his twin came to stand in the doorway to mouth a silent but gleeful "I told you so" to her brother.

Erin stared at the overflowing commode bitterly. It was definitely in need of a plumber again. She sighed as she reached for towels to mop up some of the water. Between their vacation and the plumbing bills, Brenda and Nathan would have to eat hamburger for the rest of the year!

"You spit that gum out of your mouth, Huntley, and

12

help Holly pick up all the toys you have flung about the living room. As soon as I get this cleaned up and the plumber called"—Erin turned to peep through the bathroom door pointedly at the small boy—"*again,*" she emphasized, "then we are going to eat dinner. And Huntley, it seems I didn't make myself clear this morning . . . If you throw that ball down this toilet *one more time,* I personally will grant you no mercy. You will be spanked and put to bed without your dinner. Is that perfectly clear?"

Solemn dark eyes gaped back up at her, the dire warning finding fertile ground. "I won't, Aunt Erin," he promised earnestly.

As she got down on her hands and knees to sop the water up, Erin heard the twins scurrying out of the room to head for safer ground. It wasn't that they were not totally adorable children, because they most assuredly were. It was hard not to pick them up and hug them a hundred times a day when they were not misbehaving. Holly was the least trouble of the two, a perfect lady most times, usually mortified by her brother's actions, but at other times she had been known to be the ringleader of some of their capers, standing back and looking smug when Huntley was chastised for them. Erin stood up to wring the heavy towel out in the sink. Her eyes were drawn to the reflection in the mirror, and she stared back at Erin Cecile Holmes. No ravishing, sumptuous face stared back at her. No slender, willowy curves met her eyes . . . just a very ordinary twenty-five-year-old face. She studied her soft, naturally curly brown hair, which was styled in a casual pixie cut. Her eyes were a deep pearl gray, and she had a slightly tilted perky nose with just a light smattering of freckles that popped out when she had been in the sun too long, giving her the appearance of a fresh, healthy girl-next-door type. Her mouth was neither too full nor too thin. It was just a normal mouth, or so she thought. Actually Erin was a very attractive woman, but she had convinced herself long ago that she had to work harder than most women to come across as such. All her life she had wished that she had the slim figure and lovely features of her best friend, Brenda, but instead she contented herself with the fact that she had a better personality. By the time they were in their senior year of school, the boys flocked to Brenda in droves, while Erin hung back. The boys always came to cry on her shoulder when Brenda threw them over for a new and more exciting candidate. Erin had always had a heart of pure gold, taking them under her wing, boosting their egos back to the pre-Brenda era and sending them on their way out into the cold cruel world in search of true romance once again. She had never resented her role in life—that is, not until Quinn Adams had entered the scene.

Quinn was a lot older than Brenda and Erin. His smooth, suave good looks made Erin stand in the background and dream young-girlish dreams of what it would be like to catch the eye of such a sophisticated and worldly man. Of course, she never really believed that someone like Quinn would ever look at her twice. And she was right; he didn't. Not at first. His deep, smoldering gaze fell on Brenda, and from then on they dated steadily for several months. If Erin was at Brenda's house when Quinn came to pick Brenda up for a date, Erin would stare out Brenda's window and watch the happy couple walk to the shiny new red convertible and get in, laughing together about some private joke. They would speed away happily into the night, with Brenda molded to Quinn's tall form. Erin would watch them disappear before turning away from the window despondently. It wasn't that she didn't wish Brenda all the happiness in the world; it was simply that she wished that it could be her beside Quinn just once!

Erin sighed as she gathered the wet towels and dropped them in the hamper, then started back to the kitchen. She reached up to touch her forehead, her face feeling hot and flushed. She could hear the petty squabbling of the twins as they worked diligently at restoring order to the family room, with Holly reminding Huntley that he had done the majority of the damage. After checking on the meat loaf she had put in the oven shortly before the last interruption and being satisfied that it was coming along nicely, she made the second call of the day to the plumber, then resumed peeling the potatoes. Against her will, her mind drifted back to the year she was nineteen . . . the year Brenda had married Nathan.

Brenda had graduated the year before her, and she and Quinn still continued to see each other regularly until one day Quinn's older brother, Nathan, who had just been discharged from the service, came home. Both brothers had the same handsome features and were over six feet tall, with wavy dark brown hair, their skin a dark golden bronze, but Nathan's eyes were blue, and Quinn's eyes were a light shade of green. Suddenly it was Nathan who stood on the doorstep to claim Brenda every night. As he would reach out to take her hand, their eyes would meet and the glow that surrounded Brenda seemed to light up the room. Although Nathan was indeed quite handsome, Erin couldn't believe Brenda would throw Quinn over for him.

Erin used to lie in bed at night and dream of what it would be like to be kissed by Quinn. Her young, inquisitive body would shiver in eager anticipation as she imagined him sweeping her into his arms and declaring his love for her. In her dreams she would coolly spurn his ardent advances until he was driven almost mad from wanting her. Finally, in a humane gesture of undeniable goodness, she would relent and ease his agony. It would be late when she finally dozed off, holding her pillow tight against her as she imagined Quinn lying in her arms, sated, happy and hers. Foolish, childish dreams.

Nathan and Brenda's wedding day had not only

changed their lives, it had also changed Erin's. In one short day she went from being an innocent, dreaming girl to a disheartened, frightened woman. Her foolish dream had come true. She had lain in Quinn's arms, and it was all—and more—that she had ever hoped for.

The sound of the cat's high-pitched scream made the paring knife slip from her hands as she whirled and ran into the family room. Huntley was holding a screeching, pawing, spitting cat upside down by the tail while he stood in the middle of the coffee table, his face a stern, determined mask. The cat flailed the air in panic as he hung over the bowl that housed the two goldfish swimming around lazily in the still waters.

"*Huntley Daniels!* Drop that cat instantly!" Erin bellowed, bounding down the two steps that led into the comfortable family room, her nerves stretched taut from the petrified wails coming from the furry feline.

The cat landed hastily with a thump on the table. Springing shakily to his feet, he ran for cover, his yellow body barely a blurred streak as he bolted past a harried Erin.

"He was trying to eat Buck Rogers," Huntley defended swiftly, jumping down off the table nimbly. He ran over to peer intently at the two fish in the bowl. "If he'd eat Cinderella, I wouldn't care, but he was after Buck!" he added heatedly.

"I wouldn't let him eat Cindewella!" Holly shrieked, coming over to give him a sound push. "That dumb old cat's not supposed to be in the house anyway. I'm going to tell Mama when she gets back," she vowed passionately. Her brown eyes were indignant at the prospect of the cat's choice of dinner.

"Both of you just hush!" Erin walked over and took them firmly in hand. "Now why don't you just watch cartoons until I finish making dinner. Then I'll play a game with you," she promised desperately. Anything to restore some peace and quiet. "Do *not* let the cat in again" —she looked at Huntley—"or the dog, or your pet rabbit. Got it?"

"When's Mommy and Daddy coming back?" He wasn't very discreet about whose authority he preferred.

"Not for a while," Erin told him glumly as she switched the TV set on to a loud cartoon. "Dinner will be ready in thirty minutes. See if you can sit here and stay out of trouble that long."

The twins settled back on their bean-bag seats and dismissed her with an impatient glare. If it wasn't for the color of their eyes, Erin would swear she was confronting their uncle Quinn. She had seen the same angry expression on his face when she had done something to displease him. She turned back to the twice-delayed dinner with a heavy heart. That had always been one of the big problems between her and Quinn. She had always upset him when she never meant to. After Brenda and Nathan had announced their engagement, he had started coming around to see her. Erin was never exactly sure why, but she had just assumed she was needed in the crying-shoulder category once again. Although Quinn had never said so, she knew deep down that he was resentful that Brenda had chosen his brother over him. Erin, with her soft heart, tried to make it up to him, building his ego, encouraging him to find someone new. At times it seemed to irritate rather than soothe him when Erin would try her "mother" routine. Although she constantly reminded herself that Quinn would never be seriously attracted to her, she still couldn't keep herself from hoping . . . hoping that someday *she* would be the one beside him. But when reality returned, Erin knew that somewhere in the not-too-distant future another ravishing beauty would capture his attention and that would be the end of her. Quinn Daniels would never be interested in a plain, uninteresting, twenty-pounds-overweight Erin Holmes. She was a lot of things to a lot of people, but she was definitely no dummy!

She smiled grimly to herself as she opened a package of broccoli and put it into the microwave oven. Well, almost no dummy, she thought. Any young girl with stars in her eyes could have made the same mistake she had. It had been six years ago when she had first met him. Erin bit her lower lip as she set the timer and closed the door.

The night she finally succumbed to Quinn's amorous advances had been a magical fairy tale evening for Erin. Positive that Quinn had finally seen the light, she was sure marriage to the man of her dreams was now a mere matter of time. Unfortunately, Quinn hadn't seen that night in quite the same manner. He left town the following morning, leaving a bitter and disillusioned Erin in his wake—a young, inexperienced girl who now felt very cheated, very used. She hadn't seen or heard from him again until a little over a year ago, when he had casually breezed back into town and her life. At first she fought her still-overwhelming attraction to him, telling herself over and over that she was ten times the fool for even giving him the time of day after what he had pulled on her so many years ago. But his charm and persistence won out, and slowly she found herself caught up in his alluring web. Once more her life and thoughts revolved around Quinn Daniels. For several months she allowed herself to dream and believe once again that she would one day be his wife and they would have a marriage like Brenda and Nathan's: perfect. That was what she wanted—the perfect marriage.

It didn't take long for Quinn to rob her of all her hopes and dreams. His eyes began to rove, and it wasn't very long before Erin saw the hopelessness of being involved with a man who would never be satisfied with just one woman. For Quinn there would always be an endless succession of women. Nathan and Quinn Daniels were as different as black and white.

Six months ago she had made the final break with Quinn, and he had left the country to work with an oil company in Saudi Arabia. Erin refused to let herself become bitter and disillusioned. Somewhere in this big wide world was the perfect man to fit her idea of the perfect marriage. All she had to do was find him. It certainly would not be a man even remotely similar to Quinn Daniels. She made herself a sacred promise—if she should meet a man six feet tall, she would turn her head in another direction and search for one around five feet eight. If he had green eyes, she would cross the street and look for one who had blue. Should he be unfortunate enough to have a dark complexion, she would walk two miles to find one who was fair-skinned and got sunburned at the drop of a hat. Her perfect man would be the complete opposite of Quinn. That much she had fervently promised her broken heart, and she fully intended to keep that promise.

Erin filled three glasses of milk, then went over to switch off the burners on the stove. Considering what she had gone through in the last few years, she had managed to make a fairly nice life for herself. After Quinn left town the first time, she had gone on to college, then nurse's training, graduating at the head of her class. The problem between her and Quinn had, thankfully, not interfered with her and Brenda's friendship. Brenda had been largely responsible for helping her secure her present position as head nurse of pediatrics at a large medical complex where Brenda used to work in Springfield, Missouri, some fifty miles from where Brenda and Nathan lived, after she had made her final break from Quinn six months earlier.

The blaring sound of the TV caused her to abandon her melancholy thoughts and brought her back to a happier time in her life. Brenda had called unexpectedly one day to plead with her to take some time off to stay with the twins while she and Nathan went away for a while. She had agreed readily, realizing how little time she had spent with her best friend's children. She knew she was letting herself in for trouble with the two unruly five-year-olds, but she figured she could stand anything for a week. One week! It seemed she had been with them a month already, and Brenda had just left yesterday!

The sound of another brush war reached her ears as she hurriedly spooned the potatoes, meat loaf and broccoli onto the plates.

"Red Rover, Red Rover, send Holly and Huntley right over!" Erin yelled into the midst of the miniwar. "Time to eat."

The thundering sound of four feet trying to outrace each other assaulted her in the kitchen as she placed the dinner plates on the table. Another five minutes were lost when she had to escort them back down the hall to the bathroom to wash grubby hands and faces. They finally sat down to a slightly cool dinner, the twins looking at the fare before them suspiciously.

"What's that green stuff?" Huntley asked cautiously, his ever-alert eyes falling on the broccoli.

"Try it, you'll really like it," Erin encouraged, taking a bite of her potatoes and trying to swallow them. I hope I'm not going to have another one of those horrible migraines, she thought despairingly. "See how nicely Holly's eating hers?"

Holly was daintily picking at her plate, her nose turned up sharply as she tasted the green vegetable lying next to her meat.

Huntley stared at his plate, then guardedly brought his fork down slowly to spear a piece of the broccoli. "Ohhhh . . . *YUK!*" He spit out the vegetable nastily, part of it landing next to Holly's plate. "That's sick!"

"*Huntwey!*" his sister screeched loudly, reaching over to pinch him hard on the arm. "Wook what you've done! You are simpwy out of contwol!"

"That stuff's *awful!*" he yelled back at her hotly, his arm knocking over her glass of milk.

Holly reached over and grabbed a handful of his hair as the white liquid dripped down through the cracks of the kitchen table onto the floor. A full-scale assault developed as Erin waded into the middle of the scratching, spitting, biting melee, trying to separate the warring factions. Her head began to throb harder as Huntley's glass of milk tipped over also, spilling into his plate of food.

"Stop it this minute!" Erin yelled over the screaming duo. The twins ignored her totally, each one of them trying to get in the last hit or pinch. Although she worked with children every day, she had *never* come up against such unruly ones!

The family dog started barking from its quarters in the utility room, and the house sounded like feeding time at the zoo, with the dog trying to leap over the wooden barrier that confined him. Erin was trying her best to separate the squealing, fighting twins as Huntley thrust one chubby hand into his plate, grabbed a handful of his mashed potatoes and flung it rudely at Erin. The potato missile hit her squarely in the face, and she gasped in astonishment.

"Huntley Daniels!" she sputtered wildly, wiping at the gooey, pasty mess on her face. "I've warned—" Erin's head jerked up. Through the din, she heard a man's amused voice asking loudly, "Do I need to call the riot squad, or is this just a friendly squabble?"

At the sound of his voice, the room suddenly turned deathly still. Erin could feel the blood drain out of her face as she stood in the ruins of what had once been their dinner. Nearly every dish on the table was overturned, milk was lying in deep puddles on the kitchen floor, and mashed potatoes dripped off her face, landing in wet plops on her white tennis shoes. Taking a deep breath, she

21

smiled up sickly into the amused face of a tall, handsome man.

"Where did you come from?" she whimpered weakly. His presence unnerved her even more. All she needed was a mugger to complete her day! She gazed back at his tall, heavily muscled frame leaning innocently against the doorjamb as he looked at the war-torn kitchen. His brown hair lay in rich, dark waves along the curve of his head, slightly longer than the present trend. A pair of strangely exciting eyes the color of budding leaves after a spring rain was coolly running over her soft curves. They lingered just a little too long on the swell of her breasts, their fullness obviously drawing his attention to the tight T shirt she was wearing.

When he finally spoke, his voice was deep, like rich, soft velvet, his eyes still lingering on her. "I rang the doorbell, but apparently you didn't hear it. I took the liberty of coming on in. It was obvious someone was home . . ." he added dryly, fighting to overcome the overwhelming desire to laugh out loud at her flustered countenance.

"You should have waited until I answered the door!" she snapped, suddenly coming out of her shock at seeing him standing there. She reached up hurriedly and tried to wipe more of the potatoes off her face discreetly.

"Let's see, I believe the name is—Erin, am I right?" he said, undaunted by her cool greeting.

"Yes, you're right," she answered coolly, her hands trying to straighten up some of the disorder before her. His face seemed to ring a bell in her memory, but she was powerless to come up with a name.

The twins had ceased their brawling and tumbled out of their chairs exuberantly to throw their arms around the man's legs and squeeze them tightly.

"Uncle Price, Uncle Price," they both chorused. "Did you bring us a surprise?"

Price looked down at the chattering monkeys wrapped

around his legs and grinned skeptically. "Do you think you deserve anything?"

"Yeah, yeah, we've been *good!*" they vowed seriously as they excitedly bounced up and down.

Erin glared at them in disbelief. If this man believed that, he was crazy! "Yes, I can see just how good you've been," he agreed calmly.

The twins ceased their jumping, their brown eyes guiltily surveying the demolished table and their aunt with potatoes still clinging to her face.

"It was *his* fault," Holly returned promptly, pointing her finger at Huntley accusingly. "Don't give him his present, Uncle Price," she urged, sticking her thumb in her mouth to suck on it. "He's been vewy unwuly all day," she advised between sucks.

"Take your thumb out of your mouth," Erin said as she swiped the traces of potato lingering in white, flaking patches. Her mind was in a chaotic state as she took Holly's thumb out of her mouth and wiped at the milk running down the front of her blouse. Price . . . oh, yes . . . Nathan's best man had been named Price.

"I'll tell you what I'll do," Price bargained, reaching over to set the two milk glasses upright again. "You and your brother sit back down at the table and finish your dinner—quietly," he stressed with a stern look at both of them. "Then we'll go looking for surprises. Deal?"

"Deal, deal!" they shouted excitedly, scrambling for their deserted chairs once again.

Price helped the twins back into their seats as Erin went to the cabinet for two more clean plates and glasses. In a matter of minutes sanity had been restored, and the twins were obediently and placidly eating their meal.

Price looked up from his place beside Holly, his emerald gaze capturing Erin's. "Okay, guys, now you finish eating quietly. I'd like to talk to Erin in the other room for a minute, if that's all right with her." He smiled pleasantly.

Erin's pulse leaped for a moment at the sound of his deep voice. It reminded her painfully of another man's voice . . . She nervously brushed her hands down the sides of her jeans, wondering what he would want to talk to her about.

"We will!" the twins agreed angelically, spooning their broccoli into their mouths eagerly.

Price steered Erin into the family room, sidestepping the mounds of toys scattered haphazardly around the room.

"Those children," Erin muttered helplessly as she rescued a doll from beneath Price's faltering steps. "I thought they had cleaned up this mess!"

Price laughed. "They probably did, but if I remember correctly, they can tear up a steel ball bearing in the time it takes to blink an eye."

Erin grinned back at him. "You remember very correctly."

Price extended a friendly hand toward Erin. "The name's Price Seaver. And although I do remember your first name, I'm afraid that for the life of me, I can't recall the last." He smiled in apology.

"Holmes." Erin's head began to throb painfully once more, her stomach growing queasier by the moment. Her eyes fastened on the man standing before her, and though she was totally unaware that she was gaping, that was exactly what she was doing. To her knowledge, she had seen Price Seaver only once in her life—the night of Brenda and Nathan's marriage—but for some uncanny reason he reminded her of Quinn. She mentally shook herself as she tried to concentrate on what Price was saying to her. Something about being in town and wanting to stop for a minute to visit with Nathan. The way his dark brown, wavy hair lay on his shirt collar in a careless yet very controlled manner—the unusual shade of sparkling green eyes—the thick dark lashes making them look lazy and cool—the way he towered above her medium height when he spoke to her—was she becoming paranoid?

"Erin." Price stopped in mid-sentence and looked at her self-consciously. "Am *I* the one with mashed potatoes on my face?"

"What? Uh . . . no . . . No, I'm sorry. Look, would you mind if I got a washcloth to wipe this stickiness off my face?" Erin's face blushed a deep pink as she realized she had literally been gawking at the poor man! She left the living room and returned quickly holding the wet cloth against her face.

"What did you want to see me about?" she demanded curtly.

Price looked a bit startled at her abrupt change of mood, but he recovered quickly. "Nothing, really. I just thought we'd give those two little hoodlums time to eat their dinner alone. Are you baby-sitting for the evening?"

Erin's hand went to her temple, and she massaged the throbbing area urgently. Her head felt as though it were going to burst anytime now.

"Brenda and Nathan have gone on a short vacation. I'm staying with the children until they get back."

Price let out a low whistle, his eyes watching her fingers knead her temples in concerned detachment. "You must be some kind of friend to take on a job like that," he observed with admiration.

Erin managed a weak smile at the sound of reverence in his voice. "I must admit that I had forgotten how— active the twins are."

"Active! They're like a double charge of dynamite going off every hour on the hour." Price grinned, his white teeth flashing attractively in his bronze face.

Erin groaned and buried her face in her hands. Everything about this Price Seaver reeked of Quinn Daniels!

"Is there something wrong with you?" Price asked, his voice filled with concern now.

"No, I'm just tired and I have a headache, Mr. Seaver. If you'd like, I'll tell Brenda and Nathan you stopped by. They'll be back in about a week; maybe you can come back then," Erin told him as she rose to her feet and started ushering him to the door. What she wanted most right now was to get this painful reminder of Quinn out of the house, the twins in their beds, and to collapse in her own.

"Why do I get the distinct impression you're trying to get rid of me?" Price grinned as she nearly shoved him toward the front door. Suddenly he stopped and looked at her strangely. "I promised the twins a surprise when they finished their meal, *Ms. Holmes.* Do you mind?"

"Yes, I do mind. Go home."

"I beg your pardon." He cocked a disbelieving eyebrow in her direction.

"I said, go home!" Erin knew she was being unreasonably rude, but for some strange reason she couldn't care less. "Leave the twins' surprise with me and I'll see that they get it."

"Have I done something to offend you, Ms. Holmes?"

"Don't be silly. Of course you haven't offended me." Erin started to push at his reluctant form once more. "It's getting late and I want to put the twins to bed early."

Price glanced at his watch. "At five o'clock!"

"Is it just five? It seems like it's midnight!" Erin groaned.

"Now look, Erin, I don't want to make waves, but after all, I did stop by to see the twins . . ."

"You said you came to see Brenda and Nathan!" Erin said sharply.

"Brenda and Nathan *and* the twins!" He rudely jerked her hand off his arm. "What is your problem, lady?"

"My problem, Mr. Seaver! My problem! If you want me to be completely honest, then I'll just tell you *my* problem!" Erin's temper was boiling and her head felt as if it were being squeezed in a vise, causing her to throw caution and good manners to the wind. "I don't like you, Mr. Seaver!" She opened the front door and literally shoved a bewildered Price out on the front porch.

"Will you just knock off the shoving and tell me what's going on!" Price bellowed impatiently as he was thrown out into the cool late-afternoon air. "What did I do?"

"It's not what you did but what you are. If you want to get technical, I don't like men who are six feet tall, I *detest* men with brown wavy hair, and I particularly resent a man who has your color eyes!" Her own eyes were flashing fire at the moment. "To sum it all up for you, Mr. Seaver, I can't stand the sight of you!" She slammed the door angrily in his stunned face.

No sooner had the door banged shut than a loud pounding began, followed by the persistent peal of the doorbell. Erin leaned against the door, aghast at what had just taken place. Her head hammered sickly as she covered her face with her hands and nearly wept. What in the world had gotten into her? True, Price Seaver bore a faint resemblance to Quinn Daniels, but certainly nothing strong enough to bring on an unreasonable reaction as strong as what she had just experienced.

The banging grew more heated as Erin whirled and jerked the door open furiously. "What is it now?!" she screeched.

"I want to tell the kids good-bye, *if* you don't mind." Price glared at her stormily, then shoved his way past her into the room, mumbling obscenities under his breath. "I wasn't aware when I stopped in here tonight that I was going to be dealing with a psycho—"

"Just say your good-byes and leave, Mr. Seaver. I'm not interested in a clinical diagnosis of my behavior," Erin cut him off sharply.

Price walked toward the kitchen, stopped to turn and look back at Erin. "If I had to take a guess, lady, I'd guess

27

that I remind you of one doozy of a heel," he couldn't resist adding in a nasty tone.

A swift light of pain streaked through the angry gray eyes that met his now. For one brief moment Price felt a surge of unwanted protectiveness toward the pale young woman who stood before him. Somewhere down the line she had obviously been very hurt by a man with Price's characteristics, enough to sour her on *all* men, apparently. Well, it was certainly no concern of his. He had his own problems, and the last thing he was interested in was playing nursemaid to some hot-tempered hellcat who was trying to get over an old lover.

"Well, if you'll excuse me, I hate to leave your stimulating company but I'll just see the kids before I go. Next time I'm in town I'll be sure to look you up . . ." Price's voice was sinking rapidly now as Erin blinked her eyes and stared up blankly at him. "Erin? Is there something wrong with you? Are you ill . . ." Price's temper faded quickly as he moved toward her, trying to elicit some response from her.

"Mr. Seaver . . . excuse me . . . but I'm . . . I think I'm going to be sick . . ."

A swift, terrifying black abyss began to swallow her slowly. Her last coherent thoughts were of strong arms going around her, pulling her close to a broad muscular chest. It was unexpected; it was most assuredly not wanted; but Erin Holmes was once again in the arms of a man who was six feet tall, had dark wavy hair and beautiful green eyes.

CHAPTER TWO

Erin wasn't sure how long she was unconscious, but when she awoke there were four chubby hands gently patting her cheeks. A cool cloth had been laid across her forehead, but the tight, almost unbearable pain was still pulsating in her head.

"You'll be awight, Aunt Erin," Holly assured her, tenderly patting her cheek with a greasy, meat-loaf-smelling hand. "Uncle Pwice is gonna take care of you."

Erin moaned, her stomach turning over at the faint smell of the greasy food. "Thank you, Holly, but I'll be all right." She tried to raise her head but was stopped by a firm hand.

"Just lie still, Erin. You've been out for a few minutes."

Price leaned down, the vague aroma of a very sexy aftershave reaching her nose as he carefully wiped her face with the wet cloth.

"Please . . . Price . . ." She reached to halt his hand. "I'll be fine. Thank you."

His touch sent tiny shivers rocketing through her, only adding to her pain. "That may be so, but you're going to lie there for a while anyway. What caused you to black out?" he asked, draping a light afghan around her legs gently.

"I have migraine headaches occasionally. I've felt one coming on all day," she said wearily, closing her eyes against the pain.

29

"Migraines? Those can be pretty rough," Price said softly.

"I was in a car accident several years ago, and I've had them ever since."

"Do you have any medicine with you?" he asked, pulling the twins off her. "Why don't you guys go find something to do in your room," he suggested firmly, steering them in the direction of their bedroom.

"Can we watercolor?" Huntley asked hopefully. One could practically see the wheels turning in his head.

"Sure, sure . . . Just keep the noise down, okay, pal? Your aunt Erin's not feeling well," he agreed absently.

Erin was in so much pain she was barely aware of the conversation going on around her. She was fighting hard not to disgrace herself and regurgitate on the living room floor.

"Oh boy!" Huntley made a beeline for his room, with Holly following in hot pursuit. The loud slam of their bedroom door shook the house as they gleefully searched for their paints and brushes.

"Look, why don't I carry you into your bed. This couch doesn't look very comfortable to me," Price suggested, kneeling next to her. He was being so kind, it made her hurt even more.

"Oh, Price, just go away," she moaned, fighting her nausea and losing.

"I'd like nothing better!" he snapped tensely. Gone was the tender tone that had been in his voice earlier. "But I hardly think you're in any condition to be here by yourself."

"I'll be fine . . . just give me a minute," she whimpered.

"How long are Brenda and Nathan going to be gone, did you say?"

"They won't be home for a week." Just go away, Price, she wanted to scream. This day had been a total nightmare for her.

Price stood up and began to pace the floor, rubbing the back of his neck with one large hand. "A week! How in the devil did you consent to watch those—holy terrors for a week? I can't stand to be around them one hour, let alone one week!"

A small smile flickered across Erin's face as she lay with her eyes closed. She could well imagine those twins in his care for a week. He seemed to be immaculate in his dress, and his life was probably well organized. Children would no doubt interfere very much in Price Seaver's way of life.

"I don't get to see them very often," she murmured. "I wanted to spend some time with them, so I agreed when Brenda asked me."

"You'll be sorry," he predicted grimly, increasing his pacing. "They'll have you pulling your hair out by the roots in a week."

Ha! A week, she thought dryly. How about one day!

"I love the little rascals," he hastened to add, "but that darn Nathan lets them get away with murder. They set fire to my briefcase last time I was here. Burned every damn paper in it," he reminisced incredulously, shaking his head as if he still couldn't believe it. "If they were mine, I'd take some of that out of them but quick!" he promised.

"I know," Erin commiserated, "but it certainly isn't my place to clamp down on them."

Price stopped his pacing and walked back over to peer down at her grayish green face intently. "How long do these headaches last?"

"Days," she admitted bleakly, wishing she could self-destruct.

"Well . . . darn it! You can't take care of those kids in your condition," he said.

"I'll have to."

"You couldn't if you tried," he observed. "I suppose I'll have to find someone to come and give you a hand . . ." He sounded put out at this shoddy turn of fate.

31

Erin's eyes flew open, her stomach churning violently. "You certainly will not!" Brother, that's all she would need to top her day off. Have him running around doing her favors! "I can manage—somehow," she said grimly.

"Listen, you—twerp! Someone's got to assume control here! You can't even lift your head off the pillow," he said, "let alone corral two walking time bombs!"

"I was doing fine till you came on the scene," she answered angrily, fighting her way out of the entanglement of the afghan. When she stood up, bright lights danced in front of her eyes, and she wanted to cry with humiliation as the long overdue heaves assaulted her.

Price was at her side instantly, sweeping her up in his strong arms. He made a mad dash down the hall as Erin fought to hold on until they reached the bathroom. He laid her down near the toilet, holding her head for her as she emptied her stomach over and over, disgracing herself miserably. Tears blinded her as she tried to push Price back, so embarrassed she wanted to die. But he firmly yet tenderly held her head for her, patting her comfortingly until the violent heaving subsided. Leaving for a moment, he wet another washcloth and came back to her to lay it gently on her clammy brow, wiping her flushed face. He spoke soothing words to her as she slumped weakly against his broad chest. "Take it easy, Erin. Just lie back and relax."

"Price . . . Please, you don't have to stay in here," she protested sickly.

"I know I don't," he replied softly, smoothing back the wet locks of her curly brown hair, "but I want to. Are you any better?" he asked after a moment, wrapping her warmly in his arms to still the explosive trembling of her body.

"I think so. Can you help me to my room?" She was beyond fighting now. She just wanted to bury herself in a hole and never come out.

32

"I think I can handle that." He swooped her up in his arms effortlessly and carried her back into the hall. "Which room?" he asked, looking down into her face. Erin's breath caught at the radiance of his smile.

"The first one on the right," she told him. Her heart skipped a beat—two beats—as he pressed her tightly against his chest and turned toward her bedroom. She was extremely conscious of the extra ten pounds she was carrying and mentally flayed herself for eating that extra doughnut for breakfast this morning. "You don't have to carry me," she protested. "I know I'm too heavy. I've been meaning to go on a diet," she finished lamely as he strode down the hall with her easily.

"You're not heavy," he reproached mildly.

"Yes, yes I am," she insisted, feeling like a fool. "I should take off ten pounds at least!" Her face flamed when she thought of what he must be thinking. Men did not like to carry a butterball in their arms!

"I could stand to lose a few pounds myself," he grunted as they entered her bedroom and he laid her down on the bed.

Erin stared up at his lean, trim frame and wondered where he could possibly afford to lose an ounce. He was all muscle, all virile man, and she resented it with every ounce of flab on her!

"You're just being nice," she muttered as she lay back against the pillow weakly. "I know I'm fat and—plain!"

"All right," he agreed readily, "you're a tub of lard and your face would stop a clock. Now, if that makes you feel better, maybe you'll be in the mood to tell me if you have any medicine with you."

Erin's face clouded over. He certainly didn't have to be so brutally frank. "In my purse on the vanity," she said tightly.

Price rummaged through her purse, coming up with a

brown plastic vial. "These?" He held up the bottle questioningly.

"Yes," she muttered.

"Stay right where you are, troll. I'll get you some water to take these with." Price stepped into the small bath off her room.

"I can do without the insults," she said huffily, untying her tennis shoes and kicking them to the floor miserably.

"Whatever you say," he said blandly as he returned with a glass of water and two pills. "Is this how you get your kicks? Running yourself down?"

"I'm not running myself down," she replied. "I just don't try to fool myself. I know that I'm not the raving beauty Brenda is. . . ." Her voice trailed off as she avoided his gaze, embarrassed.

He stood beside the bed staring down at her intently, his assessing eyes revealing nothing. The silence lengthened as she brought the pills to her trembling mouth and swallowed them with a small sip of water. Their eyes met again as she handed the glass back to him and lay back on her pillow.

"Feel better now?" he inquired gently.

"Not really," she said and groaned.

"Well, we need to figure out what we're going to do. I should be going soon."

"Nobody's making you stay," Erin said. "You're free to go anytime."

Price ignored her words as he walked over to gaze out the window paneled with sea-foam-green drapes. The view was breathtaking from where he stood looking out into the gathering dusk. The majestic A frame that Nathan and Brenda had built nestled in a bluff overlooking Table Rock Lake. The rising moon was glistening on the tranquil waters. A warm breeze trickled through the open window.

"I wonder if there's a neighbor who could come in and help with the children tonight," he mused. "It appears you're hard pressed to control the children even when you're well, let alone now."

She knew he was recalling the scene he had walked in on earlier. "Price," Erin said as she raised herself up on one elbow, giving him a withering glare, "if there's one thing I don't need right now, it's you telling me my faults. Now you know where the door is—please use it!"

"Get off my back, Erin. I'm stuck here for the night and you know it." He turned away from the window, his face a stony mask. "If those pills are what I think they are, you're going to be out like a light any second now."

Erin moaned. She had forgotten how powerful the medicine was. Sometimes she slept for hours after taking the pills.

"I haven't checked into a motel yet, so I'll just use Nathan and Brenda's bedroom for the night. Tomorrow I'll try to find someone to come and stay with the children until you get on your feet again."

Loud, shrilling war whoops pierced the night. The sound of running feet assaulted their ears as the bedroom door flew open and Huntley and Holly stormed in, riding their imaginary war ponies.

"Oh, good lord!" Price said with a groan, surveying the rainbow-colored faces and paint-stained clothes of the two standing before him. "What have you done to yourselves?"

"We're Indians, Uncle Price," Huntley said, letting out another loud war cry. "This is my squaw, Horseface," he said, jerking a smeared thumb at his sister. "I painted her all up!"

"Huntwey! I do not want to be Horseface! I want to be Wunning Water," Holly screeched indignantly, reaching over and thumping him smartly on his feather.

Huntley reached back and jerked her tomahawk out of her hand and swung at her wildly. "*I'm* chief and *I* give the orders, squaw!" he railed hotly.

Price stepped between them, his tall presence casting a blight over the arrogant chief's authority. "*I* happen to be the chief around here, and I'm ordering you to stop this fighting!" he told them harshly, trying to dodge the flying watercolor-painted hands that were destroying his spotless buff-color trousers. "When I told you you could watercolor, I thought you meant in your coloring books! Why in the devil did you paint yourselves up like that? Just look at this mess," he fumed, holding Holly's face between two strong fingers.

Streaks of red, blue, gold and purple were drawn all over her pretty little features, with two big round black circles drawn around each eye. "She looks like a crazed raccoon," he observed disgustedly.

Huntley leaned over and peered at his sister intently. "Yow, she does kinda, doesn't she?" he agreed in awe.

Holly set up a penetrating wail that tore through Erin's head like a buzz saw. "I don't want to look like a waccoon," she cried pitifully. "Huntwey said I could be a squaw!"

Erin covered her ears in pain. "Oh, Holly, please . . ."

"All right, you two." Price started ushering the twins out of the bedroom forcefully. "We're going to let your aunt Erin sleep now. Let's go get you cleaned up." He surveyed their condition once again. "What a mess!"

The children quieted instantly as Price led them out of the room and marched them down the hall. Erin was beginning to feel the merciful effects of the medicine taking hold as she slid down onto her pillow. She was just floating into an inky void when she dimly heard Price's astonished voice as he apparently reached the twins' bedroom.

"Good lord! What have you done to your room!"

The rest of the night was a total blank to Erin. The pills sent her into a deep, painless sleep. When she awoke the

36

next morning to the chatter of the twins playing in their room, she was surprised to find the sun barely peeking over a hill. Her head still throbbed, and her mouth felt like cotton. Glancing at the clock near her bed, she noticed it was barely six o'clock. The twins were not noted for "sleeping in." She sat up hesitantly on the side of the bed; the room whirled for a minute. With all the strength she could muster, she stood and made her way slowly into the small bath. Ten minutes later she had washed her face and brushed her teeth but still felt like someone was using a jackhammer in her head. She stepped out into the hall and walked cautiously to the door of the twins' room. The medicine had made her feel shaky and weak. "Good morning, children." She smiled softly. "Where's your uncle Price?"

"Still sweeping," Holly said irritably, her tone suggesting that it was hard to believe anyone would still be in bed at this hour.

"I'm hungry, Aunt Erin," Huntley said, his brown eyes peeping hopefully up at her from behind his large glasses. "Can we eat now?"

Erin sagged weakly against the door frame, her head begging for more medicine. "I don't know if I can fix you anything right now, Huntley. Could you wait until Price gets up?" she asked hopefully.

"Could we wake him up?" Huntley asked expectantly. "Mommy and Daddy let us wake them up when we're hungry—and we're *awful* hungry," he added for insurance.

"Well . . . I don't know. . . ."

"Oh, goody, goody, we can!" Huntley grabbed for Holly's hand. "Let's go, Holly. Maybe he'll fix us pancakes," he schemed as he bolted past Erin, heading across the hall.

"Huntley! Wait a minute," Erin said, trying to catch up with the flying feet. The twins burst into Price's room, the door slamming back against the wall, the sound reverberating around the room like an explosion. Price's head came off his pillow instantly and he looked around in confusion as the twins landed in the middle of his bed exuberantly.

"What—what's going on?" he asked, befuddled, trying to control their hugs.

"We're hungry, Uncle Price. Aunt Erin said you would fix us some pancakes!" Huntley said pitifully, getting up close to Price's face. His small hand came out to explore the heavy stubble on his uncle's face.

Erin gasped as she stood in the doorway. "Now *wait* a minute, Huntley. I did *not* say that he would fix you pancakes!" Erin had to smother a grin at the look of complete bafflement covering Price's sleepy face. Her pulse raced as he sat up and ran his fingers through his thick, tousled hair. His broad, muscular chest was covered with thick, dark brown hair that ran enticingly all the way down to where the sheet fell below his waist.

Price glanced up, seeing her in the doorway as the twins continued their early-morning chatter, filling him in on what they wanted with the pancakes.

"Okay, okay! Just pipe down for a minute," he said, gently hugging them to his chest, then glancing back at Erin's pale face. "You all right this morning?"

Erin gave him a shaky smile. "Not really. I'm afraid I'm going to have to take some more medicine . . . I'm sorry," she murmured at the bleak look that returned to his face.

Holly jumped off the bed and crossed the room to take Erin's hand in her small one. "Come on, Aunt Ewin, we all have to kiss each other good morning," she proclaimed firmly, leading her over to Price's bed.

"What?" Erin laughed questioningly as Holly pushed her down on the bed, then hopped back up to her place beside Huntley and Price. "Evewyone has to kiss each other good morning. That's what Mommy and Daddy do," she said earnestly, leaning over to kiss Price on the mouth soundly.

A frantic round of kisses was exchanged between the twins and their aunt and uncle. Erin had to laugh at their enthusiasm as they wrapped their arms around Price's neck and squeezed him tight, nearly knocking him over in the bed.

"Now you and Uncle Pwice kiss good morning," Holly instructed sweetly.

The smiles dropped from Price's and Erin's faces immediately. Erin flushed a bright red as Huntley and Holly waited for the morning ritual to be completed.

"I—don't think that's necessary," Erin hedged, lowering her eyes in embarrassment.

"But Mommy and Daddy always do," Holly said, her brown eyes puzzled.

Erin hazarded a glance at Price, who was obviously enjoying her discomfort. Holly reached up and brought the two reluctant heads together. "You gotta kiss," she issued huffily, nearly knocking their heads together. Erin's startled gray eyes stared back into Price's slightly amused emerald ones as he said teasingly, "Yeah, you gotta, Aunt Erin!"

Erin leaned forward slightly and pecked Price on the cheek quickly.

"No . . ." Holly groaned morosely. "Not like *that*. Like this!" She reached up and smacked Price hard on the mouth again. "See!" With grim determination she shoved Erin's face back into Price's amused one. "Now *weally* kiss him!" she ordered.

"Yeah, Aunt Erin," Price said as he grinned smugly. "Don't you know how to *weally* kiss a man good morning?" he taunted, his voice sounding very low and sexy.

Erin felt a strange weakness invade her as Price leaned closer and touched his mouth to hers lightly. Her eyes dropped shut as she froze for a moment, savoring the feel of his mouth on hers. His lips brushed hers gently once again, silently urging a response. She opened her eyes slowly to meet his, and with a sigh of defeat she hesitantly brought her lips to touch tremblingly against his more firmly. Price's hands reached out to clasp the back of her curly head, drawing her closer into his arms, his mouth closing over hers.

The months melted away, and suddenly Erin was back in Quinn's arms with his mouth devouring hers in searing, demanding intensity. They both seemed to forget their surroundings and the two sets of dark brown eyes that watched them, bored, as Price held her captive in his seductive embrace.

She heard him moan softly as he reluctantly broke the kiss, his hands tightening painfully around her throbbing head. It had been a long time since he had kissed a woman this way and, surprisingly, it felt good.

Impatient hands broke them apart as Erin looked into Price's lazy, slumbrous eyes, eyes that told her that if they were alone, he might ask for more than a kiss from her. "That's enough!" Huntley proclaimed. "You've got it right. That's how Mommy and Daddy do it."

Price wouldn't release her eyes from his burning gaze as he answered softly, "You're sure? I want to be sure it's *exactly* as your parents do it."

"It is!" Holly affirmed, jumping off the bed. " 'Cept sometimes Daddy wants us to go back and play in our room for a little while. He says if we're *weal* quiet and don't bother him and Mommy, he'll fix us something weeeallly special for bweakfast," she said in childlike innocence.

"I'll just bet he does," Price said, his gaze still locked with Erin's. "I wonder if that would work for me," he murmured low.

Erin snapped out of her stupor and drew back guiltily from his arms. "Don't be ridiculous. I don't plan on making *that* mistake but once in my life," she said curtly as the twins scampered out of the room, heading for the kitchen. She had not mistaken the innuendo in his veiled comment.

Price stretched like a lazy panther lying in the sun, his muscles flexing taut in the early-morning light. The sheet slipped precariously low over his hips. "Why, my dear Erin, are you saying the heel I look like took unfair advantage of you at one time?" His cool green gaze pinned her to the floor as he continued in a low, clipped tone. "You don't need to worry. A woman is the last thing I want in my life at the present, no matter how casual the encounter." His voice was very cold and indifferent now.

Erin's eyes turned as cool and glacial as his, her patience at an end with his blatant arrogance. "You cocky, pompous, egotistical—jackass! My private life is no concern of yours whatsoever!" Tears blurred her eyes as she started backing out the bedroom door, wanting only to find refuge from this hurtful man and her pounding head.

"But Erin," Price said from his bed, "surely I haven't upset you again! I don't recall making any indecent suggestion to you. You really have a problem with men, don't you? I wonder what would happen to me if I actually *did* make a pass at you." He chuckled wickedly.

"You're disgusting!" She whirled and started out the door, then paused to add briefly, "And you certainly will never find me in your bed! I may not be the raving beauty Brenda is, but I would never lower myself to sleep with a man like you, Price. Don't ever forget that!"

Price looked at her disgustedly. Why did she keep bringing her looks into their conversation! "Don't make rash statements you can't live with," he shouted as she tramped down the hall. "I may be willing to put a brown paper sack over your head and pretend that you're not a homely little—twerp!" he yelled after her as he heard her bedroom door slam. He thought about her for a moment

41

after she left the room, wondering why she seemed so hung up on her looks. He thought she was a living doll! But he wasn't interested.

Erin crawled back under her blankets miserably, cursing the day she had ever met Price Seaver. She groaned, turning over onto her stomach and burying her head deeper into the pillow, trying to block the pain and the anger but failing with both. The thought of getting up to get her medicine was just too much at the moment, so she lay in acute torment. The door to her room slid open quietly, and she heard soft footsteps coming over to her bed. Strong, compassionate arms lifted her, then turned her gently onto her back once more as a cold cloth came to rest on her forehead. The hands that ministered to her were tough, calloused hands, yet they handled her as if she were a fragile possession that would break easily if grasped too hard.

"Take these," Price ordered gruffly, yet his gentle eyes told another story. Erin groped blindly for the pills and swallowed them gratefully while he held her head up off the pillow. After offering her one more sip of water, he carefully let her head slip back down onto the pillow.

"Can't the doctors do anything about these?" he asked softly, rearranging the bedding and tucking it in close around her.

"No. It's possible they may go away someday, but right now I have to learn to live with them." In all her life she had never experienced such tenderness. Somehow, with Price sitting beside her, the pain wasn't as bad as it had been earlier.

"Do you think you can eat something?" he asked, leaning over to wipe her forehead with the cloth. "You didn't have your dinner last night."

Erin's stomach rolled at the thought of food. "No, please . . . I couldn't eat a thing. Just make sure the children are fed."

42

"They're in there putting their clothes on right now, then I'm going to try to tackle pancakes," he said grimly, removing the cloth and taking it into the bathroom to moisten it again.

The last thing in the world Erin felt like doing was carrying on a conversation, yet she didn't want to end it. It seemed nice to have a man to talk to for a change. She had steered clear of men for so many months now, she had almost forgotten how deep a male voice could sound or how nice it was to be touched by a man's hands.

Price came back out of the bathroom and went to her vanity, pulling open the top drawer and rummaging through it quietly.

"What are you doing?" she asked, startled.

"I'm looking for one of your gowns," he said absently, extracting a sheer blue one. He examined it closely, then, satisfied with his selection, closed the drawer and came back to her. "Can you sit up for a minute?" he asked, his hands pulling her upward.

"Price!" Erin struggled to clear her head as the medicine began to weave its magic. "What do you think you're doing?" she asked groggily.

"Something I should have done last night," he said, avoiding her swatting hands. "Knock it off, Erin! I'm going to get you into something more comfortable."

He threw back the cover, and Erin's face flooded with color as he stripped her jeans off with one slick motion. He had obviously had lots of practice! Then he hooked his thumbs around her bikini panties. "You'll only make your head hurt worse with all that squirming," he warned, undaunted in his task. "I don't see what the problem is. Just pretend I'm a doctor," he told her, stripping her panties just as smoothly, then letting them join her jeans on the floor.

"A doctor!" Erin protested, letting herself be handled like an infant. "No doctor ever stripped me like this!"

43

"Don't worry. I have bad eyesight," he said with a grin as he pulled her T shirt over her head indifferently. When he unsnapped her bra and her soft breasts fell loose, Price's eyes lingered uncommonly long on their feminine loveliness, his eyes turning darker. "Now I must admit this is a little harder to ignore."

"You are—horrible!" Erin sputtered, her face flaming a bright red. "If I weren't so sick I'd slap your smirking face!" she said crossly, feeling the heat from his gaze on her breasts. The dark centers began to tighten and grow taut under his continuing scrutiny.

"I'm just a disinterested bystander trying to be helpful," he said easily. His eyes dropped back to her face as he reached for her gown, slipping it over her head. "Keep telling yourself that. It'll make it easier."

"Disinterested, my foot!" she replied staunchly, slapping his hand as he brushed it over one breast tauntingly before he stood up.

"You have a nasty disposition, do you realize that?" Price said, laying her back down gently. "If I were in your boots I'd be grateful someone was kind enough to take his valuable time and help me when I needed it."

"I don't need your help," Erin replied irritably, snuggling back down.

A broad grin crossed Price's face. "Now you and I both know that's not true, so why don't you just lie back like a good girl and get over your headache so I can get back to my own life."

Erin looked up at him heatedly. "Don't kid yourself. I do not need you, Price Seaver!"

"Oh, bull! Just go to sleep, Erin. You're a hopeless case!" Price strode to the door and jerked it open. "I'm going to scour this neighborhood for someone to take over before I lose my religion with you!" He slammed the door with a disgusted whack.

Erin cringed as the door shuddered, her eyes closing

painfully at the sound. He was so rude! Her heart thudded when she thought of his parting words, but reason overtook her quickly. She hoped he did find someone!

She squeezed her eyes shut, willing herself to block out his handsome face and the thrill of his earlier kiss. No more foolish dreams, that was a promise. But was it one she could keep?

Unconsciously she balled her fists in angry protest against the unknown forces that were once again cruelly placing her in the path of a man who could cause her anesthetized heart to show some flickering signs of life. She didn't *want* to feel that exhilarating surge of awareness when he touched her. She didn't *want* her foolish heart to beat faster when his gaze nonchalantly met hers or his shoulder accidentally brushed hers as he passed her in a room. And most of all she didn't want to remember just how good it had felt to be in a man's arms, even as innocently as she had been in Price's. She could not fall in love. She would not!

CHAPTER THREE

It was barely seven o'clock when Erin opened her eyes again. She lay very still, listening for the sounds of the children's voices, but she could hear nothing. The house was wreathed in silence. Just for one delicious moment she remembered that Price was somewhere near—or perhaps that was the reason for the silent house. Maybe he had found someone to look after the children while she was sleeping and had left. A stab of fear pierced her heart at that thought. She was just being foolish again. What did it matter whether he was still here? In the end he would leave.

Reaching for the robe that Price must have draped over the foot of the bed, she rose to walk cautiously into the bathroom. Her headache was beginning to show signs of letting up, the tight band of pain releasing its grip gradually. She wet a clean cloth and ran it lightly across her face, groaning audibly as she saw her rumpled reflection in the mirror. What a mess! Her hair was standing on end, her face was pale and sickly, large black circles hung under her eyes. What Price must think of her! She caught her errant thoughts quickly. Why should she care what he thought of her. Still. . . .

In the last few years she had learned to use makeup to her advantage, and her hair was styled in a cut that was most becoming to her face. Yes, although she was still no Brenda, she might impress Price . . . But heavens! Look at her now! And this was how he had seen her from the time he had entered the door—and with the potatoes on her face!

With a disgusted shrug of her shoulders, she laid the cloth back down. If she ever did see Price again, she would make sure she looked her best. He wouldn't be interested, but it would do her ego a world of good after this disastrous meeting.

The dry cotton feeling that still lingered in her mouth even after a vigorous brushing plus mouthwash had to be appeased. On shaky legs she started down the hall in search of something cool to drink. She was distracted by the family room as she passed, taking note of its neat, orderly appearance. Nothing was out of place except— She paused and reversed her steps to walk closer to the coffee table. Kneeling, she peered unbelievingly into the small fishbowl, catching her breath in surprise. Buck Rogers and Cinderella were both floating, stiff as boards, on top of the soapy water. What could have happened, she thought in panic as her eyes searched anxiously for any sight of the twins. She didn't want to think of what their reaction would be when they found their prized pets bobbing on top of the water, cushioned in a mound of soapsuds!

E.T., the family dog, let out a pitiful yelp from his place of confinement, bringing Erin back to a standing position. He undoubtedly wanted his dinner. Price had probably been too busy trying to keep up with the children to worry about trying to feed the Daniels' menagerie. As she neared the kitchen, she heard a murmur of voices from behind the closed door to the utility room. She couldn't help but notice the spotless kitchen, everything gleaming and immaculate—a far cry from when she last saw it! Whoever Price had gotten was certainly efficient—far more so than she had been.

The sight that met her eyes as she quietly pushed open

the door to the utility room was one of calm tranquillity. Both twins were sitting next to Price, their faces and clothes sparkling clean, munching contentedly on apples. Their young, inquisitive eyes watched their uncle patiently trying to wipe green enamel off one side of the once-white dog.

They looked up as the door opened, smiling brightly at Erin.

"Hi, Aunt Erin," they greeted her. Price turned his head and surveyed her barely concealed curves as she stood in the doorway, his eyes flicking briefly over her short housecoat. Either by accident or by devious intention, he had selected the sexiest nightgown and robe she owned. The plunging neckline and sheer clinging material scarcely went past her thighs, making the outfit almost indecent to walk around in. With a barely concealed smirk he went back to scrubbing the dog.

"Feeling better, Auntie Erin?" he asked breezily.

"A little." She clutched the front of her gown closer to her, a bit disconcerted that he was still around. Her eyes followed his quick, efficient movements with the dog. "Price, what are you doing?" she asked, stepping closer to get a better look at the dog.

"It seems Huntley, our little pal there in the glasses, didn't care for the color of ole E.T., so he decided to paint him green. Real eye-catching, isn't it?" Price said, standing up to display the wet, gummy, shivering green dog.

"Huntley!" Erin scolded, looking at him in disapproval. "Didn't I tell you to stay out of that paint yesterday?"

"You said I couldn't paint my *name* on the garage door, Aunt Erin. You didn't say nothin' about the dog," he rationalized calmly, taking another bite of his apple.

"Well, no problem," Price said, pouring more paint remover on the rag. "E.T. may look a little strange to all his girlfriends for a while, but they'll probably think it's some kinky new fashion dogs are wearing nowadays."

Erin was amazed at the patience Price seemed to have with the children. In her opinion, he would have been the last person in the world to take this type of thing so calmly.

"I didn't think you were still here," she murmured quietly, her gaze fastening on his large hands as he gently massaged the paint off the white fur.

"And where did you think I would go?" he teased lightly, "with two five-year-olds, one sick aunt, one green dog and two dead goldfish?"

Erin glanced worriedly over at the twins. "So you know about—that?"

"I know about that," he said, wrapping a thick, fleecy towel around E.T. "Holly thought she saw some dirt on Cinderella's face, so she decided to give her and Buck a long-overdue bath." Price winked at Erin secretly. "To Holly's knowledge they hadn't had one in quite some time. They were both naturally quite upset to find out that fish don't take baths, but I managed to explain that accidents happen and Buck and Cinderella probably enjoyed their bubble bath . . . as long as they could." He sat the dog back down on the floor and began to rub powder into its furry body. "We thought that after you woke up, we'd have the—deceaseds' funeral. Then, if you felt like it, we'd all go down to the pet store for some new fish."

"Buck Wogers and Cindewella have gone to the big fish hatchewy in the sky," Holly explained sadly. "They're much happier now, Aunt Erin, so don't feel bad."

Erin bit her lip painfully as she tried to keep a straight face. Huntley's and Holly's features were tragic masks of composure, trying to bear up under the heavy burden Holly was carrying.

"Well, I'm happy to say I *am* feeling better, and I certainly wouldn't want to miss services for Buck and Cinderella," Erin said succinctly, turning her head away from their mournful gazes. Her eyes met Price's amused

49

ones as they both grinned knowingly at each other. "Who's giving the eulogy?" she asked sweetly.

"Reverend Seaver's been preparing notes all afternoon, ma'am," he said proudly, finally releasing the squirming dog. E.T. stood in the middle of the floor and shook his body two or three times, then began to roll on a small area rug that was lying next to his bed, trying to assuage the terrific itching from all the bath and powder he had just been subjected to.

"Really." She smiled delightedly. "I can hardly wait for the sermon! It must not be easy to find something—really special to say about two—fish." She had to bite her lip again as Price continued to grin mockingly back at her. "I mean, two fish you barely knew," she finished lamely, averting her eyes from his before she burst out laughing.

"On the contrary, some of my most stirring sermons have been given at funerals for pets," he stated smugly as he cleaned up the last remains of the paint-stained rags. "If I were you I'd go slip into something more"—his emerald gaze skipped suggestively over her skimpy gown —"conservative. Not that I don't find your attire extremely appealing, but I'm afraid the neighbors might talk," he finished, bringing his mouth close to her ear in a whisper. Shivers of delight raced through Erin's skin as his lips brushed her ear softly before turning back to the twins. "Let's go, guys. You go get the matchbox while I dig a grave site. Aunt Erin will join us out in the backyard as soon as she is dressed."

They ran off obediently to their task, leaving Price and Erin standing in the small utility room. Shyness overtook Erin as she realized that they were alone. "Price, I thought you were going to find someone to come and stay until I felt better," she reminded him, averting her eyes from his glance hurriedly.

"I tried a couple of people, but I couldn't find anyone who could stay more than one day," he replied casually, adding, "Oh, by the way, the plumber came and got the ball out of the toilet. I decided that since I'm not on any rigid schedule right now, I can hang around for a few days. Have you got any big objections to that?" His eyes finally managed to catch hers.

"What about your job?" Erin struggled to find an excuse for him not to stay.

Price gave an ironic chuckle. "Since I own my own company in Memphis, I don't think they're going to say too much. Seaver Trucking will go on for a few days whether I'm there or not."

"Aren't you rather young to have your own trucking company?" she asked in surprise.

"I'm thirty-two, Erin. I've always worked very hard for things that are important to me," he said mildly, his eyes reluctant to leave hers. "I'd be happy to stay a day or two to help you."

"That's really not necessary, Price," she answered curtly, pushing her way around him to walk into the larger space off the kitchen. His closeness unnerved her. "I'm sure you have someone waiting for you at home. I'm really feeling much better now." The thought had suddenly struck her that she didn't know if Price was married.

Price followed her into the kitchen, then leaned against the kitchen sink, crossing his arms in amusement. "Just the normal two or three hundred good-looking, ravishing women who trail me around constantly," he taunted with a devious sparkle in his green eyes. "But a man gets tired of seeing all those beautiful faces gazing at him adoringly day in and day out. I thought it might be refreshing to stay around here a few days and just gaze on you awhile."

His cocky smile infuriated her. She knew he was deliberately trying to antagonize her, playing on her insecurities.

"You may think that's very funny, Price, but I don't," she said coolly, itching to slap his face. "I may not be a

51

raving beauty, but I'm not that bad. I could attract a man if I wanted to."

Price's face grew serious as his arms dropped to his sides. "Well, well, well," he said quietly. "I was beginning to get worried about you, lady. Is it possible that you've finally taken your sackcloth and ashes off and looked in the mirror?"

"I'm sure I don't have the slightest idea what you're talking about, Price. If you mean do I realize that I'm not as unattractive as I've been babbling on about lately, then the answer is yes." Her voice was defiant as she glared back into Price's taunting eyes.

"I couldn't agree more," he said quietly. "I'd even take it a step further and admit that you're a damn appealing woman. But I suppose that's hoping for a little too much, isn't it?" he added sarcastically.

Barely aware of her actions, Erin reached out and slapped him hard across his cheek. Price's stunned look frightened her.

He instantly grabbed her hand and jerked her up close against his broad chest. Their angry eyes locked as he said from between clenched teeth, "Don't you *ever* try that again, lady. I've about had it up to here with you," he threatened in a grim voice.

"You touch me and I'll scream," she vowed hotly, trying to twist out of his iron grip. "What do you want from me!"

"Scream—see if I give a damn," he said in a controlled voice. "What you need is a man to take control of you, Erin. Someone who'll take you to bed several times a day until he proves to you that you're a desirable woman." His voice had grown husky now as he drew her angry face up next to his. "Someone who can make you *love* for a change, instead of feeling sorry for yourself."

"I'm not interested in a man—not just any man, that is," she whispered hotly.

"And what's that supposed to mean?" Price returned irritably.

"I mean I am interested in a man, but I haven't found the perf—the right one yet."

"I believe you started to say the 'perfect' one, didn't you?" Price kept her trapped against his chest, his soft breath fanning her face. "I hate to be the bearer of bad news, Erin, but if you'll pardon the expression, there ain't no such creature."

"I refuse to believe that. Look at Nathan—he's the perfect man, and he and Brenda have the perfect marriage. He totally adores the ground she walks on, and she returns that love. If I thought for one moment that I wouldn't be able to find that kind of man in my life, well, I think I would just give up. Especially after Quinn. . . ." Her voice trailed off quietly.

"Quinn? I suppose he's the guy that's got me in so much hot water?"

Erin sighed and pushed away from Price to walk to the kitchen window. She stared out at the twins as they played near their sandbox, waiting for the funeral. How could she tell Price, a man who reminded her so much of Quinn—yet Erin was beginning to see that they were really nothing alike at all—just how much Quinn Daniels had hurt her without sounding like she was feeling sorry for herself again.

"Quinn Daniels was a man I thought I loved very deeply—a man whom I dreamed of having the perfect marriage with ever since I was nineteen years old. I'm afraid I'm a person whose dreams die hard, Price. I want a per—good marriage. When I found out six months ago that I would never have that marriage with Quinn, I decided that I would not let that turn me bitter and disillusioned. Somewhere out there in the world there is a man who wants the kind of marriage I do, and I'm going to find him. It may take months, years, maybe a lifetime, but I will find him, Price. In spite of Quinn Daniels."

"Quinn Daniels! Nathan's brother?" Price's face showed surprise.

"That's right. I'm sure you know him if you know Nathan."

"I've met him a couple of times. Why would you fall for a romeo like him? You look like you'd have more common sense than that."

Erin gave a shaky laugh and sat down on the kitchen chair. "I've asked myself the same question over and over. My only consolation is the fact that I wasn't the only one. Quinn attracts girls like watermelon attracts flies!" She smiled up sheepishly at Price. "I know you think I've acted horribly—and I have. Please forgive me. It's just that I've had such a terrible headache, and the twins have been more than a handful since I got here—"

"You don't have to apologize," Price interrupted gently. "I knew that things weren't exactly going your way." He smiled. "And if it makes you feel any better, I know what you went through with Quinn." His eyes became pained, their lovely green growing dark and still. "If things had turned out differently, I wouldn't be within a hundred miles of here tonight. I would be a married man, spending a nice quiet night alone with my new wife."

Erin's eyes flew up to meet his, her heart giving an unusual lurch. For some reason the thought of Price being married suddenly upset her.

"Like you, I thought I had found the perfect woman. But it seems we didn't see eye to eye on a lot of things, so she found someone who let her have her way all the time." For the first time Erin heard bitterness creep into Price's voice.

"Did you love her?"

Price glanced at her in exasperation. "Of course I loved her! Do you think I'd marry someone I didn't love?"

54

"No. I just meant—did you love her a lot?"

"If you mean did it hurt like hell when she left me, yes, Erin, it hurt."

"I know. That's how I felt when I broke off with Quinn six months ago," Erin said sympathetically.

"Six months ago? Funny, that's when Jeannie and I broke up."

"Really, that *is* funny." They both sat staring at the sugar bowl on the kitchen table, each one lost in thought.

"Well, there's no use rehashing old memories. The past is—past. I made up my mind that I'm cut out to be a bachelor, anyway. It probably would never have worked out, and Jeannie just saw it quicker than I did. Look, I know we got off to a bad start, but if you're willing, I'd like to be your friend." His celadon gaze met hers with sincerity.

He wanted to be her friend! Erin mulled the unexpected suggestion over in her mind, then rejected it silently. Somehow she had the distinct impression that it would be extremely hard to be just a friend to such a virile, totally masculine man as Price Seaver. But if he wanted to think they could be friends, what harm could it do?

"Thank you, Price, that's very nice of you."

"One thing that should help console both of us is the fact that we can be just ourselves. I know *I'm* not looking for another involvement with a woman for a long time—if ever. And you're not likely to find your perfect man in the next few days. So how about my giving you a hand with the twins until Brenda and Nathan get back? I'm long overdue for a vacation."

"It won't be much of a vacation," Erin warned with a frown. "I'm nearly exhausted after only two days!"

"Well," Price said with another disarming grin in her direction, "it's bound to be easier with two."

"Oh, Price." Erin hung her head in shame, thinking of

how rude she had been to him since they had met. "I wish you wouldn't be so nice."

"Why not? It looks to me like it was past time a man was nice to you. You asked me what I wanted from you, Erin. My answer is nothing. I'm afraid Jeannie has spoiled my outlook on marriage and women in general for a long time to come. But if there's a perfect man out there, I hope you find him. It seems to me you deserve one."

"I think Jeannie must have been a little crazy," Erin said truthfully.

"That's funny, I was thinking the same thing about Quinn. So it's agreed; we'll be friends. I'll stick around and help with the twins for a few days, get in a little fishing, relax for a while, then I'll head back to Memphis."

"If you're sure that's how you want to spend your vacation. I must admit I could use the help." Erin paused. "I'd sincerely like to be your friend, Price—but nothing more." The whole idea suddenly seemed ridiculous. Surely he wasn't serious.

Price looked amused. "I'm not asking for anything but a few days away from the rat race, Erin. I haven't been with a woman in the last six months, so I think I'll be able to struggle through the next few days without endangering our—friendship."

Erin's heart fell. Well, holy cow! He *was* serious! "In that case, welcome aboard—friend!" Erin stuck out her hand and placed it in his large one, fighting an overwhelming surge of disappointment.

Price gripped her hand tightly, his smile growing broader. "Thanks—friend. Now I believe we have a funeral service to attend."

The intoning voice of "Reverend Seaver" held the attention of the small gathering under the tall spreading oak. Each one in his or her own special way was there to mourn the passing of Buck Rogers and Cinderella Fish. The two

56

littlest mourners stood clutching the reassuring hand of the pretty woman who stood next to the small grave site, their round eyes fixed solidly on the small cardboard box lying beside the gaping hole that read Lights Every Time matches. Erin listened reverently as Price praised the unquestionable goodness of Buck and Cinderella. Commenting that they had bubbled less than the ordinary goldfish he had known and never grew upset when they were not fed regularly, he reassured the mourners that Buck and Cinderella had a much stronger constitution than the average goldfish. Price cited as example the time Buck had lay on the coffee table for the better part of one whole afternoon when Huntley had taken him out to speak personally to him, then forgot to replace him in the bowl when his mother had called him to lunch. His comforting voice reminded Holly that Cinderella would be the cleanest fish up there, able to boast of having had a fragrant, delightful bubble bath just prior to her—long journey.

Price said a short prayer over the remains, then stuck the matchbox down into the small grave and covered it quickly with dirt. Holly stepped forward and placed a small clump of the flowers that still bloomed wild all over the banks of the lake this time of year on the lump of fresh dirt. With one long racking sigh the twins turned away from the grave site and walked morosely back toward the house.

"Hey." Price whistled shrilly. "Have you shown your aunt Erin what your dad and I built you this winter?"

Their faces lit up immediately, all gloomy thoughts dispelled as their eyes looked past Erin to a platform built about five feet off the ground on a limb of the old oak tree.

"Our tree house," they shouted joyfully. They flashed past Erin in a rush as they ran toward the tree, climbing carefully up on the small wooden ladder hooked to the platform.

"What is this?" Erin questioned, her eyes taking in the

large tree house the twins had crawled up into. It was built low to the ground, so they could easily get into it, and would present no dangers if they should become careless and tumble out. A neat thatched roof covered the large platform that had been thoughtfully covered with straw for tender knees to crawl around on. It made the perfect place to play on hot summer afternoons, a perfectly enchanting hideaway overlooking the sparkling blue waters of the lake.

"It's our very own house that Daddy and Uncle Price built," Huntley told her proudly. "You wanna come up here and sit in it for a while, Aunt Erin?" he invited graciously. "Boy, is it neat!"

Price came to stand behind her as she shaded her eyes to peer up into the tree. "No, I'll just stay down here and watch you. Be careful!" she added as she watched a minor skirmish develop between the two over territorial rights.

"Don't you want to climb up there and take a look at the view? It's spectacular," Price whispered from behind her. "Remind me to take you up there some moonlit night before you leave." He grinned at her suggestively, adding, "Friend."

"Did you help build this?" She smiled in admiration, noting that the tree house wasn't some flimsily constructed piece of work. It apparently had been well thought out and built with care.

"Designed it and helped build it," Price said, looking at the structure with pride. "Nathan and I always did want one of these things when we were kids, so one day we just decided to buy the wood and start building! Do you really like it?" he asked eagerly.

If Erin had hated it, she wouldn't have had the heart to tell him so. He was looking at her so proudly, that little-boy look surfacing on his face. But she didn't hate it—it was simply lovely and she hurriedly told him so.

The twins played happily for another five minutes while

58

Erin wandered around the area, breathing in the clean air. In the far distance she could see the white sails of several boats bobbing along on the sparkling waters. Everything seemed so peaceful—so perfect. Her gaze involuntarily sought out Price as he laughed and played with the twins in their tree house, his dark, wavy hair ruffling in the light breeze. With sudden clarity she knew that he could present a real danger to her. Nothing had ever frightened her more as that moment when she realized he was *not* Quinn. She paused, drinking in the sight of him, vowing to fight those feelings.

Price glanced up from his rowdy scuffling with Huntley and flashed her one of those devastating grins. They both waved at her boisterously, motioning for her to come up and join them. Erin smiled and waved back, starting the climb up the small embankment she had wandered down. Her hands were full of the summer flowers that blanketed the hillsides. Holly ran down to greet her, and they walked hand in hand up the hill to meet the men. Price smiled down at her as they joined them, his arm slipping around her waist as they proceeded on up the grassy rise leading to the house. To the casual onlooker they would present a picture of the perfect happy family—Mother, Daddy and children. Only the tall, handsome man holding the petite, curly brown-headed woman's hand and she knew it was a false image.

"Still feel like a hamburger?" Price asked casually, matching his strides to her smaller ones.

"Do you know what you're letting yourself in for?" she warned laughingly. "The twins' table manners are, shall we say, extremely lax."

Price ceased walking and turned to face her condescendingly, placing his hand smugly on his lean hips. "Now do I look like the kind of man who would let two five-year-olds get the best of him?"

Erin bit back a grin as she surveyed his perfectly tail-

59

ored brown designer jeans and his light brown striped oxford shirt. Price gave the appearance that he had just stepped out of a fashion magazine. He had the kind of suave sophistication that would enable him to look like a million dollars in a gunny sack. Somehow she didn't think he knew what he was letting himself in for this time.

"Well, I'm game if you are, Mr. Seaver," she said fatalistically.

"You've just got to know how to handle these kids," he reasoned sensibly as they all walked up to his new, sparkling clean car. "You have to tell children what's expected of them and then enforce it." He opened the door and the twins exploded into the backseat, their shoes leaving dust marks across the plush gray upholstery where they had walked. A funny look flooded his face as he glanced up sheepishly at Erin and reached over frantically to dust off the scuff marks. "Now you guys keep your feet on the floor," he instructed patiently, grabbing hold of one of Huntley's gouging feet. "Uncle Price gets *real* upset when you put your dirty shoes on the seats," he added nicely.

The twins immediately ceased their squirming and put their feet obediently on the floor. Price shot Erin an I-told-you-so smirk as he held the door open for her on the passenger side.

"Very impressive," she said, snickering under her breath. "You *do* have a way with a five-year-old." She couldn't wait till feeding time!

On the ride to McDonald's, the power windows in the backseat flapped up and down like window shades as Price's expensive car sped along the highway. Erin kept her face averted, gazing out the car window and pushing back her giggles as Price worriedly tolerated the windows zipping up and down. By the time they pulled into the parking lot of the restaurant, Huntley had managed to squeeze his tiny fingers between Price's seat, nimbly finding the master-control box. All four windows were buzzing up and down at the same time as Erin looked at Price sweetly. "When are you going to tell them what's expected of them?"

Price switched the engine off and turned to grab Huntley's plundering hands. "All right, you guys, let's knock it off! Huntley, let go of that switch!"

Holly set up a screech as Erin removed her hands from the once-clean glass of the back window. A smeary palm print was definitely visible. Erin glanced uneasily at Price.

"Okay, now what does everyone want to eat?" Price asked after calm was finally restored to the inside of the car.

"Are we going to eat in the car?" Erin asked in amazement.

"Don't you think we can—watch them a little closer out here?" Price asked worriedly.

"But your beautiful car. . . ." Erin's eyes surveyed the immaculate plush interior of the car. Letting the twins eat in here would be like throwing slops to a hog.

"I'd rather keep an eye on them in here than try to keep up with them in there." His eyes motioned toward the crowded dining room.

"It's your car," Erin said hesitantly. "I'll have a cheeseburger, french fries and a small Coke." She paused, thinking about her extra ten pounds. "Forget my french fries and make that a sugar-free drink. Get the children 'happy meals.' "

Price gave her a suggestive look. "No fries and a sugar-free *small* drink. I gather you're thinking about your figure again," he teased gently. "Since we're only friends, don't worry about those extra pounds and have a decent meal. You haven't eaten since last night."

"No thank you. Just the hamburger and drink."

"Suit yourself," he said resignedly. "What am I supposed to get the kids?"

"Get them 'happy meals,' " she repeated. "Just trust me, Price. They really do serve such things."

"They'd better or it's your neck," he warned with a grimace, stepping out of the car. "If I go loping up there and ask for two 'happy meals' and she looks at me as if I just rode in with a bus full of crazies, you'll pay, lady."

Within ten minutes he was back, his arms loaded with drinks and sandwiches. Erin made the twins sit quietly in the backseat while she spread napkins in their laps and carefully laid out their hamburgers and fries.

"Now be very careful and don't spill *anything* on Uncle Price's nice clean car," she cautioned, eyeing them warily.

"We won't!" They both began to devour their dinners hungrily.

Price and Erin munched contentedly on their hamburgers, exchanging smalltalk as the backseat remained calm. During one of the pauses in conversation, the distinct sound of a drink turning over, the ice sloshing onto the mats on the floor, reached their ears. Erin paused in her chewing and glanced at Price.

"Don't worry about it. I'll clean it up later," he said under his breath. "As long as they're quiet, let's not stir up a hornets' nest!"

Erin shrugged her shoulders and took another bite of her hamburger.

"Do you got any ketchup, Uncle Pwice?" Holly asked through a mouth full of hamburger.

"Do I have any ketchup," Price corrected, reaching for a plastic package lying between the seats.

"That's what I said," she replied crossly.

"Here, what do you want it on?" Price turned in his seat to help her.

"My fwench fwies. I'll do it!" She held out her chubby hand to receive the ketchup.

"I don't think so, Holly. You let *me* put it on your fries," Price said in a no-nonsense tone, visions of huge red blotches of ketchup on his gray upholstery appearing sickly in his head.

Holly plopped back in the seat disgustedly, knocking her soda over this time.

"Damn." Price groaned under his breath, squeezing out the last of the ketchup on Holly's fries. "I'd better clean both of those sodas up before they start wallowing in them."

"Here, let me help you . . ." Erin's words stuck in her throat; she watched in horror as the drink that was sitting between them tipped over and spilled in his lap. Price sucked in his breath, then sprang out of the car like a scalded cat, holding the front of his pants away from his drenched skin. Erin froze in her seat, not quite certain what to do. Price hopped beside the car for a few minutes, doing what Erin considered an admirable job of not coming unglued.

"I'm sorry," she said in a small voice, leaning over his seat to peek out the door at him. "Is there anything I can do?"

"Nothing," he said tightly, reaching for the back floor mats and dumping the ice and dirty cola on the ground. The twins stood up on the seat and watched in silent fascination as Price tried to restore some semblance of order to the car.

Erin reached over and laid Holly's fries on the driver's seat and brushed some stray crumbs off her seat. Poor Price, she thought worriedly, his car will never look the same!

"Boy, Aunt Erin sure made a mess, huh?" Huntley observed from behind his large glasses, one french fry stuck casually between his fingers like a cigarette.

Price looked up at him blandly. "Why don't you eat that french fry instead of smoking it, chum."

After brushing off the front of his jeans one more time, he opened the door and slid back into the driver's side. A frantic scream spewed out of Holly as Price came up out of his seat rapidly. "What's the matter now?" he bellowed, turning to glower at her hostilely.

"You sat on my fwench fwies and ketchup," she wailed, glaring back at him defiantly.

"Ohhhh—oh—shoot!" Price shouted, leaping out of the car and fighting to control his language in front of the children.

The twins watched in wide-eyed absorption as Price irritably picked Holly's ketchup-covered french fries off his not-so-immaculate brown jeans.

Glancing up, he saw the look of terror on all three faces. With a mean scowl on his face, he picked up some fries that were lying on the ground minus the ketchup. With great stalking strides he paced his way slowly to the car door, a growl coming from his throat.

Huntley swallowed hard and blinked back at him through his horn-rim glasses. Holly, never brave to begin with, cowered against Erin, her eyes round as saucers.

Price leered in the car door and said in a deep gruff voice, "Who put the fwench fwies in my seat!" "Was it you?" He looked straight at Holly, his eyes piercing her uneasy brown ones. She shook her head, scared. "Was it you?" he asked Huntley. The other twin swallowed hard again and shook his head nervously.

Price crawled over the seat and pressed his face up against Erin's in an exaggerated angry stance. "Then it was you!" he accused righteously.

"Yeah, want to make something out of it?" She grinned saucily.

Amid peals of relieved laughter, Price lunged at Erin, getting her down in the car seat and stuffing the french fries he carried down her blouse. The twins piled on top of him, and the car erupted in one big tickling match, squeals of laughter filling the air.

Price's hand came up under Erin's blouse and touched

one of her breasts playfully, then lingered there for a moment. Erin shot him a dirty glare as he shrugged fatalistically before removing it discreetly.

"I *thought* we were going to be friends," Erin hissed sharply under her breath.

"We are! Wasn't I being friendly enough?" he asked innocently.

"You're being too friendly," she muttered, pushing his large bulk off her, sending the twins into new fits of giggles.

"Maybe we should reconsider this friend theory," he shouted above the chattering voices of the twins as they tried to restore some order to their dinner. "And then again, maybe we shouldn't." He grinned as Erin shot him a dirty look.

By the time they had settled themselves back down and drove out of the parking lot, Price's car would have sold for half the price he had paid for it six months earlier. Erin glanced at his masculine profile as they pulled onto the highway. They had had so much fun today. Would it be this way when she found her perfect man? Of course it would! And for the first time in a very long time, Erin couldn't wait to start looking for him again. She looked at Price out of the corner of her eye. Reconsider their friendship? Never! Well . . . at least not now, anyway.

CHAPTER FOUR

By the time they arrived home, the twins and Erin were feeling the effects of the day. And Price was irritable and eager to get out of his ruined pants. The twins became crankier by the minute, and Erin's head still bore faint traces of her migraine. With Price's help, she soon had both children bathed and was helping Holly get ready for bed.

"I wanted to wear my yellow jammies," Holly fretted as Erin brushed her damp, baby-sweet-smelling locks out of her face.

"Your yellow pajamas are dirty, Holly. Remember, you wore them the first night I was here," Erin reminded her patiently, giving her another hug.

Chubby arms went around Erin's neck and squeezed tight as Holly kissed her aunt lovingly. "I wove you, Aunt Erin."

"I love you, too, Holly."

"When's Mommy and Daddy coming home? I miss them." Holly's big brown eyes grew misty. A week was a long time to a five-year-old.

"In another few days. Now that I'm feeling better, maybe we can go on a picnic or see a movie. Would you like that?"

"How long's a few days?" she persisted, her arms wrapping tighter around Erin's neck.

"Now, let's see . . . your mommy and daddy left Sunday. Today is Tuesday. Do you know the days of the week?"

Holly shook her head woefully. "No, but I can count to five."

"Well, if you can count to five, you know that you have five fingers on your hand. See!" Erin picked up her hand and pointed to each of her fingers. "Now we're going to hide your thumb, and in the morning we'll hide this finger, then the next day we'll hide another finger, and when we've hidden all your fingers but this little teeny one"— Erin wiggled a fat little finger playfully, eliciting a squeal of delight from Holly—"then the next day your mommy and daddy come home!"

Holly stopped giggling and looked down at her hand solemnly. She wiggled her little finger experimentally, hiding the other four. Looking up, she bestowed a radiant smile on Erin and said, "That won't be very wong, will it?"

"No, not very long at all. Now why don't you run on out and see if Price has Huntley ready for bed."

When Erin and Holly reached the front room, Price was in the process of buttoning a squirming Huntley's pajamas. They were a loud color of red, with MACHO MUNCHKIN written across the front.

"Hold on, macho," Price commanded as he fought to get the last button fastened. "Boy, you need a road map to get into these things," he told Erin with a frown. "Why do they put so many buttons on a kid's pajamas?"

"I don't know. I think they have one lone crazy man sitting up in a tower somewhere working for all the children's clothing companies, and his job is to design clothes that take hours to get in and out of." Erin laughed as she sat down next to him on the couch.

The twins scrambled between them, fighting over who got to sit next to Uncle Price.

Price and Erin each took a twin in their laps and snuggled down deeper in the sofa to relax before they carted

67

them off to bed. Huntley poked his finger into the beak of his slipper and made an exaggerated pretense of being bitten by the yellow bird.

"Don't you wish you had some slippers like these, Uncle Price?" he asked after his antics failed to get any response out of the older couple.

Price eyed the colorful birds for a moment. "Yeah, I was just sitting here thinking that you had all the luck. Where did you get those things?"

"Santa Kwaus brought them to him," Holly butted in. "He brought me mine, too. See!" She stuck her foot in Price's face.

"Yes, they are sure nice. Don't you wish we had a pair of bird slippers like those, Aunt Erin?" Price asked with a twinkle in his eye.

"Maybe Santa will bring you a pair," Erin encouraged playfully.

"Yeah, but you better put it on your list," Huntley warned. "You only get three things from Santa Claus." He bolted from Price's lap and ran to grab the pad and pencil lying next to the phone, returning to his seat instantly. "I'm going to write down my three things right now!"

"A little early, isn't it, chum?" Price stilled his kicking feet hurriedly. "Christmas isn't for another four months yet."

"I don't care. I might forget." He fixed his mouth in a thoughtful grimace, then began to write in big, bold letters. TRAIN, DUMS, B.B. GUM. "Here, Uncle Price, you read it and be sure I spelled everything all right." He shoved the paper at his uncle.

Price took the slip of paper and read aloud. "Let's see, you want a train, a—dum—"

"Drum!"

"Oh, right, a drum and a—oh, mercy!" He groaned under his breath, then continued, "A BB gun. Right?"

"Right!"

"They'd have to declare the neighborhood a disaster area if ole Santa comes through with this list," Price said, grinning at Erin.

"Help me write down what I want, Aunt Ewin." Holly jerked the pad and pencil out of Huntley's hand.

Huntley reached over and pinched her soundly before Price could jerk his hand away.

"This kid is faster than a speedin' bullet," Price said with a groan as Holly let out an earsplitting scream.

"Holly! That's enough! Now quiet down and tell me what you want me to write on your list," Erin said sternly.

The wails immediately ceased. "I want a lellow bicycle, a doll that wets, and uh . . . a ten-dollar bill."

"Now there's a girl after my own heart," Price said happily.

Erin looked at him teasingly. "Do you want me to write down your list, Price?"

"No. Give me the pad and pencil. I'll write my own." He wiggled his brows at Huntley smugly. "We don't want those silly women writing out our list, do we?"

Huntley began to bounce up and down. "What do you want, Uncle Price?"

"Well, now, let me think. I think I'll take a . . . lellow Maserati." He paused and made a big pretense of thinking. "I definitely don't want a doll that wets her pants." He winked at Erin suggestively. "But I would take the ten-dollar bill, and since I only have one gift left . . . that will have to be the bird slippers."

"Yeah, yeah, okay, now it's your turn, Aunt Erin!" the twins chorused.

"Oh, dear, I really don't know. I'd like to have a diamond ring, a mink coat, and . . ." She rolled her eyes upward, studying the ceiling.

"And a perfect marriage," Price finished her list for her.

Erin looked startled for a moment, then said softly,

"Yes, I would like that. A diamond ring, a mink coat—and a perfect marriage."

"Yuk! I hope Santa Claus doesn't get our gifts mixed up," Huntley said adamantly. "I want my drums!"

"And I think it's time both you little munchkins were in bed," Price announced as he rose from the couch with a twin under each arm. "Aunt Erin, why don't you fix us some iced tea while I tuck these rug rats into bed."

"Do you need any help?" Erin rose to her feet and started to follow him.

"Nope, I can handle this all by myself. You just get the iced tea."

"Night, Aunt Erin." The twins giggled.

"I'll be in to kiss you later, okay?" she called.

Price stopped and shifted his bundles more evenly. "You talking to me?"

Erin blushed. "No, I meant the twins!"

"Darn! Huntley gets the bird slippers and kisses too!" he grumbled good-naturedly as he disappeared down the hall.

By the time he returned, Erin had two large glasses of iced tea waiting. Price walked back into the room and took a seat on the sofa next to her, stretching out his tall frame in weary relief. "I think they fell asleep before their heads hit the pillow."

"You're very good with them," Erin commented as she handed him his glass, then laid her head back on the sofa and closed her eyes.

"Yeah, well, I love kids. I always thought I'd like to have four or five. I suppose I'm getting a little old for that many now."

"Oh, I don't think so. You still have plenty of time," Erin said softly.

"Well, maybe. Jeannie didn't want children. At least not right away." He stared into the cold fireplace, his mind drifting. "Not that it matters now one way or the other."

70

They sat in easy, relaxed companionship, sipping their iced teas. The house grew hushed and a sense of peacefulness washed over the couple in the small family room. Erin could see the moon reflecting off the still waters of the lake through the large glass window on the west side of the wall.

"Do you have any brothers or sisters?" Price asked conversationally.

"No, I'm an only child. I always wanted brothers and sisters, though." She laughed. "When we were making out our Christmas lists earlier, it brought to mind how I always used to start in around the first of October telling Mom and Dad that I only wanted a brother or a sister for my Christmas present. Nothing else—just a brother or a sister."

"I gather your parents decided to go along with the usual dolls and roller skates?"

"Yes." Erin smiled. "It wasn't until I reached womanhood myself that Mom told me they had never been able to have other children. In fact, they considered me a miracle child."

"That's too bad. . . . I come from a fairly large family. I have two brothers and two sisters," Price said quietly, deep in thought. "I used to come home from school every day to a house that smelled like fresh-baked cookies, pot roast, and a mom who met me at the door with a bear hug."

"I had the same thing," Erin murmured, "only I used to get so lonely. All the other kids had big brothers to protect them or sisters to argue with over clothes or boyfriends. All I had was a stuffed rabbit I used to take to bed with me every night and tell my troubles to."

"What troubles?" Price grinned affectionately. "Things like how you were the homeliest girl in the class—"

"No, I wasn't!" Erin stopped him curtly. "I was a cute *little* girl."

71

"Really? Well"—he leaned back and took another sip of his iced tea—"I was just sitting here thinking you aren't half bad now that you're all grown up."

Erin punched him playfully. "Thanks. Are you trying to tell me God doesn't make junk?"

"In your case, he didn't." Price winked. "At least the parts I've seen."

Erin blushed, her mind flashing back to when he had undressed her the other night. Price had seen everything there was to see of Erin Holmes. Her heart lifted at the thought that he had liked what he saw.

"Do you still take your rabbit to bed with you at night?"

"For lack of something better, yes." Erin grinned at him wickedly.

"Such a waste." Price shook his head regretfully, his eyes running over her feminine softness lazily. "Some rabbits have all the luck."

"I want children," Erin said, quickly turning the subject back to their previous discussion. "I used to think I wanted eight."

"Eight!" Price nearly choked on his drink. "Good grief, woman, you'd better marry a rabbit!"

Erin grinned happily. "You wouldn't want eight?"

"I hardly think so! In fact, I'm beginning to think that wanting five is bordering on insanity! Can you imagine eight Huntleys running amuck in this world?"

"Oh, my children are not going to be like the twins. They're going to be perfect," Erin said proudly.

Price watched the soft lamplight play over her lovely features. "Naturally. Perfect marriages *would* have perfect children," he said softly.

Erin opened her eyes and looked at him for a moment. "Are you teasing me about that?"

"No," he replied tiredly, leaning his head back now and staring up at the ceiling. "It's just that I hate to see you get hurt a second time, Erin."

72

"Hurt—what do you mean by that?"

"There is no perfect marriage, Erin. There's no perfect man; no perfect woman. Surely you realize that."

Erin sighed and closed her eyes again. "I can always dream, can't I?"

"As long as you realize that everything has its share of problems, and you don't go running through life looking for something that isn't there and never will be."

"What's wrong with wanting what other people have? Nathan and Brenda—"

"Nathan has had more than his share of problems, Erin. Hasn't Brenda mentioned to you that Nathan was married once before?"

Erin's eyes flew open. "What!"

"I thought you knew that. He's never made a secret of it. It was one of those crazy teenage marriages that lasted about two months. After the divorce he went into the service. He didn't meet Brenda until after his discharge."

"But Quinn never mentioned that to me." Erin was totally dumbfounded.

"Apparently Quinn didn't mention a number of things to you," Price said pointedly. "Nathan and Brenda's marriage, I'm sure, is far from perfect. In fact, I can think of two prime examples lying right in the next room!"

"That's not a good example! They love those children dearly," Erin exclaimed indignantly.

"I know they do, but I've also heard them go around and around over any discipline Nathan wants to dole out."

"At least Nathan isn't out chasing every pretty skirt in town like his brother is," Erin grumbled. "At least he's home every night with his wife and unruly children!"

"Yeah, he *is* a good husband. Good—not perfect!"

"I don't care what you say, Price. When I marry, it will be to a man who will be completely devoted to me and our children. He'll spend every night home with me, we'll do things together, we won't need other people in our lives, he will never look at another woman—we will never quarrel, and I will make his life perfect."

"Damn, I feel sorry for the poor man already!"

"Why? Isn't that the way a marriage should be? Don't you wish Jeannie would have thought a little more along those lines?"

"Leave Jeannie out of this," Price snapped.

"Why, because you still love her?" Erin pressed. "Don't you want a wife who needs only you and no one else?"

"Yes, but I don't want to live in a cell block! My wife *will* need only me, but she'll love me enough not to smother me to death. What you just described is a prison, not a healthy marriage!"

Erin's eyes began to water with unshed tears. "I didn't mean that we couldn't have other friends. I just meant—" Her voice broke as the tears started streaming down her face. "I just meant I didn't want my husband to be thinking of other women. I want to be the only woman in his life—the only one who lies in his arms at night. . . ."

Price moved toward her, and his hand reached out to pull her face against his broad chest as he whispered softly into the fragrance of her curly hair. "And you have every right to expect that from the man you love, Erin, whether it's your husband or not. I didn't mean that a marriage couldn't have all the ingredients you just listed and still be a damn good one. I only want you to see that you can't have a perfect one, because you'll go on searching until you're old and gray, and you'll never find it, honey. Quinn Daniels was no good and he's left a lot of scars in your life. You won't find a perfect man, but they won't all be Quinns either."

The tears fell harder as she pressed against him, his warmth and presence more than comforting. It had been such a very long time since she had opened up her heart and let anyone see just how deep her hurt was. The cleansing tears continued to fall, dampening the front of Price's

74

shirt. Words failed him as he held her sobbing form in his arms. What could he say? If he could have gotten the words past the lump in his throat, he would probably have told her that he had shed his own share of tears in the last few months. He had felt frustrated, and so deeply resentful of Jeannie that he thought life just plain stank and saw no purpose for going on. But he had buried his hurt and faced one day at a time. The only logical way to keep from being hurt like that again was never to become involved—deeply involved—with a woman again. If he could help Erin see that she would never find a perfect marriage—or a perfect man—then he could save her a lot of hurt in the future.

Erin's softness pressed into Price's body, and his arms tightened around her automatically. Six months; it had been six long months since he had held a woman in his arms, kissed her, smelled the fragrance of her hair. When Jeannie left, he hadn't wanted to think about a woman, let alone be with one. He knew lots of men who tried to kill the pain with other women or a bottle, but he had never been that type. Sex was not a casual thing to him, at least sex without some type of commitment. But his body seemed to know how long it had been since he had made love to a woman, as he became uncomfortably aware of the pressure mounting inside him.

He gave a deep sigh, knowing that he was going to kiss Erin. The idea of being friends had sounded reasonable at the time, but as he felt her breasts molding tightly against his chest, he knew the folly of that suggestion. He placed his hands on her head and pulled her face from his neck gently. Their eyes met in defeated recognition of what was about to happen, for they both knew what they needed at this moment—the touch of each other's lips, the feel of each other's hands, the wondrous knowledge that they were both still very much alive.

"I'm going to kiss you, Erin Holmes. Don't be afraid," he whispered huskily. "I'm only going to kiss you."

She closed her eyes once more, her fingers running across the smoothness of his jaw, and nodded quietly. "I want that, Price. I want that very much."

"Open your eyes, Erin. I want you to see me kiss you. I want you to know how incredibly lovely you are; how it wouldn't matter to me if you weighed three hundred pounds or if you were Miss America at this moment. I want you to see that the Erin Holmes I'm kissing is going to make some lucky man a nearly perfect wife someday."

Her eyes opened slowly as his mouth brushed hers lightly.

"Do you believe that?" he whispered softly.

"I feel very lovely right now," she whispered against the pressure of his kiss. "You make me feel—very lovely. Thank you."

"Then close your eyes again, lovely Erin, because I'm going to kiss you in a way you'll never forget."

She moaned low in her throat as his mouth closed over hers, and his arms crushed her tighter to his chest, the kiss becoming hungry and urgent between them. His tongue prodded gently to enter her mouth and join with hers. His restless hands searched urgently down the sides of her breasts, stopping for just the barest moment to cup the swelling fullness, savoring the feel of her. He didn't want to scare her. He knew that most likely Quinn had led her into womanhood; but that was Quinn, not Price. He had promised her friendship, nothing more, and he would not break that promise. Right now she was very vulnerable, very lonely, very hurting. From her response to him right now as her mouth eagerly accepted his kiss, he knew he could ease their sexual agony of the last six months. But was that what he really wanted? Would that be fair to her, when he had no intention of it being anything but what it was—casual sex.

She moaned again, softly, like a small kitten, as his mouth left hers abruptly. He kissed her eyelids, her nose, her cheeks before burying his face in her hair one final time.

"I think we'd better break this up—unless you want it to go further," he said quietly. It would be her decision. He wanted her right now with a deep, aching need. But he also knew he would have to face her in the morning.

"I don't know . . . what I want," she whispered painfully. "I've never been with anyone but Quinn."

Price chuckled and brushed his lips across hers again. "You don't have to tell me that. But I know if you're feeling what I'm feeling, six months is a long time. . . ." His mouth took hers in another long, lazy kiss. "You say the word. I think we could bring each other a lot of pleasure tonight." He moved her closer against him to let her feel the powerful proof of his words.

Erin's thoughts were whirling. Price had awakened a hungry need in her, one that had lain dormant for a long time now. She had given herself in love to one man and felt very disillusioned from the experience. But at least she had loved him! With Price it would be wrong, because she didn't love him. She barely knew him.

With a beaten sigh she backed away from his arms, knowing that it had to mean something to her—she had to love a man before she could ever make another commitment that serious.

"I'm sorry, Price, but I'm not Jeannie, and you're not Quinn."

A startled look crossed Price's handsome features at her words. "Quinn! Were you thinking of *him*—that no good —you were thinking of him right now when I kissed you!" he said in an incredulous voice.

"Well, sort of. And don't tell me you weren't thinking of Jeannie!" she shot back irritably. She was quite sure all that pent-up passion hadn't been strictly for her.

"No, I wasn't!" He paused, a little surprised at his own answer. He really hadn't been thinking about Jeannie. For the first time in a very long time, he had kissed a woman other than Jeannie—and enjoyed it.

"You weren't?" Erin's eyes raised to meet his.

"No, I was not! And it sure doesn't do much for a man's ego to hear that the woman he's kissing is thinking about another man!"

"Well, what are you getting upset about? If I recall our earlier conversations, neither one of us is interested in anything other than friendship at the moment, and if we happen to want to exchange a friendly kiss—" Her face turned a soft shade of pink as she thought about their earlier "friendly" kiss. To her recollection, Quinn hadn't kissed her with such mastery even in the throes of passion!

"I may not be the most experienced man in the world, lady, but I would hardly consider what we just shared a friendly kiss! I'd bet my last dollar I could have—"

"You most certainly could not have!" Erin gasped indignantly. "Are you insinuating that I'm some sex-starved woman who can't wait to fall into bed with a man!"

"Keep your voice down!" Price cautioned heatedly. "You're going to wake the children up!"

"I want you to take back what you just said," Erin hissed angrily.

"About what?"

"About me being a sex-starved woman who can't wait to fall into a man's bed!"

"You're nuts! I didn't say that, you did!"

"Mr. Seaver!" Erin drew herself up fully and stared him boldly in the eye. "I believe we are going to have to reconsider the idea of being friends. My *friends* do not talk to me in the manner in which you just addressed me."

"Nuts. You are just plain nuts!" he shouted as he jumped up from the sofa. "From the minute I walked into this house, you have ranted and raved at me just because I happen to remind you of that scum—and you're right!

I do *not* think of you as a friend. You're a damn desirable woman—"

"Don't you *dare* call Quinn scum!"

"Good lord! Are you defending him now?"

"No, but you don't hear me saying anything derogatory about that—that—floozie you're in love with!"

"Let's just keep Jeannie's name out of this!"

"See!" Erin pointed her finger at him accusingly. "See! You even admit what she is. Why would you continue to be in love with a woman who dumped you for another man—probably not half as nice as you are. Why would you let a woman like that keep you from falling in love with someone else and having your five kids!"

"How did we get onto my problems? Why don't we discuss the possibility of you getting that no-good louse Quinn Daniels out of your system, lady! What reason have you got for still carrying a torch around for a man who isn't fit to wipe your shoes, let alone deserve your love. He'll never make any woman a decent husband! You just tell me that, Erin Holmes!"

"I don't have to tell you anything, Price Seaver, except I think you should leave—right now—tonight!"

"No, thank you. I'm on my vacation. Remember?" Price's face bore a very stubborn look now as he paced in front of Erin angrily.

She stood and faced him hostilely. "You *are* going to leave! Tonight!"

"No, no, I'm not." Price casually seated himself on the sofa again and picked up his glass. "Nathan is one of my best friends, and he would be offended if I stayed anywhere else. Besides, I'm doing him a favor. I'm sure he doesn't have the least idea that he's left his children in the hands of a dingbat who doesn't seem to have any control over them—"

"And you do?" she sputtered. "What about the green dog, the dead goldfish, the painted desert in the twins' bedroom—not to mention the demolished interior of your car . . ."

"I was getting ready to trade it in anyway." He dismissed her argument with a shrug. "Besides, I think they know who's boss now."

"Well, good, then you can take care of them. I'm going back home." Erin started toward her bedroom angrily.

"Hey! Now wait a minute—come back here." Price sprang to his feet. "We can work this out like two reasonable adults, can't we? I'm just going to hang around for a couple of days, get in some fishin', then I'll leave. I haven't had a vacation in years! You wouldn't do that to a friend, would you?" he pleaded helplessly.

"A friend, no; but we are not friends, Mr. Seaver. I should never have been so gullible as to believe that we could be," Erin said tightly.

"You're upset over that kiss, aren't you? I *told* you that I was going to kiss you, and if I remember right, your exact words were"—his voice grew high and feminine—
" 'I'd like that.' But if it makes you feel any better, I'll keep my distance from you. That is, unless you signal me otherwise."

"Don't hold your breath," Erin said curtly. If she had any common sense, she would insist on him leaving tonight. But, on the other hand, it would be nice to have him around to help with the twins, and the next couple of days would be made considerably easier if he was around—and, if she would only admit it, she wanted him to stay. "All right, I'll confess I can use the help with the twins. But in two days you go home."

"Yes, ma'am," he agreed with a willing smile. "Are we semifriends again?"

"Barely," she acknowledged, the faint beginnings of a smile on her own face.

"I tell you what. Do you like fish?"

"Sure, why?"

"Well, in order to show you what a really nice guy I can be, I'll catch you a stringer of fish. Would you consent to fix them for me and the twins if I did?" His face had turned almost boyish as he tried to make amends.

"Just make it one big one and I'll consider it." She grinned.

"That's a deal, Erin." His face grew serious. "I really am sorry about a few minutes ago . . . I didn't mean to say those things about Quinn. It's none of my business how you feel about him."

"That's all right, Price. I shouldn't have said what I did about Jeannie. I know you must love her very much."

"I don't know if I do or not." The words surprised Price as well as Erin. A broad grin broke over his face. "At least right at the moment, I don't!"

"Good!" Erin grasped his hand sincerely. "You're much too nice a man to let a woman like her throw you."

"Well, I don't know about you, but I could use some sleep." Price stretched, then yawned. "How about taking the kids over to Silver Dollar City tomorrow?"

"You're not going to fish?"

"I'll get up and go early. I should be back by noon. Boy, I'd love to catch a trophy bass!" he said.

"I think that sounds like fun. I know the twins will be elated."

"Good. Then I guess I'll see you tomorrow." He walked across the room, turning out lamps as he went. Erin followed behind him, yawning. Bed would feel unusually good to her tonight.

The room was plunged into darkness, with only the faint light coming from the hallway. It seemed she was acutely aware of the broadness of his shoulders tonight, the very faint aroma of his aftershave, the way his hair looked so thick and touchable.

"Goodnight—friend," he whispered as they stopped before her bedroom door.

81

"Goodnight—friend," she whispered back, dreamily recalling the way his mouth had felt on hers, the warmth and moistness of it.

"You really are some woman," he said softly, his finger reaching out to brush away an errant lock of her hair. "Quinn Daniels is not only a rat, he's the world's biggest fool."

"No bigger than Jeannie."

"Jeannie who?" he asked, his smile growing tender.

"I'll see you tomorrow." She opened the door to her bedroom, not daring to stay in his presence a moment longer. He had awakened all those old feelings in her, and it made her very edgy.

"Yeah, see you tomorrow," Price said, his eyes lingering on the curve of her breast.

He was still leaning negligently against the doorjamb when she closed the door quietly. Jeannie who? Quinn who? At that moment Erin didn't really want to think about either one of them. At that moment neither one of them mattered. She was foolishly succumbing to Price Seaver's charms, and it suddenly scared her spitless!

CHAPTER FIVE

True to his word, Price was back shortly before noon the following day. The twins met him at the door, jabbering excitedly about their forthcoming trip to Silver Dollar City that afternoon.

"Just give me ten minutes for a quick shower, then we'll be on our way," he promised, trying to fight his way out of their clutches. He looked up and saw Erin standing in the doorway and gave her a sexy wink. "Hi, friend!"

"Hi! Any luck with the fish dinner?"

"Nope, didn't even catch a keeper this morning. The man who does a lot of guiding in this area is going out with me in the morning," he added hopefully.

"Hurry and take your shower, Uncle Pwice," Holly urged, taking his hand and pushing him toward the bathroom. "We're in an awful hurry!"

"We are, are we? Well, I'll see if I can't speed things up some," he promised her as she pushed him along.

The phone rang as Erin tried to smother a smile at the way Holly was manhandling him down the hallway, her mouth going nonstop.

"Hello," Erin said as she picked up the phone and sat down on the kitchen bar stool.

"Hello. May I speak to Price Seaver, please." A sultry voice floated over the wire. "His office said he could be reached at this number."

"Yes, he's here. Just a minute." Erin's stomach fluttered nervously as she laid the phone down and walked toward the bathroom. She couldn't imagine who was calling him, but an unreasonable surge of jealousy shot through her.

"Price, you're wanted on the phone. Are you able to take it?"

"Yo! I'll be there in a second."

Erin walked back to the phone and relayed the message. Within minutes Price walked into the room wearing only a pair of jeans. Erin forced herself to look at everything in the room but his bare, incredibly sexy chest.

"Yeah, Price Seaver here." The happy look of only moments earlier faded slowly from his face as he recognized the voice on the other end of the line. "Hello, Jeannie. How did you know I was here?" he said calmly.

A sudden feeling of nausea rose swiftly in Erin's throat as she tried to ignore the conversation. She busied herself with straightening up a few stray glasses from the kitchen counter.

"Well, I'm sorry to hear that. Maybe you two can still work things out." Price's voice remained very calm as his eyes glanced over and met Erin's.

Feeling very uncomfortable standing in the room while he was talking to Jeannie, Erin decided to see about the twins. She didn't want to hear the rest of the conversation. Apparently Jeannie's new love hadn't worked out.

It was at least another twenty minutes before Price finished his conversation, dressed, and returned to the living room. Erin was reading Huntley and Holly a story from one of their picture books, trying desperately to tell herself it didn't matter that he was talking to a woman he had loved—or still was very much in love with. It both puzzled and frightened her that she cared who he talked with. Had she jumped out of the frying pan into the fire?

"Sorry I took so long. Everybody ready to go?" Price greeted them absently. He looked over at Erin and smiled.

"We've been weady since we got up this morning," Holly grumbled, then jumped down from the sofa and wrapped her arms around Price's knee.

"Can we ride Fire in the Hole, Uncle Pwice?"

"What's a fire in the hole?" He grimaced, trying to undo her prying fingers.

"A roller coaster!" Huntley filled him in. "But I don't know if we're tall enough to ride it yet. We'll have to measure again today. You have to be th-is tall," he stretched his hands over his head as far as he could reach.

"Well, I'll make it, but I don't know about you two munchkins." He glanced at Erin. "You ready to go, Auntie Erin?"

"Yes, all ready." Every nerve in her was screaming to ask him what Jeannie had wanted, but she knew she was being completely unreasonable. It was really none of her business. They all trooped out to the front door, the twins' enthusiasm bubbling over.

"Lord, I wish I had half the energy those kids have," Price complained as he locked the front door. "If a person could bottle that, he would be a millionaire!"

"Why don't we take my car," Erin suggested as they walked down the steps. "I hate to do any more damage to yours, and they certainly can't hurt mine."

They stopped in front of her red Volkswagen and stared at the little bug. "It isn't running right, but I think it will get us over there and back," she added.

"Sure, why not. Come on, kids, get in Aunt Erin's crackerbox."

"Kwackerbox!" Holly's eyes lit up. "Is this weally a kwackerbox!"

"No, of course not. That's just your uncle Price's idea of a joke. This is a very nice, *cheap* car. Not all of us can afford a luxurious car like his." She looked at Price pointedly.

Price got in on the driver's side and started the engine.

"I'll tell you what. I'll give you the Olds when Santa Claus brings me my lellow Maserati."

"And your bird slippers," Huntley added helpfully.

"And my bird slippers," Price agreed. "I plan on wearing those everywhere I go."

It took a little over twenty minutes to drive to the amusement park. The lush Ozarks countryside was still thick with green foliage, but in another month the hills would be ablaze with the beauty of fall.

Price wheeled the small car into one of the large parking lots and they all got out, the twins barely able to control their excitement.

"Don't walk too far ahead of us," Erin called as the twins spurted forward, eager to get into the park where everything was set in the frontier days of the 1800s.

"They'll be all right. Let them work off some of that energy." Price laughed as they walked toward the tram that would take them to the entrance of the city. "Aren't you going to ask me about that phone call earlier?" he asked as he reached out and took her hand.

"It's none of my business," Erin replied, her stomach fluttering wildly at his touch.

"No, but I thought that since we were friends, you'd naturally wonder why Jeannie was calling."

They walked together in silence for a minute before Erin's curiosity overcame her. "What did she want?"

Price looked down at her and asked innocently, "Who?"

"Price!"

"Oh, you mean ole what's her name . . . Jeannie."

"Yes, ole what's her name. What did she want?"

"Well, it seems her newfound love has not worked out the way she expected."

"And she wants you back," Erin finished.

"She didn't say."

"What *did* she say?"

86

"Not a whole lot of anything, actually. I think she just wanted someone to air her gripes to, someone to feel sorry for her."

"And you obliged."

"I listened. I didn't necessarily agree with all she said."

"You would be an utter fool to take her back, Price. And mark my words, that's what she wants," Erin said bluntly, fighting that ridiculous feeling of jealousy again.

"Do tell, Auntie Erin. By the way, I've been meaning to ask you why the twins call you aunt."

"I don't know. They have always called me Aunt Erin from the moment they learned how to talk. What about you? You're not their uncle."

"Brenda started calling me that in front of them, and they just picked up on it. I don't mind; I enjoy it," he confessed. "But back to why I shouldn't go back to Jeannie. You were saying. . . ."

"I didn't say you shouldn't go back to her. I just said I thought you would be foolish to, that's all."

They walked together, Price holding her hand, both of them deep in thought. Finally Price broke the silence. "I'm flying up to Memphis tomorrow. I called my office after I hung up with Jeannie, and there's a matter that has to be taken care of. I should be back home in time for dinner."

Erin's heart sank. He was going to Memphis to see Jeannie, and he was using work as an excuse.

"I can't get a plane out until around ten in the morning. I think I'll still try to keep that fishing date with John."

"John?"

"The fishing guide. I'd sure love to get me a trophy bass while I'm down here."

Erin barely heard his words as her mind rebelled against the fact that he would soon be back in that—that woman's arms. He was such a nice guy! He deserved more than

Jeannie would ever be able to give him. Why were men such blind fools when it came to women.

The tram pulled up to the station, and they all boarded. The afternoon was perfect for an outing. The fierce heat of the summer had eased somewhat, making the day a little more comfortable for the foursome.

"When God made Missouri, he sure knew what he was doin'," Price remarked as his eyes took in the majestic hills and valleys around them. "A man would have to go a long way ever to find the beauty that's spread out here before us."

"It is beautiful," Erin agreed, pleased that he still held her hand.

The tram deposited them at the entrance gate, and Price paid their way in. For the next few hours they were visitors in the Old West, in an era when things happened at a much slower pace. A rugged sheriff met them as they entered the city and deputized the twins, much to their giggling delight. Everywhere they looked there was some type of food to tempt even the most dedicated dieter. Funnel cakes, delicious batter fried in deep fat, then sprinkled with powdered sugar; fresh pies; strawberries and ice cream; barbequed chicken; corn on the cob; gigantic hot chocolate chip cookies; homemade candies—the smells and the selections went on and on. Handmade crafts abounded and, of course, the rides that all children looked forward to.

They had just gone on The Great American Plunge, a log ride that boasted a five-story drop at the end of it, and emerged laughing and dripping wet. Erin's stomach was threatening to rid itself of the ice cream she had eaten prior to the ride.

"Let's go on Fire in the Hole, Uncle Price," Huntley urged, undaunted by the hair-raising ride they had just taken.

88

"Oh, come on, Huntley, ole pal, have a heart!" Price groaned, pulling his wet shirt away from his chest.

"You pwomised," Holly fretted, wrapping herself around his leg again.

"You know, you've got a bad habit of doing that, squirt. When you get older you're going to have to watch yourself. Some man's going to take offense when you wrap yourself around his leg like that," he said teasingly, pulling a lock of her hair playfully and winking at Erin knowingly.

"Oh, Uncle Pwice, you're siwwy." Holly giggled. "Can we wide Fire in the Hole?"

Price looked at Erin pleadingly and said, "Do we have to, Aunt Erin?"

"We better go measure and see if you're tall enough," she warned with a grin.

"Oh, brother," Price grumbled. "I haven't got a prayer. I *know* I'm tall enough!"

Price's face was almost comically relieved a few minutes later when the twins failed to make the mark by half an inch.

"Oh, dawn it," Holly complained. "I don't think I'll ever get that big." Her eyes surveyed the marker hostilely.

"Yes, you will. Next year you'll be able to ride nearly everything in the park," Erin assured her.

"Let's do something sane and logical like having our picture taken," Price suggested, scooping Holly up in his arms and nuzzling her neck with his hair. Erin was amazed at how well he handled the twins. He rarely seemed to lose his patience with them.

They wandered over to the tintype picture section, and each one selected a costume to wear. When the photographer sat them down, they looked like a typical young pioneer family. Price and Huntley wore coonskin hats and carried black-powder muzzle loaders. Erin and Holly were decked out prettily in sun bonnets and long cotton dresses.

"Now, Mommy and Daddy, you hold the children between you and group in real close together," the photographer instructed Price and Erin.

Price grinned at Erin and reached for one of the twins. "You get the other one, Mommy."

Erin felt a surge of pride for one brief moment as the real world faded away and she was indeed holding her and Price's child on her lap as the picture was taken.

Since it was going to be awhile before the picture would be developed, they decided to take a ride in the flooded mine. As they boarded the boats to ride through the cool, dark cave, Price sat Huntley and Holly in the seat in front of them. "We can keep a better eye on them this way," he explained with a devilish twinkle in his eye. Before they had each taken a twin and sat with them on a ride. "Besides, I'll probably have to protect you in that dark cave," he whispered for her benefit alone.

"I've always made out all right before." Erin grinned saucily. "Nothing's ever attacked me yet."

"Ah, then you haven't been riding with the right person." He grinned back. "Maybe your luck will change."

For once the twins sat perfectly still, never moving a muscle as the floating ride entered the dark, cool interior of the cave. The passing scenery and loud music held their complete attention, making them oblivious to everything else.

Erin was aware of Price's arms slipping around her long before he pulled her closer to him and whispered huskily in her ear, "I've been waiting all day for you to send me some sort of signal." His warm breath sent shivers racing up and down her spine.

"Signal—concerning what?" Erin pretended innocence, loving the way his arms tightened around her possessively.

"Oh, we're going to play hard to get, are we," he murmured, nuzzling her neck. "All right, I'll come right out with it. I've been going crazy all day wanting to kiss you. How about getting me out of my misery?" His mouth worked warmly along the column of her creamy neck.

"You're missing the best part of the ride," she protested weakly as her body came alive under the touch of his lips. "It's dark and scary."

"Why do you think I picked this particular ride? I'm no dummy. Besides, I've already seen all of it anyway."

The feel of his fingers gently stroking the bare flesh on her arms sent her senses reeling. She leaned her head against the comfort of his shoulder, remembering how he had looked with just his jeans on. She could almost feel the softness of that thick dark hair that stretched across the span of his broad chest.

"Um . . . what kind of perfume do you use? You always smell so good," he murmured against her hair. "Even after a day like we've put in today, you smell all fresh and clean." One large hand gently caressed the silkiness of her arm. "Forgive me, but I can't help wondering what you would feel like lying beside me in my arms at night—what it would feel like to be able to reach out and touch all those soft womanly curves . . ."

"Price, please. I don't think you should be talking this way."

"I'm not suggesting we do all those things. I was just wondering out loud," he defended meekly, his lips finding their way to her ear, taking the white lobe between his strong teeth and biting playfully. "You'd probably be real upset if I told you what I was thinking about awhile ago when you bent over to tie Holly's shoe."

"Price!"

"Oh, I know, I'm fresh, aren't I?" His tongue reached out and touched her ear now as his hand slipped around her rib cage to cup one soft breast. "But I won't tell anyone if you don't."

"I'm glad it's pitch dark in here," Erin whispered against his ear now. "We would be making a complete spectacle of ourselves."

"We? I don't see you doing anything—" His words were cut off by her mouth closing over his. For the next few minutes they exchanged long, languid kisses, their breathing becoming deeper, the kisses becoming more hungry and intense. Erin seemed to fit perfectly in his arms, and his hands tenderly explored her body, pulling her tight against him, letting her feel and exult in the effect she was having on him in their own private, dark world. In his arms she felt like a new, totally desirable woman.

Hesitantly she unbuttoned the first button of his shirt and let her hand run gently over his chest. The touch of his skin on her fingertips brought a whole new surge of longing to her. She had tasted the delights between man and woman, and her body was now crying out to be loved again.

"Erin," he whispered huskily, his mouth finding hers hotly, their tongues merging in a frenzy of ravishing kisses.

"Uncle Pwice! Wook." Holly's voice broke into their thoughts, each one forgetting where they were for the moment. "Wook at that thing!" She pointed a chubby finger at some of the passing scenery. Erin could see the light at the end of the ride and knew that they would be coming out of the cave very soon now.

"I see it, Holly." Price's voice sounded shaky as he reluctantly released Erin and buttoned his shirt. He leaned over and gave her one quick kiss. "That was one hell of a signal, lady," he said with a grin.

As their little boat shot out into the sunlight, Erin blinked at the brightness of the day. Her mind was still back in the cave and on the way she had responded to Price's kisses. What was the matter with her? Could she have fallen in love so quickly, so unexpectedly? Would she be so foolish as to lay herself wide open for new heartache and disappointment? She and Price could never make it. He was not her perfect man. He was still in love with another woman or, at best, certainly unwilling to step into another love affair so soon after the last disastrous one. He had as many hangups about love and marriage as she did at the moment.

"You've gotten awfully quiet," Price said as they walked through the park, letting the twins run toward the zoo. "Anything wrong?"

Erin smiled and reached for his hand as they walked. "No, just thinking."

"About anything in particular?"

"No, nothing."

"Do you think you could ever forget Quinn, Erin? I mean really forget him," Price asked quietly as they stopped and sat on a bench in front of the children's zoo.

Erin leaned back and looked at the cloudless blue sky, her mind trying to see Quinn's face. For some reason it wouldn't appear. Even more strange, she realized she didn't want it to.

"I spend most of my time trying to forget him. I think one of these days I might make it. Quinn was the first man I ever fell in love with, the first and only man that I . . . Well, it's just that I don't take things like that lightly. I thought I'd probably spend the rest of my life with him, and when that didn't happen, it hurt me a great deal. I don't ever want to leave myself open to that type of hurt again."

"But you do want to marry sometime in the future?" Price asked softly.

"I thought I did, but you're right: There is no perfect marriage, no perfect man. I think I'll spend the next few years just getting to know myself and what I really want out of life. Who knows—I may be cut out to be an old maid." She laughed. "If you're a bachelor and I'm an old maid, we'd make a fine pair of friends, wouldn't we? We could just sit back and be an aunt and uncle to all our friends' children and content ourselves with that—" Her voice broke off in a sob.

"I doubt that it will come to that," Price assured her. "I have a feeling you're destined for motherhood, the perfect marriage, the whole nine yards. You're just going to have to be a little patient, wait until your knight in shining armor can find you."

"If you want my true opinion, I think his horse threw him somewhere in the forest." She grinned despite her misty eyes.

"Naw, I don't think so," Price scoffed. "He'll come ridin' up someday, sweep you off your feet . . . that is, if you manage to get that ten pounds off. . . ."

"Price Seaver! You cad!"

"Come on. Let's go find the kids and eat." He laughed, dodging her punch.

"Again? You surely couldn't be hungry!" It seemed they had done nothing but eat since they entered the park.

"Starved. I'm not the one trying to lose weight. Come on, chubby, let's eat in the old mine." He grabbed her hand and pulled her toward the petting pen. "If you're good, I'll let you pet one of these stinkin' goats!"

"You're spoiling me, Price." She made a face at him. He made one back.

"For someone who couldn't eat a bite, you did a terrific job of it on all that fried chicken," Price teased an hour later as they emerged from "dining in the mine."

"Yes, but I really didn't think I was going to get that last piece of pie down," she reminded him sternly. "I told you I didn't want it."

"Sure, you didn't," he agreed, winking at Huntley and Holly. "If I hadn't bought you that piece of pie, you would have created a scene, and disgraced both the twins and me. Now admit it, chubby."

"It was good." She grinned. "Even if I did add another five pounds."

Price stood back and surveyed her curves critically. "Wherever it went, it looks good." His eyes met hers boldly. "Real good."

"Let's go get our picture, Uncle Price," Huntley said, beginning to show the first signs of slowing down.

"That's a great idea, Huntley," Erin agreed. "Let's get the picture and go home. I'm exhausted."

Fifteen minutes later they were giggling together over the picture of the very stern-looking pioneer family who stared back at them from the tintype picture.

"We look like we lost our last friend on earth," Price said with a chuckle. "Look how solemn ole Huntley looks."

They broke out in peals of laughter again as they surveyed the solemn look on the little boy's face.

"That man *said* to look serious," Huntley protested, beginning to get a bit put out at their continued laughter. It was one thing to laugh with someone and quite another to be laughed at.

"I want some popcorn," Holly yelled above the laughter.

"Oh, Holly! Surely not!" Erin collapsed against Price in another round of laughter. His strong arms caught her to him and held her tightly for a moment. Her laughter faded as their eyes met. She suddenly had the uncontrollable desire to reach out and kiss him. From the look in his eyes, he would have no objections; on the contrary, he would encourage it.

"Here, Huntley, you take the money and take your sister to that cart over there and buy her some popcorn. Think you can handle that?"

95

"Sure, Uncle Price, I'm big now." Huntley beamed at the rare opportunity to assert his masculinity.

"Hold Holly's hand," Erin called as they skipped happily away. "Do you think we should let them go alone?" she asked worriedly.

"Good grief, they'll never be out of our eyesight, worrywart!"

"I know, but they're still such babies." Erin sighed.

"Who do you think should get custody of this picture?" Price asked, turning their thoughts back to the tintype he was holding. "I suppose we should let Brenda and Nathan have it."

Erin peered over his shoulder at the photograph, a feeling of sadness coming over her. Today had been one of the most fun-filled days of her life. Being with Price had made her forget all the bad times she had experienced during the last few months. For the first time in a long time, she had laughed—really laughed. The day was drawing to an end, and she desperately wished she could make it last forever.

"We should have bought more than one," she said softly. She hated to let him know it, but she wanted that picture.

"Do you want it?" Price asked, glancing up at her.

"Oh, I don't know . . ." she hedged courteously.

"If you don't, I do." Price didn't hedge for a moment. "You sure you don't mind?"

What could she say? She should have spoken up. "No, I don't mind, but what could an old bachelor like you want with a picture like that?" she asked teasingly.

"He'll probably sit and drool over the old maid who's in it."

Erin's eyes dropped shyly. "Oh, Price. . . ."

"I got it, Uncle Price. I got the popcorn!" Huntley came dragging Holly back with him, trailing popcorn for several yards.

96

Price peered into the almost-empty box. "I think you spilled some, pal."

"I want some ice cream," Holly whined against the side of Erin's jeans.

"I don't think you know what you want," Erin said, hugging her little body close. "I think we'd better all go home before we bankrupt Uncle Price."

They left the park, a tired but happy group. Price slipped his arm around Erin and she leaned on his shoulder tiredly as they walked back to the car.

"It's been a beautiful day, Price. Thank you," she murmured as the twins ran happily ahead of them.

"I should be thanking you," he protested in a contented voice. "I can't remember when I've spent a more enjoyable day."

"I wish you didn't have to go tomorrow," she added, foolishly hoping he would forget that a woman named Jeannie had ever existed.

"I wish I didn't have to also," he replied simply. "But I'll be back."

Their eyes met each other's briefly before Erin turned away. She was overcome with the almost childish urge to make him promise—promise that he would come back. But what if he didn't come back? What if, when he saw Jeannie, all those old feelings of love resurfaced and he took her back? And if he did come back? What then? Was she even remotely close to committing herself to another man—committing her love, her very fragile feelings, her very tender and bruised heart to this tall man walking beside her.

At the moment there was only one thing Erin was sure of, one thing that would never change on her list of priorities. Before anything could ever seriously develop between her and Price, she would have to know that Jeannie was totally out of his life and his thoughts. She laughed ironically to herself. What gave her the idea Price would ever consider anything serious between them? He had been hurt just as deeply as she had been. Although they had had a wonderful time together today, could it be that he *did* think of her as only a friend? Maybe he was only letting down his reserve for a brief time while he took a few days off from work, a few days away from his own problems. Questions, questions, and for Erin, no answers.

She shook herself mentally. What was the matter with her! People didn't fall in love with each other in two days.

That thought was comforting and helped boost her sagging spirits considerably.

As they drove along the quiet countryside, dusk was just beginning to settle over the lake area. Holly sat on Erin's lap while Huntley hung over Price's seat and chattered nonstop about his pet frog, Roscoe P. Coltrane.

The little red car pulled into the Daniels' drive, and at least two of the occupants exited rowdily.

Price gave Erin a deprecatory grin. "I think I'm getting old."

"Me, too." She yawned. "I think we're both ready for a shower and something cold to drink."

Price opened the car door and got out. "Boy, that sounds great! I'll get Cathy next door to watch the kids for us."

"Watch the kids. Whatever for?" Erin paused and looked at him in surprise.

"So we can take *our* shower," Price replied with a wicked grin.

"Price," Erin gave him a tolerant smile, "*we* are not going to take a shower. *I* am."

Price's face fell. "I thought your words were too good to be true."

"Uncle Pwice, can I catch some lighties?" Holly ran over and grabbed him around the leg and hung on as he tried to walk to the house.

"I don't know, puddin'. What's a lightie?"

"Dem bugs." She pointed a pudgy finger at the fireflies swirling in the gathering twilight.

"I think dem bugs would prefer their freedom, squirt." Price gave her a hug and a gentle swat on her bottom. "Let's get you cleaned up and ready for bed."

Amid violent protests Erin and Price finally had the twins in their pajamas. A round of kisses, pleas for drinks of water, trips to the bathroom and unusually long prayers delayed their arrival in bed yet another twenty minutes.

At last, with a sigh of relief, Erin turned off the bedroom light and left two five-year-olds sleeping peacefully. Price draped his arm casually around her waist as they walked down the hallway. "You hungry?"

Erin shook her head in amusement. "No, I'm not hungry. Surprised?"

"Floored." Price smiled at her tenderly.

"I'm just tired. Being a mother is the most exhausting job in the world. You never get a day off!"

"You're a darn good mother. Did you know that?"

Erin laid her head on his shoulder as they ambled toward the living room. "Thank you. You're not bad as a father, either. Your five unborn kids don't know what they're missing," she teased.

They strolled into the living room, their eyes catching a brief view of the lake through the moon-drenched window.

"It's beautiful out there tonight. Warm enough for a swim." Price glanced at her suggestively. "If you don't want to take a shower together, how about going for a swim with me? I promise I'll behave."

"Sure you would." Erin turned away from him and sat down on the sofa.

"I would!" Price defended. "Come on, Auntie Ewin. The twins are sound asleep, and we could hear them if they woke up. The lake's practically at our back door."

"You're serious," she said with a laugh. "You really want to go out there and swim at this hour?"

Price consulted his watch. "It's not even ten o'clock."

"But we don't have any bathing suits. . . ."

"I know where Nathan and Brenda keep theirs, if you insist on using the burdensome things."

"Well, I certainly *do* insist on using them!"

Price was dragging her along behind him now. "Oh, good. Then you agree to go with me. You had me worried there for a minute, troll. I thought you'd try to tell me you looked like a blimp in your bathing suit."

"A blimp! I do not!" she protested heatedly as he stopped before Nathan and Brenda's bedroom door. "Maybe a little. . . ."

"Curvy. Curvy's the word you're looking for," Price supplied helpfully.

"Right! Curvy." Erin grinned. "*Real* curvy."

Price winked at her in a most sexy manner. "I can hardly wait to see all those curves stuffed into Brenda's bathing suit. Third drawer on the left."

"Do you promise you'll behave?" she asked with a groan as he pushed her through the door, then closed it.

"Of course," he answered dutifully, but for some reason Erin noticed his voice didn't ring true.

Erin was still grumbling ten minutes later as she made her way down the moonlit path wearing one of Brenda's outrageously skimpy bathing suits and a heavy terry cloth robe. Thank heavens it was dark and he couldn't get a good look at her attire, or what there was of it. Brenda had always been much more daring in her dress than Erin, and this string bikini emphasized the difference dramatically.

"Let's not get very far from the house," she cautioned, trying to keep up with his long-legged strides.

"We have to go far enough to reach the water," he

reasoned, catching her arm as she stumbled. "You're not only homely, you're clumsy, too, aren't you?"

"You're going to be missing some teeth, Mr. Seaver, the next time you refer to my looks," Erin warned grimly.

"Hey." Price turned around and smiled at her innocently. "*I* think you're real foxy. You're the one who keeps telling me you look like a slug."

"Some friend you are," Erin grumbled, marching behind him. "Why don't you try to humor me? Why don't you tell me how you don't think I look that bad! Maybe even outright lie to me and tell me you like fat girls!"

"I have told you that," Price said patiently, letting a tree limb slap back in her face carelessly, "but you won't believe me. Besides, I'm getting tired of this friend idea. I think I'd rather be 'lover' now," he said and grinned.

"Think again," she said curtly as they reached their destination.

Price peeled off the shirt he was wearing and reached for the button on his jeans.

"I hope you've got something on under there," Erin said, turning her face away in embarrassment.

"Am I supposed to? Gee, I'm sorry. Nathan's suits were all too big for me."

Erin clenched her teeth. "You had *better* be teasing."

"I never tease. Take a look."

"No."

"Aw, come on. Haven't you ever gone skinny-dippin'?"

"No—not with a—man." Erin was becoming nervous. Price was such a tease, she didn't know whether to take him seriously, but she was beginning to fear that for once he might be telling her the truth.

"Well," he said hastily, "I'm offering you one last chance to feast your eyes—then I'm going in."

"Don't let me keep you," Erin said tightly. Surely he was kidding!

"Aren't you going to take your robe off and join me?"

"Yes. Turn your head."

"Why? Are you going to surprise me? It's too much to hope for, isn't it, that underneath all that serious little bundle of sexy curves, there could lurk a jaded, evil woman who's going to make a man out of me."

Erin jerked the robe off, keeping her eyes anxiously averted from him. "Make a man out of you? I'm sure I'm fifteen years too late for that."

"Let's see, I'm thirty-three, so fifteen years ago I would have been eighteen . . . umm, gad! You're uncanny! How did you know? Did you know Boom-Boom Taggert?"

"No! I did not know Boom-Boom Taggert!" Erin whirled angrily at his malicious taunting, "but I gather you did!"

Price's smile vanished as he let out a low, admiring whistle. The moon shone on Erin's curvaceous body, the black string bikini revealing how truly lovely Price's little troll actually was. "Good grief, Erin, I knew you were a doll, but I must admit I never thought you'd look this good. . . ." His voice trailed off huskily as his eyes roamed over her intimately.

"Does—does it look all right?" she asked shyly, meeting his gaze in the moonlight.

"It looks fine." His eyes seemed to be devouring her now.

For the first time Erin noticed that he did have brief swimming trunks on. She couldn't make out the color, but at the moment, who cared? All she could see was the broad expanse of his chest, the way his stomach lay flat and smooth, the hard muscles of his legs.

"Then will you stop teasing me about being—a troll?"

"Probably not, but when I do, you'll know I'm only teasing you." His voice was affectionate as he reached out and gently touched her face. "Come here, troll, and kiss me."

He moved forward to take her in his arms as she ducked and stepped past him.

"You said you would behave," she reminded with a giggle. Her heart was pounding loudly in her chest, and she felt slightly breathless. There would undoubtedly be trouble if they both stood here in the moonlight and took notes on each other's bathing suits!

"Oh, so you're one of *those* kind of women!" Price reached out and scooped her up in his arms, running toward the water with her.

"No, Price!" Erin hung on for dear life as they hit the cool water with a loud splash. The shock of the cold water took her breath away as they went under, then came back up sputtering. "That was cruel!" Erin gasped, wrapping her arms tighter around his neck.

"I know. I'm a real devil! Gosh you feel good." His hands ran along her rib cage exploringly.

Erin reached down and removed his roaming fingers. "You promised to behave."

"I'm *always* making promises and not being able to keep them." Price put his hands back where they had been.

"Quinn! Stop it," Erin pleaded, pushing him away.

Price's hands fell away immediately, his face growing solemn. "I'm not Quinn, Erin," he said quietly.

Erin realized her mistake at once. She didn't know how Quinn's name had slipped out.

"I know that, Price. I'm sorry. I don't even know why I said it," she apologized sincerely.

"Could it be because I remind you of him? That you still think of him constantly?" Price's voice had a tinge of sarcasm in it.

"No," Erin replied calmly, "I don't really think of him that often anymore. And as far as you reminding me of him . . ." Erin paused and cocked her head teasingly, her hands creeping back around his neck. "You don't remind

103

me of him at all anymore. I knew you weren't a Quinn Daniels days ago."

"Oh. In what way am I *not* a Quinn Daniels?" His arms pulled her closer to him, their wet bodies meeting and clinging to each other comfortably. "I like a pretty woman as well as he does."

"You seem able to control yourself a little better." Erin's pulse skipped a beat at the feel of his solid male length against her.

"Control myself, huh?" He shifted her tighter against his mounting desire. "You call that control?"

"Price, remember, we're only friends." Erin flipped water in his face with one finger. "Too bad, huh?"

"Well, what I had in mind was very friendly," he defended, flipping water back.

"Don't get my hair wet."

"Are you serious? You look like a drowned rat!"

"There you go talking about my looks again! I suppose you never saw Jeannie with her hair wet."

Price's arms fell away from her sides as he pushed off into the dark water and swam for a few minutes, completely ignoring Erin's taunt. Erin swam toward him, feeling uneasy about being left alone in the dark water. Although the moon lit up the night, it was still a little eerie swimming in the lake at this hour. The only sounds came from the large bullfrogs croaking along the deserted shores.

She had only swum a few laps when she paused and looked hurriedly around for him. "Price? Where are you?"

The gentle lapping of the waves upon the shore was the only voice that answered her.

"Come on, Price! Answer me! I know you're there!"

Erin swam a little further out. She was becoming more uneasy by the moment. Where had he disappeared to? He had seemed like a strong swimmer. She peered ahead of her in the darkness, swallowing an urge to let out a loud, terrified scream.

Another couple of minutes went by before the scream materialized as she felt something latch onto her foot and drag her slowly beneath the water. Grasping wildly for something to hold onto, her hands came in contact with a pair of strong arms pulling her closely against a solid chest.

As they surfaced together, Price's mouth closed over hers hungrily. Although she could barely breathe, the touch of his lips was a delicious, heady sensation. His moist, firm mouth demanded a response and she freely gave it to him. He moved his mouth over hers, devouring its softness, molding her curves to the contours of his lean body. She didn't protest as his hands sought the snap on the top of her bathing suit and slowly let the scrap of fabric float away in the quiet water. His hand roamed intimately over her breast, sending cold shivers down her spine at the cool brush of his fingers on her skin.

"Don't," she managed to whisper weakly as their mouths finally broke apart.

"Why not?" he whispered back huskily. "You know I want you. Why do you keep fighting it?" His voice was filled with a curious deep longing as his mouth explored the hollow of her slender neck.

"Because . . . I don't think you're ready for this yet," she stammered helplessly as his lips moved down her shoulder sensuously. She couldn't help thinking about his trip tomorrow and the possibility that he would be seeing Jeannie. After tonight Erin might never see Price Seaver again, and although she wanted him in a way that was almost painful, she had to remember that another woman held his heart.

"I'm not?" Price drew her closer. "I know it's been a long time, but I'm nearly positive that I'm ready." He chuckled intimately.

"Oh, no, I didn't mean—" Erin broke off, embarrassed. There was certainly no doubt that he was ready. "I meant I don't think we should become this involved—this soon."

"Let me guess." Price sighed and buried his face in her neck defeatedly. "Quinn and Jeannie."

Only Jeannie, she wanted to say but didn't. Let him think she still loved Quinn. It would be easier this way. "Yes. Quinn and Jeannie," she agreed sadly.

"You know something? Right now I wish I'd never heard those two names," Price whispered tenderly against her ear. "Do you think there'll ever be a day when you get that damn man out of your system?"

"I don't know. Maybe. What about you and Jeannie?"

"What about me and Jeannie, what about me and Jeannie—you're worse than a damn cockatoo, Erin," Price said irritably. "What about me and Jeannie? We broke up over six months ago, woman! What else can I tell you?"

"You could tell me you don't love her anymore!" Erin shot back angrily.

"You could tell me the same thing about Quinn, but I don't hear you chattering nonstop about that."

"I do not chatter! And besides, why should I say that about Quinn?" Erin tossed her head haughtily.

"For the same reason I'm not going to say that about Jeannie. It's neither one of our business!" Price said just as haughtily.

"It should be!" Erin couldn't let it drop. "We're friends, remember!"

"Forget that crap! I don't want to be your friend," he said bluntly.

"You said you did!" Erin glared at him hostilely. "What have I done?"

"Nothing!" Price grumbled. "It was just a stupid idea. I've decided to stick to friends who aren't built like a brick—outhouse."

"You're holding that against me!"

106

Price looked longingly at her bare breasts in the soft moonlight. "I would be if you didn't talk so much."

"*I* do *not* talk so much! Basically I'm a very quiet, calm, level-headed person. *You're* the one who makes me a little crazy!" She sniffed disdainfully. This was one friendship she was glad to be rid of. "Kindly hand me my bathing-suit top."

"I can't."

"Why?"

"Because it's probably five miles down the lake by now."

"Then go get it!"

"No." He lay back and floated peacefully in the water. "If we were still friends, I'd think about it . . . But since we're not. . . ."

"You are making me angry, Price," Erin warned in a calm voice.

Price bobbled along happily, ignoring her temper.

Erin swam up to him and leaned down close. "I *said* you're making me *very angry,* Price. We are not going to be friends much longer unless you go get my bathing-suit top."

Price shrugged his shoulders. "I have found," he began in a philosophical tone, "that friends come and go. It's the enemies who seem to mount up. . . ." His voice began to gurgle as Erin slowly pushed his head under the water. As he was sputtering in amazement, she dove beneath him and with one angry jerk rid him of his bathing suit.

"What do you think you're doing?" he gasped indignantly.

"If you think I'm walking back up that hill half nude, then you're all wet—in more ways than one!" She scrambled hurriedly toward the bank.

He was still yelling threateningly at her as she made her way back up the moonlit path, his trunks clutched victoriously to her bare chest.

"Hey, Holmes!" he hollered. "I've changed my mind. Let's be friends again. How about it?"

"Fine with me, Seaver! Just as soon as you answer one lousy question!" she called back over her shoulder as she struggled up the vine-covered path.

"Wait a minute!" He stood up in the water, the moon glistening on his bare bottom. "What's the question?" He placed his hands on his hips arrogantly. "Don't tell me! Let me guess!"

Erin turned and her eyes met his in amusement for a moment. Then in one voice they both shouted simultaneously, *What about Jeannie?*

CHAPTER SIX

"Huntley, are you sure?"

Immense brown eyes peered back at Erin seriously. "I'm sure, Aunt Erin."

Disappointment flashed across Erin's face as she realized that she had missed Price this morning. She had wanted to see him, if only for a few minutes, before he left for Memphis.

"He's coming back tonight, isn't he?" Cathy asked as she poured a second cup of coffee for Erin.

"Yes, but I sort of wanted to talk to him before he left." She was sorry now that she had let the twins talk her into coming over to their nearest neighbor's house to play with a friend their own age.

"He put a bi-ig fish in the fwigewator," Holly lisped.

"Yeah, re-eally big!" Huntley agreed.

Erin smiled. Price must have caught a fish for their dinner this evening. She had laid out a roast this morning, but she could always use it for tomorrow's dinner. Stirring her coffee thoughtfully, she issued a silent prayer that he would be back to eat his fish dinner—that nothing—and no one—would delay his return.

"Don't forget the party tonight," Cathy was saying as she cut another slice of coffee cake and put it down in front of Erin.

"Oh, no, please. . . ." Erin pushed the plate away. "I've already eaten more than I should!"

"Are you sure?" Cathy mumbled between mouthfuls of the luscious, rich cinnamon cake.

"Positive." Erin had to be firm. She was going to get this extra weight off if it killed her. Jeannie was probably as slim as a reed, and if Erin had any hopes of competing with her—good heavens, there she went again! She wasn't going to eat another piece of coffee cake because she wanted to lose weight for herself! No one else. She was a strong, self-controlled person, and if she put her mind to it she could have ten pounds off in nothing flat. Her spirits soared as she imagined herself looking gaunt and willowy. Giving up that extra piece of cake was a snap.

"Send them over around five. I'm going to fix hot dogs before I take them to the carnival rides," Cathy added as the twins and her son Michael ran out the back door squealing like a bunch of hooligans.

"You are undoubtedly the bravest person alive." Erin laughed. For some reason she couldn't get her eyes off that darn piece of delicious, mouth-watering coffee cake. The bakery must have someone with a vicious streak to put out a dessert that looked and tasted like this!

"Thankfully, Trev will be here to help me with them. Taking six five-year-olds for the evening is not exactly my idea of fun!"

"It's very nice of you. I'm sure they'll have a wonderful time. I suppose I'll fix the fish Price caught this morning for our dinner. I have been worrying about letting the twins eat any because of the bones, so this would be a good time to get it over with." Her hand reached out and unconsciously picked up the plate of cake. "If he caught a big enough one, I'll send you and Trevor over a plateful," she offered as she forked the yummy cake into her mouth hungrily.

"That would be great. Trev loves fresh fish."

"Well, if the fish is as big as the twins say, I'll have enough to feed an army," she mused between forkfuls.

"Darn! I wish they had come in and told me Price was back from fishing!"

"You know those kids. They were too busy playing to think of anything else. Price probably called them over and showed them the fish, and their little minds dismissed it as soon as they ran out of the house again."

"I'm sure he was in a hurry," Erin reasoned as she stuck the last bite of cake into her mouth. "He had to catch a plane around ten." She glanced down at the empty plate before her. "Good grief! I ate that cake!"

Cathy peered at the barren china. "You nearly ate the dish!"

"Oh, brother," Erin moaned, shoving the plate away in disgust. "Well, the first thing in the morning *I am going on a diet* and sticking to it!"

"In the morning, huh? Well, I will too." Her eyes found the last slice of cake. "But since we already blew it for today, do you want to split that last piece?" she asked hopefully.

Erin looked at the offending beast. "Well. . . ."

"Oh, come on. I don't want to have to throw it out. Trev doesn't like sweets."

"He doesn't?" It was a shame to waste good food when there were so many starving people in the world. "Okay," she said, relenting and reaching for the last piece and dividing it between her and Cathy evenly, "but tomorrow I'm definitely going on a diet!"

It was nearly noon by the time Erin could convince the twins that they should return home and rest for the party that evening. Before she put them down for a brief afternoon nap, she hustled them into her VW and drove to the closest grocery store for a few supplies.

"Now stay close to me and don't get into anything," she warned sternly as they entered the store.

111

"We won't!" they agreed happily. "Can we have some gum, Aunt Erin?"

"I suppose, Huntley," Erin said absently as she studied her shopping list. "Go ahead and pick some out and show it to the lady at the cash register and tell her I'll pay for it along with my other groceries." Maybe that would keep them content until she finished her shopping, she thought hopefully.

They bolted away toward the candy rack and within a few minutes were arguing heatedly over what brand they wanted. Erin kept an ear tuned to the petty squabbling as she selected some fresh produce, sighing hopelessly as the squabble turned into a full-scale assault.

"Stop it this instant!" she warned as she dragged them apart. "Here, you're going to choose this flavor!" A package of banana-flavored bubble gum landed in Huntley's hand. "Now dry up, both of you!"

"What kind is it?" Huntley whined. "Is it them things?" He pointed at the clump of bananas on the wrapping.

"Yes, it's banana. Why?"

Holly set up a wail. "I hate bawnanas!"

"All right, all right! Here. What about cherry?"

Huntley and Holly turned up their noses at the package suspiciously.

"You don't like cherry? Here, try grape. Lemon? Tutti-frutti? Oh, come on! Strawberry . . . how about strawberry?" You would think they were trying to select a rare vintage wine! "It's only gum! Now pick one!"

"Maybe I'll try the bawnana," Holly said.

Erin let out an exasperated breath and handed her the package of gum. Huntley promptly ripped it out of his sister's hand and tore into the wrapper recklessly. In a few minutes they were both chomping away contentedly on wads of bubble gum.

"Stay close," Erin ordered as she went back to her shopping cart.

The meat counter held a tempting selection. Erin stopped and glanced over the fresh ground beef. The twins were getting very tired and fussy now, and she needed to get them home. They had walked beside her peacefully for the last ten minutes, but they were beginning to show signs of discontent. If they could only last a few more minutes, she would be finished. She glanced back over her shoulder and froze. They were standing at the egg case heatedly discussing their preference. Huntley liked scrambled, Holly liked fwied. At the moment neither one liked the other!

"Fwied!"

"Scrambled!"

"Fwied, Huntwey, fwied!" Holly's bubble gum dropped out of her mouth and landed at her brother's feet.

"Scrambled!" he said with deadly determination. He reached down and picked up the bubble gum and stuck it in her brown locks.

"Huntwey Daniels!" she screamed. Her fat hand went for a carton of eggs, a mean scowl on her baby face.

"Holly—no!" Erin threw down the tomato she was holding and bolted toward the egg case in a dead run.

Flying egg missiles flew through the air as a burst of hostilities erupted. Erin ran toward them, her tennis shoes sliding perilously in the sticky, slimy mess. Huntley and Holly were lobbing eggs at each other with Holly screaming at the top of her lungs, mortified at the guck running down her face.

"Don't you throw one more egg!" Erin's feet flew out from beneath her, sending her spiraling into a gigantic display of canned goods. The deafening roar of the display coming down around her shattered the air. The store manager looked up in alarm and dashed toward the melee, waving his arms wildly at the twins.

"Children! Children! My goodness. . . ." His voice died mid-sentence as an egg went sailing past him.

Erin was trying to pick her way out of a hundred cans of fruit cocktail, nearly dying from embarrassment at what was taking place. A few shoppers had pushed their carts into the battle zone but refused to enter the fracas. They stood gaping with their mouths open, occasionally dodging an errant egg.

Erin pulled herself to her feet. "I'm warning you," she swore grimly as she made her way toward the egg-drenched twins, her eyes blazing with savage intensity.

The store manager waded in and took both twins by the scuff of their necks, breaking them apart.

"I'm telling Mommy!" Holly threatened with a loud shriek toward Huntley. She had large tears running down her face, bubble gum stuck in her hair, and egg yolks dripping off every part of her body.

"I'm telling Daddy," Huntley bellowed back, precariously close to tears himself.

"I'm telling Price!" Erin threatened tearfully.

"Aunt Ewin," Holly sobbed, wrapping her arms around Erin's dripping neck, "Huntwey's being naughty again!"

"It wasn't me, Aunt Erin," he cried pitifully, grabbing her around the neck and hanging on wildly. "It was her!"

"Are you all right, lady?" the store manager asked.

"I think so," she mumbled, trying to hold the twins and remain on her feet at the same time. "I'm so sorry about all this . . ." Her voice trailed off as she surveyed the disaster area. How embarrassing!

"Don't worry about it," he said and smiled weakly. "We'll get it cleaned up." Erin knew he wanted to strangle all three of them, but he had pasted his manager's smile on his face and gritted his teeth admirably.

"May I pay for any of the damages?" she asked, shouting above the twins' bawling.

"No, there's no permanent damage," he assured her, ushering her toward the front of the store. Erin was sure he would be relieved to see the last of them.

She loaded them into the VW and left the parking lot with them both crying at the top of their lungs. For the first time in her life, she was deliriously happy that she was deprived of motherhood at the moment!

By the time she had them bathed, had washed the gum out of Holly's hair, and put them down for their afternoon nap, she was near exhaustion. Deciding that a glass of iced tea would make her feel human again, she walked to the refrigerator and opened it. Her mouth dropped open in astonishment. Staring at her was the biggest fish she had ever seen in her life. Its fat, bulgy sides looked monstrous to her as she surveyed it through the clear plastic wrap Price had put around it. My gosh! she mused silently. He really took me seriously when I said to get a large one. There was no way they could eat all that fish.

With a tired sigh she leaned against the open refrigerator door, resentment seeping into her thoughts now as she realized that the fish had not been cleaned yet. She knew he had been in a hurry this morning, but after all, it wasn't her idea to have a fish dinner, and she didn't cherish the idea of cleaning that nasty thing! The mere thought of it made her stomach churn. Cleaning a fish that big would be like slaughtering a hog!

Well, she thought tiredly as she closed the door, she was capable of giving him a meal he would never forget. She sat down at the kitchen table and sipped her iced tea thoughtfully. It seemed very lonely today without Price. She frowned as she thought about what he might be doing right now. She closed her eyes and his face appeared before her. His beautiful green eyes looked back at her, and a contagious smile lit up his handsome features. Price Seaver was a man she could fall in love with, she realized. It startled her that she was ready to admit that. But it was true. He wasn't perfect, but he was close to it. At least as close to it as she was! Okay, time to stop dreaming and start doin'!

Cleaning that fish was the hardest thing Erin had ever attempted. She wrestled it all over the kitchen, alternately holding her nose and gagging. There were very few people in this world whom she would go to this trouble for. In fact, she could only think of one right now, and her thoughts of him were not exactly friendly at the moment. She would give him fair warning, she thought rebelliously as she hacked away relentlessly at the repulsive fish. If he wanted fish again, from now on she would take him to the nearest fast-food seafood restaurant. She wouldn't go through this disgusting mess again for love or money!

After what seemed like hours she had hacked enough pieces off the monster to make a decent mess of fish and threw the remainder in the trash. Her hands were covered with small cuts and her disposition was not at its best. This day had been a nightmare so far, and she still had to get the twins dressed and over to Cathy's by five.

Around three she put a strawberry cake in the oven. A large tossed salad sat in the refrigerator, waiting for the dressing to be added as the final touch. Au gratin potatoes filled a small casserole dish, waiting to go into the oven along with the homemade bread that was rising near the window. Fresh corn on the cob and iced tea should make a meal fit for a king—or a very desirable man, she surmised proudly as she left the kitchen to get herself and the twins ready for the coming evening. Yes, Price Seaver was definitely going to be surprised!

A little before seven Price's car pulled into the drive. Erin's stomach fluttered nervously as he got out. She glanced one last time in the mirror. She had dressed in a white eyelet sundress, a perfect choice to complement her dark tan. Nervously adjusting the small pearl earrings she was wearing, she walked to the door to meet him, feeling almost shy.

"Hi, beautiful," Price said softly as he stepped up on the

porch, his eyes resting boldly on the low cut of her neckline.

"Hi," Erin responded lightly, her knees feeling very shaky all of a sudden.

"You been keepin' out of trouble, lovely lady?" he asked with a trace of affection in his voice.

"Sure . . . how about you?" She could hardly keep the words from bubbling out of her mouth. Words like, did you see Jeannie? Are you and she going to try again? All those crazy words that were really none of her business, yet the answer meant the world to her. But she said nothing.

"Now what do you think?" He grinned mischievously, watching her eyes turn stormy.

"Sorry I asked," she muttered and turned away to walk to the kitchen.

"You have a headache today?" Price asked as he trailed behind her hurriedly.

"Yes, but I believe it's spelled *t-w-i-n-s*," she tossed over her shoulder, thinking about the disastrous trip to the grocery store that afternoon.

"Bad day?" he asked sympathetically.

"Don't ask," she warned grimly.

"Where are the little munchkins?" Price glanced around the kitchen.

"Next door at a birthday party."

"You mean we're here alone!" He gave her a suggestive grin. "All by ourselves—alone?"

Dragging out a large cast-iron skillet, Erin ignored his words.

"I hope you're hungry. I fixed your fish dinner." She covered the bottom of the skillet with oil and let it heat while she dipped the pieces of fish into buttermilk, then flour.

"Fish? Well, great!" he said, a little surprised. "I'm

117

starved. I haven't had any lunch. By the time I took care of my business, I just had time to grab a candy bar."

Erin dropped the fish into the hot oil and watched the pieces as they began to sizzle and turn a mouth-watering brown.

"Hey," Price said, reaching over to take her hand. "Is something wrong? You're very quiet tonight."

Their eyes met, and Erin swallowed hard. He was so virile, so appealing to her at this moment. After the day she had just experienced, she longed to go into his arms and let him hold her, to let him whisper comforting words in her ear.

"No, nothing's wrong. I'm just tired," she murmured, turning back to the fish.

"Anything I can do to help relax you?" He grinned.

"You can sit down and eat like a horse," she said, scooping up some of the fish and laying it on a platter.

"Well, I wasn't exactly thinking along those lines, but if you insist. . . ." He reached over and took a piece of the golden-brown fish and sampled it hungrily. "Boy, this is great!"

Erin smiled smugly to herself as she put more fish in the skillet. Eat your heart out, Jeannie, wherever you are!

"I'll bet you're a little tired yourself, aren't you?" she asked.

"A little," he admitted, sneaking another piece of the fish. "Damn, this stuff's good."

"Thank you. Don't spoil your supper," she cautioned.

"Are you kidding? It would take more than one piece of fish to spoil my appetite!" He reached for another handful. Erin frowned. At this rate there wouldn't be any left to take to Cathy and Trevor.

"I'm sorry I missed you this morning," she said, motioning for him to sit down at the table. "I was next door."

"Yeah, I know. I saw the twins for a minute. Darn! Potatoes, salad, corn on the cob, bread . . . Is that homemade bread?" he asked incredulously as she sliced off thick chunks and buttered them lavishly.

"Sure. You like homemade bread, don't you?"

"I guess. I don't remember eating it very often. You're going to make some man a hell of a wife, Erin." His eyes hungrily surveyed the bountiful table.

I know, Erin thought again smugly.

Price ate hungrily for a few minutes, praising every bite. The fish was disappearing rapidly. "This is the best fish I've ever eaten in my life, Erin. No kidding!" He reached for the platter once more.

"You're going to make yourself sick." She grinned, feeling very good at the moment.

"Which reminds me," he said as he stuffed another bite in his mouth. "After supper I'm going to look in the phone book for the nearest taxidermist to mount *my* fish!" he exclaimed proudly.

Erin was spooning in her au gratin potatoes hungrily. "Your fish?" She smiled.

"I'm telling you, sweetheart, I have *never* enjoyed anything more in my life than the feel of that fish on my line. I worked for twenty minutes to get him in the boat. If John hadn't gotten the net under him when he did, I would have lost him at the last minute." He took another piece of fish. "No kidding, Erin; I wish you could have been there. It's something a man dreams of. It was a Rembrandt on a line!" He sighed proudly. "I spent one whole hour cleaning off a wall in my office where I can hang him."

Erin grinned at him excitedly. "You caught your trophy bass! When?"

Price was still stuffing fish in his mouth at an alarming rate. "When? Why, this morning. Didn't you see it?"

"See it?" Erin frowned. "No, where did you put it?"

"Where? What do you mean?" He glanced up at her in surprise.

"Where did you put your fish?" she repeated, a happy

smile still on her face. "Did John keep it for you until you got back?"

Price looked at her uneasily. "No . . . I left it here."

"Really?" She looked puzzled. "Where?"

"Well, damn, Erin. I don't see how you could have missed it. I put it right there in the refrig—" His face suddenly turned ashen as he dropped his fork and looked down at the half-eaten piece of fish on his plate.

Nausea bubbled up in Erin's throat, her eyes focusing on the empty fish platter.

"Erin," Price's voice sounded very small and childish in the deathly quiet kitchen. "What kind of fish are we eating?"

Erin laid her fork down slowly, her eyes never leaving the fish platter. "I don't know," she answered in a timid voice. "Why?"

"Where did you get it?" he asked hesitantly, his hand starting to tremble as he pushed his chair away from the table and stood up.

She rose to her feet slowly and began backing away from the table, her knees turning to jelly.

"Erin! Answer me," Price roared. "Where did you get this fish we just ate?"

Swallowing hard, she took a deep breath. "From the refrigera—"

"Oh lord, *no!*" Price practically screamed. "*Please* tell me it wasn't the fish I put in the refrigerator before I left this morning!"

Erin was beginning to get very uneasy now. Price didn't look like his normal self at all.

"But I thought you had put that in there for our supper —"

"I *told* Huntley to be *sure* and tell you *not* to touch that fish!"

"He didn't say a thing about not touching that fish, Price! How could you have left a message with a five-year-old concerning anything that important?" she asked incredulously.

"Awww . . . damn, Erin!" Price sank down in his chair. The remains of his beautiful trophy bass lying all nicely browned and greasy on his plate before him suddenly made him feel very, very sick.

"Oh, Price," Erin said, her heart nearly breaking at the agony written on his face.

She kneeled down beside him and laid a consoling hand on his leg. "I'm so sorry. I never dreamed that was your— your trophy bass." If it was possible, she felt as miserable as he did.

Price just sat staring blankly into space. "I *ate* my trophy bass."

"Price, listen," she cried, clutching his arm. "Don't worry about a thing. I'll make arrangements with Cathy to keep the twins overnight, and first thing in the morning you and I will go out and catch you another one!" She tried to keep her voice light and optimistic. He desperately needed that right now. He looked so—so—pitiful!

Price turned dull, expressionless eyes toward her. "Erin. It took me twenty years—twenty *long* years—to catch a fish that size. You think we're just going to go out there in the morning and drag another one in like it just like that?" He snapped his fingers weakly.

"I didn't say it was going to be *easy*," Erin said defensively.

"I thought you told me you were a calm, level-headed person! How could you have cut up my beautiful fish into tiny little pieces . . . and dipped them in flour . . . and throw them in grease. . . ." His voice kept trailing off until there was only a pathetic squeak. "Damn! I think I'm going to be sick!" He stood up, his napkin fluttering unheeded to the floor. "Excuse me, Erin, I think I'm going to lie down for a while. I'm really not feeling very well."

Erin watched helplessly as he walked in a daze over to

121

the sofa and lay down. As if suddenly remembering his manners, he glanced back up at her and murmured in a polite voice, "Thank you for dinner. It was . . ." Price searched unsuccessfully for the appropriate words, finding none.

"Oh, Price, I feel so awful!" she wailed. "You just get some rest and tomorrow things won't look so bad. You'll see; we'll catch another fish. Just like—"

"Erin, please. Just let me lie here and suffer in peace. Go to bed."

"Are you going to sleep out here tonight?"

"Right now all I want to do is crawl in a hole and scream."

"Would you feel better if I stayed out here with you?"

"No."

She took a deep, sniffling breath. "Are you mad at me?"

"No."

"Can't I do *anything* to help you?"

"No." His voice never changed levels. He was like a zombie.

"Well," she said with a defeated sigh, "I guess I'll go on to bed now."

As she reached the doorway, she turned and glanced back at his morose form lying on the sofa, staring blindly up at the ceiling. "Don't worry . . . darling. We'll catch your fish in the morning." She took another step forward, then paused and looked back again. "Won't we?"

She could barely hear his voice now, but she had no doubt as to what he had said. Only one brief, hopeless word. "No."

CHAPTER SEVEN

The aroma of fresh-perked coffee filled the air as Erin busily packed a small picnic hamper. Glancing toward the clock on the wall, she groaned. Five thirty! Rubbing her eyes tiredly, she slumped back down in her chair, silently willing her sleepy eyes to stay open. In the short time she had been here, she had done more for this infuriating man than she had ever done for anyone in her entire life! What was really irritating was the fact that until the last few days, she hadn't even known him. Now here she sat at five thirty in the morning, trying valiantly to keep her eyes open while she assembled a picnic lunch so she could spend the rest of the day out on a lake she didn't want to be on, fishing uselessly for a fish that had taken twenty years to catch—all because she had wanted to do something nice for a man who in all probability would be married to another woman in a short while.

Erin shook her head wonderingly. "I must have totally lost my mind through all of this!" Heaving a deep sigh, she pushed herself away from the table and reached for a cup. Life had been so much simpler a week ago.

Tiptoeing to the front door, she gazed out at the lake. It still had the same soft, moonlit look it had had when she went to bed. "I have got to try to catch that fish," she said out loud, fretting. She didn't want that bare place on his wall in Memphis on her conscience for the rest of her life! Whether he liked it or not, she was going to at least attempt to catch that stupid fish for him—with or without his help.

Price stirred restlessly on the sofa, bringing Erin back abruptly to the present. She could see the top of his dark, wavy hair barely peeping out over the blanket as he irritably pulled it over his eyes, shading them from the glaring light from the kitchen.

"Erin!" She jumped guiltily as the sound of Price's annoyed voice boomed out. "What!"

"Would you please get that damn light out of my face!" he ordered crisply, his voice muffled by the blanket over his mouth.

"I'm sorry! I'll be leaving in a few minutes," she replied in a miffed tone. She reached for her picnic hamper.

"Why don't you just take your sweet little fanny back to bed and forget that fish!" The voice from under the blanket tent was less sharp now as he turned over on his back, readjusting the pillow Erin had placed under his head the night before.

"What makes you think my mind's on the fish?" she asked resentfully, reaching for her jacket.

"I'm an exceptionally smart man," he said sarcastically. "My trained analytical mind doesn't miss a thing. Where else would you be going at five thirty in the morning with a fishing rod in one hand and a can of worms in the other?"

Throwing back the blanket, he sat up, running his hands through the thick mane of dark, sleep-tousled hair. Erin's breath caught momentarily as her eyes rested briefly on the broad expanse of his bronzed, hairy chest. His powerful muscles played across his arms as he absent-mindedly rubbed sleep-clouded emerald eyes. "I'm serious, Erin; go on back to bed," he said tiredly. He must have taken his shirt off after she covered him last night.

"No," she replied firmly. "*You* go back to sleep." Reaching for the light switch, Erin plunged the room into darkness. She fumbled for the door, banging her way across the room, catching the tip of her rod in the curtains just as she reached the front screen door. "Darn!"

She jerked the tip of the rod twice, nearly bending it double before one strong brown hand snaked out, snatching the rod from her. "I can tell this is going to be one fun day," Price muttered scathingly under his breath as he untangled the rod tip from the curtain. "Are you sure I can't change that pigheaded mind of yours?"

The room was so dark she could barely make out the tall form looming over her. She stared defiantly into the dark. "I'm going!" she hissed.

Letting out a string of expletives, Price bounded back across the room, grabbing his shirt and jerking it on as he talked. "*All right!* We're going to go out there and *prove* you can't catch another eight-pound fish any day of the week. After this useless trip"—Erin could see him pointing his finger at her accusingly—"I don't want to hear another word about it. Is that clear?"

"Perfectly, and no one asked you to go," she pointed out curtly.

"You don't know *one* thing about operating Nathan's fishing boat," Price said, tying his shoes with short, agitated jerks. "Now do you?"

"I can learn," she said, shrugging her shoulders unconcernedly.

"Yeah, sure you could! Ten boat docks could be leveled by the time you got the hang of it."

Erin stiffened, opening her mouth to speak.

"Just don't say *anything,* Erin," Price roared, reaching for the keys to the trunk of his car to get his fishing gear. "I'm going with you!"

By the time they reached the small fishing boat, which was bobbing about in the boat stall, Price was in a worse temper than when they started. Staggering up to the boat, out of breath, he dropped three fishing rods, two tackle boxes, the picnic hamper, the drink cooler, and a bag that held Erin's suntan lotion, insect repellent, sunglasses, two life jackets, her can of worms, and three paperback novels she wanted to read if things got slow.

Giving her a murderous glare, he asked sarcastically, "Are you sure you didn't forget anything?"

Looking intently over the brilliant array assembled before her, Erin's gray eyes grew perplexed. "As a matter of fact, I did mean to bring that extra top I wanted to sun in . . . but," she added quickly, seeing the eyes of the man standing before her suddenly turn violent, "I really don't need it. I can get by just fine without it," she assured him graciously. She handed him the small five-gallon gas can he didn't have room to carry. "Let's go."

Working together as a team, they quickly had the small aluminum fishing boat loaded. The sky was beginning to streak with light as the boat puttered quietly out of the cove. Erin took a deep breath of the fresh early-morning air as the smell of campers' breakfasts reached her nostrils. A large hawk swooped low over the water in front of the boat, its feet barely touching the water before gliding smoothly back up into the early-morning sky. Everywhere she looked there was a peaceful, lazy landscape waiting serenely for the approaching new day to dawn.

Price guided the boat up the lake, the small ten-horse-power motor humming along through the quiet waters, and finally pulling into a small cove some fifteen minutes later. He cut the motor and drifted silently down the quiet bank. The only sounds were the birds chattering noisily in the trees.

"Is this where you caught the other one?" Erin whispered.

Price's back was turned to her as he worked with one of the fishing rods. "Almost."

Erin glanced around, trying to locate a likely spot for a big bass. "Where?" she whispered softly.

126

"Why are you whispering?" Price asked caustically.

Erin straightened her shoulders swiftly. Why *was* she whispering? "I don't know. It just seems so quiet out here." Her voice seemed to boom across the water.

"Just talk in a normal tone," he advised, handing her a rod with a large fishing plug attached to the line.

Erin looked blankly at the rod for a moment, then back up to Price's gaze. "Where's my worm?"

"If you want those nasty worms on there, you're going to have to put them on yourself," he snapped.

"But no fish in his right mind is going to go for something that looks like that," Erin told him skeptically. "What's the name of this plug?"

"Hawg Frog."

Erin eyed him suspiciously. "You really think a fish will bite this?"

"That's what I caught the other one on," he answered curtly.

"Really?"

"Yes, really," Price mimicked, irritation showing in his voice. "Do you know how to throw it?"

"You don't have to be so hateful," she said as she studied the intricate reel attached to the rod. "Of course I know how to throw it." Brother, was she in trouble now! She had never even seen a reel like this one, let alone thrown one.

Rearing back, she cast out on her side of the boat, her gray eyes widening in fascination as she heard the whirring of the reel. The line snarled in a large, matted ball on the spool.

Price didn't move a muscle, his eyes resignedly taking in the tangled mess. "I thought you said you knew how to throw one," he said in a frosty voice.

"I do!" Erin shot back. "It's just—been awhile, that's all," she finished in a defensive voice. "Just give me a few minutes to get the hang of it."

Price gave a short snort of disgust as she began to unwind the miles of tangled line in the bottom of the boat. Turning back to his rod, he cast smoothly out of the boat, his plug landing neatly at the edge of the bank.

For the next fifteen minutes the little boat drifted down the bank of the cove while Erin worked diligently on her snarled line and Price plugged the shores systematically.

Finally she had a neat reel once more in her hand. She stood up and zealously flung the line out her side of the boat again, making an almost perfect cast. She smiled smugly at Price. "Did you see that?"

"Yes," he answered blandly. "Now which one of us is going to untangle your line off mine?"

Erin's mouth dropped open, her eyes focusing on the two lines tangled together in the water. Immediately one of the two plugs floating together took a sudden dip under the water. Price's reel made a high-pitched whine as line started running through it at a rapid speed. Jumping to his feet, he nearly knocked Erin down as he started cursing, trying desperately to gain control of his rod. Erin began reeling in her line, her fascinated eyes never leaving the churning water as he fought the tangled lines, their eyes catching a glimpse of a large fish breaking the water occasionally.

"Don't reel in, Erin," he screamed in near-hysteria, pushing her firmly down to sit in the boat seat. His fishing line was growing taut now as the fish went deeper into the water. Making his way to the front of the boat, he gave the fish more line, his face a mask of worry. "Boy, this baby's a beauty," he breathed.

Erin's rod began to slide across the bottom of the boat, the tangled lines pulling it along. Picking up the rod, she secretly turned the handle a couple of times, hoping to take some of the slack out to help him.

A sudden snap was heard, then the line on Price's rod flapped loosely in the air, both plug and fish gone!

With a disgusted snort he turned quickly and saw Erin's rod in her hand. "Did you reel in your line?"

Crossing both fingers, Erin hedged slightly. "No, my rod just started sliding across the boat, so I picked it up."

He sat back down on the front boat seat, skeptically watching her as he opened his tackle box for another plug. "That was a hell of a fish," he muttered under his breath.

Erin sheepishly rolled her line back in, her plug still intact. "Did your other one really weigh eight pounds?" she asked conversationally.

"Nearly nine," he confirmed gloomily.

"Wow, that *was* a nice one, wasn't it," she complimented him.

"Wasn't it though," he remarked dryly, casting out once again on his side of the boat. "Look, you fish toward the back on your side; I'm going to throw up toward the front," he instructed. "That way there shouldn't be any reason for a repeat of what just happened, should there?" he finished pointedly.

"None whatsoever!" she agreed enthusiastically.

For the next two hours they fished together quietly, saying very little to each other except for the two times her line got hung up, plus the three times she lost her plug.

As Price was tying on her fourth plug of the day, he gave her some friendly advice. "You'd better marry a millionaire if you intend to fish any after you're married!"

Later in the morning Price caught a nice-size bass and Erin held the net for him as he brought it up alongside the boat. "Ooooh," she squealed excitedly, "that's a *big* one."

Price held it up with his hands for closer inspection. "Yeah, that's not bad."

"How much do you think this one weighs? Almost as much as the other one?" she asked hopefully.

He shot her a disgusted look. "This bass won't weigh over two pounds, Erin."

"It certainly looks bigger than that," she told him, hoping to boost his confidence. "Don't you think you could have this one mounted to put on the empty wall in your office?"

Price turned incredulous green eyes on her. "Mount a two-pound fish?"

"Well . . . it might look impressive on your wall," she said, still holding to the slim hope that this fish might satisfy him.

"Yes, I could also nail ten minnows on a board and draw big mouths on them for a conversation piece, but I'd rather hold out for a bigger bass, if you don't mind," he said, throwing the smaller fish back into the water.

"Why did you let him go?" Erin protested. "I could have fried him for sup—oh," she said, sitting back down in her seat. "I guess you've lost your taste for fish, huh?"

"Forever," he agreed bluntly.

Erin reached down, resignedly opening the picnic hamper. "Are you getting hungry?"

"I could probably eat. What have you got in there?" he asked, peering into the wicker basket.

"Tuna salad sandwich," Erin admitted. "Remember, I didn't know you were coming," she added defensively.

"Haven't you got anything else?"

"Crackers, a candy bar, a doughnut and some pretzels."

"Good lord, do you eat like that all the time?" he questioned disgustedly. "You must have a cast-iron stomach."

Erin was munching along contentedly on her sandwich now, unruffled by his criticism. "Do you want half this sandwich or not?" she asked him again patiently. "It's going fast."

"Give me half of the stupid thing," Price said roughly.

Erin broke the sandwich in two pieces and handed him one. "I suppose Jeannie packs a more nutritionally balanced lunch," she said snidely, handing him a can of soda she had extracted from the cooler.

"That wouldn't be too hard," he responded, grinning for the first time today. "But come to think of it—yes, she's a real good cook."

"Naturally," Erin said curtly.

"And," Price added, "she dresses nice, she can sew her own clothes, she dances well, she. . . ." He paused and grinned. "Come to think of it," he said, pondering, "I don't know of a thing she doesn't do well." He wadded his napkin and pitched it playfully at her. "Want to split your doughnut?"

"You can have all of it," Erin offered, her appetite fading. "Did you have a nice time in Memphis?"

"Not particularly," Price returned, tearing the doughnut in two and biting into the soft, cream-filled center.

"Did you see Jeannie?" Erin cast her eyes down to her half-eaten sandwich. She had to know.

Price was silent for a moment as he chewed thoughtfully on his dessert, staring out across the water. The silence was uncomfortable until he decided to answer her question. "Yes, she came to the office."

An acute pain tore through Erin. She had known deep down that he would see her. So why did it hurt so badly? "Did you have a long talk?" she asked quietly.

"I suppose we did." He was still staring out at the blue water, his face an unreadable mask. He glanced up at Erin. "We had a long talk . . . and I kissed her."

Erin flinched and turned away from him. Why was he doing this? She didn't want to know that. She laid her sandwich down on the boat seat, her appetite completely gone now.

"Don't you want to know what happened after that?" he asked softly.

"No," she answered honestly, fighting the tears that threatened to form in her eyes.

"Well, I'm going to tell you anyway. I kissed her—and I didn't feel anything. Nothing, Erin."

"I'm sorry," Erin said, still keeping her eyes from him. "Maybe the feeling will come back. She wants to try again, doesn't she?"

"Yes, she suggested that."

"What did you say?" Erin's gaze finally found his.

"I told her I'd have to think about it."

"Oh." Her stomach felt queasy.

"What would you say, Erin, if Quinn wanted you back?" he asked calmly.

Erin was surprised by his question. What would she say? At one time she would have given her very life for that opportunity. But now?

"I don't want him to ask me back," she admitted tiredly. "I don't love him any longer. Maybe I never really did. Maybe it was a silly high school crush that took six years to get over."

Price reached out and touched her face with his hand, his eyes caressing her tenderly. "I'm glad to hear that, lovely lady. When I said that I kissed Jeannie and didn't feel anything, I meant that, Erin. It surprised the hell out of me, but I didn't feel a thing for her."

Tears were threatening to overflow as she brought her hand up to touch his. "I'm glad." She smiled.

"You are? As old friends, I thought you might want me to get back with Jeannie and you could meet her sometime," he said, stroking the line of her jaw lightly.

"As an old *friend,* I might. We could even ask Quinn to join us," she replied. "I'm sure you'd really like him once you got to know him, Price."

"I doubt that!" Price said irritably, his hand dropping from her cheek rapidly. "Well, back to the old grind, Holmes. I want to get this silly fishin' trip over with."

The afternoon dragged by in a blaze of heat. Erin had on a layer of suntan lotion an inch thick, yet her nose was still bright red. The hot sun beat down on them unmercifully. She took an empty soda can, filled it with water from

132

the lake and poured the cooling liquid over her steaming body, giving her some relief from the scorching sun. Price glanced up, his eyes going to the front of her wet blouse. The water had turned the fabric into a transparent delight, bringing a wicked grin to his already flushed face.

"What are we doing? Having dessert again?" he asked dryly as he languorously let his gaze roam seductively over the outline of her generous breasts.

Erin had been deep in thought as she looked up and met his intense scrutiny. "What?"

"I said, what are you doing?"

"Sitting here sweating. What are you doing?" she returned shortly, wondering if the sun had finally cooked his brain.

"I'll tell you what I'm *going* to be doing if you don't stop pouring water over the front of your blouse," he answered with a devious grin.

Erin gasped and swiftly raised her arms protectively across the front of her blouse. "I'm sorry! I didn't realize. . . ."

"Don't let it worry you. I probably wouldn't have mentioned it, except I knew you would be wondering why I was panting and drooling in another five minutes," he dismissed grumpily. "For a troll, you've got one of the best sets of—"

"Price!"

"What?"

"Just stick to your fishing," she warned grimly.

"Is your line tangled again?" Price asked, changing the subject abruptly.

"I think so," she said meekly, heaving a sigh. "I'll just sit here until you're ready to go."

Price cast a few more times, ignoring her. He wouldn't care if I sat here and rotted, she thought miserably.

Finally he laid his rod down carefully and asked, "You ready to throw in the towel yet?"

133

"Yes," Erin acknowledged gratefully. She would go to her grave with the black stigma of having fried his irreplaceable fish! She might as well face it.

"Hand me your rod, then," he said tiredly, his face flushed from the heat.

Gladly relinquishing the hated stick, she handed it to him gingerly, not wanting to tangle it more than it already was. He gave a few quick, agitated jerks, but the line remained securely buried, hooked to a dead limb sticking out of the water. Growing increasingly impatient, he worked fruitlessly for the next five minutes, muttering selected uncomplimentary phrases under his breath, giving one final authoritative and no-nonsense jerk. The plug came careening back toward the occupants of the small boat with lightning speed. Erin ducked rapidly as she heard the whistle of the plug sailing past her head. It ricocheted off the stern light at the very moment that Price swung his head around to watch the path of the flying missile, which came sailing back, catching him squarely on the arm. Erin's gasp of disbelief echoed through the quiet cove as Price stood stunned in the front end of the boat, the plug embedded above his elbow.

Springing into action, she lunged for him. "Oh, Price, darling, hold still," she cried sympathetically. "I'll try to get it out!"

Price's shocked expression changed to one of pure terror now as he backed frantically away from her outstretched hands. "*No!*" he gasped. "Don't you dare touch it!"

"But Price," she said with a shudder, "it's stuck in your arm. We *have* to do something!" Although Erin was a nurse and supposed to remain calm in situations such as this, it was an entirely different story when someone you loved was involved!

Snapping out of his stunned state, Price reached out, putting his uninjured arm around her, the fishing plug

134

hanging grotesquely off his other arm. "Calm down, sweetheart. I'm all right. You can't just try to get it out. It has several barbs in it."

Patting him tenderly, she said consolingly, "Just relax and we'll go back to the house. Then I'll run you over to the hospital. They'll take it out in five minutes." She sucked in her breath and gave him a sympathetic pained look, concern clouding her troubled eyes as he seated himself back at the motor. "Oh, darling, does it hurt very much?"

Price chuckled ironically. "Only when I move it. But I don't plan on moving it around too much in the next couple of hours," he assured her solemnly.

He started the small engine and drove using his good hand, heading for the boat dock as fast as the undersize fishing rig would take them. They had barely reached the dock before Erin was out of the boat and racing up the hill for the keys to her car, with Price following slowly behind. Bolting back through the front door of the house, she practically shoved him into the passenger side of the Volkswagen, despite his loud protests. "I'm not hurt, I tell you. Just calm down!"

The red bug sprang into life as Erin ground it into gear, peeling out of the drive, floorboarding the gas pedal and flying out onto the blacktop road. Price grabbed frantically for the handle on the car's dash for support. The little car's motor still had a miss in it, causing Erin to really have to give it gas to get up any speed. Driving faster than she had ever dreamed she could, Erin screeched the Volkswagen around curves, up and down hills, making her small car a red blur on the winding roads.

Price was clutching the dash, his face growing paler by the minute.

For the next forty-five minutes she fought her way through the heavy resort traffic, her pace sometimes slowing to a crawl, and at one point sitting for a full ten

135

minutes without moving, drumming her nails on the steering wheel. Heaving an exasperated sigh, she spied a small space on the right-hand side and swung the Volkswagen around the piled-up traffic, leaning on her horn as she careened madly around the sitting cars. Price groaned audibly, laying his head back on the headrest, clamping his eyes tightly shut.

"Don't worry, darling," she mumbled reassuringly. "We're almost there!"

Irate drivers blared their horns and shook their fists as Erin gunned her way past them, loose gravel flying up on all their windshields.

Wheeling breathlessly up to the emergency entrance, Erin skidded to a sliding halt. Price opened his eyes cautiously, letting out a relieved sigh. "Do you always drive like that?" he asked in a shaky voice.

Looking earnestly into his pained gaze, she answered piteously, "I'm sorry it took so long—my car's not running right!"

Price's face was a mask of disbelief as she helped him from the car. "Erin," he snapped briskly, "there's nothing wrong with my legs. I can walk!" She nevertheless put a protective arm around him and urged him to lean on her as they pushed open the doors to the emergency room.

The nurse on duty glanced up, quickly assessed the situation and handed Erin a clipboard for her to fill out for hospital records, instructing firmly, "You fill these out, and"—pointing to Price—"you follow me." They disappeared behind a closed door, leaving Erin standing alone in the antiseptic-smelling waiting room. She sank down on the straight-backed chair and stared blankly at the papers before her.

Beginning to laugh almost hysterically, her mind mocked this impossible situation. She couldn't fill out any of these papers; she didn't know anything about him! Wasn't that crazy! She giggled. This man who had walked into her life barely four days ago and quietly stolen her heart hadn't even told her where he lived in Memphis or anything personal about himself at all. Jeannie would know these things, but Erin didn't.

She brushed away a stray tear and filled in his name and the address he was staying at presently, leaving the rest of the sheet blank. She watched a white-coated doctor walk swiftly through the door Price had entered a few minutes before. Thirty minutes later the uniformed nurse walked back out the door, a smile lighting her motherly face.

"Everything's just fine, Mrs. Seaver. Your husband will be ready to leave shortly. The doctor's just finishing up."

Erin smiled weakly, her emotions totally drained. "Is he all right?"

"Why, he's just fine, honey," the nurse assured her. "These things happen all the time down here." Noting the strained look on Erin's face, she asked concernedly, "Mrs. Seaver, are *you* all right?"

"I'm all right," Erin said tiredly, not bothering to correct her mistake. "I'm afraid my—uh—husband will have to fill the remainder of these papers out." Her gray eyes briefly met the puzzled ones of the nurse. "We haven't been married very long," Erin explained meekly.

"Well, no problem," the nurse said. "Here he comes now."

Jumping to her feet, Erin hurried to Price. His arm came out to enfold her in a comforting hug. "It's all right, honey," he said softly. "You can get that terrified look off your face now."

"Are you sure you're all right?" she asked, hugging him in a tight, possessive embrace.

"Well," he told her in a low tone, "I may need some private nursing after a while, but let's get out of here first."

"Not so fast, Mr. Seaver," the nurse piped up. "Your wife wasn't able to complete the hospital forms." She motioned for him to step over to her desk, where Price filled in the needed information.

As they walked back out into the cooler air of the fall night, he looked down at her and grinned. "Wife, huh?"

Erin blushed. "I didn't want to embarrass her."

He gave her a reassuring squeeze. "I kind of liked it. Where's the car keys?"

She looked up swiftly, surprise clouding her features. "Why?"

"Because I'm driving home!"

"Well, for heaven's sake, why? And what about your arm?" She thought she had done a tremendous job of driving to get him here.

Price glanced at her sternly. "My arm is fine, and you drive like a demented jockey!"

Erin stiffened, resentment overcoming her. That was gratitude for you! She had practically risked her life to get him here in record time, and he was standing there criticizing her driving!

Hooking one arm around her neck, he pulled her head over to his. Grinning cockily, he lightly kissed her pouting mouth. "Now don't get your feathers ruffled. I'd just rather drive home and let you rest. You've had a hell of a day," he added tenderly.

Too tired to argue, Erin laid her head down on his broad shoulder, only too glad to turn things back over to his strong, capable hands. She slept during the drive home, snuggled close against him.

Her last coherent thought was that she had made such a terrible mess out of things. True, she had set out to impress Price. And undoubtedly she had impressed him, although not in the way she had hoped to. But at least he had come back from Memphis . . . at least she had that much.

CHAPTER EIGHT

The peaceful sounds of night floated quietly through the open window as Erin tossed restlessly back and forth. Since coming to bed an hour ago, she had been unable to turn her thoughts off and go to sleep. Her nerves were tense from the harrowing day she had just been through. By the time she had gotten the twins in bed, she had been almost numb with fatigue. Price had helped her tuck them in, then retired to his bedroom, the strain of the traumatic day showing on his sunburned face.

Erin sat up and tossed the light blanket back, then listened to the croaking tree frogs for a moment. Why couldn't she sleep? Why did her mind refuse to shut down and grant her some peace? After all the solemn promises she had made to herself about not becoming involved with another man—especially one who reminded her so vividly of the past—she found herself right back in the same old prison—a prison in which she loved the man and he didn't return that love.

Heaving a long sigh, she ran her fingers through her hair. At least Price had been honest. She had known from the start that he was in love with another woman. Her only mistake had been allowing her defenses to break down and open her heart to another man. It was a humdinger of a mistake, no doubt, but nonetheless she had made it!

Realizing that sleep was impossible, she slipped out of

bed and into her housecoat. She couldn't keep lying here, her mind running over all her mistakes. The house was quiet as she tiptoed through the kitchen and let herself out the back door silently. The moon lit the night brightly as she walked down the path leading to the bluff that over-looked the lake.

A gentle breeze ruffled her hair as she stopped and stared out over the water. The lake lay shimmering in the muted darkness like a rare and beautiful jewel. The lights of hundreds of other homes in the area twinkled back at her brightly. Leaning against a tree, she tried to envision who lived in those houses and if they were happy. Her hand brushed against the steps of a wooden ladder as her eyes caught the shadowy form of the twins' tree house in its branches . . . the one Price had helped to build. Tucking the hem of her gown up around her waist, she began to climb up the stairs slowly, feeling her way ahead of herself in the dark with one hand. When she reached the level platform, her heart nearly stopped as her fingers came in contact with a bare foot! A loud gasp filled the night air as a dark form shot up, grabbing her groping hand. Erin let out a terrified scream and shoved frantically at the scary bulk, sending it spiraling over the side of the hay-covered platform. A man's voice, mouthing some very unfriendly phrases, could be heard as he hit the ground with a jarring thud.

Erin's heart was pounding as she crawled to the side and peeked over, trying to make out the identity of the intruder.

"Price! Is that you?" she hissed.

"Damn it, Erin! What are you doing out here at this hour of night?" Price sat up and rubbed the small of his back, obviously in pain.

"What am *I* doing out here? What are *you* doing out here? I thought you were asleep hours ago," she whispered loudly.

"I couldn't sleep," he said as he pushed himself to his feet slowly, "so I came out here to think."

About Jeannie, I'll bet! Erin fumed as she scooted over to make room for him as he climbed back up the ladder.

Price reached the hay-covered platform and stretched out with a groan. "Damn . . . I think you've broken my back!"

"You should have let me know you were up here!" she snapped. "You nearly scared me to death!"

"I didn't even hear you walk up! I must have finally dozed off," he muttered defensively, still rubbing his aching back.

"Oh, here! Turn over," she grumbled, shoving him on his side. "I'll rub it for you."

Price rolled over on his stomach gratefully. She pulled his shirt up and began to massage his lower back. Erin's hands worked slowly, and the feel of his bare skin against her fingertips sent tiny shivers racing up her spine. He felt so warm and vibrantly alive. She wondered what it would feel like to touch him everywhere.

"What are you doing out here?" he asked contentedly. "I thought you were asleep."

"No, I couldn't sleep," she admitted, stroking him gently.

"Any particular reason?"

"No, I suppose I was too tired."

"Your hands feel good," he said softly. "If I married you, would you promise in the wedding vows to do this to me at least twice a day?" he asked lightly.

Among other things. She grinned silently to herself but ignored his question. "It's really pretty out here at night," she said as she gazed out over the water. "Is that a boat sitting out there in that cove?"

Price turned his head so he could see the lake. "Yeah, that's a sailboat . . . it's anchored out there. Can you hear that bell?"

Erin listened above the sounds of the night and could hear the faint tinkle of a bell as the boat bobbed up and down in the water. "Yes, I hear it."

"It's tied to the top of the mast. I had a heck of a time figuring out where the sound was coming from," Price whispered.

"It sounds nice." She sighed. "Everything sounds so peaceful and quiet out here. I'll miss it when I go back to the city."

"When are you going back?" he asked quietly.

"Sunday. Brenda and Nathan should be home sometime late in the afternoon."

Her hands slipped sensuously across his broad shoulders. She could feel the strong columns of muscle as she kneaded the bare, warm flesh. It struck her that she would like to kiss along the same path that her fingers had just covered. She wanted to taste the saltiness of his skin to see if he tasted as good as he smelled.

"What's waiting for you at home, Erin Holmes?" he inquired in a drowsy voice.

"My job at the hospital, a little apartment, some very nice friends . . ."

"Men?"

"All kinds," she said evasively. "I have both men and women friends."

"What's your job at the hospital?" He rolled over on his back and took her hands in his, his eyes meeting hers in the moonlight. "Tell me about yourself, lovely lady. What makes you tick?"

"Oh, you don't want to hear the boring story of my life." She laughed. Her hands trembled slightly in his.

"Yes, I do," he insisted. "I want to know all about you."

"Really?" she asked, staring into the magical depths of his sleepy eyes.

"Yeah, really." He pulled her head down on his chest and lay back. "Now . . . are you a janitor at the hospital, do you clean bedpans, or do you do brain surgery?" he coaxed as he gently stroked her hair.

"I'm a nurse in a pediatrics ward. A very good one, I might add."

"I figured as much. You're much too good with children never to have been around them before. Do you like your job?"

"Very much. I love children. There are times when I think I'll die with grief over some of their terrible illnesses, but at other times I thank God that I can be there to hold them in my arms and love them when they're alone and frightened in the middle of the night."

"And who holds *you* in their arms and tells you they love you when you're alone and frightened at night?" he asked gently.

"No one," she admitted. "But someday somebody will."

"Someday when the perfect man comes along."

"He will," she said firmly. "I used to lie in bed at night when Brenda and I were in high school and build the perfect man in my mind. He would be tall, dark and handsome. We would live in a little house outside the city and I would take care of his children. We would grow old together. After our children were grown, we'd still love each other as much as the first day we married. No—more! Much more. When we were ninety, he would still be my only love. We would live a simple, full life, and when it was time for us to leave this old earth, we would simply lie down somewhere together and never wake up."

"And you thought you had found that in Quinn?" he asked tenderly.

"Yes. Oh, *now* I know that I didn't, but then . . . well, you see, I never did attract the boys like Brenda did," she admitted readily. "Brenda was always the one with the looks, and boys used to flock to her."

Price shook his head thoughtfully. "Brenda's okay, but

I don't see where you think she's anything exceptional. In my opinion, you're the good-looking one!"

Erin raised up and looked at him in amazement. "Are you teasing me again?"

"Hell, no, I'm not teasing you! Why do you always come down so hard on yourself?"

"I don't know," she said with a deep sigh, laying her head back down on his broad chest. "I've always been very insecure about my looks."

"Well, don't be. You're the prettiest woman I've ever held like this," he assured her as his hands drew her tighter to him.

"I suppose you've held a lot . . . I mean, other than Jeannie." She closed her eyes and savored the feel of being in his arms.

"Can't say that I have. I'm usually a one-woman man. To be honest, I can't handle more than one at a time." He chuckled intimately.

Erin's hold on him tightened. "Please, Price, I don't want to talk about you being—intimate with anyone." Her voice trailed off weakly.

"Why?"

"I don't know why . . . I just don't."

"Well, I hadn't planned on giving you a detailed account of my previous love life, but it intrigues me to know why it would upset you."

"I told you, I don't know either!" She shifted around irritably. "Let's drop the subject."

"Nope. I want to talk about it. Why should you care how many women I've gone to bed with?" he persisted.

"Price!" Erin sat up and glared angrily at him. "This is crazy!"

"So? Mark it off to being alone in the moonlight with a beautiful woman." Erin was shocked when he grinned and reached for her. "Come here and kiss me, troll."

"You're scaring me," she warned, but she went willingly into his outstretched arms.

They kissed for a moment, a warm, exploring kiss.

"You're scaring me now," he whispered huskily as their mouths began to search hungrily for each other.

"Why?"

"Erin, I just came out of one damn mess. I don't know if I'm ready to jump right back into another one." His breathing took on a quickened pace as she pressed her body tightly against his.

"Are you going back to Jeannie?"

"Oh, brother! Do we have to talk about Jeannie right now?" His eyes found hers in the moonlight. "Don't look at me that way."

"What way? I'm only *looking* at you." Erin kissed his eyes closed. "There, does that help?"

"No. I think you need to kiss here." He pointed to his cheek. "And here, and here. . . ."

"And here, and here. . . ." Erin took over, her hands wrapping securely around his neck. She was tired of fighting her feelings. She was hopelessly in love with this man, and after tonight he would probably suspect it. He might not be able to make a commitment, but her heart had already made hers.

"Uh, I think you'd better be careful. . . ." Price whispered against her lips. "It's been awhile since I've—"

"I told you I don't want to talk about that!"

"But I'm afraid you're going to take advantage of me." He grinned sweetly.

"And you'd care?" Her tongue traced the outline of his lips.

"No, if you promise you'll still respect me in the morning." His teeth nipped playfully at her nose.

"I'll respect you as much as I always have."

Price frowned. "What do you mean by—" His words were cut off by her mouth closing over his.

Five minutes later they lay in each other's arms completely nude, bare skin pressed against bare skin yearningly. It hadn't taken them long to undress each other. As each item of clothing had fallen away from Erin's body, Price had kissed that area tenderly, his hands running gently over her feminine curves.

The feel of his hair-roughened chest mashed tightly against the fullness of her breasts now made Price and Erin realize just how long it had been for both of them. Erin's fingers lovingly touched the bare skin of his back, her lips tasting the hollows of his neck, breathing in the clean, male scent of him. For one small moment sanity returned to Erin as she thought about what the consequences could be from the spontaneous lovemaking, but she soon relaxed, remembering she would be safe.

"I knew your skin would feel like this," he said with a groan as his hands ran down the length of her satiny thighs. He gave her a long, lazy kiss, stoking the growing fire between them even higher. Cupping her bare bottom with one large hand, he pulled her against the proof of his desire for her. "I want you, Erin. I want you more than I've even let myself believe."

Waves of desire coursed through her as she pressed against the male length of him, his body imprisoning hers in a web of growing arousal. His lips brushed her nipples before his tongue explored the rosy peaks with slow expertise, bringing them to pebble hardness.

Slowly his hands moved downward, skimming the sides of her rib cage, dropping down to tenderly caress her firm stomach.

"Do you honestly not realize how very lovely and desirable you are to a man, Erin? Hasn't a man ever told you how your skin feels like silk, how your hair smells like roses, how your lips taste honey sweet. . . ." He moaned as his mouth took hers again roughly.

Her hand reached out shyly to touch him, and his body

146

tensed, then melted against hers as he groaned once more, his kisses growing more urgent, more uncontrolled.

She didn't protest as he slid her beneath him and she felt him inside her, gently at first, then he began to move slowly. Together they shared a height of passion both had never known before, one they had only dreamed they would someday find. Price was a tender yet masterful lover, blending his body with hers in an act of love. Soaring higher and higher, their bodies met in perfect rhythm, perfect harmony. At this moment he was her perfect man in every way that mattered.

As Erin cried out for release, Price's arms held her tight as tremors shook their bodies, melting away the last of their tension and frustration. When at last they were able to speak, it was in whispered murmurs as they lay wrapped in each other's arms. Contentment and peace flowed between them as she lay in the haven of his embrace.

The bright moon played across her face as she opened her eyes and stared up into the sky filled with a million glittering stars. There was no need for words. What had just taken place between them was a rare and beautiful thing, and she only wanted to savor the hour.

"Price."

"Humm."

"I—was it—I mean—"

"Was it something special?" he supplied drowsily. "Was it something other than the fact I haven't been with a woman in a very long time? Yes, lovely Erin, it was something special."

Erin rolled back over to look at him. "Were you *really* celibate all that time?"

Price chuckled. "Don't look at me like it was hereditary. Yes, I was. I haven't had any particular interest in a woman since Jean—in a long time."

"I know, since Jeannie—oh, my gosh!" Erin gasped and

sat straight up. "Your arm! I completely forgot about your hurt arm. Why didn't you say something, Price? Why didn't you stop me!"

"Now, Erin," Price said calmly, cocking a dark eyebrow at her seriously. "Do I look like a stupid man to you?"

"Well, no, but the way we've been holding each other—well, that had to hurt!" She was flabbergasted that she could have forgotten his injury. "Didn't it?"

"Like hell. But it was worth it."

Her fingers reached out to touch the swelling on his arm. "I can't believe you wouldn't say something," she murmured.

"If you're waiting for me to kick you out of my bed, you'll be waiting a long time," he warned, nipping at her fingers.

"Are you sure you're not hurt?"

"Kiss it here." He pointed to his arm.

Erin touched her lips to the spot he pointed at and breathed a kiss there. "Better?"

"I think I feel better all over." He sighed, pulling her across his muscled chest. "You didn't bring any blankets with you by any chance, did you? This is the first time I can recall lying out on a riverbank in September, nude, with an oversexed troll, a swollen arm and a broken back. Are you getting a little chilly?"

"Here, put my housecoat over you," she offered, scooting around on the hay to find her discarded robe.

"That thing! Oh, come on, Erin!" Price grumbled as she found the garment and laid it over both of them.

"Stop squirming around, Price, or you're going to fall out again," she warned.

"What if someone would happen to see us? I look like a fool with this flimsy thing thrown over me. Besides, I'd have more warmth with just a pair of socks on," he said fretfully as she lay back down and hugged him close.

148

"You didn't wear your socks, remember?"

"Ahh . . . yes, I remember. Did I wear my pants?"

"Of course you did. Silly!"

"Then why am I lying here wrapped in a woman's negligee half-naked?"

"Because you just made love to a very—needy woman," she teased, brushing her lips against his lightly.

"That's right, I did, didn't I? And she made me a very happy man."

They exchanged several long kisses, happy to be in each other's arms.

"I wonder if Brenda and Nathan are having as much fun as we are right now," Price whispered.

"Sure they are. They have a perfect marriage, no matter what you say," Erin reminded him.

"Oh, yes, I'm sure they've spent the entire week in tranquil bliss," Price said. "You're a dreamer, lovely lady!"

"So? What can it hurt? Someday I'll find my perfect man, Price Seaver, and when I do, you'll be the first to know." She caressed his smooth jaw lovingly. "Yes, you'll be the first to know," she finished softly to herself.

Price lay quietly, his hand stroking the bare flesh of her arm thoughtfully. "I hope you do." He closed his eyes regretfully. Why couldn't he tell her what he was feeling right now? Had Jeannie made him so bitter about life that he couldn't tell this wonderful woman how he really felt? Would he ever be able to commit himself again?

"Maybe I'd better go in and check on the twins," Erin said sleepily. "I know we can hear them, but if they woke up and were frightened of the dark . . ."

"Not for another few minutes," Price pleaded huskily, his arms tightening possessively around her. "It's late and they're sleeping soundly. Stay in my arms for just a little longer, Erin."

She leaned down and kissed him, the fires of passion

building quietly in them once more. His hands reached out to bring her body back to his. Their gazes met, and the world stopped spinning as his eyes sent her a private message, one that only a man can send to a woman. It spoke of love, of wanting, of uncertainty, of pain. The gentleness of his gaze was like a soft caress as she lay with him again on the sweet-smelling hay. It was a gentle coming together this time, a slow, languid time of making love to each other, of discovering each other's likes, dislikes. When the ecstasy had again mounted to unbearable proportions, the world shattered into a million glowing stars once more. They lay in each other's arms, spent and exhausted, their legs intertwined, and listened to the sound of the water lapping gently against the shoreline.

"What should we do tomorrow?" Price asked as Erin threatened to succumb to the numbed sleep of a satisfied lover.

"I don't know. Any suggestions?"

"It's Saturday. Let's take the twins on a picnic, maybe go swimming. I'd like to spend another day with them before I leave for Memphis."

Erin tensed at his words. Tomorrow would be their last day together. "Whatever you want. Maybe we could take them out to eat tomorrow night, then to a movie?"

"I don't think we'd better plan on taking them out, sweetheart. If I remember right, Huntley eats like a bulldozer out of control."

Erin giggled, thinking about the twins' less than perfect table manners. Price rolled over and faced her. "Why don't you and I spend the evening alone. I'll arrange for a baby-sitter and we'll go to some quiet, secluded, out-of-the-way place—just you and me. What do you say, Auntie Ewin?"

"I say that sounds wovewy, Uncle Pwice," she lisped. "We'll spend the day with the children, and the night will be for—each other." Her hand traced the outline of his face affectionately. "Thank you for making me feel like a woman again tonight. I haven't felt that way for a very long time."

"My pleasure. Remind me to give you my business card, and if I can ever be of assistance, give me a call." He gave her a sexy wink.

Erin pushed him playfully as he reached out and poked her in the ribs.

"Price! Don't do that. I'm ticklish!"

"Oh, really?" He grinned at her wickedly. "Where? Here?"

"Price!" she gasped, grabbing for both his hands.

"How about here? Here?"

"Stop, you fool!" Erin reached out and grabbed thin air as she felt herself teetering on the edge of the small platform. "Price! We're going to fa—" Her voice faltered in mid-air as they both tumbled out of the tree house simultaneously. Erin landed on top of Price in a heap, nearly knocking the breath out of both of them.

"Oh, damn! I *know* you broke my back this time—and my arm" he said with a moan as she tried to get up off him but developed a strange case of the giggles.

"Stop laughing and get off me!" he thundered, making her laugh even harder. If anyone found them in this ridiculous situation, she would die of embarrassment!

"*What is so funny!* Get your elbow out of my stomach—Erin!" Tears were running down her face now, she was laughing so hard. "I'm going to make it a cardinal rule never to go to bed with anyone crazier than I am," Price said with a snort, her laughter growing contagious. "Erin! Get your hands off my—you're nuts, lady, right down nuts!"

She reached over and hugged his neck tightly, her body shaking with hilarity. "Oh, Price, I like you so very much!" She didn't want to say "love." It would scare him to death. "You're the best friend I've ever had!"

151

"Yeah, well, I like you, too, you crazy woman."

"Really?" Her laughter was losing momentum now as she wiped at the tears in her eyes.

"Really." His gaze met hers again tenderly. "I just don't know what in the devil I'm going to do about it."

"Will you let me know when you find out?" she asked solemnly.

"Oh, I'm sure you'll be the first to know, lovely lady. I'm sure you'll be the first to know."

CHAPTER NINE

"Aunt Ewin, Huntwey's eatin' the stick of budder."

Erin turned from the stove and gave him a stern look. "Huntley, put the butter back down on the dish and eat your cereal—please."

"When is Mommy comin' home?" he asked as he laid the stick of margarine back on the dish obediently.

Holly dropped her fork and swiftly brought her hand out in front of her, folding down all her fingers until she only had the small one left. "Tomowwow."

"That's right, tomorrow." Erin tried not to let her voice sound too relieved. "How would the two of you like to go on a picnic today?"

Neither one exhibited much enthusiasm as they spooned their hot cereal into their mouths.

"Is this Saturday?" Huntley asked worriedly.

"Yes, why?" Erin sat down at the table with her cup of coffee.

"Do we gotta go to Sunday school in the morning?" Holly asked with a long sigh.

"Don't you go every Sunday?"

"Yes, but Huntwey's unwuly there—weally bad!"

"I am not!" he denied indignantly.

"You are too! You're not supposed to talk out woud, and you *always* do!"

"Why not? Who's going to stop me?" He cocked his head arrogantly.

"Aunt Ewin will have to make them daddies stop you!"

"What daddies?" he scoffed.

"Them daddies that always come by with them dishes and make people put money in them. Them daddies called hushers, Huntwey!" she scolded in a loud, no-nonsense tone.

"Children, stop your arguing and eat your breakfast. When Uncle Price gets up, he's going to take us on a picnic," Erin interrupted hurriedly.

"Is he *still* sweepin'?" Holly bit into her toast disinterestedly.

"Yes, he was up very late last night." Erin let her thoughts run deliciously back to a few hours earlier. It had been close to dawn when they finally came back into the house. She smiled lovingly as she recalled how passionate, how demanding, yet how very sweet Price had been.

"I wike him," Holly decided, licking the jelly off her sticky fingers. "Don't you wike him too, Aunt Ewin?"

"Very much, Holly. He's a nice man."

The sound of a car coming up the drive and the angry slam of a door caught Erin's attention. As she started toward the window to peer out, the kitchen door flew open and Brenda stormed in.

"Mommy!" The twins scrambled from the table excitedly.

"Brenda!"

"Hello, my little sweeties," Brenda said, gathering the twins in her arms affectionately. "Did you miss Mommy?"

"Yeah, yeah," they chorused, tumbling over each other to get their arms wrapped around her neck.

"Brenda! What are you doing home today? I didn't expect you until late tomorrow afternoon," Erin said with surprise. "Where's Nathan?"

"Don't mention that man's name to me!" Brenda's face was furious now. "I never want to see him again!"

"What? What in the world's going on—"

154

"Where's Daddy?" Huntley stopped squeezing her neck and showering her face with kisses long enough to remember his father.

"Uh—he'll probably be along anytime," Brenda hedged, drawing him back to her for another round of hugs and kisses.

"He gonna have to paddle Huntwey, Mommy. He's been a bad boy," Holly told her mother primly. "But *I've* been good."

"Have they been bad?" Brenda glanced up at Erin worriedly.

"No. Just normal five-year-olds." Erin was thankful that she had always been a tactful person. It came in unusually handy at the moment.

All of a sudden Brenda's face clouded. She buried it in her hands and started to bawl like a baby.

The twins immediately puckered up and looked very close to tears themselves as Erin hurried over to Brenda and put her arms around her. "Brenda, my goodness, what's the matter?"

"It's that darn, infuriating—pigheaded Nathan!" She sobbed wildly, losing all control now.

"Have you had a quarrel?" Erin bit her tongue, thinking how stupid that must sound! It was apparent that Brenda and Nathan were not on the best of terms at present.

"Yesss!" She sobbed pitifully.

The twins set up a loud howl as they fell around their mother's neck again, confused and frightened by her tears.

"Good lord, what's going on down here?" Price asked as he walked into the bawling, sobbing, puzzled foursome.

"Oh, Price," Erin said, running over to him, whispering worriedly. "I think Brenda and Nathan have had a terrible argument."

"Where's Nathan?" Price glanced around the kitchen.

"Beats me. Brenda arrived here alone a few minutes ago."

"Hey, you guys." Price walked over and untangled the twins from Brenda's neck while Erin tried to console their mother. "Let's go over and see if Michael can play for a while." He picked a child up in each arm and started toward the door. "Be right back, Auntie Ewin."

As the door closed behind him, Erin sat Brenda down in a chair and poured her a cup of strong coffee. "Now, Brenda, calm down and tell me what's happened."

Brenda dissolved in a fresh round of tears. "This has been the most miserable week of my life! Nathan and I have done nothing but fight since we left."

Erin couldn't believe her ears. Brenda and Nathan fighting? They couldn't! They had a perfect marriage!

"I thought we would spend the whole week together, just the two of us, one long romantic week. But that—that —jackass has done nothing but gripe and grumble all blessed week long, totally ignoring me!"

"But where *is* Nathan?" Erin persisted worriedly.

"How do I know? I drove off and left him standing at the last gas station we stopped at." Brenda sniffed haughtily.

"Brenda! You didn't!" Erin was astounded.

"I certainly did! I warned him if he barked at me one more time, I would come home by myself!" Brenda blew her nose loudly.

This was absolutely ridiculous. Brenda and Nathan, who always got along so beautifully, were nearly in the divorce courts over his barking at her? Erin shook her head wonderingly. What was this world coming to?

"You just drove off and left him standing in—in—"

"Arkansas."

"Arkansas!" Erin groaned. "You surely didn't!"

"You're lucky, Erin. You're *so* lucky that you're not married and have to put up with a stubborn man every day of your life." She blew her nose loudly again. "I have *had it* with Nathan Daniels!"

"Now, Brenda, you don't mean that. You love Nathan
—"

"I know I do!" she gulped in a childish voice before
dissolving in a new round of tears. "But I don't *like* him!"

"Oh, good grief, will you stop it!" Erin wet a paper
towel and wiped Brenda's flushed and puffy face. "Please
calm down."

"What's Price doing here?" she said with a hiccup,
gratefully letting Erin mother her. "Do you know Price?"

"We've met." Boy, have we met, Erin thought ironically. "He stopped by to visit with you and Nathan a few days
ago and . . . oh, it's too long a story to go into now, Brenda.
I'll tell you all about it when you're more—later."

Brenda clutched Erin's hand frantically. "Don't ever
marry, Erin! All husbands are nothing but—rat finks!"

"Brenda, you can't mean that! You and Nathan have a
wonderful marriage."

"We did—up until this week. Oh, Erin, I'm so miserable!" She laid her head down on the kitchen table and
cried.

Erin patted her head absently, wondering how poor
Nathan was going to get home from Arkansas.

Price opened the back door and stepped into the kitch-
en. "Cathy said the twins could stay over there for a
while." He glanced nervously at the woman sobbing helplessly in the chair. "Everything all right here?"

"Just ducky," Erin said with a shaky smile. "Brenda
never wants to see her rat finky husband again, and he's
standing somewhere in Arkansas trying to hitchhike his
way back home."

"Ohhhh—he's not going to get away with this!" Brenda
declared angrily, pushing her chair back from the table.
"Nathan—stubborn, mule-headed Daniels is not going to
get away with this!" She stomped heatedly out of the
kitchen, muttering vilely under her breath.

157

Price grinned at Erin. "Somehow I get the distinct feeling that the perfect marriage has soured."

"You don't have to look so gleeful, Price. Brenda is really mad at him!"

Price's smile faded slowly. "Yeah, I know. What should we do?"

"I'm worried about Nathan," Erin confessed. "She left him standing at a gas station somewhere in Arkansas!"

"Damn!" Price whistled low. "That's a rotten thing to do."

Erin glanced at him sharply. "It was his fault! He crabbed at her all week!"

"And I suppose she was perfect all week?" He crossed his arms arrogantly.

"Men! They *always* stick together," Erin said disgustedly. "So what do you think we should do? Maybe you should drive toward Arkansa—"

Erin was interrupted by Brenda entering the kitchen once more, dragging two heavy suitcases behind her. "*If* you should happen to see *your* friend, tell him he's moved!" She threw the suitcases at Price's feet and huffed angrily back out of the kitchen.

"Oh, brother!" Price groaned. "This is one hell of a mess!"

"Look, Price, there's a bread truck pulling up in the drive." Erin glanced out the window anxiously.

Price leaned over her shoulder and mumbled glumly. "Well, brace yourself. It looks like the rat fink has hitched a ride home—and he doesn't look too happy. I'd better go out and break the news to him that he no longer resides here."

Price let himself out through the back screen door, a worried frown on his handsome features. Erin could hear him and Nathan talking to each other, Nathan raising his voice angrily at times.

"He's here, isn't he?" Brenda hissed from the doorway.

Erin turned around, startled, to face her. "I didn't hear you come back! Yes, Nathan just drove up a few minutes ago. Do you want me and Price to leave—"

"No! I don't ever want to see that man again!" she hissed shrilly in a loud whisper. "Promise me you won't leave me here alone, Erin. Promise!"

"Brenda, don't start crying again!" Erin warned with a trace of impatience creeping into her voice. "I'm not going anywhere." She was beginning to grow a little tired of Brenda's theatrics.

"What are they saying? Is Nathan upset?"

"Wouldn't *you* be if you just rode in from Arkansas in a bread truck?"

"Oh . . . he'll probably kill me!" Brenda said, wringing her hands and peering over Erin's shoulder anxiously.

"He's not going to kill you, but that *was* pretty rotten, Brenda!"

"He deserved it," she muttered defensively. "Oh, look! He's starting toward the house! What should I do? Tell him he can't come in, Erin!"

"I can't tell him he can't come in!" Erin said exasperatedly. "It's his house!"

"Then we'll leave! Come on, Erin, let's get out of here before I blow my top again."

Erin sighed defeatedly as Brenda pulled her toward the door. How did she get herself into messes like this?

They passed the two men in practically a dead run on the way to Erin's car. Erin smiled sheepishly as she encountered a puzzled Price. "We're leaving."

"Brenda Daniels, I want to talk to you—" Nathan's face turned an angry red as he reached out to capture his wife's fleeing form.

"Well, I don't want to talk to you, you—heel!" She broke his grasp and ran for the car, sobbing furiously.

"Brenda . . . damn it!"

"Nathan, maybe it's best if you let her alone until she

159

cools off," Erin said gently. "I'll try to talk some sense into her."

"Would you?" Nathan looked relieved and tired. "I don't know what the hell has gotten into her this week. She's been as cranky as an old bear!"

Erin and Price smiled at each other. Now where had they heard that recently? "Don't worry," Erin said consolingly, patting Nathan on the arm reassuringly. "I'll take care of everything."

"How do you figure a woman?" Nathan mumbled to Price as Erin turned and walked away. "If Erin manages to calm that hellcat down, it will be a miracle!"

"Oh, don't worry," Price said absently as he watched the red VW fade into the distance. "Erin will get that hellish streak out of her." He turned and gave Nathan an encouraging grin. "If nothing else, Erin's driving will scare it out of her!"

"Don't you think we should stop somewhere?" Erin pleaded wearily. "We've driven for hours!"

Brenda dried her eyes for what seemed like the hundredth time and looked at Erin pathetically. "I don't care what we do."

"Are you hungry?"

"No." She sobbed loudly.

"Thirsty? Don't you at least need to go to the bathroom?" Erin searched for any plausible excuse to stop the car.

"I don't care, Erin! Do anything you want to, but I'm not going back home!" she warned with a large hiccup.

Naturally! Erin fumed silently. So far she had been extremely unsuccessful in bringing Brenda to her senses.

In another twenty minutes Erin impatiently pulled into a truck stop and shut the motor off. "I am going to at least have a cup of coffee!" She got out of the car and walked into the café, hoping that Brenda would follow. This was

160

to have been a nice, quiet day with a picnic, laughter, an eagerly awaited romantic evening with Price . . . Suddenly she resented Brenda very much.

Brenda came dragging in behind Erin, lamenting dramatically as they sat down opposite each other in a booth, "Why is life so cruel?"

"Why is there air?" Erin said, sounding more surly than she intended. "I don't know the answer to your question, Brenda, but I honestly think you are blowing this argument all out of proportion."

"You don't understand, Erin." Brenda stared morosely at the ceiling. "Nathan used to spend hours alone with me. He used to tell me over and over again how much he loved me, how pretty I was, how he couldn't live without me."

"And he doesn't anymore?"

"Well . . . yes . . . occasionally, but not like he used to!"

Erin gave the waitress their order, then turned back to Brenda. "Nathan loves you very much, Brenda. Don't you think that a couple just naturally tends to take the other for granted after they've been married as long as you and Nathan have?"

"They shouldn't," Brenda shot back irritably.

"I know, but they do," Erin returned quietly. "I don't think that means that Nathan loves you any less than the day he married you. Do you tell him how much you love him every day, how you can't live without him?"

Brenda was quiet for a moment. "Not every day. But he knows I do. I love him, Erin, more than anything in the world," she admitted in a small, childish voice.

"I know you do," Erin said tenderly. "And he loves you just as much."

"He'll probably never speak to me again after what I did to him this morning." She let out a weak giggle. "You should have seen the look on his face when I pulled out of the gas station!"

"I can imagine."

161

"Oh, I've made such a mess of things, Erin." Brenda gave a long, shuddering sigh. "Don't ever give your love to a man," she warned again sadly.

"You don't think it's worth it?" Erin asked, thinking of last night in Price's strong arms. The point in question was beside the fact now. Her heart had already been given. "You don't think you'd miss having a man to come home to you each evening, a man whose arms you can lie in at night, someone to tell your problems to at the end of each day, someone to share your life with? I can't believe you'd want to give that up, Brenda."

Tears had begun to slip silently down Brenda's cheeks now. "No, I don't want to give that up."

"No marriage can be perfect." Erin stopped for a moment and laughed ironically. "Listen to me! I'm the one who's been looking for the perfect marriage, determined to settle for nothing less!"

"Nathan's and mine is nearly perfect," Brenda said, a little life creeping back into her voice now. "Oh, we have our fights, but most of the time I wouldn't trade my marriage for a million dollars."

"That's what I've been trying to tell Price, but he won't believe it!" Erin laughed again.

"Price?" Brenda took a sip of the coffee the waitress had brought. "Is there something going on between you and Price?"

"I don't know, Brenda. I try to tell myself there isn't . . . at least, nothing serious, but. . . ."

"I didn't think Price would be ready for another commitment so soon after Jean—"

"Jeannie? I know all about her," Erin confessed tiredly.

"To be truthful, I didn't think *you* would be ready for one so soon after Quinn."

Erin shrugged her shoulders. "I didn't, either. Maybe I'm not. Then again, maybe I am. Anyway, that's all

162

beside the point. Price has an opportunity to go back to Jeannie. He may take it."

"Surely not!" Brenda gasped indignantly. "She really dumped on that poor man!"

"Well, then I can only surmise he enjoys being dumped on, because her new love affair fell flat and she called him this week. They even saw each other."

"Men! Aren't they disgusting! Well, you're not just going to sit there and let her have him again, are you?"

"What can I do? After all, we didn't even know each other until five days ago!"

"Oh, but you did! Don't you remember—you thought he was a living doll at our wedding!"

"When I was that age, Brenda, I thought *anything* that wore pants was a living doll! No, I barely remember meeting him."

"Well, he remembers you. Every once in a while he used to ask me where you were and if we were still good friends."

"No kidding?" Erin sat up to face her. "I wonder why."

"I heard him tell Nathan one day he thought you were a good-lookin' chick, and he'd like to—" Brenda blushed. "Well, they didn't know I was listening, and you know how blunt men can be sometimes," she excused embarrassedly.

Erin's smile was radiant. Price had thought of her in the most intimate way years ago! This was absolutely wonderful! And that was *before* Jeannie! "I know!" Erin agreed happily, absently stirring five tablespoons of sugar into her coffee. "Extremely blunt!"

"I'm exhausted," Brenda admitted with a yawn. "Let's finish our coffee, then we can go back home. I'm going to make all this up to Nathan tonight."

"Well, I should hope so. . . ."

"Excuse me, ladies," a brawny-looking man said, walking up to their table as he wiped the sweat off his brow with a grimy handkerchief. "Do one of you chicks own that red VW sitting out in front?"

"That chick does," Brenda said, pointing at Erin.

Erin shot her an exasperated glare.

"Well, there's a feller out there that said to tell whoever owned it that they got a flat." He stuffed the soiled handkerchief back into his pocket.

"Oh, darn it! That's all I need now," Erin said and groaned, trying to see the VW out one of the truck stop windows but failing. "Is there someone around who can change it for me?"

"I don't know. You'll have to ask," he replied as he calmly walked away from the table and pounced on one of the empty bar stools at the counter.

"Why didn't you ask *him* to fix it?" Brenda suggested worriedly.

"I thought he would offer to," Erin said in a disgusted voice as she watched the man from the corner of her eye unconcernedly order a cup of coffee and a piece of pie. "Let's go see if we can find someone to change it for us."

They slid out of the booth and walked to the register to pay their bill, both of them feeling painfully self-conscious of being two girls alone in a truck stop. Other than the waitress, the café was filled with men.

"Have I got a hole in my jeans?" Brenda whispered, clinging to Erin's small form.

"No, have I?"

"Get a load of the way that man on the third bar stool is looking at us," she muttered uneasily under her breath.

Erin nonchalantly let her eyes rove down the row of seats and linger for a moment on the gorilla who was sitting on the third seat. She smiled weakly as his face broke into a wide, licentious grin, exposing two yellow gold teeth and one rotten one.

"Oh, lord! Let's get out of here!" Erin forced herself to

smile brightly at the big brute as she and Brenda nearly tripped over each other in their haste to exit.

They tumbled out the front door and rounded the building, heading for the spot where they had parked the VW. "I hope that man doesn't decide to follow us," Brenda said, fretting. "If he does, you stall him while I run for help—" Brenda's voice broke off in a scream as one arm came out from behind the VW and literally jerked her off her feet.

Erin's heart nearly stopped as she felt someone grab her from behind and pull her up against a broad wall of a chest. One large hand closed over her mouth as she started to scream at the top of her lungs.

"Shhhh—you want to bring the cops down on us?"

"Price!"

His hands loosened on her mouth and he spun her around to face him. "You called?"

"Price Seaver! You dirty—"

"Now wait a minute, this wasn't *my* idea. It was all Nathan's," Price said quickly. "I was for coming in there and carrying you out of the restaurant like a man, but Nathan wanted to do it a little quieter."

"Why didn't you just let us know you were here?" she sputtered, still trying to convince her legs to support her. Her heart was beating like a jackhammer from the fright he had just given her.

"Oh, sure. With Brenda in the mood she's in!"

Erin looked around frantically. "Where is Brenda?" All Erin had heard was Brenda's terrified scream shortly before Price had grabbed her.

"Nathan took her to their car. I think the lovebirds need to talk." He grinned as the sound of flying gravel and tires squealing on pavement reached their ears.

"And you had to go to these drastic means?" She gasped, prying his hands away from her waist angrily.

"It worked, didn't it?" He looked extremely proud of

himself at the moment. "Darn. Give us a little credit. It took us three hours to find your car—and cost fifty dollars to get that guy to tell you your car had a flat!"

"Price, you are horrible!" Erin scolded with a relieved laugh.

"Yeah, I know it." He cringed at the sound of Brenda's voice screaming one last time as Nathan pulled out of the truck stop. "Ah! Ain't love grand!"

"They really do love each other." She smiled tenderly at him, wanting to kiss him so badly she ached.

"It sounds like it," he agreed blandly. "Come here, troll, and give me a kiss."

Erin went into his arms happily and they exchanged a long, lazy kiss.

"How did you ever find us?" she finally managed to ask.

"Drove into every café and truck stop for the last fifty miles." He kissed her on the tip of her nose playfully.

"How nice. But why all the bother? I would have brought Brenda home later."

"I missed having our picnic today," he whispered huskily as their mouths merged again. "And I was determined I wasn't going to miss our date tonight."

"You sound like you might be takin' a likin' to plain little ole trollish me," Erin teased in a hillbilly twang.

"Naw. Never! Nathan and I drew straws and he got the good-looking, ravishing doll, and I got the troll." He sighed disappointedly, brushing his lips across hers tantalizingly.

"I don't believe you for one minute! I happen to know for a fact that you noticed me at Brenda and Nathan's wedding all those years ago. You've even asked Brenda about me occasionally," she revealed smugly.

"Now who's been feeding you all that bull? I've never looked at an ugly, homely girl like you in my whole life." He winked and pinched her on the fanny.

"Just what *did* you tell Nathan you'd like to do to me?

166

Brenda said she overheard you and Nathan talking one day—"

Price stopped her with a masterful kiss. When she was finally able to catch her breath, she asked again, "What did you tell him?"

"Promise you won't get mad." He grinned cockily.

"I won't get mad."

He leaned over and pulled her up against his long male length and rubbed against her suggestively as he whispered in her ear.

"Good heavens, Price! You *are* unbelievable!"

"I know. I really can be when I put my heart into it!" he said proudly, his hand lazily stroking her back. "Come on, I passed a little motel about ten miles down the road where we can check in and I'll prove it," he murmured against the silken mass of her hair.

"Don't be silly. We're not going to spend the night in a motel. . . ." Her voice trailed off weakly as his hand caressed the side of her breast.

"Why not?" He kissed her slowly. "I want to hold you in my arms again, kiss you, touch you, have you touch me the way we did last night."

Erin felt her defenses crumbling fast as he pleaded against her mouth softly. "What's wrong with a man wanting to be with his woman?" he whispered persuasively.

His woman! That sounded so very, very wonderful. Had it only been a phrase that popped into his head, or did he realize what he had said? At the moment it made very little difference to her. She loved him, and that was all that mattered. The smoldering flame that she saw in his eyes comforted her. Price Seaver was a doomed man—doomed to a lifetime with her—only she wasn't about to tell him so right now. She sighed, running her hands through the thick hair on his broad chest. She'd let him discover that all by himself.

Parting her lips, she raised her mouth to meet his kisses as his hands continued to explore her soft body. So much love and warmth seemed to flow between them at the moment that it held them both in awe.

"Don't you think we'd better go before we make a public spectacle of ourselves?" he urged in an unsteady voice, his eyes growing dark and slumbrous with desire.

He reached behind him and opened the car door, his mouth never leaving hers for an instant. Together they got in and he pulled her over close on the seat as he started the engine.

"Can you drive with both of us in one seat?" she asked between his long lazy kisses. A strange feeling of languor began to invade her body.

"If I can't, we'll walk the rest of the way," he promised in a ragged breath.

They drove to the motel exchanging heated kisses, their growing need for each other causing a sense of urgency in them, yet each one wanting to prolong the inevitable as long as possible. Erin wanted to touch him, to explore every inch of this man she loved. She wanted to kiss him, to feel his naked skin next to hers, to hear his voice raggedly pleading for more.

Although the ride took only ten minutes, to Erin it seemed like ten hours. As the door swung shut in the small motel room Price had rented, he scooped her up in his arms and carried her to the bed, then laid her down gently. Her breathing quickened and her cheeks became warm as he began slowly to undress her, kissing each naked area as her clothes fell away. His emerald green gaze moved over her feminine loveliness, and his breathing deepened to match hers.

"Shouldn't we close the blinds—there's so much light in here," she protested weakly as his mouth found its way home to hers once more.

"Maybe we'd better," he agreed huskily as his hands

168

lovingly traced the curve of her hip, "but we're going to turn on a light. I want to see my beautiful troll when I make love to her."

"Do you really find me beautiful?" she asked in awe.

Price pulled away from her long enough to meet her eyes, his serious gaze telling her all she needed to know. "That's about the silliest question you've ever asked me. Of course I find you beautiful. I always have."

"I think you're very beautiful, too—" She laughed at his instant frown. "Well, you know what I mean."

"No. Why don't you show me." He grinned back, reaching over to close the blinds and switch on the lamp next to the bed.

Her hands reached out and methodically began to unbutton his shirt as she whispered softly against his mouth, "I may not do this as well as you do, but I think you're *very* handsome." Her hands stroked his broad chest, her finger trailing playfully down the thin line of dark hair that ran below his trousers. "I love the sexy way you look with your shirt off. . . ."

"You noticed?"

"I noticed."

"Do go on," he urged. "I could listen to this all night long."

"Well, I love the color of your eyes. . . ."

"You hate men with green eyes. Your words, not mine," he said teasingly, kissing her tenderly.

"And I love the color of your hair, and the way your skin tastes after we've made love . . . and I love the way you go all limp when I kiss you here—and here—and here—"

Price groaned, his breathing growing heavier.

"And I think your legs are incredibly cute," she continued as she helped him slip out of his pants and underwear, discarding them in a heap on the floor. She ran her hands lightly over his legs, touching and savoring the feel of his long, muscular length against her bare flesh. "I love the size of your hands. Do you know that one of your hands would make two of mine?" She picked up his hand and kissed it reverently. "I love the way your hands touch me, all soft and gentle, yet firm and knowledgeable."

Taking her hand, he guided it to himself, moaning pleasurably as her touch sent shivers of delight coursing through his body. His kisses grew hungry, then demanding as the gathering twilight filtered through the tiny room.

"Make me your man, Erin Holmes," he urged passionately.

Suddenly they could no longer control their overpowering need for each other and they became lost in an outpouring of fiery sensations, each giving deep and loving pleasure to the other. His kisses sent a wild torrent of desire racing through her as he moved his large body to cover her smaller one. The flames of passion burned within both of them as he entered her, and they moved together slowly at first. Then the dam opened and she surrendered completely to his lovemaking, striving to show him her overwhelming need for him, just how much she loved his touch, the feel of him, the musky male scent of him.

They didn't want to yield to the burning sweetness that seemed captive within them. They both fought to stave off the inevitable, but all too soon they were caught up in a bursting blaze of sensations. She gasped in sweet agony as he moaned softly, their pleasure pure and explosive. Price cried out her name as they both reached their fulfillment simultaneously, his embrace tightening almost painfully before he fell limp beside her.

Slowly they drifted back to earth and she snuggled close in his arms. She could never remember feeling as peaceful, content and satisfied as she did now. For the first time she realized that Quinn Daniels had only been a foolish young girl's dream. She had never loved Quinn with the awesome, overpowering certainty that she now felt for Price Seaver.

Burying her face against the corded muscles of his chest, she spoke first. "I suppose that what I've been trying to say is, most of all, I love *you*, Price."

The room was quiet; only the sounds of the passing traffic outside shattered the stillness occasionally. Price didn't speak for a few moments, but when he did, his voice was soft but not alarming. "I don't know what to say, Erin. I'm afraid"—his voice broke with huskiness—"this has all happened so fast. . . ."

"I know." She patted his chest reassuringly. "I know. I'm not asking for anything, Price. I just wanted you to know that I love you."

Reclaiming her lips, he crushed her to him almost painfully, her calm shattered by the hunger of his kisses once more. His kisses became heated, almost angry at times as he made love to her again almost savagely, yet with incredible tenderness. As wave after wave of ecstasy washed over them, they cried out each other's names, clinging to one another helplessly as the world spun crazily, then finally slowed, then returned to normal.

It was hours later when they finally drifted off to sleep in each other's arms. Tomorrow she would go home. If Price decided he wanted her, she would be waiting for him. It might take a week, a month, a lifetime, but her perfect man would come for her, she reminded herself tearfully. Well, maybe not perfect, but Price *would* come for her! He simply had to. Love, will you ever remember me, was her last coherent question as she dropped off into a numbed, peaceful sleep.

CHAPTER TEN

"I still say you're being a silly fool." Brenda sat on the bed and watched Erin pack the remaining articles of her clothing, then close the lid and snap the lock shut. "Are you even listening to me?"

"Yes, but you're not saying anything," Erin replied calmly.

"How can you be so serene about all this! If you love Price, how can you just let him get in his car and drive back to—to that woman!"

Erin sighed tiredly. "First of all, there is nothing in the world that I could do to prevent it. Second, I don't know for certain that he *is* going back to Jeannie, and third, all he would have to do is ask me for some type of commitment—which he isn't about to do—and then I'd gladly say yes. But, as you can plainly see, I seem to be butting my head against a brick wall."

"Well, you *know* he cares for you, Erin! You spent the night with him last night, didn't you?" Brenda asked.

Erin's face turned a warm pink. "No—Price rented me a separate—"

"Oh, come on!"

"All right! Yes! I spent the night with him So what? It's my business. I'm over twenty-one," Erin defended weakly.

Brenda lay back across the bed and stared up at the ceiling dreamily. "I hope he was as wonderful, as exciting, as passionate as my darling Nathan was."

Erin looked at her friend warily. "Darling Nathan? You seem to have changed your tune since we last discussed that—uh—I believe rat fink was the term you used."

"But that was yesterday and this is today!" Brenda said brightly. "He managed to sway my opinion of him to a more favorable one."

"Well," Erin said as she glanced around the room one last time, "I should be on my way. I'd like to get home before too late."

"You're being foolish," Brenda warned once more as she followed Erin out the bedroom door. "You're going to be sorry!"

"I usually am," her friend agreed.

As they reached the kitchen, where Price and Nathan sat having a cup of coffee, Price stood and took her bag from her hand.

"Hi. All ready?"

"All ready." Erin smiled at him affectionately. They had said practically nothing to each other since they came home this morning.

"I'll walk to the car with you." Price's gaze met hers for a moment, then skipped away quickly.

Erin kneeled and hugged the twins, giggling delightedly as they showered her face with sloppy kisses. "You make Mommy bring you up to visit with me soon. We'll take an afternoon and go to the zoo. Would you like that?"

"Sure!" they replied enthusiastically.

The entire Daniels family escorted Erin and Price out to the small VW, much to both their dismay. Erin had desperately wanted a few minutes alone with Price. Not that she expected anything to come out of those few minutes, but at least she would be able to kiss him good-bye in private.

"You dwive careful in this kwackerbox," Holly cautioned in an adult tone. "This kwar just doesn't wook vewy safe to me!"

Everyone laughed as Erin got in behind the wheel. "I will, Holly. You can count on it."

Price and Erin looked at each other anxiously.

"Oh . . . hey." Nathan suddenly remembered the circumstances. "Why don't we go into the house and find something to eat. I'm starving."

"Hungry! Nathan you couldn't be—" Brenda saw the distress signal Nathan shot her with his eyes. "Oh! Yes, well . . . you didn't eat your dessert. Come on, kids," she said, leaning in the car and kissing Erin on the cheek. "Call me!"

"I will. See you later." Erin hugged her.

Price leaned on the car window frame for a moment, an uneasy silence settling over the couple as the Daniels family ran back toward the house, laughing noisily.

"How long will it take you to drive home?" His eyes finally found hers.

"Just an hour or so. It depends on the traffic. When are you leaving?"

"As soon as you pull out of the drive. I have a good six-hour drive ahead of me."

"That will make it very late when you get home then." Erin gazed back at him lovingly.

"Yeah, it will. I think I love you, too, Erin."

Erin's mouth dropped open. "What?"

"I said—I think I love you, too, Erin—but I want us both to be very sure this time." His eyes were tender as he picked up her hand and stroked it gently. "Let's give ourselves some time away from each other. Time to assess things in a new light. I can't seem to think straight when you're with me or when you're in my arms. . . ." His voice was soft and deep as he stared at her for many long moments.

"All right, Price, how long? A week, a month—a year?" Erin agreed softly.

"However long it takes. We'll both know when the time

174

is right." He put his hand under her chin, turning her toward him. "Right now I want to kiss you, lovely lady, but if I do, I'll never let you out of this drive." One long finger gently traced the outline of her troubled features. "Wait for me, Erin."

"I will, but don't take too long, Price. I've waited twenty-five years to find you. I need you."

"We should know within a month," he said quietly, a promise shining in his eyes.

Erin reached down and turned the key to start the engine. "I'd better be going." She was fighting tears that threatened to overtake her. The last thing she wanted was to make him feel pressed into a commitment he wasn't ready to make.

"I'll be seeing you, Erin Holmes."

"I'll be waiting, Price Seaver."

Tears were nearly blinding her as she backed her car out of the drive and started for home. One month! He had said one month. But did he mean it? If he really loved her, he would know now. It wouldn't take a month.

As the red car sped steadily toward home, Erin knew without a doubt that she loved him. She sighed deeply. Maybe women knew these things quicker than men did. Maybe it was because women matured faster than men did. Maybe it was something in their genes. Erin shook herself mentally. Maybe it was because she was such a stupid fool and fell in love with the wrong man again! Whatever the reason, she would know in a month. If Price lucked out and her knight in shining armor didn't show up sooner and whisk her off to blissville! She wasn't going to be stupid enough to wait around forever for him. She could spare a month—but that was all.

It was late afternoon when Erin pulled into her own garage. Reaching down to turn off the ignition, she leaned her head on the steering wheel in weary gratitude. It felt good to be back home.

The apartment was dusty after being neglected for a week, so she went right to work. Two hours later everything was clean once more. It was considerably easier to work without four additional chubby hands helping. Once again her mind traveled back to Price's words this afternoon. Could she bear to wait a month for him? Would life be worth living the next month without the feel of his arms around her, the touch of his mouth, being able to look into that lazy, slumbrous green-eyed gaze of his? For her it wouldn't be. And what if the unthinkable should happen and he went back to Jeannie?

Erin suddenly felt tears streaming down her cheeks and dropping off her nose in rivers. Here she was, crying over a man again! All the promises, all the vows she had made to herself were as useless as the tears that fell steadily down the front of her blouse.

Well, she would go after him. If he didn't come in a month—maybe three weeks—she would shamelessly go to Memphis and . . . and . . . and what?

With a tired sigh of resignation, she buried her face in her hands and cried for hours.

By ten o'clock she was tired, tearless and hungry. Deciding to have a pizza delivered, she phoned in her order, then took her bath quickly. By the time she had blown her hair dry, the doorbell rang. "Mercy, that was fast!" she thought, reaching for her money and hurrying toward the door.

When she opened it, her heart nearly stopped. Instead of a pizza delivery boy standing before her, it was a tall, brown-haired man with the most lovely green eyes she had ever seen. He was holding a large bouquet of roses and carrying three packages wrapped in Christmas paper.

Erin caught her breath and leaned against the doorjamb, her heart suddenly feeling very light and happy. With an amused grin she asked, "Yes?"

176

"Excuse me, ma'am. Does Erin Holmes live here?" the man asked indifferently.

"Yes, she does. Who wants to know?"

"I'm here to deliver one knight in shining armor, one perfect husband, these flowers"—he shoved the bouquet into her hand unceremoniously—"and three Christmas presents. Does she accept?"

"Well, now, that depends." Erin crossed her arms arrogantly and surveyed the "knight" suspiciously.

"On what?" came the sexy reply.

"On who's sending them."

He reached out and kissed her tenderly. "Price Seaver, ma'am."

"Oh." Erin smiled at him sweetly. "Sorry, but there's some mistake. He's not due for another month!" she said, then slammed the door in his startled face.

"Erin!" Price pounded on the door loudly. "Open this door, woman. I would have been here earlier, sweetheart, but my damn horse threw me in the forest and I almost never got back on the stupid thing!"

Gales of laughter erupted from Erin as tears ran freely down her face. Price was here! He had come after her. Her knight in shining armor had finally shown up!

The door swung back open and she was in his arms, laughing, crying, kissing, her salty tears mixing with his.

"Oh, Erin, sweetheart. I knew five minutes after you left that you were the only woman I wanted in my life." His kisses were a hungry reaffirmation of his love for her. "I may not be the perfect husband, but I'm damn sure going to work hard at it."

"Oh, Price. I don't want a perfect marriage! All I want is to spend the rest of my life as your wife. For me, that *will* be the perfect marriage!"

"Help me get into the apartment," he murmured between heated kisses. "Your neighbors will have a field day with this!"

Erin had completely forgotten she was standing out in the hall locked in a passionate embrace with Price. "Oh, darling, I couldn't care less. But maybe we should go in," she agreed as the woman across the hall opened her door and glared at Erin.

They kissed their way into the apartment and sank down on the sofa together. Erin took the Christmas packages from his hands and laid them on the coffee table.

Turning back to him, she gave Price a wicked grin. "Now, let me see. I always dreamed what I would do to my knight when he finally showed up." She winked at him broadly. "Just sit back and enjoy this, knighty. I'm going to do something I've fantasized about since I reached puberty!"

"Hallelujah! So you are *that* kind of woman!" Price groaned pleasurably as she swiftly rid him of his shirt and everything else he was wearing.

They walked to the bedroom and lay on the bed, kissing with reckless abandon as their bodies melted against each other's. She felt her breasts crush against the hardness of his chest as her hands explored his body lovingly, exulting in the familiar smell of him.

"I was so afraid I'd have to wait a month—one long month—before I could kiss you again," she confessed as his mouth moved along the dusky peaks of her breasts, outlining them with the tip of his tongue.

"That was about as stupid as my asking you to be my friend," Price agreed with a low gasp as her hand found him intimately.

"You changed your mind again? We're not friends anymore?" Erin caressed him gently.

"No, from now on we're strictly lovers," he murmured, taking her mouth hungrily with his. His hand searched out the pleasure points of her body, teasing her senses to throbbing awareness.

"I haven't heard you say the words yet, Price," she whispered urgently. "You haven't said—"

"I love you? I *love* you, my beautiful, adorable little troll. There must be at least a hundred different ways to say I love you, Erin, and if you give me your love, I'll find the way to say them all to you," he vowed adamantly, kissing her with every sentence.

"And you're not still mad at me because I fried your beautiful fish—"

"I said I loved you, sweetheart, I didn't say I'd lost my memory! I could still wring your neck every time I think about—"

"I'll make it up to you," she promised, hurriedly kissing him in a way that took his mind off the subject.

"You'd better," he told her huskily as he pulled her on top of him. "I'm going to make you apologize to me at least twice a day in this manner," he pulled her tighter against him, "for the next year."

"Oh, my goodness," she said in mock despair. "Why, I'll *simply* die!"

"Yeah, but what a way to go!" He grinned.

"Gee, since you've doled out such severe punishment, maybe I should get started on my sentence. Now let's see, do I conduct myself in the standard procedures, or should I get aggressive, wanton, wild. . . ."

"Yeah-h-h-h, all of the above," he agreed in a languid tone as her fingers and hands miraculously found all the places that pleased and excited him. "Let's just love each other for the rest of our lives, and enjoy it," he murmured tenderly, his mouth closing sweetly over hers again.

She knew the flooding of uncontrolled joy as she lay in his arms. At last love had remembered her! In a most wondrous and fulfilling way.

Restlessly Price's hands wandered down her sides, skimming her body, drawing her upward to meet his overpowering need of her. Her whole being flooded with desire for the man she so dearly loved as they came together in an act as old as time. Their bodies vibrated with liquid fire for each other as he became one with her. All else ceased to exist in the world as together they poured out their love for each other in murmured words, with heated touches, and finally anguished cries of emotion as they scaled the top of the mountain and slid passionately over.

"Oh, my lovely Erin, I love you so much," Price said in a low, throaty voice when he was able to speak once more.

Erin's eyes grew serious. "I want you to love me, Price. More than anyone or anything in this world. I won't smother you with that love, but I do want to feel secure in it."

His steady gaze bore into her silent expectation. "I told you once before, Erin, I'm a one-woman man. You can trust your love to me without ever fearing that I'll do anything to destroy it. I think that in some ways what Quinn and Jeannie put us through will strengthen our marriage. We know now when love is good, and when it's all wrong. We're lucky. We found each other, and our love *is* good, Erin."

They exchanged a kiss of mutual love, still wrapped tightly in each other's arms.

Later—much, much later—they lay together in each other's arms, their bodies still moist from their lovemaking. Price refused to loosen his hold on her as he kissed her lazily, his hand gently stroking the crests of each breast.

"How long was it after you left that you realized it was the real thing?" he whispered against the perfume of her hair.

"Days before."

Price raised up on his elbow and looked at her. "Are you serious?"

"Yes, I'm serious. I think I fell in love with you the night you carried me into the bathroom and sat by while I heaved my socks up." Her hand ran lightly through the thick hair on his chest. "But then again, it might have been the next morning, when I saw you in bed and noticed your incredibly sexy, hairy chest. . . ." She recaptured his mouth with hers. They kissed hotly for several minutes before she spoke again. "Price, I know that I'm beginning to sound like a broken record, but—"

"But what about Jeannie?" he mocked teasingly.

"Yes! What about Jeannie!"

"What about her?" He crossed his hands behind his head and stared up at the ceiling. "I wished I smoked. This would be the perfect time for a cigarette."

Erin sat up and glared at him angrily. "Will you be serious! I want to know what she said when you gave her your answer!" Erin looked at him suspiciously. "You did give her your answer, didn't you?"

"In the movies it always looks so good when the man lights a cigarette and hands it to the woman. Then they both take a long drag—" His words were interrupted by a pillow hitting him in the face.

Rolling over on her, he captured her flailing hands with his large ones. "All right, if you must know—she took a gun and blew her brains out. Right there in my office. It was disgusting. It took the janitor an hour to get the place back in shape."

"Price," Erin gasped, "you're surely kidding me."

Price grinned down at her, kissing the tip of her nose. "I surely am."

"Did you tell her?" Erin demanded, biting his lip painfully.

"Ouch! Yes, I told her!"

"When?"

"The same day she asked me!"

Erin's face softened. "You mean you didn't even have

to think about it? You told her the same day you were in Memphis?"

Price chuckled. "I had thought about it, Erin, constantly for the last six months. I realized that it was over a long time ago." He kissed her again lovingly. "If it makes you feel any better, I never loved her in the way I love you. You're the first woman in my life who ever made me feel the way I do at this moment, Ms. Holmes. I love you very, very much."

"It does make me feel better, Mr. Knight. I love you, too."

"And Quinn?"

"I've forgotten what he even looks like!" she admitted honestly.

"Good, because from now on you're my woman, like it or not!"

"I like it!"

His hand slid down the length of her silken thigh. "Oh, yeah? Prove it." His mouth swooped down to capture hers, forcing her lips open to his thrusting tongue as the peal of the doorbell seeped through their passion-clouded senses.

"Who is that?" Price grumbled disgustedly.

"Pizza man," Erin murmured, bringing his mouth down to meet hers once more. "Oh, my gosh, it's the pizza man!" She scrambled out of bed and fumbled for her robe. "I called for pizza over two hours ago!"

The happy couple sat on her living room couch, kissing and munching contentedly on the pizza.

"This is good." Erin sighed between mouthfuls. "I shouldn't be eating this . . . I *have* to lose ten pounds."

Price frowned at her and took another bite out of his slice. "You shift one ounce of flab around on all those sexy curves and you'll have me to fight."

"No," Erin said firmly, reaching for her third piece. "I

mean it. I'm going to go on a diet first thing in the morning. I'm very strong-willed. I can do it if I set my mind to it. Do you want the last piece?"

"No, you eat it."

"Thanks. As I was saying, I'll have this weight off in no time flat." She bit into the last piece and rolled her eyes. "Gosh, this tastes good!"

"Whatever you say. Just so you can get into a wedding dress."

Erin paused in the middle of a bite. "Wedding dress?"

"You know, for a girl who's a born romantic, you're not very curious when your knight in shining armor finally does ride up. Don't you want to know what the fool brought you?"

Erin grinned sweetly. "I thought he already gave it to me. Twice."

"Naughty woman. Now you don't get your Christmas presents."

Erin eyed the gaily wrapped boxes greedily. "Are those really for me?"

"I don't know who else I'd be taking them to at this time of year."

Erin laid her pizza down and scooted closer to him, wrapping her arms around his neck. "But why do I get Christmas presents in August?" She kissed his neck, snuggling against him contentedly.

"Because you're such a troll, Santa probably always flew right over your little house." He reached out and grabbed her hands that were exploring now. "And if you don't stop it, it's going to be another hour before you get to open them."

"I'll stop." Erin ceased her actions after one final intimate pinch. "I want to open the big one first."

Price grinned at her devilishly. "Oh! You mean the box?"

"Price!" She tore into the wrapping excitedly. "How did you know what I wanted?"

"We made out our lists last week, don't you remember?" Price was beaming at her in undisguised love as the paper fell away and she lifted a sable brown full-length mink coat out.

"Oh, Price," she whispered in awe. "You can't be serious."

"I'm very serious, my lovely Erin."

"But it's so expensive—I couldn't take this. . . ."

"You're going to be my wife. You'd better get used to being pampered. I plan on doing a lot of this." He kissed her again. "Now, open the small box next."

Erin's fingers were trembling so, she could hardly get the tiny box unwrapped. Her eyes filled with tears as she opened the lid and a large diamond engagement ring sparkled back at her.

Price reached in and took the ring out of the box and tenderly slipped it on the third finger of her left hand. "We've both waited a long time for this day, Erin. Will you trust the rest of your life to my loving care? I promise you that I'll never give you cause to regret it."

"I would be very happy to be your wife, Price."

"It won't be a perfect marriage, sweetheart, but it will be a damn good one." His voice had an infinitely compassionate tone as his lips met hers in love. Erin leaned against his solid form, giving herself freely up to his love and protection for the rest of her life.

"Now, how about opening that last gift. I would have been here two hours sooner if I hadn't turned the town upside down looking for the last item," Price said minutes later as they broke apart reluctantly.

Erin looked at him and smiled puzzledly. What other gift was there? He had given her a mink coat, a diamond ring, and the promise of a near-perfect marriage. Everything on her gift list. She unwrapped the paper hurriedly and opened the box. Her face lit up in a radiant smile as she surveyed the contents. Her life was now complete!

It was very very late as Erin and Price sat on the sofa, still wrapped in each other's arms.

Four yellow bird slippers stared back at them sightlessly.

"Don't you think we'd better go to bed? It's getting late." Price kissed her softly. "We have a big day ahead of us tomorrow."

"Are you going home?" Erin asked sleepily.

"No, if you don't mind quitting your job suddenly, we're going to find a justice of the peace, get married, spend the next three days making love, then we'll both go home together." He kissed her long and lazily. "But for right now, what do you say we get started on a family of our own?"

"Do you still want five children?"

"At the moment I'd give strong consideration to ten." He nuzzled her neck affectionately.

"And if we have twins?"

Price's lips paused in mid-air. "Twins?"

"It's possible, you know. They run on my father's side of the family."

Price's hands ceased their roaming, a frown forming on his handsome face. "Is there an all-night drugstore open near here?"

Erin grinned. "You're just a little late on your thinking, Uncle Pwice. But don't worry, I've been on the pill for several months," she told him reassuringly.

Price eyed her suspiciously. "Oh?"

"You can get that look off your face, Mr. Seaver. It's under doctor's orders for a small problem I've been having," she said with an outright laugh. "I only have three more to take, then I'm through with them."

185

"Where are they?" he asked politely as his hands resumed their wandering.

"In my purse. Why?"

"Because before I make love to you again, I'm going to run in there and pour them all down the drain," he replied firmly, slipping her robe off her shoulders and kissing his way down her neck.

"Price!" Erin sputtered against his plundering mouth. "The doctor said—"

"What's three days," he pleaded. "I'm getting older by the minute! I want to make some babies now—tonight!"

"Well, you're simply going to have to wait three more days," she said matter-of-factly, her knees going weak as his mouth trailed down to capture one breast lazily. "Don't you think you could *force* yourself to make the best of the situation and just concentrate on making love to your future wife," she added persuasively as her hands reached over to unbutton his shirt slowly.

Price heaved a long sigh as he stood and gently scooped her up in his arms, bird slippers and all. "Gosh, I'll try, Auntie Ewin," he said with a decidedly wicked grin on his handsome face, "I'm certainly going to try."

A WINNING COMBINATION

To my brothers,
Dan, Pat, and John Smart.
And my sister, Sue Authur.
In case I've forgotten to
mention it—I love you.

CHAPTER ONE

The blustery March wind was sailing men's hats off and making the women grab modestly for their billowing skirts this afternoon, but Kayla Marshall didn't mind at all as she hurried back to her office from her scandalously long lunch hour. She closed her eyes and took a deep breath, assuring herself once again that the air most definitely did have that deliciously magic smell of spring in it. Her feet were fairly flying along the sidewalk as she glanced down anxiously at her thin gold watch and noted the lateness of the hour. She hadn't meant to spend so much time at the little boutique she had found, but they were running such an enticing sale she hadn't been able to resist stopping in for a minute, and time had gotten away from her.

As she rounded the corner another sharp gust of wind tore at her, angrily jerking one of the small sacks out of her arms and sending it soaring through the air. Kayla came to an abrupt halt and watched the errant sack whipping around mindlessly, her good humor disappearing rapidly. Out of the corner of her eye she saw a large dark sedan drive up in front of her office, Trahern Tool and Die, and brake to a halt.

Her feet began moving again, her attention riveted to the

11

drifting package as she edged toward her destination once more. The wind showed no signs of setting its hostage free as Kayla trailed helplessly along behind, mutely mouthing all the naughty words she had been punished for as a child.

Another violent burst out of the north sent the small pink sack careening wildly toward the tall blond-headed man who was just stepping out of his car. He glanced up only seconds before the sack hit him squarely in his handsome face. The impact sent him reeling back against his car as Kayla raced forward frantically, trying to ward off the inevitable. Her feet faltered, and her blue eyes widened, first in astonishment, then in outright horror as the thin paper sack began to tear and all three pairs of the shockingly brief bikini panties she had just bought came tumbling down the front of the man's broad chest. Both dismayed gazes fell to the panties strung across his chest, the wind keeping them firmly plastered in place. If Kayla could have dug a hole, she would have gratefully crawled into it.

"I assume these belong to you?" The man's voice was deep, very masculine, with just a tinge of amusement evident.

Kayla forced her eyes away from the frilly unmentionables and slowly raised her head. Her gaze ran up the strong column of a tanned neck, a firm smoothly shaven jawline, lips that were well shaped and looked very, very, kissable, a nose that was not too large, eyes the color of storm clouds on a summer day, hair the color of wheat in the morning sunshine—just an average man, she thought fleetingly as her embarrassed features came face to face with his. Well, maybe more than average, she added on second thought.

"Yes. I'm terribly sorry . . ." Her voice trailed off weakly. She felt like such a fool! "Here, let me get these things off . . ." Kayla reached out to snatch the panties from his chest.

"No, here. I think I can . . ." It was his voice that trailed off this time as his large fingers worked unsuccessfully to untangle the lace of one pair from the button of his rust-colored corduroy suit jacket. "It seems to be caught," he mumbled sheepishly as the pair of white panties resisted his attempts to free it.

"Here, let me try," Kayla offered again, reaching up to undo the entanglement. Her hands were shaking from nervousness as she drew a deep breath, trying to calm herself and get this humiliating experience over with quickly. After working diligently for a few moments Kayla noticed the man was getting a bit antsy, shifting from one foot to the other.

Sighing with annoyance, he grabbed her hands and said sharply, "Look, why don't you just tear the damn things off and get this over with!" His tone of voice was suddenly almost rude.

Kayla glared at him anxiously. "These are brand new panties. I just bought them not fifteen minutes ago." She had always had a practical side.

"Lady, I'll buy you a new pair," he gritted out in a low growl. "Just get the damn things off me!"

With a sigh of defeat Kayla jerked hard on the lacy undies, cringing as she heard the fabric tear, along with his button.

"There. I hope you're satisfied," she said briskly as she plucked the other two pairs from his shoulders and stuffed them into one of the other sacks she was carrying. "That's five dollars down the drain."

"My heart bleeds for you," he said as he dismally surveyed his suit jacket.

Kayla was busily gathering up her purse and other packages, the offending pair of briefs still clasped tightly in her hand. She was now twenty minutes late, and she certainly didn't have time to stand here and argue with this stranger over a pair of panties.

One large hand snaked out and took the scrap of white lace from her hands and held it up for a closer inspection. He emitted a low whistle between his teeth. "Holeeee Moses! Do you actually wear these things?" he asked incredulously.

Kayla paused and surveyed him arrogantly. "Is there something wrong with them?" He had such a cocky look on his face!

"They look to me like they'd be a torture chamber," he said

bluntly, his eyes assessing the skimpiness of them. Then, as if a new, more agreeable thought had occurred to him, his gaze sauntered over her feminine curves, a small grin creeping over his handsome features. "Although I'll admit they could start a man's motor running with no problem."

"I am not interested in starting any man's motor, as you so crudely put it, and I certainly don't have time to be carrying on this ridiculous conversation," Kayla told him irritably as she gathered the last of her packages together. "I'm late for work as it is."

"Hey, wait a minute," he called as she brushed rudely by him and started up the set of stairs leading to her office. "How do I know what size . . . uh . . . these things to buy you?"

"Forget it," she said tightly as she unlocked the door to the office and started in. "I'll buy my own . . . torture chambers!" The door closed with an irritated bang. That had to be the single most embarrassing incident in Kayla's life. If she never saw that man again, it would be too soon!

Hurriedly dumping her parcels in the small closet next to her desk, she silently thanked her lucky stars that she was working in a one-girl office. When she had agreed to replace Paula for a couple of weeks so she could go on vacation with her husband, Doug, Kayla had known that her office skills would be a little rusty, but she was shocked when she found out just how rusty. The last few days had been chaos, and one of the contributing culprits was frantically flashing its lights at her from the console on her desk.

"Good afternoon, Trahern Tool and Die." She forced her voice to sound pleasant as she punched down the first blinking button. "Yes, sir, I'll connect you. One moment, please" Biting her lip, she studied the typewritten sheet next to her, looking for the right extension. Holding her breath, she pressed down on a second button and, she hoped, transferred the call. Repeating the process with fumbling fingers, she answered the five calls that were coming through. Kayla was so engrossed in her work, she was barely aware of the front door opening and the tall blond-haired man stepping into the room.

"Good afternoon, Trahern Tool and . . . Oh, I'm sorry, sir! I didn't realize I cut you off. I'll transfer your call again." Exasperatedly she searched the extension sheet and frantically poked another button.

"Excuse me, ma'am, I know you're busy, but . . ."

Kayla barely glanced up as she tried to keep track of the lights going on and off. She flushed miserably as she recognized the man from the street. "What do *you* want?" she said curtly. She needed him right now like she needed another incoming call.

"What do I want? My, what receptionist school did you flunk out of?" he chided in a condescending tone.

"None. I owned a dress shop in Florida until a few months ago," she said sharply, still punching buttons, not knowing which call to answer first. "Please, just go away. I'm terribly busy right now. I told you, you don't owe me anything."

"Owned a dress shop," he mused thoughtfully, ignoring her request. "What happened? Did you develop a case of amnesia and stumble in here by mistake?"

Kayla glared up at him.

"Where's Paula?"

"Lolling around somewhere in the Bahamas right about now. I'm just filling in for her. She won't be back for another week yet. May I help you? Oh, darn!" Kayla snapped as she severed another phone conversation cleanly.

The stranger leaned against her desk, boyish grin on his tanned, handsome face. He was clearly enjoying her frustration. "Why don't you let that thing ring. Nobody's going to reach their party anyway."

With a sigh Kayla leaned back and let the lights blink. "You're right. This thing's giving me fits," she admitted glumly. "Did you really want something?" Her large blue eyes rose to meet his smoky gaze. For a moment, just one slight moment, her heart fluttered. She was looking into Tony's eyes. Eyes that could

15

turn dark and sensual when he was sexually aroused, cold and hard when he was angry. Tony's beautiful eyes had enchanted, thrilled, and excited her. At one time Tony Platto had meant the whole world to her. Then he had destroyed that world, and her along with it.

"You really don't know who I am, do you?" the man smiled questioningly.

"No. Thrill me," she said churlishly.

The man leaned forward, his smile turning into a broad grin. Crossing his arms negligently, he surveyed her with a slow, easy familiarity. "I probably could."

"I'm sorry, but I'm not familiar with the regular salesmen that come in here. Do you have an appointment?" she asked sharply. She was uneasily watching the increasing array of blinking lights before her, ignoring his sexy innuendo.

"I'm here to see Mr. Trahern," he answered, suddenly very businesslike, playing along with her professional tone of voice.

"If you're referring to the elder Mr. Trahern, he's out of town for the next month. If you mean 'Romeo' Trahern, I wouldn't have the slightest idea where he might be." Her tone left no doubt she cared even less where *that* one was. "It's my understanding he doesn't work out of this office and is rarely in town."

"Romeo? My, do I detect a note of animosity toward the son?"

Disarmed, Kayla looked up and, realizing what she had just said, put her hand over her mouth. "Oh, excuse me. That's just one of the things I've heard him called. I'm so rattled today, I'm not thinking straight. Look, honestly, I don't have time to sit here and idly chat with you. Did you have an appointment, Mr. . . ." Kayla looked up expectantly at him.

"Uh, Franklin. That's my name, Franklin. And, no, I don't have an actual appointment. Mr. Trahern just usually lets me drop in on him from time to time. Why don't you like Nicholas?"

"Who?"

"Nicholas—Nicholas Trahern, the son. What's wrong with him?" His eyes had turned slightly mistrustful now.

16

"Good heavens!" Kayla said in exasperation. "I didn't say I didn't like the man. In fact, I wasn't even aware his name was Nicholas." She giggled. "I've always heard him referred to as Romeo, Hot Lips, Don Juan, and—" she stopped, and her cheeks reddened again as she offered him a small shy smile.

"And?" he persisted, standing up straighter now.

"Superfly!"

His left eyebrow shot surprisedly upward. "Super *what?*"

Her face clouded with embarrassment, and she lowered her eyes back to the top of the desk, aghast at her easy familiarity with this total stranger.

"Guy!" she amended hurriedly. "And I don't even *know* the louse . . . man. I only know what I've heard about him. But you're right, I don't particularly like what I've heard. I suppose you're a friend of his." She had probably stuck her foot in her big mouth again.

"You might say that. You still haven't said exactly what you don't like about the man." She clearly had him worried.

"*Mr.* Franklin!" Kayla stood up and put both of her hands flat on the desk and glared at him beligerently.

"Franklin . . . just call me Franklin," he suggested sweetly.

"I just did!"

"No, I mean drop the Mr. and just call me by my first name."

"What is your first name?" Kayla was losing her patience rapidly.

"Franklin!" He grinned boyishly.

Kayla let out a snort of disbelief. "Your name is Franklin Franklin?"

Franklin shrugged his broad shoulders, and his grin broadened. "Catchy, isn't it? But look, you don't have to raise your voice to me." He lowered his head timidly, and a shy expression came over his face. "I know you're upset by all this talk about that . . . disgusting Nicholas and what happened outside a few minutes ago. Believe me, that was the most embarrassing thing that has ever happened to me." His earnest gray eyes peered at

17

her soulfully. "But it was just an unfortunate accident, and I told you I'd be more than happy to buy you another pair." She could have sworn he blushed as he dropped his head down and stared at the floor. He looked like a whipped dog.

Kayla regarded him suspiciously, surprised at the sudden change that had come over him. When she was satisfied that his discomfort and repentance were real, the anger drained out of her, and she sank back down in her chair tiredly.

"I'm sorry, Franklin, I didn't mean to raise my voice, but this has been a bad day. First of all, I've never met Nicholas Trahern. In fact, I've never even seen a picture of the man. I've *heard* certain things about him that could only lead me to believe that I would never like the man personally. If he's a close friend of yours, then I apologize, and I'm sorry if I've embarrassed you by . . . by his nicknames."

"Oh, yes, I know the things you're referring to," Franklin agreed, his eyes growing round and sincere. He came around the desk and sat down on it in front of her. "You've probably heard all those nasty stories about him being a womanizer, a rake, a spoiled playboy who does nothing but gamble, play with his racehorse, drink too much." He searched his memory for more scurrilous faults. "Steal candy from small children, beat dogs—"

"Yes, well, I hadn't heard the part about children and dogs," Kayla had to admit in all honesty, "but I had heard all the other things."

"Well, I hate to say it, but he is *all* those despicable things, and more! I cannot understand what a decent woman would see in him." He reached over and casually picked up Kayla's hand, enclosing it in his large tanned one. "Why in the world would a woman be interested in a man like that, Ms." It was he who was now searching for a name.

Kayla glanced down uneasily at her small hand engulfed in his large one, wondering whether to pull it back or let it remain where it was. The sudden change in his manner had her a bit confused. Deciding that he was probably very harmless, and suddenly aware of the fact that for some reason her hand felt very comfortable in his, she decided to let it pass for the moment.

"Marshall. Kayla Marshall," she offered pleasantly.

"Kayla Marshall. Very pretty." The timbre of his voice was very deep with an almost musical quality to it. Smoky eyes gazed into sky-blue ones for a fraction of a minute before he continued softly. "As I was saying, Kayla Marshall, what makes a woman fall for a man like Nicholas Trahern? I have to admit, I've always been . . . very shy, very ill at ease, insecure around women"—his voice dropped even lower, and he began to gently massage her hand, lulling her into a state of placidity—"so I'm simply amazed to see how smoothly the cad operates. We've been friends for years, and I can't help but like the guy. But it's outrageous how women flock to him. It's simply uncanny," he said with a depressed sigh, shaking his head in disbelief.

Strange, but Kayla would not have thought Franklin would ever have any trouble attracting women. He certainly was nice-looking enough—downright handsome, in fact—and the way he was caressing her hand, sending little shivers of delight up her arm . . . that certainly didn't indicate any shyness on his part.

As if reading her thoughts, he dropped her hand, sending it thudding back down on the desk painfully, his head drooping shamefully once again. "Oh, my! I don't know what's come over me," he apologized. "You must think . . . It's just that for some reason, you make me feel so . . . so comfortable with you. I hope that you don't think that I'm the sort of man who would try to take advantage of a girl, like my good friend Nicholas? . . ." His voice trailed off.

"No, no, really, Franklin." Kayla reached over to pat his hand reassuringly with her still stinging one. "I don't think that at all . . . really." This poor man definitely did seem to have problems relating to a woman! "And as for your friend Nicholas, some women are attracted to the rich, spoiled, playboy type. I've heard he's extremely good-looking and personable . . . and, well"—she shrugged her shoulders and smiled apologetically at him—"add all that together, and to some women he *would* be totally irresistible!"

"Yes, I suppose he is. You'd fall for him, too, if you ever met him, wouldn't you?" He raised one brow hopefully.

"Afraid not. His type are a pain in the—" Kayla caught herself before she embarrassed Franklin further. "No, I'd never be attracted to Nicholas Trahern! Now, if you'll excuse me, Franklin, I really do have to get back to answering these calls. If you'll leave your card, I'll see that the elder Mr. Trahern gets it."

Franklin looked momentarily disconcerted as he began to rummage through his suit pocket, trying unsuccessfully to come up with a card. "Sorry." He grinned innocently. "I seem to be all out of my business cards."

"Then I'll be happy to leave a note for him. Was this strictly a social call, or do you do business with the company?"

"Uh . . . sort of a combined call," he hedged nervously.

"Oh, then you *are* a salesman. Do you sell machinery?" she asked pleasantly, inwardly cringing at the ever increasing flash of lights before her.

"No, I sell"—Franklin's eyes darted around the room, finally coming to rest on the mound of books lying on the table in the small reception area—"books . . . encyclopedias."

"Encyclopedias?" Kayla asked blankly.

"Well, not just strictly encyclopedias." He beamed enchantingly. "I sell other types of reference materials . . . but let's not talk shop. You know, Kayla Marshall, I'm about to do something that's totally out of character for me," he said hastily, changing the subject. "You've given me the nerve to do something I've always dreamed of doing. I'm going to ask a beautiful woman to have dinner with me tonight."

"Good for you, Franklin," Kayla said hurriedly as she took his arm and tried discreetly to escort him to the front door. "I'm sure that *any* woman would be happy to have dinner with you this evening."

"Thanks. What time should I pick you up?"

Kayla's mouth dropped open, and her arm dropped limply to her side. "Me? You're asking me?"

"Oh, I know." Franklin's wide shoulders dropped dejectedly, his beautiful eyes painfully resigned. "You're going to fib to me and say you already have other plans tonight—"

"Franklin . . ." Kayla was so softhearted, it really disturbed her to see the bleak look in his eyes. But really! She didn't want to spend an entire evening with some salesman she had just barely met. In fact, she didn't want to spend an evening with a man, period.

"Don't worry about it. I'm used to women refusing my invitations," he said graciously. "I'll just go back to my motel and have some peanut butter and crackers . . . no, I had that last night. Maybe I'll open a can of soup and heat it up on the hot plate I carry with me. It really doesn't matter—I'll find something." He grinned bravely.

Kayla's heart sank. She opened her mouth and forced the words out. "I'd be delighted to go to dinner with you this evening, Franklin. I was just going to say that I might be a little late getting out of here tonight, that's all."

"Really?" His face lit up like a Christmas tree. "Now, don't you worry about how late you are. I haven't got another thing to do," he assured her elatedly. "Just tell me what time to pick you up, and I'll be here!"

Kayla bit her lip nervously, wondering how in the world she had gotten herself into this mess. "If you don't mind, Franklin, I'd like to go home and change first." Reaching for a small pad and pencil, she scribbled her address down, then handed it to him hesitantly. "I'll be ready by seven."

"Great!" His handsome face beamed angelically. "Kayla, I . . . thanks for doing this. And I want to assure you, you'll be perfectly safe in my company. I'm not like . . . my good friend Nicholas." He showed her his most serious face.

"Thank you, Franklin. I'm sure we'll have a lovely evening."
She smiled valiantly.

Kayla stood at the door and watched Franklin walk jauntily to his dark sedan, whistling softly under his breath. He seemed like such a nice, sincere man, and anyway, what was one night? She could put up with anything for one night. Besides, it had been a very long time since she had been treated like a woman. It had been over a year since she and Tony had broken off their relationship. She closed her eyes against the swift shaft of pain that coursed through her heart at the thought of Tony and Maggie. By now their baby would be around six months old, probably working on cutting his first tooth. Kayla stood in the doorway fighting the overwhelming urge to let the tears fall unchecked again as the gusty wind tossed her hair around wildly. For what seemed the millionth time, she tortured herself with the mental picture of a little dark-haired baby with eyes the color of smoke. It could have been her and Tony's baby. Tony had been her first and only love. She didn't want an involvement with another man. Not now, not ever. When Tony had come to her with tears in his eyes, begging her understanding about a one-night indiscretion, as he had so elegantly phrased it, with another woman that had resulted in her pregnancy, Kayla's world had fallen apart. Honesty was high on the list of qualities she admired, but oh, how she had wished that he could somehow have found a less painful way to let her know. If he had just walked out on her and let her believe he was in love with another woman, how much easier that would have been than for him to plead that he loved *her*, that his life was being torn apart by the situation he found himself in. But Tony had felt a very definite responsibility toward his child, so he had married its mother, still promising that there would someday be a future for him and Kayla. But Kayla had vowed just as passionately that there would not be.

She had immediately put her small dress shop up for sale and been lucky enough to sell it within a month. Without leaving a

22

trace of Kayla Marshall behind, she had moved to Little Rock, Arkansas, where Paula, her best friend from college, now lived with her husband, and began the slow agonizing task of starting a new life. She had always been a gullible, trusting girl, but she had sworn that never again would she believe in a man's promises.

For the last few months she had drifted aimlessly in a void, her interest in life at an all-time low. Luckily she had made a tidy little profit on the sale of her business, allowing her the luxury of simply existing for a while. When Paula had approached Kayla with the suggestion that she fill in for her at Trahern Tool and Die while she and Doug went to the Bahamas for a couple of weeks, Kayla had agreed readily, happy to feel useful once again. Happy to just feel anything again. That was some improvement over the last year. Not much, but at least she was beginning to make some progress.

Snapping back to reality, Kayla closed the door and strolled back across the small room. Yes, it might be nice to be in the company of a man like Franklin Franklin. She grimaced at the "catchy" name. He might be a shy, timid man—although for some reason that didn't ring quite true to her—but she was almost pleased by the prospect. Let the Tony Plattos and the Nicholas Traherns of the world go to hell! And besides, she consoled herself one last time, what was one night? She could afford to be generous. She had nothing to lose. She had already lost it all!

CHAPTER TWO

By the time Kayla arrived back at her apartment that afternoon, it was quite late. Balancing her packages on her knee, she fumbled in her purse for her key, vowing to start putting it in one certain compartment rather than merely throwing it in haphazardly, as she had a habit of doing. She spent the better part of five minutes every day rummaging in her purse before coming up with the elusive key. Finally locating it, she let herself into the small apartment and dumped her parcels on the nearest chair. Pushing back a wayward strand of blond hair, she sank wearily down on the sofa and kicked off her shoes, wiggling her toes in delicious freedom. Her periwinkle eyes lighted a little as she thumbed through the day's mail, smiling as she surveyed the postcard from the Bahamas with Paula's familiar handwriting scrawled across it. "Having a ball, wish you were here!" Kayla grinned and stretched languidly on the couch, closing her eyes for a moment and imagining the steamy tropical climate, the softly swaying palms, the warm sandy beaches. Paula wasn't the only one who wished she was there.

With a long exhausted sigh she unwillingly pushed herself off the sofa and headed toward the bathroom and a quick shower before Franklin came to pick her up. Twenty minutes later she was applying the last touches to her makeup when she heard the peal of the doorbell. Glancing down at her watch, she noted that the man was very punctual. It was seven o'clock on the dot.

I can stand anything for one night, she reminded herself for at least the tenth time since he had left the office that afternoon. Pasting a weak but completely believable smile on her face, she opened the door.

There was something about Franklin Franklin that for one brief moment made her heart thump erratically. Of course, it could very well be the way she suddenly became acutely aware of his tall, athletic physique, or the way his casual red V-neck sweater revealed a muscular chest covered with crisp blond hair. Behind large horn-rimmed glasses gun-metal-gray eyes met her blueberry ones magnetically. With a look of faint amusement he lazily inspected the suggestion of nubile curves beneath the midnight-blue dress she wore. An easy smile played at the corners of his mouth as he spoke, his deep, sensual voice sending a ripple of awareness coursing through her.

"Good evening, ma'am. You look . . . very pretty tonight." He extended a small beautifully wrapped package, along with a tiny bouquet of forget-me-nots. "These reminded me of the color of your eyes," he explained with an irresistible grin.

"Franklin . . . you really shouldn't have"—she smiled tenderly—"but I'm glad you did! Don't tell me you brought me candy too." She was examining the pink bow adorning the little package.

"Only in the eye of the beholder. Go ahead and open it."

Kayla felt a little embarrassed at his attentiveness. It was so very sad that such a nice man had not met a woman who would give him the affection and acceptance he so obviously needed. Hurriedly slipping the bow off the pink box, she undid the paper and opened the box. She had to struggle hard to keep her face from displaying her dismay. Lying between the layers of flimsy tissue paper were several pairs of bikini panties—even more shockingly brief than the ones she had purchased earlier that day.

"Do you like them?" Franklin asked earnestly, pride spreading pleasurably over his face at his, as he evidently thought, excellent taste.

"Yes . . . well . . . Franklin, you shouldn't have . . ." Kayla didn't know what to say. Apparently Franklin had changed his mind about the panties being "torture chambers"—or else he was intent on harsher punishment. The panties nestled in the box would scarcely cover the bare essentials, let alone be comfortable! With inquisitive eyes she discreetly noted that the size was perfect. Now, how in the world could he have guessed what size she wore if he wasn't used to being around women?

"Franklin, how did you know what size to buy?"

"Lucky guess." He beamed proudly.

Kayla's eyes narrowed suspiciously. What was it about this man that made her a bit uneasy? Just because he happened to make a lucky guess about the size underwear she wore? . . . "Well, again, thank you. But it was really unnecessary."

"But I wanted to, Kayla Marshall," he said sincerely, his deep voice once again making her extremely conscious of his overwhelmingly virile appeal. He came a few steps closer to her, and his eyes swept over her face approvingly. "Lovely women should have lovely things. It's been all my pleasure, I assure you."

There was something lazily seductive in his look which made her catch her breath. The sudden strange surge of affection she was feeling for him made her very nervous. He was standing very close now. She could smell his clean manly scent, the sexy, tantalizing smell of his aftershave, and it was making her feel almost giddy. His eyes caressed her softness, and had it been any other man but Franklin, she would have sworn he was debating about whether to kiss her!

"Well"—she laughed nervously—"thanks, again." Good heavens! How many times was she going to thank the guy?

"Again, you're most welcome." With one last admiring glance

he stepped back and became all business once more. "I hope you're hungry, Ms. Marshall. Do you like Mexican food?"

Reaching for the light sweater that was draped over the arm of the chair, she picked up her purse, and they exchanged polite smiles.

"I love Mexican food, and please, just call me Kayla."

"Oh, ma'am"—he managed to look mildly embarrassed—"I really don't feel I know you well enough to call you . . . Kayla."

Her sense of humor surfaced, and she laughed openly. "You buy me three pairs of the most, uh, delicate panties you can find, and you feel you don't know me well enough to call me by my first name!" Her bubbly laughter filled the room as Franklin stood before her grinning sheepishly. What a perfectly wonderful man! "Forgive me, Franklin," she managed to get out between fits of giggles, afraid she would hurt his feelings, "but I find you—"

"I know." His face suddenly turned grave. "Dull and old-fashioned. But I'm afraid that's just the kind of man I am. To me a woman is special. She should be treated with respect and reverence." He reached out to touch her hand gently. "Especially a woman like you."

"Certainly *not!* You're not dull or old-fashioned, Franklin." Kayla took his hand in hers and squeezed it affectionately. "You're . . . you're a delightfully refreshing change from the men I've known. Not that I've known very many . . ." Her voice trailed off as thoughts of Tony flashed through her mind.

"Is there one special man in your life, ma'am?" Franklin's hand increased the pressure on hers, his sooty gray eyes darkening dangerously. For the first time that day he began to wonder at the wisdom of the path he was pursuing with this lovely lady.

"Once there was—but that was a long time ago. Now, come on, Franklin, I believe you mentioned something about enchiladas, tacos, burritos." She slipped her arm through his and walked toward the door.

"Enchiladas, tacos, burritos . . . mercy, you must eat a lot more than you look like you do. I'll have to check my wallet!"

"No way. You're such a nice person, I'm going to take you out tonight." Kayla grinned happily. "Order anything you want. The meal's on me."

From behind the large horn-rimmed glasses Franklin gave Kayla a withering glare. "You'll do no such thing!" he shot back huffily, a note of impatience in his voice. "I was only teasing you. I can afford to pay for your dinner."

Kayla was instantly contrite. The last thing she had meant to do was imply that he didn't have the money to take her to dinner. She had just thought that he was probably a struggling salesman and would welcome going dutch for the evening.

"Of course, Franklin. Whatever you say." She smiled with pleasure. He was really nice! "I'll put my flowers in water, and then I'll be ready to go."

"You know, I didn't notice you wearing glasses earlier today," she said brightly as he helped her into the sedate four-door sedan. "They look nice on you." Actually, when she stopped to think about it, a wart would look nice on him. But he really didn't seem to have the slightest idea what a devastatingly handsome man he was. He had a sweet personality, too, she mused as he got in on the driver's side and backed out onto the street. Maybe he had a problem in the bedroom. Her eyes sneakily surveyed his legs, which were encased in a tight pair of brown corduroy pants, the fabric fitting snugly over their firm, muscly contours. It was all she could do to keep her inquisitive eyes from roaming from the thighs to a quite different and personal area. Out of sheer respect for Franklin she forced herself to look out the windshield. *Well, maybe just a fast peek,* she thought hurriedly. No, he didn't have a problem in the bedroom. She'd bet her last nickel on that!

"I don't wear them all the time," he was saying as they sped down the street headed for the freeway. "Only when my eyes feel strained."

"Do you come to Little Rock very often?" she asked as he expertly pulled off the ramp and merged into the stream of heavy traffic. He seemed to know right where he was going.

"Fairly often. Damn," he muttered softly under his breath as the traffic began to slow. "The races must have had a big turnout today."

Kayla looked out the window at the line of cars coming from Hot Springs. Paula had said that during horse racing season the traffic was heavy, especially on weekends.

"I wonder how many Snyder brought across the wire today," Franklin mused to himself as he switched over to the faster lane. Kayla knew just enough about horse racing to know that Snyder was one of the more popular jockeys.

"Do you like horse racing?" Kayla asked in surprise. Somehow he didn't seem the type.

Franklin looked momentarily edgy. "Nick owns racehorses. I've always tried to follow his wins."

"I've never even been to a horse race," Kayla admitted. "I'm not much of a gambler."

Franklin glanced over at her, the even whiteness of his smile dazzling. "I can see you at the window now, placing your two dollar bet on a shoo in to show!" He chuckled. His eyes were bright with merriment as he surveyed her honey-blond curls, blown appealingly around her face by the breeze from the open car window.

"I'm afraid I don't know what that means," she confessed.

"When you go to the horse races, you place bets on a horse to win, place, or show, or a combination of all three," he explained patiently, keeping his eyes on the cars ahead of him. "When you bet on show, it's usually a pretty safe bet if you pick a good horse. Of course, it would take a long time to get rich that way."

"Really? Why?" she asked, fascinated at the way his face seemed to beam when he was talking about something he so obviously enjoyed.

29

"Well, if you win, and you've placed your two dollars on a favorite, you get your initial bet back, plus, oh, a little profit. Now, if you bet on a long shot with your two bucks, that's a little more profitable, but still a slow way to get rich."

"Yes, but at least I'd get my two dollars back!" she reasoned pertly. "I suppose you bet everything—the whole two dollars—on a long shot to win."

"The whole two dollars," he agreed, grinning broadly, "on the nose."

"And I'll bet your friend Nicholas bets on the nose, the rump, and the tail." She laughed, not having the least idea what his track lingo meant, thinking how ridiculous her two dollar bet would be in Nicholas's eyes.

The smile faded rapidly from Franklin's face. "He's not a compulsive gambler, if that's what you mean. He does take a certain amount of pride and satisfaction in his horses, though," he defended curtly. "What's wrong with that?"

Kayla glanced over at him, a bit surprised at his tone of voice. "Nothing. It just struck me funny when I thought of how much he would bet and how much you and I would."

It amazed her how protective Franklin seemed to be of his friend. Perhaps he had lived in awe of him for so many years that he resented anyone's saying anything the least critical about him. "I'm sorry. I wasn't criticizing him," Kayla pointed out. "Only thinking out loud."

"You've got the wrong impression of him, Kayla. He's not such a bad guy," Franklin said defensively. "You can't believe all that smutty gossip you hear about him."

"But *you* admitted most of it was true," Kayla argued.

"Did I say that?" he asked in mock surprise, realizing the conversation had grown too serious. "Well, maybe part of it's true."

"Oh, and what part is that, Franklin?" Kayla laughed, enjoying his look of discomfort. Nicholas Trahern might be a conceited snob, but he had managed to find a very valuable asset in his life—a true friend, in the form of one Franklin Franklin.

Flashing her a devilishly handsome grin, he winked broadly. "He most definitely is a Superfly . . . *guy!*"

Kayla's mouth dropped open at sweet, shy Franklin's risqúe statement. Then, recovering from her shock, she began to laugh so infectiously that Franklin joined in. She wasn't sure if Franklin was good for her, or the other way around. She only knew she hadn't felt so lighthearted in a very long time, and it felt so very, very good. Amid peals of laughter they pulled into the Mexican restaurant, laughing even harder when they saw the puzzled stares they were attracting. They got out of the car, Franklin came around to her side, and it seemed quite natural when he slipped his arm around her waist. They walked into the Spanish building before them, still smiling at each other happily.

Somewhere between the refried beans and the last bowl of tortilla chips, Kayla was sure she was going to explode. For the last half hour they had eaten with the zeal of a condemned man consuming his last meal. As they sat in the small booth in the dimly lit room, she begged off when Franklin asked if she'd like another taco.

"Please, have a heart," she said, puffing both cheeks out like a chipmunk. "I em about to die, señor. Have you no mercy?"

"You need to fatten up a little bit," Franklin chided, his eyes running lazily over her feminine curves.

"Now, that does it," Kayla said in mock annoyance. "I should stand up and gun you down for that remark," she threatened. "All the long, grueling days I've lived on nothing but salads and yogurt just so I can be thin, willowy, and oh, so appealing, and you sit there and have the gall to say I ought to fatten up! Bah, a curse on you!"

"You don't have to watch that lovely figure," he said admiringly, his eyes roving intimately over her exquisite form. "Why don't you leave that pleasant task to the men." His strong features had a certain sensuality to them as he picked up her hand and brought it casually to his lips.

Kayla was mesmerized as she felt the light touch of his lips play across her fingertips before he placed a fleeting kiss on them.

"Franklin," she whispered a little breathlessly, "it's so hard to believe you have any difficulty with women—not when you're so . . . affectionate with me. . . ." Her voice trailed off, weak and shaky, as his smoke-colored eyes captured hers, his lips still playing sensuously over her fingers.

"I'm amazed myself," he said lightly. "Let's just say you make me glad I'm a man and can enjoy such a lovely woman's company tonight."

His thick blond hair tapered neatly to his collar, giving Kayla the overwhelming urge to reach forward and touch its lustrous sheen. The rippling of his muscles under the V-neck sweater as he gently but firmly kept her hand in control made her pulse quicken and her heart pound erratically. His disturbing virility caused her great confusion. At the moment she could not recall ever feeling this attracted to a man. Not even Tony. That thought scared her more than all the other thoughts put together.

Pulling her hand away gently, she forced her eyes to leave his, murmuring softly, "Franklin, I . . . I don't want to see you get hurt, so I feel that I have to say this. You're a very dear, dear man, but we could never be anything but friends."

"Why?" Franklin asked calmly, picking her hand up again. "Because of the guy that hurt you?"

"Hurt me? How did you know a guy hurt me?" Kayla gave an ironic laugh. She apparently hadn't given him enough credit for being able to read between lines. "*Hurt* seems like such a small word, but yes, because of that guy."

"What happened?" he asked quietly.

It was hard for her to think straight with him gazing at her that way. He had slowly brought her fingers back to his lips again, tantalizing her with whisper-soft kisses.

"Does it matter?" she said tiredly, wishing desperately she would never have to think about Tony again.

"It does to me. What was the guy's name?"

"Tony. Tony Platto." Her stomach fluttered as Franklin's tongue touched first one fingertip, then another. She would swear he had had a lot of practice at this sort of thing if he didn't look so angelic behind those large glasses of his.

"What did he do to you?" he persisted firmly.

"We were engaged. He got another girl pregnant and had to marry her." Funny, that didn't hurt as much as the last time she had told someone about it.

"Did you love him?"

"I certainly thought I did," she admitted painfully.

"Did?" he pursued gently.

"Did, do, I don't know. But it doesn't matter anyway. What we had is over and gone." Her eyes had lost their sparkle and glow. In its place was defeat. Cold, hard defeat.

"And you're going to let one son of a—" Franklin caught himself. ". . . one bad experience sour you on men for life?"

Kayla's blue gaze pleaded with him for understanding. "Franklin, I believed what Tony and I had together was something sacred and special. I believed the sun rose and set in him. I would have gladly laid my life down for him. I trusted him implicitly. I gave him my all. I encouraged him in whatever he dreamed of. I wanted what he wanted. He took all that love and trust and threw it back in my face the night he decided to go to bed with another woman. Yes, Tony soured me on other men, and I just don't know if I can ever care for anyone again. Right now I choose to live my life without men."

"You're sure you can do that?" Franklin cocked one blond eyebrow questioningly. "Don't you think it's possible for you to be attracted to another man? Say, a man like my good friend Nicholas?"

Kayla answered curtly, "Are you kidding? He would be the last man on earth I'd be attracted to!" For some unexplained reason Franklin was stirring up a lot of old longings that she had thought had died along with her love for Tony, and she didn't like it. "Why do you find it so unusual that I don't want a man in my life right now? I was under the impression you weren't"— Kayla paused, searching for the right words—"that you didn't have a lot of experience with women. You apparently are living successfully without women."

"Oh . . . well, yes, to be totally honest—" He leaned forward, bringing his face very close to hers, his eyes dead-serious behind the large horn-rimmed glasses. "I *can* be totally honest with you, can't I?"

"You certainly can," she said encouragingly, her fingers beginning to tremble in his strong grasp.

"Uh . . ." He looked around uneasily to see if their whispered conversation could be heard by anyone. "To be absolutely honest, I have never—" His voice broke off embarrassedly.

Kayla's blue eyes widened as his words hit pay dirt. "Never?" she whispered incredulously.

"Shhhh!" he threatened in a mortified tone. "I've never told another soul that!"

"Oh, I'm sorry, Franklin," she soothed, grasping his hand tighter in hers. "I was just so . . . so shocked to think . . . How old are you, anyway?"

"Thirty-six."

"Thirty-six! And you've never—"

"Shhhhh!"

"Sorry!" Kayla glanced around nervously, then continued in a hushed tone. "Haven't you ever even wanted to?" This was too much!

Franklin shrugged his massive shoulders and admitted in a meek voice, "I've thought about it sometimes."

I should hope to shout, Kayla thought irritably. *Thirty-six years old and never . . . Well, he must hold some kind of record!*

"Do you have some sort of problem," she asked conspiratorially. There had to be some reason for this . . . this gross case of injustice!

"No!" Franklin fired back instantly. "No, no problem. It's, well, I wanted to save myself for my wife . . . that's all. I told you, I'm an old-fashioned guy," he said defensively.

Kayla drummed her fingers on the table and stared at Franklin critically, wondering if this guy was for real. She halfway wished he hadn't been so candid and told her *all* about his life. Now, suddenly, he began to seem like a challenge. Thirty-six years old . . . and never! Shish!

"Perhaps I've been too straitlaced," he said guiltily, reaching for her hand again, "but Mother always warned me against . . . bad girls." He cocked one eyebrow and peeked from behind his glasses at her studious face. "Of course, I don't know *why* I'm telling you all of this. We're both going to be in the same boat now, since you've sworn off men."

Troubled blue eyes met bleak gray ones. "Aw, come on. You're puttin' me on, aren't you, Franklin?" She smirked accusingly, absolutely refusing to believe her ears.

"I'm telling you the truth!" he insisted adamantly. "Franklin Franklin has *never* gone to bed with a woman in his life." Doom was written all over his handsome features.

"Well, try not to worry about it," she urged optimistically as she patted his hand in sympathy. "Someday the right girl will come along, and you'll be glad you waited." What else could she say to a thirty-six-year-old male virgin? *Hang in there, fellow, and try not to think about it?*

"Well, I suppose if you're ready, we should be starting home," Franklin said gloomily, dropping her hand back onto the table.

Trying not to let her strong feelings of sympathy for him show, she made herself smile brightly. "It's been such a nice evening, I hate to see it end."

"You're just saying that," he replied glumly as he scooped up the check and threw a hefty tip onto the table. Kayla's eyes broadened as she glimpsed the wad of bills he carried. He must carry his life savings with him!

The drive home was very different from the rest of the evening with its lighthearted banter. Kayla was lost in her own thoughts as she stared out at the passing streetlights. Franklin seemed to be thoughtful, making only a minimal attempt at any meaningful conversation. Her heart ached for him in so many ways. She had known him barely a few hours, yet she felt an unusual closeness to him. How she wished he could find some nice girl who would . . . She sat up suddenly, alarmed at her outrageous thoughts. For some crazy reason the thought of him with someone else sent a wild stab of jealousy through her. For heaven sakes! What was wrong with her. She certainly didn't want to get involved with this man. No, what she was feeling was pure sympathy for a nice guy who seemed to be having a hard time. Emotionally she couldn't afford to let herself become involved in Franklin's troubles. She just couldn't! He had had these problems for thirty-six years; surely he could live with them a little longer. When he took her home tonight, she would discourage any future involvement with him. Her mind was made up. She wouldn't trust a man with her feelings ever again.

As they pulled up in the drive Franklin killed the motor and sat with his hands draped over the steering wheel. "Well, I guess this is good night," he observed dejectedly.

"Yes, I guess so," she agreed. "I meant it when I said I've had a nice time, Franklin. I wish you'd believe that."

"There's only one way on earth that you could make me believe that, and that's if you'd let me—" His voice broke off.

Oh, good grief! Surely he wouldn't have the guts to ask her to go to bed with him, she thought frantically. Not after thirty-six years of abstinence.

"Let you what?" she asked helplessly. She was ready to scream. If he did ask her such an utterly ridiculous question, she honestly didn't know how she would answer him. He was so . . . good-looking and virile!

36

Almost before she knew what was happening, he slid her over next to him smoothly, one large hand taking her face and holding it gently. "Let me kiss you good night," he finished sweetly. "Oh, I know I'm being much too bold," he went on apologetically, "but you're just so . . . so . . . special." He began to run his thumb deliciously up and down the satin creaminess of her cheek, his eyes pleading silently with hers. In one forward motion she came into his arms. Not for a moment did she consider denying his request. She wanted this kiss. She had all evening.

"Franklin, you're not bold. Really, I don't mind," she said eagerly. He pressed his lips to hers, caressing her mouth more than kissing it at first, his mouth feather-touching hers tantalizingly.

"You mean you'll really let me?" he asked hopefully, and his tongue reached out to touch hers warmly. You would have thought she'd given him a million dollars!

"Just a kiss," she reminded him . . . and herself.

"Oh, ma'am, I wouldn't *dream* of asking for anything else," he said in a horrified tone, peering down angelically at her from behind the large frames.

She felt the heady sensation of his lips against her neck, and then he slowly brought his mouth around to capture hers. She kissed him with a hunger that belied her previous thoughts of giving up men. With a soft groan he smothered her lips with demanding mastery, his kiss sending a wild swirling into the pit of her stomach. If Franklin was as inexperienced at lovemaking as he said he was, then he was a real natural at it! Her hand moved from his cheek to his jawline, stroking the clean-shaven smoothness, then running on up to greedily entwine itself in the thick mass of dark-blond hair that curled so enticingly at the back of his tanned neck. He pulled her closer to him, wrapping his arms around her waist, his strength molding her against his granite frame.

When his lips left hers, what seemed like only moments later, she felt an acute sense of disappointment. She had forgotten how nice it was to be held and kissed.

"I suppose this is not only good night but good-bye," he reminded her sadly, his lips leaving hers and searing a path down her neck again.

"Are you leaving tomorrow?" she whispered shakily, her hands tightening in his hair as his mouth reached the curve of her neckline, his tongue flicking lightly at her fragrant skin.

"No, I'm going to be in town for a while. I just thought since you were off men permanently, you probably wouldn't want me hanging around your doorstep." His mouth recaptured hers more demandingly this time. She kissed him lingeringly, savoring every delicious moment of his hands moving seductively along her back.

"I wouldn't mind," she said hopelessly, all previous thoughts of discouraging him down the drain. "I mean, as long as you're going to be here for a few days, I wouldn't care if you called me."

"Umm . . . well, if you're sure, ma'am. What are you doing tomorrow?" he asked, sipping at her lips as though they were a rich, full-bodied wine.

"Nothing! I'm free all day. It's Saturday," she murmured between heady kisses.

"Will you go on a picnic with me?"

"In March?" she asked weakly as his lips continued to play over hers lightly.

"In March," he confirmed seductively.

"I'd love to." Why fight it. She was definitely attracted to this man.

"Then, I think you'd better let go of my neck," he murmured sexily, "or I'll have to tell my mother on you, Kayla Marshall."

Kayla blushed heatedly, releasing her death lock on his neck, her mouth still mingling with his. "Tell her what?"

"Tell her I *finally* met up with one of those 'bad girls' who is supposed to lead me down the garden path," he teased. "Should I fear for my virtue?"

"Do you honestly think I'd deny your wife the surprise of her life on her wedding night? Not a chance." She grinned as she gathered up her purse and slid over to the passenger side. "See you in the morning, Franklin Franklin."

"Good night, ma'am." He grinned sweetly.

She was still smiling as she turned out the light thirty minutes later and laid her head down on the cool linen pillow. Maybe life could begin to hold new meaning for her again. When she had broken off with Tony, she had honestly thought her life was over. Until today she had had no reason to believe otherwise. But a matter of hours had brought a very shy, very honest man into her life. What would it hurt to pursue the possibility of falling in love again? Franklin was not like other men—he was sweet, kind, considerate, and a thirty-six-year-old virgin! With an un-believing shake of her blond head she pulled the blanket up closer to her chin. Oh, well, if she came to care about him like she strongly suspected she would, there was a good possibility that she would consider changing that too. For his sake as well as her own.

CHAPTER THREE

Saturday dawned bright and beautiful, the perfect day for a picnic in March. Kayla awoke with a new lease on life, and she found herself humming happily as she fixed a basket lunch for her and Franklin. She had just wrapped the last ham sandwich and hard-boiled eggs when she heard the doorbell ring. Her breath quickened and her cheeks warmed as she realized just how much she was looking forward to spending the day with him.

With a happy little skip she walked to the door and swung it open, welcoming Franklin with a radiant smile. "Hi!"

His whole face lit up as he surveyed her. "Hi, yourself, ma'am."

"I'm almost ready," she told him, stepping aside to let him in. As he brushed past her her heart thudded, then settled back down to its normal rhythm. "Where are we having our picnic in March?" She smiled.

"I know a nice little place I think you'll enjoy," he said absently, admiring the nice way her slacks hugged her rounded bottom. "Want me to carry anything?"

"If you'll take the hamper, I'll get the blanket and my sweater.

40

I hope you're hungry. I've packed a big lunch," she called from the hall closet.

"Starved," he called back, glancing around the small, neat living room. It had a feeling of warmth and cheerfulness to it. The touch of a woman—a very lovely woman.

"Well, I'm ready if you are." Kayla was standing before him again, her face eager and excited.

"Kayla . . ." Franklin's face had grown serious now, his eyes troubled. "I think there's something you should know."

"Franklin." Kayla took his arm and steered him toward the front door. "You don't have to tell me anything about yourself. I like you just the way you are. For today let's just enjoy each other's company." Poor Franklin was so insecure around women he felt he had to always give them his pitiful life story!

"But—"

"No *buts*," she stated firmly.

"Whatever you say." He let out a deep breath. What a hell of a mess he had gotten himself into this time!

"Your car's nice," Kayla commented as he helped her into the passenger side. She thought she might try to boost his morale by pointing out all the good things he had going for himself.

"It's not mine," he said, curt to the point of rudeness.

These abrupt changes of manner were beginning to baffle Kayla, but then, maybe that was his problem—he was unpredictable! "Oh, well, it's nice anyway," she said. "Whose is it?"

"Hertz's."

"Oh."

"Don't you want to know what kind I drive?" he snapped impatiently.

Kayla turned and looked at him in surprise. "What kind do you have, Franklin?" she asked, a bit tense. He didn't seem to be in the best of moods at the moment.

"A damn Ferrari!"

"That's nice," she said coolly. "I have a damn Ford." If he

41

meant to impress her, he was going at it in the wrong tone of voice. "Does your 'damn' Ferrari get good gas mileage?"

He whirled to glare at her, anger showing in his eyes. "Doesn't it strike you the least bit odd that a book salesman would be driving a Ferrari?" he demanded irritably.

Brother! He must have gotten up on the wrong side of the bed this morning. What did he want her to say? That he wasn't good enough to go into debt for the rest of his life for an extravagant car that was apparently in the shop for repairs? She felt her anger rising as she glared back at him coldly. "Does it strike you odd that I drive a Ford? Good grief, Franklin, I don't *care* what kind of car you drive. Those things don't mean a hill of beans to me. I like a person for what they are, not for what they have!"

The tenseness disappeared swiftly from the set of his broad shoulders, and she found it impossible to resist his disarming smile. "Sorry I came on so strong," he apologized. As they waited at a stoplight, he reached over to tilt her face around to meet his gently. "For a woman who's been hurt once, you're too damn trusting of men, Kayla," he said softly.

The soft brushing of his fingers against her cheek sent explosive currents through her, and once again she experienced mixed emotions about the man looking at her so intently.

"What a strange thing for you to say, Franklin. Why shouldn't I trust you? Aren't we friends?"

"Kayla!" Franklin said, irritability creeping into his voice once more.

There it was again. That lightning switch of moods! "Franklin, if you'd like to change your mind about our picnic today, it's perfectly all right with me," she told him, getting a little irritable herself. It was going to be a miserable day if this kept up!

His voice, though quiet, had a melancholy tone as his beautiful smoke-colored eyes captured hers. "No, I haven't changed my mind. I want very badly to spend this day with you, Kayla."

Her large blue eyes were misty and wistful as she responded quietly, "And I want to spend the day with you." His fingers slid sensuously from her cheek to barely touch her lips. He read in her eyes a longing, an honesty that he had never before encountered in a human being. Kayla Marshall was a rare and beautiful woman, and for the first time in his life he felt the faint stirrings of love.

Kayla drowned in the gentleness of his gray gaze, his eyes caressing hers. She hesitantly leaned forward to receive his lips on hers as the loud, impatient blare of a car horn spun them back into their immediate surroundings. They laughed with released tension, and Franklin set the car in motion again. All traces of the previous friction between them were gone. It was going to be a beautiful day after all. Kayla's heart sang joyously as she resumed her vigil out the car window. A truly beautiful day!

They drove for over twenty minutes through the rolling hills. Kayla noticed the way the grass was beginning to green up. It was one of those glorious days that occasionally come along in March. A day when the temperature climbed toward seventy degrees and the wind was simply perfect for soaring a kite toward the teal blue of the heavens. Franklin turned off the main highway, driving along a graveled road for the next mile, talking to her casually about first one thing, then another. They drove over a cattle guard rail, and the car took off over a grassy pasture, heading in a southeasterly direction. Kayla could see rows of white fences in the distance and several sleek Thoroughbred horses standing in the thick carpet of grass.

"Oh, look at those horses," she said excitedly, reaching out to grasp Franklin's arm. "Aren't they beautiful?"

Franklin was gazing out at the spirited, healthy animals as the car sped over the bumpy terrain, a look of pride in his eyes.

"Yeah, they certainly are," he agreed softly. "Those are some of Arkansas's finest. Born and bred right here. Look! See that gray standing over there to the left?"

Kayla leaned forward, peering out his window to catch a glimpse of the horse he had pointed out. Franklin slowed the car to a crawl as they both studied the animal's smooth, glossy coat, evident even at this distance.

"Yes, I see it. That's a racehorse, isn't it?" she guessed accurately. "It looks so . . . majestic! Look how dainty its legs are, and the way it holds its head so proudly!"

"That one should be proud," Franklin said paternally. "She's won the last six races she's run in. She's one of the best fillies racing right now."

Kayla glanced over at him in surprise. "Do you own these horses?" she asked.

"No . . . no." Franklin picked up speed and sent the car on its way again. "They belong to Nick."

Oh, brother, him again, Kayla thought as she scooted back to her side of the car. "Well, even if they are his, they're still beautiful. Does Nick live around here?" she asked. Not that she really cared, but Franklin seemed to dote on his rakish friend so.

"He owns that ranch over there, but he's rarely around to run things. He has a good foreman who keeps the ranch operating smoothly."

"Wonder why he would even bother to have such a large spread when he is obviously too busy off doing whatever he does all the time," she pondered out loud.

"He's off trying to make a living," Franklin said, slightly perturbed again. "He plans to come back here someday and settle down. He's getting to the age—" He gave a short ironic laugh. "Actually he's long past the age when he should have found himself a wife and started having all those children he's always thought he might like to have."

"Nicholas Trahern wants children?" Kayla was shocked. "I mean *legal* children? From what I've heard, he probably has one in every state," she scoffed.

"And what you've 'heard' is just that!" he said gruffly. "Nothing but gossip and hearsay. He does not have a child in every state. He is a little more selective than that, Kayla. Hell, give the man *some* credit!"

44

Kayla brought one hand up and bonked herself hard on the head. "I'm sorreeee. I didn't mean to malign your perfect Nicholas! Personally I wouldn't give the man the time of day, but if it makes you happy, I'll consider him a monk!"

"He's not perfect," Franklin conceded in a milder tone, "but he's certainly not the SOB you think he is."

"Okay," she admitted. "One of these days, when the great Nicholas Trahern is in town, you can take me to meet him. But I guarantee I will not like him nearly as much as I like his friend. I'm willing to bet that he isn't half the man Franklin Franklin is. I know that you think he's everything a woman would ever want in a man, but you're wrong." Kayla scooted over close and captured his arm tightly. "The kind of man that most women want is as honest and as caring as you are. I certainly wouldn't want a man who had slept with every woman he came in contact with."

"Nick has *not* slept with every woman he's come in contact with," he gritted out impatiently.

"I know, I know." She patted his arm consolingly. When was she going to learn! "What I meant was . . . well, *your* wife is going to be the luckiest woman alive. To think that she will be the only one to . . . to . . ."

Franklin broke in heatedly. "Look, Kayla, surely you wouldn't expect your husband to come to you pure as the driven snow! A man has his needs, just as a woman does. Take you for instance. Didn't you sleep with Tony?"

"Well, yes . . . but he's the only man I've ever . . . And we were going to be married, or so I thought."

"There, see? There are certain things in one's past that one can't change. It shouldn't really matter what's happened before in two people's lives. It's what happens *after* they meet each other that should concern them!"

Kayla blinked her eyes and shook her head. "What are we talking about, Franklin? I was merely trying to point out the difference between you and Nicholas Trahern! I just wanted you to see that not *every* woman goes for a man like him." This man simply would not let a woman help him over his insecurities, or say one bad thing about his idol friend. "And besides," she added irritably, "why shouldn't a woman be thrilled about her husband coming to her a . . . a virgin? Your wife's going to be getting one!"

"Whoopee!" he grumbled quarrelsomely as he pulled the car up under an old oak tree and braked to a halt. "I would think that she would have enough brains to want him to come to her as someone who had looked them all over and wanted no one but her. A man who loved her and wanted her to be the mother of his children. A man who wanted to spend the rest of his life with no one but her beside him. Wouldn't that make more sense than worrying about what he had done when he was out sowing his wild oats?"

"I suppose," she said thoughtfully, and then her blue eyes brightened. "But don't you see, that's the beauty of it. Your wife's going to have it all!"

Franklin groaned and knocked his head on the steering wheel. "Let's just drop the subject," he said tiredly.

"Fine with me," she said, glancing around at their surroundings. "This is nice. You have good taste, Franklin." She had to bolster his morale.

The next few hours were the happiest Kayla had spent in over a year. To be honest, maybe they were even happier than all the hours she had spent with Tony. Franklin had an easy persuasive way about him. He had spread the blanket out on the ground, and they had talked for hours about their childhoods, the things they liked, didn't like. Actually Kayla did most of the talking, at his insistence. He seemed very hesitant to talk about his life, only commenting on minor, impersonal aspects of it. As the afternoon deepened, Kayla began to have the nagging suspicion that Franklin was becoming more than a friend to her. Was it possible for a woman to fall in love with a man she had met less than twenty-four hours ago? She had heard of such things but had personally always thought the idea was a little farfetched.

Still, when she looked at the man stretched out before her on the blanket, a deep peace entered her being. The nearness of him gave her such comfort, such happiness—not to mention the way her pulse quickened every time he looked at her and smiled that open, friendly smile at her. And the way the warmth of his laughter sent little cold shivers racing up her spine. No, this afternoon was a turning point in her life. After the hell she had been through during the last year, she could finally see the light at the end of the tunnel. Franklin Franklin was about to capture her heart, and she felt no fear. He was good, he was honest. He would never do anything to hurt her. It almost brought tears to her eyes.

"Why the serious look, Kayla Marshall?" he asked drowsily as he turned over on his back and looked up at her. They were both lying sleepily in the warming rays of the early spring sun, feeling stuffed and lazy from their picnic lunch.

"Just thinking what a nice man you are and how glad I am I met you," she answered honestly, reaching out to push back an errant lock of his dark blond hair.

Two deep lines of worry appeared between his brows, and his eyes filled with a curious deep longing. "Have you ever wished you could live a day over in your life, Kayla?"

"Oh . . . I suppose so. Why?" she asked, still absently stroking his hair.

"If I could, I'd live yesterday over," he said truthfully.

"Yesterday?" That seemed an odd thing to say—they had met yesterday.

With one efficient turn he rolled over onto his side and propped himself up on an elbow, gazing at her intently. "There's things that I would do differently."

"Well"—she sighed contentedly, then lay down on her back to stare up at the cloudless sky "—I suppose we all could say that. Not just about yesterday but about other days in our life." Her thoughts wickedly led her back to Tony. "Did you have a bad selling day yesterday?" she murmured sleepily.

47

"No," he said gravely. "I think I outdid myself." *She has such a nice voice,* he thought fleetingly. *All soft and clear and low.* Everything about her spoke of warmth, love, and understanding. If he ever encountered the man who had hurt her so badly, he would be hard pressed to keep from bashing his head in! Just the mere thought of anyone causing her pain twisted his insides painfully. The ever-nagging thought of what he was doing to her caused that pain to twist deeper in his gut, but he found himself in a position that he had no control over. What had started out to be a lark, a challenge, a silly game had now developed into something that frightened and disturbed him. Never had a woman turned his head nor touched his heart as this lovely creature lying next to him gazing up at the sky had done. He had always been told that when the right woman came along, he'd know it. For thirty-six years he had waited patiently, and suddenly there she was, cutting off phone calls before she could answer them. But he was everything that she despised in a man, or so she thought. And what would her reaction be when she found out that the quiet, shy Franklin Franklin was the notorious womanizer, Nicholas Franklin Trahern. Nick groaned softly. Somehow he had to keep her from finding that out just yet. For he needed more time with her—time to make her fall in love with the man, not the name. It was his only hope. It sickened him to see the look of trust that radiated from her lovely eyes every time she gazed at him, but he was just going to have to bear it until he could figure a way out of this nightmare.

"Umm . . . Then what would you change?" she asked dreamily. "I thought it was a pretty nice day. I know I certainly enjoyed our dinner last night." She reached over and playfully removed his glasses as she ran a piece of grass across his nose. She discerned the merest twinkle in his eyes as he balanced one of the fresh strawberries she had packed for their lunch on the tip of her nose. "You did?" he whispered huskily, wisely changing the subject. His tongue flicked out to catch the succulent berry in his mouth.

She instantly responded to his seductive gesture, and her senses reeled as if short-circuited. With a voice as steady as she could manage, she answered weakly, "Didn't you?"

"Are you serious?" he said, raising one eyebrow skeptically. "Of course I enjoyed last night. Want to share this with me?" He stuck part of the plump red strawberry out of his mouth in invitation to her. In answer her pulse thudded rapidly. His mouth slowly descended to meet hers, leaving her little time to refuse his offer. As if she would even consider such a refusal! She bit into it daintily with her small, even white teeth, and the juice squirted out over them, dripping down the corners of their mouths.

"Umm . . . good," she agreed with a breathless laugh, her voice sounding tinkling clear in the afternoon's quietness.

"Very," he murmured as his tongue flicked out to catch some of the juice falling from her red lips. "I think I like this better, though," he observed, and his lips slowly met hers one more time. Suddenly she was lifted into the cradle of his arms, and his lips parted hers in an exploring, sensual kiss. His tongue probed the sweet recesses of her mouth as her arms came up around his neck to draw him closer. The world faded from existence as Kayla's last shreds of doubt crumbled and she gave herself up to the sheer joy of being in his arms. They lay locked in each other's embrace, his mouth holding hers a very willing captive. When they finally broke away from each other, their breaths were coming in soft, short spurts.

He gazed at her longingly, his smile as intimate as his kiss had just been. "Ma'am, you do strange things to me," he said hoarsely, his eyes following the uneven rise and fall of her breasts.

"You do strange things to *me!*" Kayla said, her voice uneven. She could still feel the delicious imprint of his lips on hers. "Are you sure you haven't had years of experience at that sort of thing? It's hard to believe you're shy."

"I've just been waiting for the right woman to help me get over that little obstacle . . ." His last words were smothered by her

49

lips as he claimed them once more. Forcing her mouth open to accept his thrusting tongue, he pulled her roughly against his rigid frame, his mouth eagerly devouring hers again and again. Rockets, bells, horns, flashing lights, everything Kayla had ever read about clanged in her head as this overpowering virile male staked an undeniable claim upon her. Wrapping her arms around him, she pulled him closer, acutely aware of the hardness of his muscular thighs pressing against her. His large hands locked against her spine as his ardor ignited in a searing blaze of passion. Her body melted against his, and her world was filled with nothing but him. He began murmuring her name almost incoherently as his hand lightly touched her through the soft material of her blouse. Her mind was spinning in confusion. She was drowning in his touch, yet concerned at how quickly this was getting out of hand.

"Franklin," she gasped in sweet agony," your wife . . ."

"My what?" he breathed hotly as his lips seared a path down her neck, across her delicate shoulders.

"Your future wife . . . It seems such a shame to have made it all these years, and then—" Kayla's breathing was coming hard and fast as his kisses fairly sang through her veins.

What was the matter with her! Why should she worry about some future wife when she was practically begging for his touch, the undeniable maleness of him.

Franklin broke away, fighting to bring his passion under control. "Yes . . . yes, my wife. I've got to think of my wife!" His voice sounded nearly strangled.

"Oh, Franklin," she whispered, burying her face in his neck and breathing a kiss there, "it isn't that I don't . . . want you. It's just that I think it would be best for the both of us if this didn't go any further right now." She couldn't stand for him to think that she didn't desire him, because she certainly did. "We've just met, and . . . although I feel very close to you, I . . . I . . . things are just moving too fast," she ended helplessly. The poor man must think he really *did* have one of those girls his mother had warned him about. Kayla had probably scared him to death by responding so wantonly to his kisses! His hands felt so warm, so gentle as he cradled her in this arms and buried his face in the mass of her fragrant hair.

"It's all right, sweetheart . . . shhh . . . I understand. I'm sorry," he apologized sincerely.

"Oh, it wasn't you, Franklin," she hastened to assure him. "It was me! I don't know what came over me. I don't want you to think that I'm . . . well, that I act like this with every man I meet." Her lovely face was filled with consternation.

"I don't think that," he whispered tenderly. "And I should be kicked for getting out of hand." He gathered her more tightly to him. "Forgive me, Kayla?"

"Of course," she whispered shyly, breathing in the sexy smell of his aftershave. "But I think we've proved something good today, Franklin."

"Really? Now, what would that be?" He grinned uncomfortably, trying to keep her squirming body away from the blatant evidence of her effect on him.

"I think you're starting to pull out of your shyness around women," she said encouragingly. "There certainly wasn't anything shy about the man who was kissing me a few moments ago," she continued. "Your friend Nicholas would undoubtedly be very proud of you."

"Kayla, you're too nice for your own good . . ." His voice trailed off as he leaned down and touched her lips lightly with his one final time. "I don't think even old SOB Trahern would be proud of me at this moment."

"Well, he might not be, but I surely am, Franklin Franklin. All my friends say that I'm too accepting, but my parents always taught me that the important things in life are love, trust, and always having something to hope for. I think I'm ready to start thinking about those things again. I feel we're going to be very good for each other. You did say you lived close to here, didn't you?"

"Yes."

"Then we'll have plenty of opportunity to explore our feelings for each other in the next few weeks," she said as she sat up and began to gather together their picnic items. "Who knows?" She grinned saucily. "This may be the start of something big." Her face grew serious once more. "Someone to love, something to hope for. That's all that's really important in life. And maybe, just maybe we can find those things together, Franklin."

"Yes, maybe we can," he murmured uneasily. She was right, it was the start of something big. It was going to be the biggest thing he had ever encountered.

An old saying his parents had always hammered into him popped into his head as he helped her into the car and stowed the picnic basket in the back seat. You can never change the past, but you can ruin a perfectly good present by worrying about tomorrow!

He'd have to take his chances.

CHAPTER FOUR

The following days were ideal for Kayla. Hours sped by rapidly as she fell into the pattern of efficiently handling the office work of Trahern Tool and Die, then spending the evening with Franklin. Although he still showed definite traces of shyness, Kayla noticed a new exciting dimension developing in Franklin. Always the perfect gentleman, he proceeded to court her with the tenderness and affection she had always longed for. Not that Tony hadn't shown her affection—he had; but not in the same way. Franklin never failed to have some small gift in his pocket when he showed up on her doorstep each night—ranging from her favorite candy bar to the ridiculously expensive diamond locket he had given her last night. His offerings never failed to elicit a shower of kisses and affectionate hugs from Kayla. As the days passed, her fondness grew for the man who had accidentally happened into her life such a short time ago.

They had been seeing each other regularly for over a week and a half when Franklin telephoned on a Wednesday afternoon to remind Kayla what time he would pick her up that evening. The mere sound of his voice sent her stomach fluttering.

"Hi, pretty lady. Do you know I find it next to impossible to keep my mind on work lately," Franklin began in a low, suggestive voice.

"Funny. I've found that hard too. What do you think's causing the problem?" She leaned back in her chair and closed her eyes dreamily, picturing Franklin's face.

"I don't know. Maybe it's because I keep seeing a pair of big blue eyes looking at me, or I keep imagining the taste of that pink lipstick you wear. What flavor is that?"

Kayla laughed softly. "It doesn't have a flavor. Besides I resent the fact that your mind is on such trite and inconsequential things as the flavor of a woman's lipstick when you're kissing her. Can't you think of anything more imaginative that that?"

"Oh, my imagination runs wild when I'm kissing her," he assured her seductively, "which, by the way, I'm dying to do right now."

"Kiss me?"

"Among other things."

Kayla chuckled wickedly. "By the way, who is this calling?"

"Kayla!"

"Oh, Franklin! I didn't recognize your voice."

"You're turning into a tease," he growled playfully.

"I know, and I'm sorry."

"I'm not. I kind of like it. Want to go to a carnival tonight?"

"A carnival? I didn't know there was one in town."

"There's a small one passing through. I noticed it on the outskirts of town this morning as I came to work. You know what else I noticed?"

"No, tell me." She loved the small-boy tone of his voice when he was excited about something.

"Well, I noticed they had a big double-wheeled Ferris wheel."

Kayla's stomach turned over as she thought about the height of one of those contraptions. "And?"

"And I was thinking about how nice it would be to get you up there all alone, and maybe if my luck held out, there would be some minor mechanical problem—"

"I hate heights," she warned.

"Trust me. If that happens, your mind is *not* going to be on heights," he said blandly.

"Promise?"

"You're teasing again, you little witch. What time do you want me to pick you up tonight?"

"Same as usual, I suppose. Things have been very light around here today."

"Old man Trahern still gone?" he asked quietly.

"Both senior and junior, thank goodness. As I mentioned before, Paula said Nicholas is rarely in the office, and the elder Trahern is out of the country. You know, I rather wish Romeo *would* drop in sometime during the day. He keeps the strangest hours. Apparently he comes in at night and catches up on his work, because there's always a pile of paper work to be typed and filed every morning," she mused thoughtfully. "I'm dying to get a look at this man who has most of the women who know him practically drooling."

"I'm sure the guy has a real problem on his hands," Franklin snapped. "Look, I've got to get back to work. I'll pick you up around seven."

Kayla was a bit surprised as she heard the rather sharp click at the other end of the line. Frowning irritably at the receiver, she replaced it in its cradle and sighed. Franklin sounded as if he was in another of his strange moods today. Regretfully turning back to her own pile of work, she hoped she could change that tonight.

When the sporty red Ferrari pulled up in her drive that evening, Kayla had to do a double take to be sure it was Franklin. Up until this moment she had forgotten Franklin's car was in the shop for repairs.

"Boy, this is what I call real class," she said admiringly, circling the automobile slowly. "How long have you had it?"

55

"A year or so. Do you like it?" Franklin's pride was ill concealed.

"It's gorgeous. It must have cost a fortune," Kayla surmised, wondering how Franklin could swing the payments on a car like this one.

"Get in. It rides like a dream," he boasted as he took her arm and helped her into the passenger seat. Minutes later they were zooming down the highway, with Kayla agreeing that it did indeed ride like a dream.

"Where do you want to eat tonight?" Franklin asked, reaching over to give her a quick kiss.

Kayla's gaze met his lovingly. "Anywhere's fine with me."

The sound of squealing brakes filled the air as Franklin impulsively cut across two lanes of traffic and pulled onto the shoulder of the highway. In one swift movement he pulled Kayla over to his side and crushed his mouth down on hers in a kiss that made her senses reel. His lips moved against hers in an urgent, exploring welcome, devouring their softness. She was powerless to resist his mastery, nor did she want to. His body felt heavy and warm pressed up against hers in the small car, arousing a deep longing in her. He buried his fingers in her soft flesh and moaned almost painfully as his kiss branded her with fiery possession. When she finally broke the embrace, she could feel his ragged breathing on her cheek. She buried her face in his broad chest contentedly.

"Oh, Franklin, I've missed you today," she murmured, trying to regain control of her erratic pulse. "I know it's crazy to . . . to . . ." She didn't want to say "fall in love," but that was exactly what had happened to her. Kayla had fallen in love with Franklin so quickly that she hadn't had time to set up any defenses against him. It wasn't something she had wanted to happen, but since it obviously had, she had no intention of fighting it.

The strong arms that were holding her close tightened in their clasp as Franklin buried his face in the fragrance of her hair.

"To what?" he prompted.

"To . . . feel so . . . close to you. We barely know each other, and yet . . ."

It was impossible to find the words she was searching for. These new and disturbing feelings she had for Franklin were engulfing her, and yet she couldn't think of anything that she wanted more than to simply turn herself over to him—body, mind, and soul.

Franklin was silent as he held her tightly, his eyes closed in shameful misery at what was taking place in his life. It was almost laughable. For thirty-six years women had meant very little to him. Not that he disrespected them. It was simply he hadn't needed them, except for the obvious. But the short time he had spent with Kayla had made him yearn for a different sort of life. A life with a woman like the one he now held in his arms—a woman who would have his children, share his dreams. Would all these hopes be shattered when she found out who he was? He had been so careful. He had taken her only to the most out of the way restaurants. Instead of going to the movies or to disco clubs he had elected to take her on long moonlit drives or secluded picnics, always fearing that they would run into someone who knew him not as Franklin Franklin but as Nicholas Trahern. When that moment came . . . His large frame shuddered to think of the consequences.

"Are you cold?" Kayla hugged him closer.

"No. Far from it," he teased in a voice made shaky by emotion.

"Hungry?" she pursued with concern.

He drew her face up to meet his. "Only for you." He sighed, bringing his lips coaxingly to hers. They kissed with slow intoxicating kisses until their ardor began to mount to simmering proportions.

"I think," Franklin rasped, pulling away from Kayla forcibly, "that we had better put a stop to this. You realize we're providing quite a show for every motorist out there."

57

"I couldn't care less." She grinned, kissing him on the tip of his nose. "But I suppose we should be going."

After one last kiss Kayla scooted back to her seat. The car pulled out onto the highway and merged with the other traffic smoothly.

"What are you in the mood for?" Franklin asked innocently, referring to his original question about where they should eat that evening.

Kayla wickedly slid back over and playfully nipped at his ear. "Do you really want to know?"

"You are making it next to impossible for me to keep my mind where it should be," Franklin scolded, trying to keep his eye on the heavy traffic and steal hurried snatches of kisses from her at the same time. "Have you no shame, woman?"

"Uh-uh. None at all." She teased the lobe of his ear with her tongue.

"Kayla," he protested weakly, his body growing taut and tense from her playful actions. "This is pure torture."

"Oh, all right," she relented, but not before her mouth found his with another searing kiss. "I'll behave."

"At least for the moment," he pleaded. "You have me at a distinct disadvantage, you know. Wait until I can enjoy your little games with you. Then we'll see who begs for mercy." His eyes told her exactly which one of them it would be.

They chatted comfortably as they drove to the restaurant, a small steak house on the outskirts of town.

"You undoubtedly know the quaintest, darkest places," Kayla teased, squinting her eyes as she tried to read the menu in the dim light.

"I like dark places," Franklin assured her quietly.

"You must. I don't think we've eaten in one place where I could read the menu . . . not even once!" She laughed. "What sounds good to you?"

"I think I'm going to have the prime ribs. How about you?"

"The same. And I want a huge baked potato." For the last few days Kayla's appetite had run rampant. At the rate she was going, she would gain back the weight she had lost after her breakup with Tony in no time at all.

After the waitress had taken their order, Kayla turned to Franklin, her eyes sparkling with excitement. "Guess what?"

"I can't imagine." Franklin smiled tenderly, picking up her hand and kissing each finger slowly.

"Franklin," Kayla protested, her senses springing achingly to life, "I want to tell you my news."

"Fire away."

"I can't think when you're kissing me like that," she complained, yet she loved every minute of it.

"Good. Then we're even. I haven't been able to think straight since the day I met you." He brought his tongue across the palm of her hand in feather-light strokes.

"Oh, Franklin," she said softly, her eyes devouring his handsome features, "I wish I had met you years ago."

Before he could answer, the waitress was back, setting their salads before them. With resigned smiles they picked up their forks and began eating.

"What were you going to tell me?" Franklin asked, opening his package of crackers and offering her one.

"Well, I just had this marvelous idea this afternoon. I think I mentioned that I used to own a small dress shop when I lived in Florida."

Franklin nodded, offering her another cracker. "You said something about it."

"I loved that shop." A look of pain crossed Kayla's face. "But when Tony and I broke up . . . well . . . I didn't feel like I could stay there any longer, so I sold it and moved here. I made a tidy little profit on it—in fact, I really haven't had to work since I moved here. Up until lately I wasn't sure I was going to stay here. But now I'm ready to think about starting another shop here in Little Rock. I don't know if getting back into the business world has spurred me on, or what. All I know is that I called a real estate agency this afternoon, and they gave me a list of several available shops to look at." Her face became animated as she laid down her fork and picked up Franklin's hand. "Will you help me look for a new shop?"

"Don't you think you should think about this a little longer, Kayla? Maybe you'll meet some rich man who'll marry you, and you'll never have to work another day in your life," he said seriously, stroking her hand gently.

"Oh, that isn't what I want at all, Franklin! A rich man has never been my goal in life. I would be perfectly happy with just a nice ordinary man. Together we can both work for the things in life that seem important to us." *An encyclopedia salesman would do just fine*, she thought wistfully, but discreetly refrained from saying so. "Besides, if I open a shop here, then we'll be able to go on seeing each other. You did say you lived near here, didn't you?"

"Sort of."

"Sort of! Why are you so evasive about where you live?" Kayla suspected that Franklin had a small apartment somewhere and didn't want her to see it for fear it wouldn't seem prosperous enough. She was sure that his car ate up most of his earnings, although he always carried a large amount of money with him.

"I'm not being evasive. I'll take you there someday," he returned in a passive tone.

"Franklin, I don't *care* where you live, or how you dress, or what you drive. It's *you* I care about." He certainly didn't have anything to worry about so far as the car and clothes went, and she was sure his apartment was clean and presentable.

"Kayla . . . look"—he threw his fork angrily down on the table—"we have got to talk."

"About what?" Kayla gazed at him seriously. So seriously that his nerve failed him totally. Somehow this just wasn't the right time to tell her. He had to do it with diplomacy and tact. If he didn't, he would lose her. He suddenly had no doubt in his mind about that. What else could he expect? He had deliberately misled and lied to her. Come what may, he would eventually have to face the fact and suffer the consequences. But for as long as possible he was going to delay the inevitable.

"About . . . the advisability of going into business on your own right now," he faltered.

"Oh, I can make it, Franklin! My shop was thriving in Florida. I used to carry these darling dresses—"

"Damn it, Kayla! There are businesses going under by the hundreds right now." He didn't want her going into business by herself. He was a rich man, and *he* wanted to take care of her.

"My goodness, Franklin," she teased, "I'm not a rich woman. I have to work for a living. Granted, I could probably survive for another few months on my savings, but I do have to start thinking about the future. Anyway, if I should happen to marry a man who wasn't rich, then I would already have a nice profitable business established, and I'd be able to help us buy a home sooner," she said with a glint in her eye. "After the children came along, I might be persuaded to stay home, but until then it would seem senseless," she reasoned, desperately hoping she wasn't scaring him to death with this talk of marriage and children.

The plate of beef that had been set before him suddenly looked very unappetizing to Franklin as his mind tried to find fault with her reasoning but failed. Unexpectedly he had to control the powerful urge to slam his fists against the table and blurt out the terrible truth to her. The truth being he was a low-down SOB who didn't deserve the love and complete trust that shone so brightly in her eyes.

Kayla seemed unaware of his dilemma as she dove into her meat, complimenting Franklin on his choice of food, as usual. Whatever avenging angel had decided to get even with Nicholas Trahern was indeed doing a superior job, he lamented glumly as he disheartedly picked up his fork and punched at his meat. In fact, he would probably be given a gold medal!

* * *

61

Hours later they were still wandering around on the small carnival ground they had driven to after dinner. Kayla had noticed that Franklin's pensive mood was lingering. He was such a strange man. Tender and loving one minute, harsh and almost angry at others.

She desperately wished she knew what bothered him so at times. She had done everything within her power to boost his confidence and assure him that he was a completely desirable man. Everything except . . . Her mind toyed with the idea that had been forming in it all evening. There had only been one man in Kayla's life, and she had loved him with her entire being. Now a second man had taken Tony's place in her heart. Could she do less than offer the same love to Franklin? Although Franklin had proven to be a very ardent suitor, he had never overstepped the bounds he had established, and he had touched her only in controlled passion. She knew that at times that had been very hard for him. More than once she had felt his overpowering need for her as he pressed her tightly against his lean body. His kisses would grow hot and urgent, but always at a certain point he would firmly though lovingly push her aside, his breathing ragged and desirous. Many times she had wanted to tell him that it was all right, that she loved him and would gladly give herself to him. But he had not asked for such privileges, and she was embarrassed to offer them to him. Instead she would go in the house with a deep need unfulfilled and spend the night in restless dreams. Dreams that always featured a tall, tawny-haired man whose kisses could set her blood aflame.

All night the tiny thought had been chasing around in her mind that maybe Franklin was simply too shy to make the first move. Still a virgin, he probably wouldn't have the least idea where to start; he might even be shy about undressing in front of a woman. If that were the case, then she would have to be the one to initiate their lovemaking. That particular thought sent shivers down her spine and set her pulse racing erratically. In fact, the mere thought of Franklin undressed and lying naked in her arms sent her stomach into a mad whirl. She had seen very little of his body, but what she had seen turned her knees to water and sent a shaft of longing coursing through her. Making love to Franklin would be no hardship whatsoever. She was sure of that. So sure that she had made up her mind to make the first move. Now all she had to do was concentrate on getting him to leave this amusement park and take her home. From then on it would be up to her.

"Franklin, I'm getting tired. Aren't you about ready to go home?" Kayla asked, not for the first time, as she shifted the two panda bears and the one long, monstrous stuffed snake around in her arms. Franklin's aim was deadly with anything you could throw or shoot. Consequently she had had to give some of the prizes that he had beamingly bestowed upon her to a couple of children who had watched his expertise with awe.

"What's your hurry? Let's ride the Ferris wheel again," Franklin protested, never once dreaming what delights lay in store for him.

"Absolutely not! We've ridden that thing four times, and it's made me ill every time!"

"Are you sure? That's my favorite ride." Obviously Franklin felt that all his inhibitions flew right out into space when they were stopped at the very top. For those few minutes Kayla was hard pressed to believe that Franklin was as inexperienced as he claimed to be.

"I'm positive. Nothing could get me on that wheel again. Let's go home."

"Okay, but just one more ride first." He eyed the Bullet interestedly.

"Not that thing either," she said irritably, cringing at the screams of pure terror that erupted from the spinning cars on the ride.

He took her arm and they strolled through the park, stopping at each ride for her to put the final quietus on each one. They were down to the Mad Mouse when she finally decided to bargain with him.

"If we ride one more, can we go home then?"

"I agree." He grinned angelically. It was amazing how amusement parks could bring out the small boy in grown men. "I choose, though!"

Five minutes later Kayla was zooming up in the air on the Ferris wheel once more, hating every minute of it. Clutching her stuffed toys, she buried her face in them as they climbed higher and higher, then slid over the top, her stomach dropping to her toes.

"Aren't the lights pretty from up here?" Franklin observed, leaning over to stare down on the gaily lighted fairgrounds.

"Sit still!" Kayla warned, her knuckles turning white as she gripped the bar across her lap.

Franklin chuckled wickedly, then set the car into motion, rocking it deviously.

"Oh, good grief!" Kayla threw her arms around his neck and buried her face in his chest. "Franklin, please!" she pleaded helplessly.

"Franklin, please what?" he whispered, catching her chin and tilting her mouth up to meet his.

His nearness suddenly made her forget where she was and what was happening as her blue eyes met his silver-colored ones.

"Franklin, please kiss me," she finished, aware of only him.

They kissed for the rest of the ride, her soft curves molding to the hard contours of his body. It was with extreme disappointment that she realized their ride was over. For once that stupid ride had not made her sick!

It was growing late when the Ferrari pulled up in front of Kayla's apartment. Franklin had insisted she share his seat, and they had exchanged interminable sultry kisses on the slow drive home. Shutting the engine off, Franklin continued to kiss her until his control was pushed nearly to the limit. With resigned patience he released his hold on her and brought his hands back to grip the steering wheel.

"Well, I guess this is good night."

"Good night?" Kayla was surprised. "Aren't you coming in?" As a rule he came in for a while after bringing her home.

"I don't think I'd better tonight, honey." He knew that if he went through that door now, he wouldn't be coming back out—tonight. Kayla was like a powerful drug invading his senses, and his desire to make love to her was rapidly growing out of control. But he knew he couldn't touch her until the truth had been revealed. Then and only then would he allow himself the luxury of taking her in his arms, stripping her clothes off piece by torturous piece . . . He forced his mind to snap back to what she was saying.

"Why not?" She kissed him again softly, teasingly. "It isn't very late."

"I know it isn't," he agreed weakly, tracing the outline of her lips with his tongue. "I just think it wouldn't be wise right now."

"It couldn't hurt," she pleaded, knowing how hard it must be for him to refuse, yet feeling compassion for his naïveté. Yet, how was she going to remedy his inexperience if she couldn't coax him into the house? This car was hardly conducive to making love, and besides, she wanted his first time to be something special . . . something he would remember for the rest of his life. She would not want to cheapen the experience by forcing the issue in the front seat of a car.

He groaned as her fingers easily unbuttoned the first button of his shirt and slipped beneath the material to gently caress the coarse mat of hair on his chest.

"I like all that hair," she noted suggestively, her lips following the path of her fingers.

"Kayla . . ." Franklin's voice was a low moan as he caught her hands and drew them gently out of his shirt. "I've changed my mind. Let's go in." He had to get out of this car or all his gallant vows would go straight down the drain.

"Oh, great!" Kayla agreed readily, reaching for her door handle. Her spirits soared as she realized that now her plan for tonight would not have to be aborted after all.

"Only for a minute," Franklin added quickly, picking up his suit jacket and discreetly draping it over the telltale front of his trousers.

Kayla wrapped her arm around his waist as they walked up the walk, silently offering him any encouragement that he needed. Taking her key from her purse, she unlocked the door and they stepped inside the dark apartment.

Franklin reached anxiously for the light switch next to the door, but a small hand stopped his in midair. "Don't turn on the light, Franklin," she ordered softly.

The room was silent; only the sound of a clock ticking caught Kayla's attention. She was so nervous! Never had she tried to seduce a man, and she realized with a sinking heart that she didn't know the first thing about where to begin. Tony had always initiated their lovemaking.

Franklin didn't speak for a moment, and when he finally did, his voice was cautious and unsteady. "Why?"

Kayla took a deep breath and swallowed her pride. "Because I want us to make love."

"*No!*" Franklin pushed away from her angrily.

Summoning every ounce of strength she possessed, Kayla stepped in front of Franklin and blocked his path. "Yes," she said calmly. "I think you want that too."

"No, no, I don't," Franklin protested firmly, backing away from her fearfully.

"Yes, you do," she insisted quietly, taking each step with him. "I know that you're painfully shy and you'd never ask me . . . but that doesn't matter. I've . . . I've fallen in love with you, Franklin, and I want to share that love with you. It doesn't matter if you don't return the feeling right now—"

"Damn it, Kayla, I do return the feeling—"

"You love me?" Her face lit up with radiance.

"I do. So damn much it's tearing me apart. That's exactly why I won't let this happen."

"But if we both love each other, it's only natural for this to happen, Franklin," she argued in a gentle tone, slowly backing him up against the wall. "It isn't as if we were strangers. I think I fell in love with you the first time you brought me those beautiful blue forget-me-nots," she said soothingly as her fingers slid up his chest and began to take off his shirt. "I never forget you, Franklin. Not for one moment. I dream about you at night, daydream about you in the daytime . . ."

"Kayla, have mercy," he pleaded huskily as his hands struggled to still her working ones. "There are things you don't understand—"

"I understand that I love you, and you just said you loved me." She was working the buttons open one by one. "I don't need to know any more than that."

"Yes, you do. You don't know anything about me."

"I know I love you. Anything beyond that isn't important. At least not at the moment. Take your arm out of your sleeve," she coaxed firmly.

"No . . . and stop that!" He yanked his shirt closed. "This is insane."

Kayla paused, her doubts surfacing. "You honestly don't want to make love to me?"

"Now, Kayla, I didn't say that!" he moaned, relenting for the moment and pulling her close to his broad chest. "Of course I want to make love to you. I have from the minute I first laid eyes on you, but . . . the time just isn't right," he whispered in a ragged plea. He closed his eyes against the shaft of pain that sliced through his middle. It was taking everything he had not to sweep her up in his arms and carry her to the bedroom, prove to her how much power she was beginning to have over him. Just the thought of having her in his arms, willing and eager to let him sample the delights of her young slim body, sent his passion

67

soaring. And yet he could not find the words to tell her of his deception.

"I love you, Franklin. Doesn't that mean anything to you?" she asked solemnly. "I thought that when Tony left me, I would never love again. But you came along, and suddenly I wanted to live again. To love again. I know how hard it is for a man with your morals to accept the idea of sex out of marriage, and ordinarily I would agree with you," she hastened to add. "I'm still rather old-fashioned myself. But Tony taught me that when you love someone, you want to be with them . . . to share with them . . ."

"If you *don't mind*, I'm not too crazy about hearing what Tony taught you," he growled, pulling her tighter in his embrace, wrestling with the streak of jealousy that had bolted through him.

"Oh, you don't *ever* have to be jealous of Tony," she chastised lovingly, understanding his feelings completely. "That's all behind me now. It's you I love!" Once more her hands moved to rid him of his shirt. As she peeled the fabric back to expose the thick hair on his muscular chest, her breath caught slightly at the magnificence of his body.

"Oh, Franklin, let me love you," she pleaded tenderly, hoping fleetingly that his mother would never find out about her wantonness. Kayla could feel his uneven breathing on her cheek, and she sensed a raging battle in him, one that he was losing with every passing minute. Taking his hand, she tugged him gently toward the bedroom, her heart pounding wildly. Drawing him next to the bed, she carefully removed his glasses, laying them on the bedside table, then hesitantly reached out and unbuckled his belt, slipping it slowly through the loops of his pants. In another few minutes his trousers joined his shirt on the floor, and then the last remaining piece of clothing was peeled away and her eyes hungrily devoured the man she loved. Only the dim light from the streetlamp filtered through the bedroom window, but it was enough to let her know that she would be hard pressed to find another specimen of manhood quite so magnificent anywhere on this earth. He looked so powerful to her, standing there in the dim light. His chest was broad and well-developed, his waist slim, his legs long and sturdy like those of some long-ago Viking. The hair that covered his body was the same color as that on his head, only thicker. Her fingers trembled as she reached out to touch him, to feel his bare skin against the softness of hers.

"This is sheer madness," he whispered huskily, his voice growing uneven as her hands began to run freely over him, his taut body awakening to her fleeting touches.

"No, it isn't, darling. Don't you want to touch me? Undress me, Franklin," she demanded, firmly placing one of his hands over the top button of her blouse.

"No! I really don't want to . . ." His voice cracked as his fingers involuntarily unfastened the first button, then the second. "Well, maybe for just a minute."

"I know how hard this must be for you, darling, and believe me, I wouldn't be doing this with just any man, but you have brought so much joy and happiness into my life, Franklin, I . . . I want to make you as happy as you've made me," she pleaded against the pressure of his lips.

By now Franklin had managed to undo all the buttons on her blouse, and he slipped it off her shoulders with trembling fingers. His mind was desperately searching for a way out of this situation, and yet his heart was crying out for him to let go and make love to her the way he had dreamed of so often in the last few days.

"See how easy it is," she murmured as his mouth started a slow search down her neck and over her shoulders, his lips devouring the rose-scented softness of her. "Touch me here, Franklin." She guided his hands to her budding fullness. "And here . . ." She continued to move his hands to places where she found his touch pleasurable.

He complied eagerly, suddenly more than willing to be the pupil.

Kayla gasped as his hands came alive, touching her intimately with sure, deft strokes. He certainly was a fast learner!

"How am I doing?" he asked a few moments later as they broke apart from a long, heated kiss. "Is there something more I should be doing?"

"No, darling," she gulped, nearly breathless from his overpoweringly virile assault on her body and senses. "You're doing . . . magnificently!"

"Are you sure?" His hands ran smoothly over the velvet texture of her fragrant skin, his lips following lazily in their path. "I always thought that a woman would love for a man to . . ." He pulled her closer to him, whispering something quite seductive in her ear while his hands proceeded to most deliciously demonstrate what he had just described in words.

"Franklin!" she panted, shocked yet thrilled at his aggressiveness. "Oh, Franklin!"

They had only been together a few minutes, but he was already close to achieving near perfection in his first attempt to make love to a woman. It was truly amazing. And she hurriedly told him so, complimenting him as he conquered new territory after territory like a seasoned warrior.

With a groan of defeat Franklin drew her down on the bed beside him, his mouth finding hers again in the darkness, and sought to unfold the beauty of Kayla Marshall for his own selfish pleasure. Her breasts were generous and firm, her waist small and easily engulfed by his large hands. Her legs were slender and willowy, and silken to the touch. He couldn't remember a time in his life when he had felt more self-revulsion than he did now for what he was doing to this lovely woman. Yet he was incapable of stopping.

Their lips met time and time again as they drew from each other a wondrous sense of love and fulfillment. Franklin's touch was more than Kayla had dreamed it would be, tenderly seeking out all her secret places, thrilling and arousing her to the point of madness.

70

"Make love to me . . . now, Franklin," she urged, sensing that he was at last ready, after thirty-six long, miserable years, to taste the delights of manhood.

Franklin's conscience managed to rear its head in one final thrust of condemnation, but only briefly.

"I can't, Kayla," he begged, rolling away from her and miserably sitting up on the side of the bed. Again his mind fought for a way out of this nightmare. "You have got to help me," he pleaded raggedly. "I'm not going to be able to do this on my own."

Mistaking his words for yet another expression of his shyness with women, Kayla came daintily to her knees and crawled over to his side of the bed. Wrapping her arms around his trim waist, she planted moist, seductive kisses along his neck, soothing him gently.

"It's all right, Franklin. I understand."

"No, you *don't* understand, Kayla. Believe me, you don't understand. But, so help me God, I love you." He turned to her, his face an agonized mask, his cheeks surprisingly moist.

She pulled him down on the bed with her, the fight totally drained out of him now. Her slight frame slid on top of his, her lips, her mouth, her hands beginning the slow, sensual explorations of love.

With every ounce of love she possessed, she poured her heart into making love to him. Gently she whispered instructions in his ear, encouraging him to relax and enjoy their lovemaking. She stroked his body to rigid firmness, eliciting groans of pleasure from him. His large form trembled as she led him into manhood, praying that it would mean as much to him as it did to her.

When at last their desire reached the point where there was no turning back, he joined with her in a union that was explosive, fiery, and oh, so sweet. The feeling that washed over them and engulfed them was mutual as they clung to each other long after their passion had peaked, then subsided. Once more love had

71

walked into Kayla's life, only this time the result would be different. This time the man she chose to give her trust, her faith, her very life to returned that love. In her heart she had no doubt of that. Kayla Franklin. It sounded nice. And with that thought floating lazily through her mind she drifted off to sleep in the arms of her love.

The sound of muted thunder and the first drops of rain hitting the window woke Kayla the next morning. They were in for a spring thunderstorm, she mused, snuggling down tighter against Franklin's warm body. She loved thunderstorms and the sound of the wind whipping savagely through the branches outside her window.

A gentle smile found her lips as Franklin's hand reached out to cup her rounded softness. At first she had feared that last night had only been a dream, that when she awoke, Franklin would be gone. But he wasn't. He was here, pulling her against the muscled hardness of his body, kissing her awake with kisses that went from gentle to savage almost in a heartbeat. Their appetite for each other had not nearly been appeased in the night, and it was a different Franklin who made love to her this morning. Gone was the shy, gentle man, and in his place was a smooth, experienced lover who knew how to bring her to the very brink of fulfillment but refused to let her topple over until both their bodies were crying for release.

The storm outside their window was pale in comparison to the tempest inside as their muted cries of pleasure filled the small room. Franklin's mouth muffled her whimpers of satisfaction as together they once more reached the ultimate goal in their lovemaking. A million stars shattered into the universe as they soared to awesome and shuddering heights.

When it was over, the storm still raged on outside, but inside only the soft whisperings of love could be heard.

"I never had a chance to ask you last night. Was everything . . . as you expected?" Kayla murmured against his ear, her passion ebbing away slowly.

"Are you serious? It was wonderful," he whispered back sleepily. "I love you, lady."

She felt a strong sense of elation that his "first time" had been completely successful. She grinned smugly. The second wasn't shabby either!

"Umm. . . I love you too. What time is it?"

Franklin picked up the clock on the bedside table and tried to see the hands. "A little before five."

"Oh," she groaned, wrapping her arms more snugly around his waist, "it's way too early to get up yet."

"Not for me it isn't. I have to be on the road in another hour." He yawned drowsily.

"Oh, do you have to go out of town today?"

"Yes. I was going to tell you last night before you so . . . uh . . . delightfully distracted me." He grinned, finally rolling off her and pulling the covers up over them warmly. "Maybe I'll just lie here a few more minutes," he reasoned tiredly. "I think you wore me out last night. But thanks," he added politely with a smile in his voice.

"You're most welcome," she acknowledged lovingly. "Will you be back tonight?"

"No." His voice grew solemn. "I won't be back in town until Sunday."

"Sunday!" Kayla opened her eyes. "Why so long?"

"It's . . . business."

Business? Kayla found that unusual. Usually Franklin's business trips were only for a day. Or at least they had been since she had known him. Her voice revealed her disappointment as she replied, "Darn. I wanted you to help me look for a place to open my shop."

"I told you you didn't have to open a shop. I can take care of you," he reminded her curtly, but he tempered it with another long kiss.

"I know you can, but I meant it when I said I wanted to help us get a house. No problem, though. Paula will be back Monday, and then I'll have every day free to look for a shop." Marriage hadn't been mentioned yet, but Kayla felt sure that it would be soon.

"Whatever you say," he agreed, dismissing her words immediately. When all this misunderstanding was cleared up, he could change her mind. But before he proposed, he needed a little more time to find a way to straighten things out.

A hard, cold lump of fear rose in his throat as he heard the quiet sound of her breathing. She had fallen asleep while they were still talking, her arms wrapped lovingly around his neck. He would have to find a way soon. He couldn't keep running the chance that she would find out accidentally who he was. The only person likely to spill the beans was Paula, but surely Paula would never associate Franklin Franklin with Nicholas Trahern. He would be extremely careful and stay out of the office even more than he had done for the last week and a half. He could run Trahern Tool and Die by going in late in the evenings, just as he had been doing, and working half the night to catch up on paper work he had promised his dad he would do while the elder Trahern was away. It would all work out, he told himself grimly as his hold on the lovely bundle in his arms tightened possessively. It had to.

CHAPTER FIVE

"I can't tell you how wonderful it is to see the sparkle back in your eyes." Paula leaned forward in her chair and grasped her friend's hand tightly. "You know, I was really beginning to get worried about you."

"I know." Kayla's smile was glowing. "You've been such a good friend. I don't know how you've put up with me the last few months."

"You had reason to act the way you did," Paula assured her, squeezing her hand once more before releasing it, "but whoever this Franklin is, I could personally hug his neck."

"Oh, no, you don't. No one hugs my Franklin's neck but me." Kayla laughed. "Oh, Paula. I know I loved Tony . . . but I can see now that what I feel for Franklin is so different . . . so . . ." Kayla searched for the words to explain her feelings and there simply were none. She was head over heels in love with Franklin, and life was nothing but pure joy.

"So wonderful? I can see it in your every move," Paula told her. "And I couldn't be happier for you. Where did you say you met him?"

"Right where you're sitting," Kayla exclaimed. "Don't you

honestly remember him?" Kayla couldn't see how Paula could forget a salesman as good-looking as Franklin was, even if she was married!

"No"—Paula's face was a mask of concentration—"I don't recall any encyclopedia salesman of Franklin's description. Maybe he's new with his company."

"No, I don't think so. He asked where you were the first time he came in. Oh, well, you'll probably recognize the face when you meet him."

"And when do you think Doug and I will have that titillating experience?" Paula teased.

"Soon. Very soon, I promise. Franklin's work schedule is rather odd, and he travels a lot." Kayla thought back over the frequent two- and three-day trips he had made during the last few weeks.

"There's always weekends," Paula prompted, anxious to meet the man who had so vastly improved her best friend's life. "What about this weekend?"

"No, I don't think so," Kayla replied with a frown. Franklin had told her only last night that he would have to be gone again this weekend. "Franklin is going to be away on business this weekend."

"Franklin must really be a go-getter if he devotes all his weekends to business too." Paula sighed, tossing the last of her sandwich into the waste can.

Since Paula had returned from her vacation they had been too busy to have a long conversation, and while Kayla had been out looking at shops this morning, she had decided to stop by Trahern Tool and Die to have lunch with her friend.

"Yes, that's what I've thought too," Kayla admitted, "but he does seem like such a timid man. Oh, well, I'm sure we can get together soon."

"How's the shop hunting coming along?"

"Slowly. If I find the right size, the rent is too high, and if I find the right rent, the shop's too small." Kayla shrugged. "I seem to be running in circles. I hope Franklin can help me look sometime next week, although I must admit, he is very little help in that area. He doesn't want me to open a shop at all."

"Why not?"

"Oh, something to do with the fact that *if* I find someone to marry, I'll probably want to stay home and have babies." She grinned happily.

Paula smiled knowingly. "Do you think he's trying to tell you something?"

"I think so!" Kayla chuckled. "He hasn't come right out and asked me to marry him yet, but he sure makes a lot of veiled comments about how much he loves me and how he would love to start a family. I think he's trying to get up the courage to ask me."

"Kayla! You should help the poor guy out," Paula scolded.

"Are you serious! I've done everything but write down the words *Will you marry me, Kayla?* on a slip of paper and hand it to him!" Kayla protested.

"Well, I'm sure he'll finally summon up the nerve to ask you one of these days. Are you sure you're willing to devote all your time to being a housewife with three or four babies to care for?" Paula asked with a challenge in her voice.

"I would be if they were all Franklin's," Kayla said with a dreamy sigh.

"I certainly hope you have the good sense to name them something other than Franklin Franklin, Jr. Ugh. No offense intended, but that's the most gosh-awful name I've ever heard of," Paula said bluntly.

Kayla frowned. "Boy, it is, isn't it? But names don't matter. Only the man matters, and I would marry him if his name was Mortimer Snerd."

Paula shook her head. "I can see you're a hopeless case."

Kayla smiled brightly. "Guilty!"

Paula glanced at the clock on the wall, then hurriedly downed the last of her milk. "This has been fun, but I've got to get back to work. Don't you miss this nice little office?"

"Not really. It wasn't all that hard, but I barely got all of the younger Trahern's typing finished before he had another stack on my desk each morning," Kayla confessed, gathering up her purse and the remains of her own lunch.

"Isn't he a doll?" Paula asked absently, applying lip gloss to her mouth.

"Who?"

"Nicholas. Isn't that who you were talking about?"

"Oh. Yes, that's who I was talking about, but I wouldn't know if he's a doll or not. I never saw him. He always came in late in the evenings after I left. By the way, did you know that Franklin and Nicholas are the best of friends? It's almost impossible to believe, but they are. Two more different men you could never hope to meet!"

"Honest?" Paula paused in combing her hair. "That does sound like an unlikely friendship."

"I'll say! I'm only thankful that Nicholas's rakish ways haven't rubbed off on Franklin," Kayla observed thoughtfully.

"Oh, Nick isn't so bad. His reputation far exceeds the reality, I think. Actually, he's rather nice. I think you should meet him. In fact"—Paula sized her friend up—"you two would probably make a perfect couple. All Nick needs is the right woman to come along and make him sit up and take notice."

"No, thanks!" Kayla refused quickly. "If Bowser wants to sit up and take notice, he'll have to find someone other than me. I hope I'm taken! But you know what? I *would* like to know what the guy looks like."

"You've never seen a picture of him?" Paula asked with surprise.

"No. Is there one around here?"

"I think so. Nicholas and his father had some PR pictures taken several years ago. Wait a minute. I'll see if I can find one."

Paula rose and went over to the metal file cabinet. She browsed for several minutes before she closed it slowly. "Darn, there don't seem to be any left. I've sent a lot out lately—I guess I'll have to call the printer for more." She shrugged. "Sorry."

"That's all right," Kayla assured her. "It isn't important. I just thought it would be fun to see what all the fuss was about."

"Nicholas *is* a darn nice-looking man . . . and rich to boot," Paula said thoughtfully. "No wonder women drive him crazy all the time. He's to the point where he practically won't accept a call in the daytime from any woman unless I swear it isn't a personal one."

"Poor baby," Kayla said snidely. "It must be awful to be so sought after!"

"It must," Paula agreed laughingly. "Now will you kindly get out of here and let me do my work!"

"Only if you promise to ask Doug about Saturday."

"Oh, rats! I'd forgotten about that."

"Do you think he'd mind?" Kayla asked worriedly.

"No, I'm sure he won't. I'll let you know what time we'll pick you up. Doug doesn't miss an opportunity to go to the horse races, let alone the chance to go to the last one of the season. Saturday is the Arkansas Derby!"

"Really? Is that something special?"

"All I know is that it's one of the four quarter-million-dollar races they have each year, and they run three-year-olds on the mile-and-one-eighth track. Oh, hey! I bet some of Nicholas's horses will be running Saturday. I'm sure of it. He goes to Hot Springs almost every week. Instead of a picture you can meet him in person."

"Not interested," Kayla said with an airy dismissive gesture. "All I want to do is learn more about horse racing so I can talk intelligently with Franklin about his favorite subject."

"Undoubtedly Doug can help you there. I'll call you tonight and tell you what time we'll leave. Okay?"

"Fine. Talk to you later."

Kayla left Trahern Tool and Die humming softly under her

79

breath. She had some shopping to do before Franklin came by to pick her up that evening. Tonight she wanted to look extra special. For the last six weeks they had spent nearly every night together, excluding the ones when he was out of town. As of yet she hadn't seen his apartment, since it was much easier for Franklin to stay overnight at her place, eliminating the long drive back into town each morning. Kayla shivered as she recalled the nights spent in Franklin's arms. Somewhere along the way the teacher and student roles had been reversed, and now Kayla was the pupil in their lovemaking. Somehow Franklin had turned pro, and Kayla was delighted that she had been responsible for introducing him to the pleasures that a man and woman can share. His lovemaking was more thrilling than she had ever dreamed of, and her happiness knew no bounds. Since she was always on the alert to make herself more knowledgeable about his life, she had asked Paula if Doug would mind taking her to the racetrack this weekend and explaining some of the finer points of horse racing. Since Franklin would be gone all weekend, she would surprise him with her newfound knowledge when he returned. He would be so proud! She just knew it. She was so sure of it that she discreetly refrained from letting him know her plans for the weekend as they lay in bed that night, lazily kissing in the mellow afterglow of their lovemaking.

Her weekend plans were not the only thing she was keeping secret. Her hand moved down to gently touch her stomach, hoping that by the time Franklin returned, she would have other news to give him . . . news that would make him ecstatic. But it was too soon. She wouldn't go to the doctor until Friday, but then . . .

Heaving a long sigh, she rolled over onto his broad chest, her fingers tiptoeing up through the mat of hair. "Have I told you yet today how much I love you?" she whispered.

"I believe you did mention it a couple of hundred times, but I never grow tired of hearing it," he teased, catching her fingers and kissing them gently.

"Oh. You think I'm too obvious about how crazy I am about you?" she asked with a mock pout.

"Not to me you're not. But I'm not sure what all your friends will say when you put on the 'I love Franklin Franklin' T-shirt you bought at the mall today."

"Oh, pooh. I couldn't care less what they say. I *do* love Franklin Franklin."

"And *he* do love you too," he assured her, kissing the tip of her nose. "And he's going to miss you like hell this weekend. I'll be glad when you can start going with me on . . ."

"On what?"

"On . . . these business trips."

"When will that be?" She kissed him seductively, her hand wandering aimlessly over his solid flesh. "Why can't I go now?"

"Honey, I've told you . . . in a few weeks you can start going with me." He had made up his mind. When he returned Monday, he was going to take her somewhere where they could be alone for a couple of days, and in that time he was going to find a way to tell her who he was. Well aware of what the consequences could be, he was still determined to go through with his plans. No longer could he live with the lie between them. He loved her, and he would make her believe that. It wouldn't be easy, but he knew that she loved him, and he hoped that she would understand when he explained that although it was a foolish thing for him to do, he had lied to her on the spur of the moment, then dug his way deeper and deeper into the deceit until there was no longer a way to tell her the truth. Whatever the risk, it had to be brought out in the open now. Living from day to day with the knowledge that at anytime she might discover his identity was taking its toll on him. The dark circles under his eyes were not from the long hours he had been working. His clothes fit looser—he had lost his appetite. Only his continuing interest in his racehorses made his life bearable at the moment. But to go to the races, he was again forced to lie and tell Kayla he was off on business. Well, in a way it was business, although not business as she perceived it. No, he had to take the chance and tell her the truth, then ask her to marry him. With that all behind him Nicholas Trahern would be the happiest man alive!

"Kayla, listen to me, sweetheart." Franklin stilled her exploring hands. "I can't take you with me this time, but when I get back Monday, I want us to go away for a few days. What do you say? Just you and me." His gray gaze was solemn . . . and very serious.

"Can you take off work for that long?" she asked with concern.

"That's no problem," he said. "Will you go with me?" Reaching out with one hand, he pushed back a lock of her golden hair, his fingers lingering poignantly at the side of her face.

"I'd go anywhere with you, Franklin. I thought you knew that," she said quietly.

"That's what I'm counting on, Kayla."

She cocked her head at him and smiled. "What do you mean by that?"

"I mean I love you . . . remember that. When you look back on this hour, I want you to always remember one thing, I love you. From the bottom of my heart. I love you. Always remember that."

With a groan he pulled her mouth back down to meet his, and for the moment all else was nonexistent. How much longer would their world be secure? Nicholas wouldn't allow himself to think past tonight. Bringing everything he possessed to it, he made love to the woman he held in his arms with almost savage intensity, leaving her both shaken and puzzled by what had suddenly overcome him.

Franklin was such a strange but wonderful man. Kayla wondered if she would ever cease to be amazed at his rapid changes of mood. But it didn't really matter, she reminded herself as she snuggled down in the shelter of his arms. She loved him, whether he was plagued by moods or not. Franklin was the best thing that had ever happened in her life, and if he wasn't perfect . . . so what? She wasn't either.

Kayla was thinking similar thoughts when she emerged from the doctor's office Friday morning. A baby! It was true, she was carrying Franklin's baby, and she had not the slightest doubt that he would be thrilled and overjoyed at the prospect of becoming a father. Naturally he would insist on marriage right away. Kayla smiled and touched her stomach wonderingly. Her baby would be lucky enough to have one of the most honest, sincere men in the world to call Daddy. At that moment, in the middle of a bustling, crowded, street corner, Kayla let out a whoop of sheer joy for the baby and her love for its father. Mrs. Franklin Franklin! What more could any woman want?

For ten weeks every spring the little town of Hot Springs, Arkansas, some forty-seven miles southwest of Little Rock, reeled under the impact of twenty-three thousand race fans daily. From the second week of February until the third week in April the ardent race fans thronged their way into the beautiful Oaklawn Race Track, their spirits soaring at the anticipated sound of "They're off!"

Today was no different as Kayla, Paula, and Doug surged through the entrance gates, caught up in the air of excitement that prevailed in the stadium. The day was a gorgeous one, the sun streaming brightly over the beautifully landscaped track. Kayla would have loved to sit outside for the races, but Doug had already purchased tickets in one of the two five-story glass-enclosed grandstands.

"Boy, this is great," Kayla said excitedly, rummaging in her purse for more money to buy yet another "hot tip sheet" from one of the numerous barkers milling through the crowd, hawking their wares. "Anyone got an extra dollar?"

Doug fished in his pocket and extracted the asked-for currency. "Hey, Kayla, that's the sixth tip sheet you've bought. Don't you think you've got enough?"

"But each of those men said if I followed their tips, the horses they had picked would win today," Kayla protested.

"Ri-ght!" Doug said with a skeptical smile.

Kayla looked confused. "Isn't that right?"

Paula took her arm and steered her through the crowd, laughing at her gullibility. "Lesson number one. Anytime anyone tells you he has a 'sure thing,' run as fast as you can in the *opposite* direction!" she warned.

"The only sure bet around here is the hot dogs," Doug contributed. "Anyone want one?"

Paula and Kayla agreed to wait until later, but Doug's mouth was watering for one of the plump, juicy dogs served in a warm bun and smothered with mustard and relish, so he left the women and made his way to one of the concession stands on the third level.

"Come on, we can go to our seats," Kayla called over the noise of the crowd. "He can find us when he's finished."

Kayla followed Paula down the aisle of steps until they came to the row they were to be seated in. They were going to have an excellent view of the racetrack and Kayla's pulse quickened at the prospect of what was to come. All around her people were studying their racing forms, trying to decide where to place their first bet of the day—the daily double.

"What's a daily double?" Kayla mused, studying her tip sheets and program.

"That's one you're going to love! It only costs you a two-dollar bet. You try to pick the horses that will win the first two races," Paula explained patiently. "For instance, I think I'll bet on this horse, Molly's Mother, to win the first race, and then I think I'll take . . . umm . . . Bold Mary to win the second. If both those horses win, I'll win."

"How do you know which ones to bet on?" Kayla asked, overwhelmed by the choices before her.

"Oh, I pick the jockey with the cutest name, and bet on the horse he's riding," Paula said knowledgeably.

Kayla glanced at her skeptically. "Does that work?"

"It works as well as any system I use. Usually nothing works for me," Paula confessed.

"Well, I don't know." Kayla wasn't too impressed with her friend's betting system. "I wish I could see some of the horses before I bet any money."

"Oh, we will. We'll go down to the paddock before the races start, and you can see some of them. Oh, Yes. Lesson number two. The paddock is the place where they take all the horses to saddle them before the races. I think all horses are supposed to be saddled in view of the public. Then, of course, you'll see the jockeys and their horses in the post parade too."

"Post parade?"

"The jockeys parade the horses in front of the stands before each race. It's neat. I've brought some binoculars so we can see which one of the jockeys is the cutest, and then we can run up and place our bet."

"Oh, good grief, Paula. Isn't there a little surer way to bet?" Kayla could see her two-dollar bets going down the tube if one of those "cute" jockeys turned out to have an off day!

Paula looked hurt. "It's as good as any other system, I tell you!"

Doug returned, carrying cold drinks for each of them and two hot dogs for himself. The threesome sipped their drinks and read the tote board in front of the stands. Kayla watched as the computerized board flashed the names of dignitaries who were in the park today, the time of the first race, post time, and the time of day. One section of the board showed the total bets in separate pools for win, place, and show, along with the odds and pay-off prices. Kayla could easily see why Franklin loved the exhilaration of horse racing. Although she'd barely arrived, she was already eager for the first race to begin.

"Have you lovely ladies decided where to put your money for the daily double?" Doug asked between bites of his hot dog.

"Not yet. I haven't gotten a good look at the . . . horses yet," Paula amended swiftly. "What about you?"

"No question," he answered. "Trahern has a horse running in each race. That's where my money's going."

Kayla studied her program and saw that Nicholas Trahern was the owner of My Pretty Baby in the first race and Getha Leadout in the second.

"Getha Leadout? What kind of a name is that for a horse?" Kayla asked disgustedly.

Doug leaned over and looked at her seriously. "It's pronounced 'get-the-lead-out.' I can tell *you've* never been on your feet screaming at the top of your lungs as the horses come around that quarter pole and your horse is barely in the lead, straining for the finish wire. Personally I can't think of a more appropriate name for a horse at that time," he added with a devilish grin.

"What's the jockey look like who rides him?" Paula asked attentively.

"How should I know." Doug glanced over at his wife irritably. "Anyway, the track is fast today, so you ladies better make your bets carefully. There'll be some tough competition out there today."

"Do you mind if I ask what a 'fast track' is?" Kayla hated to be so dumb, yet the reason she was here was to learn.

"Oh, I'm sorry, Kayla. I was talking about the condition of the track. A fast track is one that's dry and ideal for racing. At least I prefer to bet a fast track. Other times the track can be classified as muddy, heavy, good, slow, or sloppy. I usually bet accordingly."

"Who makes up all these rules for horse racing?" Kayla asked interestedly. "The owners? The jockeys?"

"Good heavens, no. The State Racing Commission sets the rules, along with The Jockey Club. Now, mind you, I'm not an authority on any of this, but I'll try to fumble through your questions," he told her seriously.

Kayla grimaced. She would never be able to remember any of this when she needed it!

"And what about the horses themselves? How would I tell if a horse was a Thoroughbred or not?" she pursued doggedly.

"Oh, my, you'd have to see their papers. At least, that's the only way I could tell. I do know something about horses' markings, though—but surely you're not interested in hearing about that."

"Yes, I am. Now, come on, what are some of the markings?" Kayla persisted.

"Well, now, let me think. Some horses have a sock. That's a white band around the foot above the coronet."

"Coronet?"

"Top of the hoof. Then there's a white marking on the forehead called a star, and a blaze is a large white patch on the face. A snip is a small white or flesh-colored marking on the nose or lips, and a 'bald' horse has an entirely white face, including the skin around the eyes and nose. A stripe, which is usually narrow, extends from between the eyes to the bridge of the nose. And, of course, there's the stocking. That's where the lower part of the horse's leg is all white."

Paula let out a loud fake yawn and fell over into Kayla's lap in boredom. "*Never* ask Doug a simple question without expecting a detailed answer!"

"Well, she wanted to know!" Doug said defensively.

"Honestly, Paula. I *do* want to hear this. Go on, Doug," Kayla insisted.

Doug shot his wife a superior look, then continued. "Then, of course, Thoroughbreds can have different colors. Chestnut, roan, gray, bay, black, and brown are all recognized by The Jockey Club."

"Goodness!" Kayla frowned and decided to change the subject. "I noticed when I was reading the program that all the horses running today are three years old."

"That's right," Doug said, studying the sheet before him. "Wednesday they ran the fillies and mares—"

"Whoa! Explain!"

"A filly is a female horse under five years old. A yearling is between one and two years old. A colt is under five years old and male. Then a horse is male and over five years old," Doug explained patiently, "and a mare is female and over five years old. As I was saying, on Thursday and Friday they ran the four-year-olds and up, and today they'll be running all three-year-olds. Clear?"

"As mud," Kayla said glumly.

"I know it's confusing." Doug laughed. "Look, a lot of this information would be easier to digest if I could point out some of the horses to you. The races don't start until one, so let's walk down to the paddock, and I'll try to show you what I've just been talking about. Anyone in the mood for a hot dog yet?"

"Doug!" Paula scolded. "Surely you don't want another hot dog this soon!"

Doug looked properly shamefaced, but that didn't deter him from an honest answer. "I could probably eat three more."

Paula shook her head disbelievingly. "We are going to have to carry you out of here today."

"Oh, all right. I'll eat a pretzel with cheese on it instead," he grumbled.

They all decided that pretzels sounded good. Paula and Kayla waited as Doug made the purchase, and then the three of them took the stairs down to the lower level. As they approached what looked to Kayla like a concrete pit with stalls, Doug observed excitedly, "Gosh, take a look at those beauties!"

No one could argue that the horses being led in and the ones already standing in the stalls were not real beauties. Their healthy, sleek coats glistened as the grooms put on their pads, number cloths, and saddles and tightened their girths.

"Aren't their legs delicate," Paula said admiringly. "I don't see how they stand up under the pressures of racing."

"That's usually where a racehorse is most prone to injuries," Doug told them. "In their knees, hocks, legs, and fetlocks. The way they have to pound so hard on the track accounts for a lot of injuries."

"I can imagine," Kayla said, wincing at the thought of the weight those slender limbs had to support.

Kayla watched the far corner of the paddock as they brought in a stunning gray filly. Her eyes feasted on its gracefulness, and she thought how much it looked like the one Franklin had pointed out to her the day of their first picnic. The filly pranced in sassily, giving the firm impression that the race *it* was running in was all over but the shouting. That particular Thoroughbred certainly looked like a—what had Franklin called it?—a shoo out?"

The groom led the horse to one of the stalls nearest the entrance to the paddock as another man followed, carrying its tack. Distracted for a moment by the restless movements of a chestnut in the stall directly in front of where they were standing, Kayla failed to see a tall third man enter and walk to the gray filly's stall and kneel down to check the wrappings on the animal's hind leg.

"Oh, hey, look! There's Nicholas right down there!" Paula pointed toward gray filly's stall. "I thought he would probably be here today!"

Kayla glanced toward the far corner of the paddock, halfway expecting to see a harem waving palm leaves above the head of their "master."

"Really? Where?" she asked disinterestedly.

"Right over there by that gray horse. The good-looking one kneeling down in back, checking the horse's legs."

Kayla's eyes followed Paula's pointed finger, and her face lit up brightly. "Oh, gosh, Paula! There's Franklin! He must be here with Nicholas today!" Kayla said excitedly. "I wonder if he can hear me if I yell at him!"

"I don't know. It's pretty noisy in here," Paula said. "Which one's Franklin?"

"The handsome devil in the blue slacks and blue shirt, silly! Isn't he a doll?" Kayla's voice was filled with undisguised love and adoration.

"Blue slacks and shirt . . . I don't see anyone in blue slacks and a blue shirt except Nicholas. Is Franklin standing in the stall with the gray filly?"

"Yes, Paula, he's standing right there, talking to the man who's putting that thing on the gray horse's head!"

Both sets of eyes were trained on the men in the far stall. Slowly Paula's face lost its smile as a nagging suspicion began to creep through her mind.

"Is . . . Franklin . . ." Paula swallowed hard. "Is Franklin . . ."

Kayla looked at her friend in concern. "What's the matter with you, Paula? Is Franklin what?"

Paula cleared her throat and started again. "Is Franklin the one kneeling down again?"

Kayla glanced back down at the stall. "Yeah. That's him. Isn't he cute?"

"Oh . . . Kayla." Paula's heart sank. "There must be some mistake."

"Mistake? What do you mean?" Kayla smiled.

"That's . . . that isn't . . . that man leaning down is Nicholas Trahern." Paula didn't know anything to say but the truth. Surely Kayla was teasing her.

Suddenly the bright, exciting day turned cold and dismal. Kayla looked back at the man in question. "That's not funny, Paula," she said in a near whisper.

"I never meant it to be, Kayla." Paula reached out and grasped her friend's hand.

"Now, look, there's got to be some reasonable explanation for all this. Don't start jumping to conclusions," Doug cautioned.

Kayla turned a blank face toward them. "I don't know what you two are talking about. Franklin wouldn't lie to me. He wouldn't do that to me . . ." Her voice trailed off painfully as her eyes once more returned to the paddock. It felt as if someone had slammed a hard fist into the middle of her stomach. Surely this was some cruel, vicious joke.

As if experiencing a rare perception, the tall man in the blue slacks stood up and glanced toward the crowd, his eyes trying to locate what was bothering him. Then his features froze and his face grew pale as his gaze encountered the confused, stunned face of the pretty girl standing next to the railing. In one forward motion he raced to the retaining wall, shouting her name. The sound of his voice had the effect of someone throwing a bucket of ice water in her face, and she whirled and bolted through the crowd. Her mind was one chaotic mass of bewilderment. Her wonderful, shy, loving Franklin had lied to her. He wasn't Franklin at all, he was Nicholas Trahern! The despicable womanizing cad Nicholas Trahern! How he must have laughed at her all these weeks . . . all the nights when she had patiently led him in the acts of love, showing him what pleased a woman . . . the nights when she had whispered how much she loved him. Her stomach threatened to empty itself as she blindly pushed her way through the maze of bodies, searching for a way out of the stadium. Tears were rendering her nearly sightless as she ran from the entrance and fled down the street in the direction of the motel where she and Doug and Paula had rented rooms this morning. They had planned on spending the entire weekend in Hot Springs, but now . . .

The impatient blare of a car horn made her swerve wildly as she ran on down the street. It was happening all over again, the almost unbelievable pain that sliced through her when she thought of his deceit, the lies that he had told her. She thought it had hurt when Tony had betrayed her, but that had been nothing compared to the bitter, excruciating pain that overtook her now. Somewhere in the far corners of her mind she heard her name being shouted, but it barely registered as she ran mindlessly down the sidewalk.

"Kayla! Dammit . . . stop!" Nick's voice thundered through the air, but she had no intentions of stopping. She would never stop if she could help it. She would run to the ends of the earth if it meant she could for one moment erase men like Tony Platto and Nicholas Trahern from her tortured mind.

Blindly she ran on until she came to the motel. The key delayed her momentarily, her fingers shaking so hard she couldn't insert it into the lock. When she finally managed to get the door open, she rushed into the room and bolted the door securely behind her. Her side was aching from the long, hard run, and salty tears were streaming down her cheeks as she leaned miserably against the door and grasped her stomach. The baby. She had to think of the baby right now! All that running might have hurt it, and this hysterical crying surely couldn't be good for her in her condition.

"Oh, God." She sank down on the floor and buried her face in her hands. "Why have you let this happen to me again?" she questioned pleadingly. "What have I done to deserve your anger and your wrath?" She lifted her face in a plea to her heavenly Father. "I loved him. I truly loved him. How could he have done this to me?" She prayed for an answer, *any* answer, that would ease the pain in her heart. Only the quiet sound of the muted traffic outside filled the room. There were no answers for Kayla Marshall today. And the desolate thought crossed her mind that there might never *be* an answer. Not even tomorrow.

With feigned calmness she straightened her shoulders and began to wipe at the cascading tears. She had to get herself under control. No matter what had happened, she would be able to live through it. She had before, she would again. Only this time she would have something left of her misplaced love. Her hand went back down to tenderly touch her abdomen. This time she would have one thing that couldn't be taken from her. Not ever.

The calm was shattered by a loud fist slamming against the door. Kayla jumped as if she had been shot with a gun, her mind jerking back to the present.

"Kayla, open this door!" Nick demanded hotly.

"Go away, you . . . you snake in the grass," she hissed.

"I'm warning you, Kayla, open this door. I don't want to make a scene, but I will," he warned in a grim voice.

"You'll have to burn this place down before you'll get me to open that door, *Mr. Trahern!*" she shouted. "I don't ever want to see your lying face again as long as I live! Do you hear me?" she yelled at the top of her lungs.

"Yes, I hear you," he acknowledged in a muffled tone, "along with every other damn person standing out here. Now, open the door, and let's talk this over quietly."

"Over my dead body," she announced flatly.

"Have it your way," he said angrily. Kayla flinched as she heard his foot hit the door, splintering the wood violently.

"Don't you dare come in here, Franklin . . . Nicholas . . . whatever your name is. I'll call the desk and have them send the police—" Her words were interrupted as the door shook on its hinges once more, sending wood chips flying all over the room.

Kayla ran for the telephone and was frantically dialing the desk when the door finally gave way and Nicholas stormed into the room. Jerking the receiver from her hand, he slammed it back in its cradle, his face a violent mask of anger.

"Sit down, *Ms. Marshall,*" he roared.

"I don't have to sit down—" Nicholas pushed her roughly onto the bed and landed next to her, his eyes warning her that she *would* sit down, *and* like it! "You can't treat me like this! Someone will hear you and call the management," she argued.

"I told the bystanders that we were on our honeymoon and having our first quarrel. I don't think anyone's going to be com-

93

ing to your rescue." His breathing was labored as he tried to still her squirming body. "I think I convinced them."

"Oh, that's right. I'd forgotten for a moment what an excellent *liar* you are . . . Nicholas," she spat out.

A look of pain blanketed his face as his eyes turned stormy. "I want to talk to you about that," he said quietly.

For a moment the struggling ceased as their eyes met in mute anguish. Unwanted tears welled up in Kayla's as she looked at the face that had come to haunt her days and nights. It looked innocent enough. It still had all the features she loved. The smooth, tanned skin, the beautiful silvery eyes, the soft golden hair, the firm, almost rigid jawline that she had kissed so often . . . it was all still there. All those familiar landmarks, yet she had the feeling that she was staring at a stranger. A cold, lying stranger.

CHAPTER SIX

"Don't look at me that way, Kayla." Nick's gaze was pained as his eyes met hers. He leaned forward as if to kiss her, and she jerked back angrily.

"Don't you touch me, you dog in the manger!"

"Stop calling me snake in the grass and dog in the manger!" he snapped, struggling with her heatedly. "You haven't even given me a chance to explain!"

"Ha! As if you could!"

"I can. Are you willing to listen?"

"No! I don't want to spend another minute with you, let alone the time it would take for you to explain your little deception," she cried, wrestling with him for possession of her wrists. "I'm warning you, I'm going to resort to violence if you don't let me go!"

Nicholas rolled her over onto her stomach and threw his large frame on top of her, pinning her tightly to the mattress. "We are going to discuss this if I have to sit on you all night, Kayla!"

Kayla pounded the bed with her clenched fists, powerless to move. "I hate you. Do you realize that? I hate you!"

"I know you think you do right now—"

"I don't think it! I know it."

Nicholas closed his eyes in agony. "Don't say that, sweetheart."

"And don't *ever* refer to me as 'sweetheart' again. I'm not your sweetheart . . . I'm nothing to you—" Her voice broke off in a sob.

"That's not true. Good Lord, Kayla, you're everything to me," he said in a husky tone. "I was afraid this was going to happen. I knew I should have told you sooner, but that first day . . . you remember the first day we met?"

Kayla lay silently, her mind painfully recalling their first meeting. The way she had picked her silly panties off his broad chest . . .

Nicholas took her silence for a sign that she was listening. "Remember how you let me know in no uncertain terms how you felt about men like me . . . Nicholas Trahern. I knew that I would never get to first base with you if you found out that I . . . Well . . . *that's* what made me say my name was Franklin."

Kayla grunted disgustedly and buried her face deeper in the pillow.

"And that *is* my name . . . in a way. Nicholas *Franklin* Trahern. That part wasn't entirely a lie," he said lamely, a trace of self-righteousness in his voice.

Kayla refused to answer him.

"Are you listening, sweetheart?"

"No. Let me up. I want to go home."

"No. Not until I make you understand that what's happened between us in the last six weeks has not been a lie. I am in love with you, Kayla."

Kayla's anger overcame her, and she shoved against him violently, knocking him off her. She scrambled over to the side of the bed and glared at him coldly. "You actually want me to believe that what you did to me you did from love? Well, I'm sorry, Frank— Well, I'm sorry. That is certainly not my idea of love. You must have had a good laugh at the way I believed that you had never been with another woman." Her voice cracked and she swallowed hard. "Did I amuse you, *Nicholas*, when I coached you in all the things that please me?"

"Don't do this, Kayla," Nick said harshly, his eyes growing misty. "Don't cheapen what we had. I know what I did was wrong."

"Well, at least you're man enough to admit that. Yes, Nicholas. What you did was cruel and despicable . . . and I will *never* forgive you for it."

"Don't say that. You don't really mean it."

"I don't think I'm getting through to you, Nick. After today I hope I never see you again. As far as I'm concerned, I've never met Nicholas Trahern. The man I loved, Franklin Franklin"— her voice broke, and tears threatened to overtake her— "the man I loved with all my heart and soul died today. That's the way I'm going to look at it. I will grieve over the loss of Franklin until the day *I* die, but as far as *you're* concerned, I feel nothing!"

Nicholas reached out and turned her over and pulled her roughly up against his chest, his mouth grinding into her lips hurtfully. For a moment Kayla was too stunned to try and break the embrace, but when she realized what he was trying to do, she jerked away angrily and slapped his face. "Don't *ever* do that to me again!" she warned in a deadly tone.

"Are you trying to say that you don't still respond to me . . . that what we had is gone because of some stupid misunderstanding?" Nick's face was a tortured mask as he released her and they backed off from each other.

"That's exactly what I'm saying. I detest you. It's as simple as that."

"I will not believe that, Kayla. You don't detest me . . . you detest what I have done to you, and I can't blame you. I know I'm going to have to give you some time . . . I know this has been a terrible shock . . ."

"I mean it, Nick. Don't ever try to see me after today. You've had your fun. Now the game is over—I don't want to play anymore," Kayla sobbed.

"Kayla, look. Remember when I said that I wanted us to go away for a few days when I got home Monday? Honey, I was going to tell you then, honest I was. I knew that this couldn't go on indefinitely. I was going to tell you who I was and ask you to marry me. You have *got* to believe that, Kayla."

"I wouldn't believe a word you said, Nicholas. Why can't you get that through your stubborn head. Go back to your world of women and horses . . . and lies . . . or whatever a man like you does, and leave me alone!"

Nick's face became cold and proud as her words began to sink in. "Is that what you really want?"

"Yes." Kayla turned away from him and walked over to the window. "That's exactly what I want."

"Then I'll be damned if I'll bother you again! I guess I was wrong about you, Kayla. You're just like all other women. Selfish, cold, with not an understanding bone in your body. You've put on quite an act, haven't you? Making me think you were a warm, lovely, unselfish—"

"I want you to leave, Nicholas. Now!"

"With pleasure!" He strode angrily to the door and yanked it open. "I tried to tell you—"

Kayla staunched the flow of words by slamming the door in his face. "You should have tried harder!" she yelled through the splintered wood.

The silence in the room was unbearable as Kayla walked back over to the bed and miserably threw herself down. No matter how hard she tried to believe that she hated Nicholas Trahern, the awful truth kept bleeding through. She didn't hate him. Disappointment, a sense of betrayal, loneliness, she felt all of those at the moment . . . but hate? Could such a final and forceful word be used to describe her feelings for Nicholas Trahern? There was supposed to be such a fine line between hate and love. On which side did her feelings lie? Rolling over onto her back, she stared at the ceiling in blind apathy. Right now she couldn't tell what she felt. Only one thing was clear in her mind. She would never see Nicholas again if she could possibly avoid it. He would never know about the baby. Luckily she had no ties to this city. Nothing to prevent her from pulling up her roots once more and leaving. Thank heavens she had been unable to find a shop that suited her. As it was, she could leave immediately. There was nothing to prevent her from going home and packing all her belongings and putting the past behind her. And that's exactly what she would do.

The ride back to Little Rock was strained. Doug and Paula had returned to the motel shortly after Nicholas had departed. They said very little, only that they would pack their bags and take Kayla home. Paula had put her arms around Kayla and hugged her in mute commiseration. Words failed both of them. This had happened twice in a very short span of time, and Paula couldn't give Kayla the comfort that she needed. Kayla felt like an utter fool, and she knew Paula felt totally incapable of dealing with this unexpected turn of events.

Once a fool, always a fool kept running through Kayla's mind as she rode back to the city. It wasn't a very pleasant thought, but now the signs were unmistakably clear. All the times Franklin had acted preoccupied, as if something was on his mind, all the times he had told her they needed to talk, the way his lovemaking had become expert almost overnight, his strange moods . . . it all fit together now. She must have been a blind fool to miss the cues, because he had certainly given her enough over the past weeks. Obviously the furthest thought from her mind had been that Franklin was not who he said he was. Love had made her sightless, deaf, and most assuredly stupid. The nagging nausea that had plagued her all afternoon threatened to overcome her as she laid her head against the back of the seat and closed her eyes. Her nerves were a mass of quivering jelly, and she longed to be home where she could let her emotions spill out in private.

When they reached her apartment, she said her good-byes hurriedly, promising to talk to Paula tomorrow. The moment she was inside her apartment, she bolted for the bathroom, thankful that she had escaped the embarrassment of having to ask Doug to stop the car.

Afterward she was too drained even to switch on the light as she walked into the bedroom and fell across the bed. Deciding to lie there until she could get her dazed feelings under control, she closed her eyes and let the tears fall.

When she awoke, it was morning. She was still lying in the same position she had been in when she fell asleep. As she slowly raised herself up another bout of nausea assailed her. Reeling under the intensity of it, she ran for the bathroom at full speed. Ten minutes later she flopped weakly down on the bed and placed a wet washcloth over her forehead. Of all the stupid times to come down with a case of the flu, this was undoubtedly the worst. So many things to do, and she didn't have the strength to raise her head off the pillow. With a tired sigh she closed her eyes again, fighting the new surge of sickness that washed over her. Today was definitely out. Packing and leaving would have to wait until tomorrow. At the moment she felt she would be lucky to see the dawning of a new day, period.

A week later Kayla still lay staring up at the same stain on the ceiling, wishing someone would have mercy and shoot her. Hour after hour of sickness had blurred into days. At first she was sure she had contracted some rare tropical disease that was undoubtedly fatal. Having no idea where she could have picked up such a debilitating illness, she quickly surmised that the germ must have been carried in on the last bunch of bananas she had bought at the store. After several days of not being able to keep even a simple glass of water down, she went to the doctor. It gave her little satisfaction to find out that her rare tropical disease was only a typical reaction to pregnancy. Clutching the morning sickness pills the doctor had prescribed, she had hurried back home to the sanctity of her bed and bathroom, grateful that her days were not numbered, as she had secretly feared. Although she had little desire to go on living at the moment, she had less desire for the alternative.

Paula had been a saint during the last week, stopping by every evening after work to check on Kayla and bring her something to tempt her appetite. Kayla who was still unable even to think about food, much less eat anything, had lost a great deal of weight.

"Hi. I brought you a chocolate shake," Paula called merrily as she breezed into Kayla's bedroom.

Kayla's stomach lurched at the thought of the milkshake, and the smell of Paula's perfume made her grit her teeth.

"Thanks, Paula, just put it in the freezer. Maybe I can drink some of it later on."

"Come on, Kayla. Can't you try to just get a little of it down? You didn't eat any dinner last night, or breakfast this morning."

"I know." Kayla sighed. "I'm sorry, Paula. I appreciate all you're doing for me, but I simply can't eat a thing."

"Does the doctor know how sick you are?" Paula asked worriedly, taking the washcloth off Kayla's forehead and going into the bathroom to run cold water over it.

"He says that some women have a harder time than others at first. The baby and I are healthy, and hopefully in a few more weeks the nausea will pass. If I live a few more weeks!" she added sickly.

"I worry about you," Paula confided, placing the washcloth back on her head. Sitting down on the edge of the bed, Paula peered at her friend's pale features. "Are you all right . . . otherwise?" Nicholas Trahern's name had been mentioned rarely since the day they had come home from Hot Springs. Kayla had been too sick to discuss her problems with Paula, desiring only to get through each day without adding the extra pain of thinking about Franklin. Nights had been the hardest to endure. There had been times when she had cried for hours, longing for his presence beside her, confused by her body's changes . . . wishing with all her might that things could have been what they first seemed to be—that Franklin could be here with her, that he could help her through these long days and give her the love and support she so badly needed.

"I'm fine," she answered quietly.

Paula noticed her voice didn't sound fine. "He's asked about you . . . several times." Paula bit her lip, knowing that the subject was painful, yet feeling that Kayla needed the assurance that he hadn't forgotten her.

Kayla didn't answer, only turned her face toward the wall and closed her eyes.

"I think he cares, Kayla. His feelings and pride have been hurt too. Don't you think it would be only fair to let him know about the—"

"No! I do not want him to know about this baby, Paula." Kayla's voice was calm, yet firm.

"But you need his help, his support right now," Paula reasoned. "You *can't* go through this by yourself!"

"Thousands of women do every day. I'm no different. I don't need Nicholas Trahern's support, nor do I want it."

"You're being pigheaded about this, Kayla. Who's going to take care of you while I'm gone?"

"Where are you going?" Kayla opened her eyes.

"I told you . . . Mother is being operated on Friday morning. I promised I'd be there with her. I'll be gone a week or more. Someone has to look after you. You can't take care of yourself right now."

"I'll make it all right. I've always been able to care for myself. You worry too much. Excuse me for a minute."

Kayla jumped up and ran to the bathroom. By the time she returned shakily to her bed, Paula had fixed her a glass of 7-Up and placed it on her bedside stand.

"This is awful." Kayla laughed weakly, her eyes filling with tears. "I feel so . . . so helpless!" She lay across the bed and cried like a baby. All her senses seemed to be out of whack, and it was the most frustrating experience she had ever had to deal with.

"Let me call Nick," Paula pleaded.

"No."

"Then let me take you to the hospital and have you admitted until I get back. I don't know why the doctor hasn't put you in before now."

"Oh, Paula! Stop!" Kayla covered her ears. "I'll be all right! I really appreciate all you've done for me, but please, please, stop worrying about me. I can't stand all of this fuss!"

"I don't care what you say, I'm going to call Nick—"

"No! You do and I'll never speak to you again. I mean it, Paula! Promise me you'll not even *think* about calling Nicholas."

Paula thought for a moment, then mentally crossed her fingers. "I promise."

"Good." Kayla closed her eyes once more, nausea building again in the pit of her stomach. "At least that's one worry off my mind!"

After Paula left, Kayla lay thinking about her promise. Surely she wouldn't lie to a sick person. That would be unthinkable. No, she had always been able to trust Paula, and she saw no reason to doubt her now. Kayla's secret was safe, and just as soon as she was able to stand on her feet five minutes without throwing up her socks, she would leave this town, as she'd originally intended, and put thousands of miles between her and the father of her baby. All she needed was a little more time.

Bolting off the bed, she ran for the bathroom once again. Just a few more days and she would be her old self again. If not, she was reasonably sure she would be dead. Either way, it would all work out!

The night before Paula left for her mother's, both she and Doug came by to check on Kayla. By now Kayla's hair was limp and scraggly, and her complexion an ash gray. She was in no mood for company, yet she did appreciate all that was being done for her.

"Now, I've left five cans of chicken noodle soup—" Paula began.

"Paula, please. Just leave me a note. I'll read it when my stomach feels up to it," Kayla moaned. The mention of chicken noodle soup had made her queasy. Her mind instantly conjured up all those greasy little noodles floating around in a yucky yellow broth . . .

"Excuse me, Doug," Kayla mumbled, grabbing for her robe and streaking past him.

It was another thirty minutes before Kayla could convince her friends to leave for Paula's mother's. By the time they let themselves out the door, Kayla was feeling drained and irritable, but pleased to be by herself once more. She dozed off and on for the remainder of the evening, waking occasionally to glance out the window by her bed. In the distance she could hear the rolling thunder, which reminded her of the early morning thunderstorm that had awakened her and Franklin the first night they had spent together. For a brief, painful moment she remembered the feel of his lips on hers.

Assuming that another storm was on its way, she rolled over onto her stomach and buried her head under the pillow. She didn't want any reminder of Franklin . . . however remote. During the past week she had intentionally blocked out all thoughts of him, and she felt much too vulnerable at the moment to let her mind dwell on the past. Drifting in and out of sleep, she heard the storm lashing at her windows and the loud peals of thunder literally rattling the room.

Calm returned with the passing of the deluge, and only the methodical dripping of the rainspouts could be heard when Kayla awakened much later. The peal of the doorbell startled her. Glancing at the clock on her bedside table, she saw that it was nearly midnight. Surmising that Paula and Doug had decided to drive to her mother's in the morning instead of tonight, she lay there in bed waiting for the sound of the key in the lock. Paula probably wanted to check on her one final time. She had been letting herself in lately to keep Kayla from having to get up. And sure enough, a moment later Kayla heard the sound of the door being opened and footsteps entering her apartment.

"Paula?" Kayla called out softly.

There was no answer, but Kayla could hear the footsteps drawing nearer to the bedroom door. Her heart raced as she realized that Paula would surely have answered her by now. Sitting up in bed, she peered through the darkness toward her bedroom doorway. "Paula," she tried again.

"No, it's not Paula." Nick's voice came to her quietly through the shadows.

That traitorous, conniving ratfink Paula had betrayed her!

"How did *you* get the key to my apartment? It was Paula, wasn't it?" Kayla said disgustedly. "You can just turn around and let yourself back out, or I'll call the police," she ordered impolitely.

"Just dry up. I'm here, and you're not going to call the police," Nick said irritably. "Where in hell is the light switch?"

"Find it yourself," Kayla said crossly, then flopped back down on the bed and covered her head with the pillow. Great balls of fire! How much had Paula told him? Surely she wouldn't have told him everything! Even if she hadn't, Kayla would never forgive her for giving Nick her apartment key and letting him come over here tonight. What a perfectly rotten trick to play on a friend. Kayla's hand crept up under the cover and tried to push her stringy hair into some semblance of order. She looked like death warmed over, and here Nick was standing in her bedroom, searching for a light switch!

"Don't turn on the light," she hissed from beneath the covers in a muffled voice. There was enough light streaming in from the lamp Paula had left on in the living room for him to see. What did he need—floodlights?

105

"Why not?" His familiar voice brought back a flood of unwanted memories.

"Just leave it off! What do you want?"

The sound of footsteps moving closer to her bed caused Kayla's breathing to quicken. Although he didn't make a move to touch her, she was acutely aware of his presence in the room.

"Take that sheet off your head. I want to talk to you."

"You can talk to me like this. What do you want?" She wasn't about to let him see her looking this bad.

He moved closer to the white lump on the bed. Kayla cringed as she heard his foot land in the large pan she kept by her bed in case she couldn't make it to the bathroom in time.

"What in hell—"

"That's my 'urp' pan! Get your foot out of it!"

He jumped back like he had been burned. "Your . . . I hope it wasn't . . . full!"

She would have gladly given everything she owned to be able to tell him "Yes, it was . . . filled to the brim!" But unfortunately it wasn't. She decided to do the second most cruel thing and simply not say anything. Just let him wonder if it had been used or not.

"Well, was it?"

"I can't remember."

"I'm turning on the light," he said authoritatively.

"You turn on that light and I'll scream the rafters down," she warned, pulling the sheet up higher over her head.

"Okay, okay," he relented. "Don't make a scene." He felt his way over to a chair and sat down, slipping his shoes off quietly. Before he put them back on again, he wanted to get a good look at them in the light.

They sat in the dark for a few minutes, neither of them speaking. As the silence deepened, Kayla became more irritable. What did he think he was doing? Coming over here in the middle of the night and sitting down next to her bed without saying a word! Any minute now she was going to have to make her hourly trip to the bathroom, and she would have to crawl over his lap to reach her goal. The thought was revolting.

"Have you had any dinner?" Nicholas broke the silence at last.

"Yes. I had chop suey and then went dancing with a friend," she lied.

"Be serious. Have you eaten anything or not?"

"No, I haven't eaten anything! And I don't *want* to eat anything. You just wait until I get my hands on Paula!" she fumed, trying to raise the sheet up at its corner for a breath of air.

Reaching over, Nick quickly ripped the sheet off her head and tucked it neatly around her chin. "*If* you don't mind! I felt like I was confronting a member of the Ku Klux Klan!" he explained dryly.

His hand lingered for just a moment as it came into contact with the softness of her cheek. "How are you, babe?" he whispered softly.

Maybe it was from being so sick for so long. Maybe it was the touch of his hand. Maybe it was the never-ending hours of loneliness. Kayla didn't know. All she knew was that suddenly, her defenses started to crumble as she tried to see in the dim light the face she once had loved so dearly.

"Oh, Franklin . . . I've been so sick," she cried, forgetting for the moment that Franklin no longer existed.

"I know, and I'm so sorry, sweetheart." He pulled her head against his broad chest, and the sobs tore out of her, long racking sobs that she had held in for weeks, sobs that shook her body violently and cleansed her soul. Holding her close, he murmured words of comfort into her ear, assuring her that he was here now, that she wasn't alone any longer. When there were no more tears left, he switched on the bedside lamp and went to the bathroom for a cold washcloth. She lay limply on the bed, her face a molten red, hiccups jarring her body, and wished she didn't have to face him yet. Bringing the cloth back, he placed it on her face and sat down on the bed next to her.

107

"Why didn't you tell me about the baby?"

"It's none of . . . *hic* . . . your . . . *hic* . . . business!"

"None of my business! Dammit. That's *my* baby you're carrying, too, you know," he said sternly.

"I don't . . . *hic* . . . look at it that . . . *hic* . . . way!" she returned with as much dignity as the situation would allow.

"Well, I *do* look at it that way. We'll get married immediately." There was no particular emotion in his voice as he said the words, Kayla noted. Not "I love you, Kayla, baby or no baby" or "You're going to marry me because I can't live without you." No! Just the cold, indifferent "We'll get married immediately."

"I wouldn't marry you if you were the last man on . . . *hic* . . . Earth," she told him bluntly. "I could wring Paula's neck for telling you!"

"You're not being sensible, Kayla. If you think I'm going to let my baby be brought into this world without the benefit of my name—"

"There is absolutely *nothing* you can do about it, Nicholas." She spit the words out at him nastily.

"What do you mean, there's nothing I can do about it? There's plenty I can do about it. You watch me!"

"I'll be happy to watch you. It so happens that I called a lawyer shortly after I found out about my pregnancy . . . just in case this situation should arise. You're an unwed father, Nick. In essence you have very few rights . . . practically none at all! Not unless you can prove me an unfit mother, and it will be a cold day in hell when that happens," she told him heatedly.

"You forget, Kayla. I have the power and the *money* to fight you every step of the way on this. I'll take you to court and make your life miserable if you try to play dirty with me." His face was contorted with anger now, his gray eyes snapping. "I want *my* baby!"

"Go ahead! Waste your money if you want to! It is not *your* baby. This baby's father was named Franklin Franklin. I had never met a Nicholas Trahern when this baby was conceived. What do you think a judge would say to that, Nick?"

Nick looked uneasy for a moment but quickly regained the upper hand. "All right, so I don't get anywhere in court. Either you marry me and let me give our baby a name, or I'll camp on your doorstep until the kid is eighteen years old! I won't allow you a moment's peace, Kayla. I can be pretty damn stubborn when something of mine is in jeopardy. Think about it, Kayla!"

"I don't need to think about it. Face it, Nick. For once in your life neither your money nor your power *nor* your lies will benefit you. No judge would give you custody of a child under these circumstances. And I certainly would never marry a man simply to give my child a name. My baby will carry *my* name."

Nick sprang up from the bed and stalked to the window. He stood looking out into the night, a tense muscle working along his jawline. "How in hell do you think you're going to support a baby by yourself? You don't even have a job right now!"

"I have some savings. Enough to last until the baby comes," she replied quietly.

"What about hospitalization?"

"I have . . . a little for that. Look! I didn't say that I wouldn't let you help me through this." It went against Kayla's grain to acknowledge that she might need financial help during her pregnancy, but she wasn't stupid. She knew that even with her savings, money was going to be extremely tight, and she wouldn't be able to open her own business now.

"You're willing to take my money but not my name—is that what you're saying?" Nick asked snidely.

"No. I'm not willing to take either one now. Forget I mentioned it! I don't want or need your help, Nick. All I want is for you to forget that we ever met. I'm certainly going to."

"You are crazy as hell if you think for one minute I plan on stepping out of your life," Nick said grimly, turning back around to face her. "Whether you like it or not, that baby you're carrying is just as much mine as it is yours. It's my flesh and blood, and if you think I'm going to walk off and leave it, then you're just plain off your rocker. You can refuse to marry me, you can scream your head off that you hate my guts, but that isn't going to change one thing. That baby's half mine, and it's going to know it has a father who loves it, and *wants* it. Do I make myself clear, Kayla?"

Kayla glared at him angrily. "Perfectly! But you can't torment me and my baby if you can't find us! I'll run away, Nicholas. I'll run so far you'll never find me!" she threatened.

"Go ahead and run. I'll find you. I'll hire a man to watch you twenty-four hours a day. Starting *before* I leave this house tonight. You're going to get tired of running, Kayla. Especially with a small baby who needs a home and love and care. Are you willing to treat our baby like that?"

"I hate you, Nicholas," she cried, her nausea rising up in her throat again. His coming here had upset her all over again.

"I'm sorry about that. But you're forcing me into a situation that is not going to be pleasant for either one of us. I'd suggest you reconsider my offer of marriage."

"Never! I'd rather die first."

"Then you better reconcile yourself to the fact that until that baby's born, I'm going to be around to see that you *live* to give birth to it. When it's born, I'll *talk* to *you* in court. Now, are you going to throw up again?"

"Yes. Get out of my way!" She got out of bed and shoved past him.

"I thought so. Your face looks green."

"I don't want to hear your nasty observations," she said sourly as she slammed the bathroom door in his face.

"Good. I wasn't wanting to tell you your hair looks like a chicken's roost."

Kayla slammed the stool lid up and pretended it was Nicholas Trahern she was bending over.

On her way back to bed, she stopped dead in her tracks. Nick was calmly making up the sofa in the front room.

110

"Just what do you think you're doing?" she asked incredulously.

"Going to bed. Why?"

"Not in *this* house, you're not."

"Oh, yes, I am. It's an hour's drive to the ranch. If I have to fix your breakfast in the morning, I'm not going to drive home, then back."

"Who said you were fixing my breakfast in the morning?" she sputtered.

"Look at you. You must have lost ten pounds in the last week. That can't be good for my baby!" Nick snapped. "I'm going to see that you get some decent meals down you, starting with breakfast in the morning."

"Food won't stay down, Nick!" Kayla said between clenched teeth. "Do you think I'm an idiot? I *try* to eat for the baby's sake."

"Together we'll work on getting something down you that your stomach won't reject. Now, why don't you go to bed and get some sleep. You look like hell."

Kayla could have stomped her foot in anger, screamed, and pulled out all her hair, but she realized how determined Nick was to assert his authority tonight. With a cry of disgust she slammed the bedroom door and climbed back into her bed. When she got back on her feet, she was physically going to throw that ill-tempered, conceited jackanapes right out on his ear! He could bank on that!

CHAPTER SEVEN

April drifted lazily into May, then May into June. Kayla's days were nearly all identical, varying only in the degree to which she was sick each particular day.

Nicholas came by the apartment every morning and evening and patiently tried to coax meals down Kayla's throat. There were many days when barely a civil word was exchanged between them as Nicholas calmly spooned soup or pudding into her mouth, her blue eyes glaring defiantly into his slate-gray ones. The only reason she allowed this outrage at all was that she was still too sick to do anything about it; she was living for the day when she had the strength to boot him out.

As Nicholas straightened up the apartment each day he would talk quietly about his ranch, about some remodeling that he was having done. He took to bringing decorating books by for Kayla to look through in the daytime and asked her to jot down pages that she liked or disliked. For the first six weeks she had hatefully jotted down every page she looked at in the "dislike" column. She wasn't about to help him redecorate his house! Nick would patiently look the list over, then hand her a new batch of magazines with the instructions to "browse through these today."

112

Kayla did notice one thing. He was always there when she needed him. It was uncanny how she would run to the bathroom and he would be beside her, holding out a wet washcloth when she was finished being sick. He knew when every doctor's appointment was and never failed to show up an hour before she was due so that he could drive her there. Occasionally he would leave her sitting in the waiting room while he went in and visited with the doctor himself. He did all the shopping and all her laundry and fixed all her meals. Kayla wondered when he had time for a life of his own, but he still went to work every day and only occasionally left early after dinner. Kayla assumed he probably had dates on those evenings, but since they rarely said anything personal to each other, the subject was never broached.

She tried to tell herself she didn't care what he did with his time as long as he didn't bother her. And that he didn't do. Never once since he had started taking care of her had he touched her in any way or made any move that wasn't entirely above reproach. Nor did he tell her he loved her, and he certainly never mentioned marriage again. He was a nice, polite . . . servant. The baby was always politely referred to as "our baby," and he never failed to bring home some ridiculous toy that the child couldn't use until it was in grade school! A considerable assortment of dump trucks, toy trains, footballs, and tricycles occupied a huge corner of Kayla's apartment now, and each time she glanced over at what she now referred to as "Santa's workshop," she seethed anew. He would never even *see* the baby, let alone watch it grow to an age at which it could use those toys, if she had her way. Daily she nursed her original idea of running away. One day she even went so far as to pack a bag and lug it out to her car. The heat had been atrocious, and the longer she sat there in the driver's seat, the sicker she became, until finally she gave up and went back in the house. When Nicholas came by that evening, he eyed the suitcase suspiciously but said nothing to her. Instead he unpacked it and put it back in the closet. His courteous conduct was driving her batty.

113

At least he wasn't staying overnight like he had the first night. He did allow her a few hours of privacy before he came back in the morning to fix her breakfast. At first she totally ignored his comings and goings. That part was easy. The Loch Ness monster could have swum through her living room and she seriously doubted whether she would have noticed, as sick as she was.

But as the weeks passed she caught herself watching him as he did the dishes or ran the sweeper. Every once in a while she would catch a whiff of his aftershave, the one he had always worn as Franklin, and her insides would tighten at the memory of the nights they had spent in each other's arms. Nights when he would whisper all sorts of indecent suggestions to her and she would willingly and lovingly comply.

Nicholas dressed immaculately, and now that he had abandoned his horn-rimmed glasses, he was breathtakingly handsome. At times she had to will her eyes to look away from him, traitorously intent as they were on staring at him.

One night after dinner he had slumped into the chair next to her bed and drew a magazine on horse racing out of his briefcase. It seemed he wasn't in any particular hurry tonight.

"I'll bet you don't have the slightest idea what a horse eats while it's in training, do you?" he asked, opening the conversation congenially.

"No." Kayla's curt answer left no doubt that she didn't care what a horse ate while it was in training. "Why don't you go home?" she said crossly.

"I don't want to. Now, take a guess. What would you think a horse would eat?"

"Bacon and tomato sandwiches." Kayla leafed through her romance novel and found the page she had stopped on the night before.

"Wrong. Bran, oats, and hay."

"Whoopee."

"Okay. Take a guess what a filly would weigh. Wait a minute

—that isn't a fair question. You probably don't know what a filly is," Nick said apologetically.

"Oh, yes I do." Kayla didn't want to play his little game, but she spoke before she thought.

Nick glanced up in surprise. "What is it?"

"A female horse under five years old."

Again he looked surprised. "That's right. How did you know that?"

Kayla shrugged and went back to her novel. "Doug told me the day we went to the races." A swift shaft of pain sliced through her when she thought back to that horrible day.

"Oh." He looked thoughtful. "Do you know how much one would weigh?"

"Nope. I didn't have my scales with me that day."

He shot her a dirty look. "A little over a half a ton. All right, here's another. Do you have any idea on what date of the year a horse has its birthday?"

"Beats me." She turned over toward the wall and began reading.

"First of January. I can tell this quiz is really turning you on, isn't it?" he said dryly.

"You noticed."

"Hey, how about this one? How much does a jockey usually weigh?"

"A little over a half a ton. No, wait, that was the horse, wasn't it?"

Nick snapped the magazine closed and stood up to leave. "I get the distinct feeling you're not interested in racehorses."

"That's right. I don't *ever* plan on being around any."

"Our baby will be raised around a stable full of them. Don't you think you should take an interest at least for its sake?"

Kayla ignored his question, keeping her face turned to the wall. With a sigh he leaned over and asked, "Do you need anything before I leave?"

"No. Nothing. Thank you."

"Well, then, I guess I'll see you in the morning."

Kayla heard his footsteps walking toward the door. Taking a deep breath, she closed her eyes and called out softly, "Nicholas?"

He paused, then looked back. "Yes?"

"How . . . how much does a jockey usually weigh?"

A flicker of tenderness crossed Nick's face, but Kayla couldn't see it. Her face was still turned steadfastly toward the wall.

"Somewhere between a hundred and ten and a hundred and sixteen pounds."

"Oh . . . that's interesting," she returned nicely.

"Are you sure there isn't anything I can do before I leave?" he asked again.

"No, nothing."

"Good night, then."

"Good night." For the first time Kayla really didn't want him to leave, and for the life of her she didn't know why.

As the bedroom door closed she laid her book aside and salty tears ran down her cheeks. She rolled over onto her back and covered her eyes with her arm. She had been depressed all day. That was the only reason she hadn't wanted him to leave tonight, she told herself.

Suddenly she sat up, her hand going to her stomach. She had felt a tiny flutter! Her baby had moved for the first time! The tears mixed with her laughter as it fluttered again, letting her know that within her body she carried another life. It gave her a feeling of awe and reverence to know that someday that tiny life would call her mother. Nick! He would want to feel the baby move too! She sprang to her feet and ran to the door. Peering out, she could see the red taillights of his car going down the street. Her face crumpled as she let the curtain drop back into place. It didn't matter, she told herself as she returned to her "prison." It had been a foolish idea to begin with. He was the man who was going to try to *take* her baby from her when it was born! Why should she care if he felt his baby move for the first time.

116

With a relieved sigh at having missed him she lay back down on the bed and switched off the light. Tomorrow was another day. Another painful, endless day.

"You're eating better this morning," Nick observed as he got up to pour them another cup of coffee.

Kayla finished the last of her bacon and eggs and sat back in her chair. "You know, I think I do feel a little better this morning." It was the first of August and for the past few days Kayla had noticed that the bouts of nausea were coming much less frequently now.

"Let's see. You're how far along now?" Nick asked, buttering another slice of toast and handing it to her.

"It's more than four months now. I don't think I can eat another piece of toast, Nick," she protested.

"Sure you can . . . put some strawberry jam on it. The baby loves strawberry jam." He smiled coaxingly.

"The baby and I won't be able to get through the kitchen door if I keep feeding it all this strawberry jam." She grinned back, smearing her toast liberally with the red preserves.

"Say, I've noticed you're beginning to pooch out in front a little," Nick observed teasingly.

"Yes, look at this." Kayla pushed back from the table and stuck her slightly rounded stomach out. "I'm going to go shopping for maternity clothes soon. I can't get into anything I own."

"Good. Let me know when you need some money," Nick told her, adding cream to his coffee.

"I don't need any of your money." Kayla's smile disappeared. "I'll buy my own clothes."

"No, you won't," he replied calmly. "Have you felt the baby move yet? It should be getting close to the time when you can feel it. The baby books say sometime in the fifth month."

"Yes, I've felt it." Kayla picked up her toast and started eating again, dismissing the subject of clothes for the moment.

"You did? When?"

117

"A couple of weeks ago," she said with a shrug.

"Two weeks ago! And you haven't said anything about it?" he asked incredulously.

"That's right. I still don't consider it any of your business." She put the toast back down on her plate, her appetite suddenly gone.

"Well, I'll be damned. I thought you'd at least tell me when you felt it move for the first time." He sounded rather put out with her.

"I didn't think about it," she fibbed.

Nick sat coldly assessing her, his eyes running lazily over her breasts, which had suddenly become fuller, along with her pudgy stomach.

"Will you at least tell me the next time it happens?"

Kayla shrugged again. "It happened just a few minutes ago."

"Honestly?" He slipped out of his chair and reached to lay a hand on her belly. "Do you mind?" He glanced at her questioningly.

She couldn't bring herself to meet his expectant gaze. "I don't suppose so. Though it might not do it again for a while."

They sat for a moment watching his hand, neither one saying a word. In a few minutes a broad grin broke across Nick's face. "There! It moved, didn't it?" he said excitedly.

Kayla's grin nearly matched his. "Yes! Could you really feel it?"

"Sure, I felt it. That kid's going to be tough! Hey, there it went again!"

Baby Trahern was indeed putting on quite a show for its mom and dad.

"Does it hurt?" Nick asked, suddenly concerned about Kayla's discomfort.

"No, I can barely feel it," she assured him, "although I'm sure that in another few months he'll get a lot rowdier."

"He? Do you think it's a boy?"

"Oh, I don't have the slightest idea. A little girl would be nice too. Don't you think?"

"Oh, damn, I don't care if it's a boy or a girl," Nick said. "All I want is for you to come through this with flying colors and for the baby to be good and healthy."

Abruptly, as their gazes met and held, the mood changed. For one brief unguarded moment love flickered brightly in Kayla's eyes.

"Please don't take this baby from me, Nicholas . . . it's all I have," she begged, forgetting her pride. "You'll have other children. Let me have this one."

"Don't ask me to do that, Kayla." His eyes grew deeply distressed. "I don't want to hurt you any more than I already have, but you *can't* ask me to give up this baby. I love it every bit as much as you do. I would despise myself if I knew that somewhere in the world I had a son or daughter who thought its father had deserted it. All I'm asking is for you to share this baby with me," he pleaded. "Let me take care of my baby, Kayla."

"No, it isn't fair! You have the money to buy anything in the world it takes to make you happy. Why can't you be content with that and leave me alone!" she blazed.

"I can't buy happiness," he protested. "As I said, I don't want to hurt you, but you're not going to take this baby away from me. Not without one hell of a fight."

Kayla shoved away from the table angrily. "You are one insensitive clod, Nicholas Trahern!" She glanced around the table wildly, looking for something to throw at him.

Both their eyes lit on the piece of discarded toast covered with strawberry jam.

"Oh, no, you don't! You throw that at me—" He ducked as the toast and jam sailed by his head, splatting up against the wall nastily.

"Ha! You missed!" he yelled smugly.

"Oh, yeah! Well, I won't this time!" She snatched up the jar

119

of jam and pitched it all over the front of his white dress shirt. Angrily she whirled and started to leave the kitchen.

"Hey! Did anyone ever tell you motherhood has given you one mean, nasty disposition!" he yelled after her.

"Blow it out your ear . . . Superfly!" she shouted back.

"Blow it out yours . . . Mommy." The anger drained out of him as he ran one long finger along the front of his shirt and scooped up the dripping strawberry jam. "Say, this isn't bad," he observed after licking his finger. "I can see why the baby likes it." He grinned and winked mischievously at Kayla.

She gave him a withering glare and stalked out of the kitchen in a huff.

"Oh, well," he said with a sigh and peeled off his stained shirt. "The baby book said there would be days like this!"

"What do you want for breakfast this morning?" Nick was standing at the stove with a spatula in his hand when she entered the kitchen the next morning. She hadn't spoken to him since breakfast the previous day, totally ignoring him when he brought her dinner by last night.

"Bacon and eggs." She sat down at the table and picked up her fork, waiting expectantly for her food.

"You *can't* have bacon and eggs."

"Why not!"

"We are completely out of jam," he pointed out resentfully, "and I know you don't want bacon and eggs without toast and jam to go with it."

Kayla looked sheepish. "Pancakes?"

"How about French toast?"

"Umm . . . I suppose so." He was spoiling her rotten.

Nick walked over to pour her a glass of orange juice and a glass of milk.

"You know," she said, "this is silly. I'm beginning to feel good enough to make my own breakfast. You don't need to keep coming over here every morning."

"You wouldn't eat a bite if I didn't fix it," he told her firmly. "I intend to see that you take care of yourself until the baby's born."

A surge of anger went through Kayla. Until the baby's born! Always the baby! "I don't want you around until this baby's born!" she complained. "You're *not* taking my baby, Nick. Somehow I'll find a way to prevent you from ever doing that! And I want a cup of coffee instead of this horrible milk!" She shoved her glass irritably toward him.

"You can't have coffee this morning. Not until you drink your milk," he replied patiently, wiping up the drops of milk that had sloshed out of the glass. "We go through this every morning, Kayla. You need to drink milk for the baby's sake."

Kayla gritted her teeth and slammed her fork down on the table. She knew perfectly well she was acting like a spoiled brat, but she didn't care. His slightest word could set her off.

"How many pieces of toast do you want?" Nick asked calmly, walking back over to the stove.

Kayla refused to answer.

"Two? Good. You must be feeling fine this morning." He dumped a wad of butter in the skillet and turned on the burner. "Did you sleep well last night?"

Kayla sighed, then reached for her glass of juice. "Not very. It seemed awfully hot in my room."

"I don't think your air-conditioner is working properly. I'll call your landlady today," he replied absently.

The word landlady instantly rang a bell in Kayla's head. "My landlady! Good heavens, I just thought of something. I've been so sick I haven't paid any bills for months. It's a wonder I haven't been pitched out in the street for not paying my rent." She was shocked that she could have let something that important slip by her, but she had barely been aware of the days, let alone her financial responsibilities.

"I took care of the bills," Nick answered lightly.

"You what?" Kayla set her glass down and stared at him.

"I said, I took care of your bills while you were sick. Here, you can start on this while I fix the other one." He handed her a plate with a slice of French toast on it, then turned back to the stove.

"What gave you the right to interfere in my personal business?" she snapped.

"Now, look. We are not going to get into a big hassle over the fact that I kept things running smoothly while you were flat on your back, carrying *my* baby. If it's going to upset you, you can pay me back."

"I most assuredly will!" Kayla picked up the jar of syrup and angrily drenched her French toast. "You write down *every* cent you've spent, plus all the groceries you've been buying lately," she ordered.

"All right, I will. I'll have Paula send you an itemized statement," he agreed blandly. "Now eat your breakfast."

"Don't have Paula send me anything!" Kayla mumbled between bites of toast. "She's nothing but a ratfink. *You* send it to me."

"I thought I was a ratfink too," he mocked, dishing up his slice of toast.

"You both are."

"There's a sale in the babies' department at Sears today. Are you going to go?" he asked, reaching for the syrup.

"I might," she replied crossly. "I need to start buying some things for the baby."

"No, you don't. I've bought enough to supply six babies. Did you see that frilly little thing I brought home yesterday?"

"Yes. And I just hope you can find some needy little baby to give all those beautiful things to, because you're *not* giving them to mine!"

"Ours. And, yes, I am." He stuck a piece of his toast in her mouth.

"Stop it!" She brushed his hand away.

"Okay. Let's change the subject. Since you're feeling better, how about going out to the ranch with me tonight after work.

122

The carpenters have reached a point where I have to okay some changes."

"I'm not going anywhere with you," she said stubbornly.

"What would it hurt to take a drive in the cool of the evening. You haven't been out of this house for weeks," Nick reasoned. "If it's a matter of being with me, I can't see what difference it would make. Whether it's here or riding in the car I'm going to be with you."

Kayla mulled over the tempting proposal. It *would* be nice to get out of the house. It had been so long since she had done anything but lie in bed.

"How long would we be gone?"

"Just a few hours. I promise I won't wear you out."

With a sigh of resignation Kayla gave in. "All right."

"Good." He smiled happily. "We'll have dinner somewhere on the road."

"Great. And now that you're not trying to hide from the world, I hope it will be in a restaurant where there's enough light to read the menu."

Nick looked properly put in his place. "I would have taken you to the darkest places I knew whether I was Franklin *or* Nick. I remember some pretty pleasant times in those dimly lit booths." He grinned one of those smug, infuriating grins he could manage so well.

Kayla blushed, her stomach fluttering at the innuendo in his voice. This was the first time he had said anything really intimate to her since this mess all began.

"Another thing I'd like for you to do is meet my parents one of these days," he said decisively.

Once again Kayla's face flamed a bright red. "Nick! I wouldn't think of it!"

"Why not?" He glanced at her in surprise.

"Meet your parents! With me as big as a barn with your child . . . Well, I simply wouldn't do that! Besides, what would be the sense of it?"

"You're carrying their grandchild, Kayla. Don't you think they would want to meet you?"

"You told them about . . . about the baby?" she gasped.

"No, not yet. Mom and Dad are out of the country right now, but as soon as they return, of course I'm going to tell them," he returned calmly.

"No, I *don't* want to meet them. I would be embarrassed to death. And so should you be," she scolded. "Or am I not the first woman you've brought home to meet them carrying your child."

"That's ridiculous and you know it. Have you told your aunt?"

Kayla had once remarked that she had been raised by her aunt after the untimely death of both her parents when she was eight years old.

"No, and I don't know if I will," she returned uneasily. "We're really not very close. I haven't seen her in years. I should have been more careful," Kayla murmured, glancing down at her lap shamefacedly. "Or if *I* didn't have the sense to be, *you* should have taken care of it." Kayla knew why she had left herself wide open for this pregnancy. At the time she had had every intention of marrying *Franklin*, had he asked. But for *Nick* to have been so careless puzzled her. Surely with his vast experience with women he hadn't always been so neglectful!

Nick had picked up the morning paper and was looking at the ad for the sale at Sears, having lost interest with their conversation.

"Well, why didn't you?" she demanded, knocking his paper out of his hand in exasperation.

"Will you cut that out?" He mopped up his spilt coffee with a napkin. "Why didn't I what?"

"Why didn't you take precautions about getting me pregnant?"

Nick lifted his shoulders in an indifferent shrug. "I thought you were."

124

"You thought! You thought! Why didn't you ask?" she insisted.

"Because it didn't really make a whole hell of a lot of difference to me, Kayla. At the time . . . at the time you felt a lot differently about me than you do now, and I assumed that if anything happened, we'd get married. I had no objections to your having my children. I had every intention of taking care of you if anything happened."

"Are you like that with *all* women?" she asked incredulously.

"No. Only you," he admitted sullenly.

Kayla's breath caught at his words. They were very direct, sincere, and honest. Why did he have to be so nice after he had been so deceitful? For that matter, why couldn't he have played it straight with her from the first so this horrible situation would never have arisen.

"Why did you have to lie to me, Nick?" she asked in a hurt voice.

"I told you. It was a spur-of-the-moment, asinine joke. One I'll regret the rest of my life. But I can't change it, Kayla," he said impatiently.

He rose from the table and looked down at her. "Until the day comes when you can forgive me, there's no way I can make it up to you."

Kayla shook her head negatively. "I'm sorry. I want to forgive you, but I can't. No . . . that isn't true. Maybe I have forgiven you." She realized that might be true. At some point during the last few weeks his kindness and tender care had forced her heart to forgive him. "But I can't *forget* what you've done."

His eyes were sad as he reached for his suit jacket and slipped it on. "I know, and I'm very sorry you feel that way. But the fact remains, we have a baby that's a part of both of us, and I intend to claim my part." Kayla held her breath, hoping he would tell her once again that he loved her and wanted to marry her, but he remained silent. Apparently what little affection he had felt for her had died in the last few weeks. Well, it didn't matter, she told herself defiantly. She wouldn't marry him if he got down on his hands and knees and crawled!

"I'll see you tonight," he said with a tired sigh. "Call me if you need anything today."

"I'm sure I won't." She avoided his gaze, trying not to notice how virile and handsome he looked this morning.

Kayla had to work very hard at keeping the tears at bay as he left the room. For one wild moment she had considered flinging herself into his strong arms and letting him hold her, give her the strength she needed to face the day. But of course she hadn't. He would have thought she was a fool, and she would have been. Her feelings had been turbulent throughout this entire pregnancy, and today was no different. At times she felt as if she loved Nick as deeply as she had loved Franklin. In truth they were the same man in so many ways. Except that Franklin had been shy and insecure, whereas Nick was bold and always in control. Nick was capable of the same tenderness that Franklin had shown her. He brought small gifts to her even though she steadfastly refused them. There was a pile of candy bars and little trinkets a mile high next to her bed. He had spent hours reading to her at night, and watching TV with her when she had been so ill, and he had brought home her favorite flavor of ice cream at least twice a week. All these things he did without expressing any particular feeling for her in words; only for the baby.

But the main ingredient of a happy relationship was sadly missing. Trust. Kayla didn't trust Nick. She was always looking for an ulterior motive and usually had no trouble coming up with one. He was doing all these things for her because of the baby he wanted so badly. If it weren't for the pregnancy, she would never have seen Nicholas Trahern after the day when they had broken up in Hot Springs. She was convinced of that. Although he had offered to marry her, Kayla was sure that he was merely being gallant. He wouldn't leave any woman out in the cold. If he got her pregnant, he would face up to that responsibility. It was as simple as that.

Lately she had begun to wonder if she had been too hasty in refusing his offer of marriage. Although it burned her to think of taking anything from him, she knew that it was going to be terribly hard to raise a baby alone. Especially if he carried out his threat to make her life miserable if she didn't let him have custody of the child. Would that be the best thing for her child? Her hand went lovingly to her rounded belly. Already she loved this child with all her might. She couldn't give it up! He had no right to try and take something that was so precious away from her. He simply had no right! Somewhere she would find a lawyer who would prolong the fight for years, if it came to that. She still didn't believe that Nick could actually take the baby, but as he threatened repeatedly, he did have the power and the money . . .

Tiredly she left the kitchen and went to take a shower. She *would* go to that sale at Sears today. Maybe if she had her own layette for the baby, it would help her to pull out of her depression. At least it was worth a try.

The department store was hot and crowded, making Kayla wish she had stayed at home. It occurred to her that she didn't feel as well as she had earlier thought, but since she was already here, she might as well take advantage of the sale. With a feeling of apathy she sorted through the tiny baby clothes, trying to picture her baby in her mind. Would it have Nick's proud nose, or his smoke-colored eyes? Quickly she caught herself and deliberately made her mind go blank. She would not spend the whole afternoon mooning over him!

Absently she studied the different brands of prefolded diapers arrayed before her, glancing up in embarrassment as she stepped on the foot of a man standing next to the baby rattles.

"Pardon me." Kayla's eyes suddenly narrowed suspiciously. "What are *you* doing here?" she hissed between clenched teeth.

Nick's silvery eyes focused on her small form, lingering for a

127

moment on her rounded stomach. "Buying *my* baby a bed," he said matter-of-factly.

"A bed! Well, you can just take it back. I'm buying one!" she said sharply. "Besides, it won't be with you at all, let alone lie in a bed!"

"I'm not getting into this with you again," he retorted stubbornly, reaching for a large crib mobile lying on the display rack. "You'd better save your money for the custody suit. You're going to need it."

Kayla's temper simmered as she watched him pick up one of the boxes of diapers that *she* had planned on buying and stuff it under his arm authoritatively. She noted with extreme irritation that he had reverted to his "Franklin" disguise for the afternoon. He had on the large horn-rimmed glasses he had worn during his masquerade, and he peered interestedly at the price of a teething ring. Obviously he was in hot pursuit of another unsuspecting woman, using that shy, inexperienced act he was so good at.

Jealousy ripped through Kayla painfully at the thought of Nick and another woman. Undoubtedly he had been seeing other women all along. A man with his strong appetite would certainly never remain celibate for all these months, and he sure hadn't been sleeping in her bed! The thought was torturous. Nick kissing another woman . . . his hands roaming intimately over her body as they had done so often and so deliciously over hers.

Her anger was close to the boiling point. Tapping her foot agitatedly, Kayla warned him tensely, "Put it down, Nicholas! I've already bought one of those too. You're going to be stuck with a thousand dollars' worth of baby items that you'll have no need for."

His answer was to pick up a set of nursing bottles and add them to his growing pile on the counter. "Let me worry about that," he said with saccharine sweetness, turning back around to stare at her pointedly. "Why don't you run on home. You look washed out."

That was the wrong thing to say at this particular moment. Kayla's temper blew. "Nicholas Trahern, you're treading on thin ice with me," she said hotly. "And take those *ridiculous* glasses off. Who are you trying to impress with your meek act today?" She reached up and viciously snatched his glasses off his nose and threw them onto the floor.

Nich stared down at his glasses, his mouth open in consternation. "Now, Kayla, dammit . . . that was my best pair of glasses!" he complained in a hurt tone. Damn, but she'd been touchy since she got pregnant; and he was getting pretty tired of these rampages she had been going on lately.

"I suppose you're going to tell me you really *do* have to wear glasses!" she said in near hysteria, as though daring him to make something out of her temper tantrum.

"Yes, I do," he said defensively. "I wasn't lying about that. When my eyes are strained, the doctor said I have to wear them."

Kayla glared at him witheringly, all his previous fibs running through her mind. She knew she was being totally irrational, but he was simply pushing her too far!

With one deliberate stomp she shattered first one lens of the glasses, then the other. Looking back up at him belligerently, she said in a menacing tone, "Tell me another one, Nicholas!"

"Well . . . I'll be damned! That takes the cake!" he railed.

Feeling considerably better after her act of violence, Kayla whirled and fled the department store, leaving Nicholas and the saleslady standing staring in mortification at the pile of twisted frames and shattered rubble lying on the floor.

Nick looked at the saleslady sheepishly, then shrugged his broad shoulders philosophically. "Hormones," he offered lamely.

By the time Kayla arrived back at her apartment, she was furious. To think that she had been having second thoughts about Nicholas this morning! She must have been crazy to think that they could ever live with each other. Her anger only increased as she saw the dozen or so boxes lying on the sofa with the name of a local maternity shop printed on the sides.

Angrily she ripped the boxes open, irritably surveying the lovely maternity fashions lying in the boxes. Superfly had struck again! Well, she would return every last one of them. He would *not* patronize her in this flagrant manner.

Shoving her shoes back onto her swollen feet, she gathered up every box and carried them out to her car. For the rest of the afternoon she returned the despised items and got his money back. He had paid a king's ransom for the wardrobe. Then she went to her bank and withdrew from her savings enough money to pay Nick back for the last few months' rent, groceries, and other miscellaneous bills that he had paid for her, and some extra to buy three or four modestly priced dresses and pairs of slacks to see her through the remainder of her pregnancy. When she had finished her shopping, she climbed wearily back into her car and drove home, feeling very proud of her independence and accomplishment. It had nearly killed her, but she had managed to stand on her own two feet once more!

CHAPTER EIGHT

"I'm warning you, I'm tired and I'm cranky, and I don't want to be gone all evening." Kayla followed Nick out the front door, wishing she had never promised to go with him to the ranch. The long day of shopping had worn her out completely, and her back ached, her feet were swollen, and the nausea had returned to a slight degree.

"I know, I know. You've warned me six times already and we haven't even gotten in the car yet," Nick said. "And don't talk to me about being cranky. You didn't have to spend the last three hours at the optician's."

Kayla noticed he was wearing a new set of glasses. The sight of the old Franklin was achingly familiar, and it caused her to close her eyes briefly in the pain of remembrance.

They approached a Renegade sitting at the curb, and Nick opened the door for her. "Hop in."

Eyeing the vehicle disdainly, she taunted, "How many cars do you have, anyway?"

"Only two. I just bought this Renegade to keep at the ranch. Why?" Nick slid behind the wheel and started the engine.

Kayla tried to ignore the fact that he had a pair of cutoff jeans

131

on and his bare legs were sending her into fits. "It must be nice to be filthy rich," she observed resentfully.

"It certainly is," he agreed. "You could be, too, you know. I've offered to make things easier for you." He pulled the Renegade out onto the street. "Take that dress you're wearing, for instance."

Kayla glanced down at her new maternity outfit. "What's wrong with it?"

"Well, I keep waiting for elephants and clowns to come walking out from beneath it," he said bluntly. "Now, why in hell would you return all those lovely clothes I bought you and go buy something like that?"

"Because I distinctly told you *not* to buy me any clothes. You know that. And there's nothing wrong with this dress!" Actually Kayla had considered the red and white stripes a little colorful herself, but it had been a good buy on the sales rack.

"Suit yourself, but you'd better run as fast as your little legs will carry you if you see a circus truck coming down the street," he warned.

They stopped for Chinese food on the outskirts of town. During the meal they managed to refrain from snapping at each other. Nick talked about some of the problems he was having with a couple of his Thoroughbreds. Kayla found herself listening more attentively when he discussed the horses. To her surprise she had begun to grow interested in horse racing and had made a promise to herself that one day she would go back to the races and actually see the horses run.

After dinner they left the restaurant in a more mellow mood. The August evening had begun to cool as they drove toward the ranch. All around them the sounds of summer could be heard as the jarflies and katydids tuned up.

Kayla was reminded of the first picnic she and Franklin had gone on as Nick turned the Renegade into the large gateway and drove across the cattle guard. Tonight Kayla couldn't see any horses standing around in the fields, as she had the previous time.

132

"Oh, I was hoping some of the horses would be out," she said, disappointment in her voice.

"They're down at the stables. I'll take you there later tonight if you'd like." Nick reached over and pinched her nose playfully.

"I'd love it. I'm surprised they're here at all. Aren't you racing them?"

"Not this week. I'm going to go to Ak-Sar-Ben next weekend and watch a couple of them run."

"Where?" Kayla grimaced at the strange name.

"Ak-Sar-Ben. Think about it. What does Ak-Sar-Ben spell backward?"

Kayla thought for a moment, then smiled. "Nebraska?"

"Right. Omaha. Do you think you'd feel well enough to go with me?"

Kayla's smile vanished. "No."

"Not so fast." He tweaked her nose again. "Are you sure you don't want to think about it? I'll only be gone a couple of days. They have a beautiful racetrack up there and rumor has it that the last horse races you attended turned out to be a less than enjoyable." Nick's voice turned husky. "I'd like to make that up to you, Kayla . . . if you'd let me. I'd like to show you a part of my life that's very important to me."

Suddenly the months peeled away and they were back to the old Franklin and Kayla. The atmosphere was almost congenial as they drove along the winding lane leading to Nick's ranch. Kayla considered his proposal silently, wondering where the intense irritation she had felt only a little while ago had gone. How could she forget that the man who sat beside her was going to try to take a large part of her life with him when they separated in a few months. For they would eventually have to separate. After the baby was born, Kayla knew she couldn't live in the same town as Nick. But for now, would it hurt to let down her defenses for just a moment and accept his offer to accompany him to Nebraska? She would love to see his horses race, and it did seem senseless to keep refusing to go anywhere with him when he was with her the greater part of every day anyway. And, she theorized, that too would probably stop before very much longer, since she was beginning to feel so much better now.

"Are you thinking it over?" he asked softly.

"I'm . . . thinking," she answered.

"I promise you'll have a good time."

"Where will we stay?" That thought had occurred to her belatedly.

"In a motel." He glanced at her angelically. "We'll rent two rooms. Strictly on the up and up," he added.

"And if I don't go, what then? Would I actually get to spend two whole days of glorious freedom from all that obnoxious milk you make me drink?" Her smile was mischievous.

"No. I'll just ask that ratfink, Paula, to come over and sit with you while I'm gone."

"You certainly will not. I'm still not speaking to her."

"You're going to have to get over that too. Paula was only looking out for your best interests. I would eventually have found out about the baby whether she told me or not," he replied seriously.

"I don't see how," she argued. "If I hadn't gotten so sick, I would have left town the day after I returned from Hot Springs."

By now they had reached the sprawling ranch house, and Nick pulled up in front of it and shut off the engine. "I wouldn't have let you just walk out of my life like that, Kayla," he said quietly.

Her breath caught at his look of . . . of what? Tenderness? Love? She wasn't sure. The moment passed, and Nick forced his gaze away from her and opened the Renegade's door. "Come on, let's take a look at what the carpenters have done."

"Why are you redecorating?" Kayla asked as he came around and helped her out of the passenger side.

"I bought this house several years ago," he told her, taking her arm and steering her up the walk. A profusion of marigolds, zinnias, cosmos, and pinks lined the concrete path, their colors riotous in the late summer evening. "At the time I had neither

134

the chance nor the inclination to fix it up the way I wanted to. It's funny." He paused and surveyed the house and emerald green pastures that surrounded it. "I fell in love with this house the minute I saw it. I knew this was where I wanted to spend the rest of my life and raise my children."

Kayla's eyes followed his line of vision, and she could easily see the beauty he was referring to. The ranch had a peacefulness about it, a tranquility that could only be found in the lush, rolling Arkansas hills with their tall, majestic maples and oaks.

"That is funny," she said thoughtfully. "Somehow I wouldn't have thought you were the type who would take an interest in a home and family." She didn't mean to sound critical or sarcastic. His words had merely surprised her.

"That only goes to show how little you really know about me, doesn't it?" he remarked curtly.

"I didn't mean that to be offensive, Nick. It's just that I've always had a different opinion of you—"

"I know what your opinion of me has been." He reached into the pocket of his cutoffs and withdrew a key. "My problem is I just don't know how to change it."

The front door swung open, and Nick ushered her inside. Kayla's eyes widened as she stepped inside the redwood house with its chocolate-brown trim, and she stared openly at the homey interior. A large combination dining room, kitchen, and family room met her gaze, and she noticed with delight that the ceilings had exposed wood beams. Several colorful handloomed rugs lay about on the wooden floor at the end of the room where a huge open fireplace stood. Antique pots and cooking utensils sat on the hearth, and one large cooking urn hung over the cold ashes in the grate. Two rust-colored sofas sat facing each other in front of the fireplace with a monstrous round pine coffee table separating them. Kayla had never seen a room so beautiful. Only in magazines had she ever seen such elegance, yet it was all done with such simplicity that she knew that anyone would feel at home and comfortable in these surroundings. Four large win-

135

dows and a French door let in the light from outdoors, making the room warm and cozy in the gathering dusk.

"Oh, Nicholas . . . this is lovely," she breathed, walking over to touch the charming bow-backed pine settee closest to her.

"Do you like it?" He looked at her, trying to read her face.

"Like it? It's . . . I've never seen a house like this one," she said with awe.

Kayla paused in the dining area to take in the beautiful replica of an old-fashioned harvest table and the marvelous antique pie safe.

"Where did you find these chairs?" she exclaimed. "I love them!"

Nick glanced at the classic cane and chrome side chairs and smiled. "You picked them out, don't you remember?"

Kayla looked at the chairs more closely. "Me? When did I pick them out?" She had no doubts that she would have chosen these chairs but to her knowledge she had never seen this furniture before.

"Don't you remember all the books I had you go through? These chairs were about the only thing you had on your 'like' list!"

"You bought them because *I* liked them?" she asked wondrously.

"That's right." He took her arm and propelled her forward before she could protest. "There's a lot more I want to do with the house," he told her excitedly. "I haven't even begun on the bedrooms yet, and there's two of the baths that still need redoing." As they approached each room he offered detailed explanations of what he would like to have done with it.

Kayla could do little more than take in all the beautiful furnishings, and she was soon caught up in Nick's enthusiasm. "And a big four-poster bed with one of those lovely old-fashioned patchwork quilts would really set this room off," she told him happily when Nick led her into the guest bedroom.

136

"That's exactly what I had been thinking," Nick agreed. "Something in blues and reds. I love those two colors."

As they walked down the hall he draped his arm casually around her protruding waist. "Then I thought I'd like to have some of those frilly, sheer curtains hanging at the window and maybe a big wooden rocker sitting next to the window where our guests could look out over the pastures and horses."

Kayla noticed the word *our* but thought that it was a slip of the tongue on Nicholas's part. He was totally absorbed in planning the house.

Strolling on down the hall, they came to a room on the right, close to the master bedroom. Opening the door carefully, he stood back and waited for Kayla to walk in. "Now, don't get mad," he cautioned leerily.

Kayla looked at the room filled with toys, Ethan Allen baby furniture, rocking chairs, and toy trains.

"Nick." That was all she could say. She meant for her tone to be accusatory but failed miserably. Instead it came out very weak and unimposing. "Why are you doing this?" Her eyes took in the large toy giraffe leaning in the corner, looking very lonely as it waited for its master.

"You know why." Nick leaned against the door and watched her carefully. "I want my baby to have everything I can possibly give him."

Kayla sighed and walked over to lovingly touch the yellow comforter that was lying in the crib. It was so dainty and beautiful. The whole room was. It had obviously been planned with care and love. Again it occurred to her that she wished things could be different—that this was going to be her home, that this would be the room where she would love and care for her baby. She could visualize herself sitting in the wooden rocking chair, holding their baby close and crooning a soft lullaby to help it go to sleep. Nick would come in, and together they would put the baby gently in its bed and tuck the lovely yellow comforter around its sweet-smelling body. Together they would kiss it good night, then leave the room quietly, Nick's arm around her waist. He would lead her to their bedroom and close the door, the look of love and desire on his face causing her to turn weak with longing—

"A penny for your thoughts." Nick's soft voice interrupted her daydream.

She laughed quietly. "Not worth it. I was only thinking."

"About what?"

"About what a pretty room this is. I hope you'll have many babies to bring home to it. But I hope you won't try to spoil them all to the degree you are . . . to the degree you're planning on." She had started to say "this one" but couldn't manage the words.

"Spoil them? I'm not going to spoil them," he said indignantly.

"Yes, you are," she insisted, walking over to the rocker and sitting down. She began to rock. "My parents died when I was very young. I went to live with my aunt, who wasn't exactly thrilled to have an eight-year-old thrust upon her. She fed me, clothed me, sent me to school, and did all the things that were expected of her, but there was one thing lacking in my life. She never loved me. When I was fourteen, I got my first job. Between school and working I had little time to spend under her feet, so we got along better. When I was sixteen, I moved out of her house and into a little apartment behind the house of an elderly woman whom I worked for. I took care of Mrs. Swain's house and lawn, went to school, then worked six hours at night at a nearby clothing factory."

"I had no idea you came from that sort of background," Nick said quietly from the doorway as he watched her begin to rock faster. "The only thing you ever told me was that your parents died and you lived with your aunt."

Kayla shrugged. "I've never talked about it. Anyway, when I became eighteen, I received a small inheritance from my parents. I stuck it away in the bank, and after college I bought my own dress shop. I worked very hard, Nick, and I made that shop successful. I probably would still be there today if it hadn't been for Tony . . . ." She paused and blinked. "Well, what I'm trying to say is, I don't want my child handed everything on a silver platter. Naturally I would never want him to go through what I did, but I want him to live in the real world, Nick. A world where you earn what you have and it isn't simply given to you. I'm sure you have no idea what I'm talking about, do you?" The sound of the rocker made a rhythmic click on the wooden floor as Kayla stared out the window at the gathering twilight.

"I never wanted for anything, if that's what you mean. But my parents didn't throw money around like it was water. Dad has poured his life's blood into the business, and he's taught me the value of a dollar. The Trahern money is the result of a lot of hard work, some very wise investments, and a steady hand at the helm. My son or daughter will be taught the same things, Kayla, but I do have enough money to make life a little easier for my child. Surely you wouldn't want to see it any differently."

"I don't want to see *it* at all," she replied firmly. "I really wish we didn't have to face a long-drawn-out battle over the baby, Nicholas."

"We don't. All you have to do is be reasonable," he returned quietly.

"Reasonable? What you mean is, all I have to do is give up my baby."

"No, I didn't say that. There are other alternatives."

"Marriage?"

"That *was* one." The stubborn muscle of Nick's jaw was working now as he stared past her toward the open window. He was in love with her, but he would be damned if he would ask her to marry him again until she showed some sign of loving him back! "But you've ruled that out!"

If he had asked her to marry him at that moment, she would gladly have flung herself into his arms and agreed. She was tired of fighting him, and yet her pride would never allow her to beg him to marry her. Apparently he wasn't going to renew his offer.

"So what's left?" she asked tiredly.

Nick sighed wearily. "You realize, don't you, Kayla, that if I wanted to, I could make this pretty dirty. With a good lawyer and enough money I could bring in witnesses who would not be favorable to you." He paused, then continued, "But I think too much of you to do that. What I am going to do, though, is this. If marriage is out of the picture, then as soon as the baby's born, I'm going to legally declare that the child is mine and ask the court to grant me reasonable visitation rights. I intend to fully support the child financially."

"Bring in witnesses! I haven't done anything . . . immoral, Nick!"

Nick's eyes grew cold. "I *said* with enough money I could do a lot of things, Kayla."

Kayla closed her eyes painfully. "That is going to be nothing but a headache for both of us, Nick. What happens when we both marry? I may want to move out of the state."

"Forget it! I'll never permit that, Kayla." His angry words shattered the night air.

"You can't stop me!" Kayla rocked faster, her thoughts tumbling together. "And suppose I *don't* get married. How do you think I'll feel when you and your . . . wife take my baby for weeks at a time."

"You're crossing too many bridges at one time. I don't have any intention of marrying right away," he snapped.

"You're not seeing anyone right now?" Kayla was mortified that she had blurted out her thoughts like that.

"You mean lately?" Nick looked surprised at the abrupt question. "Since I met you?"

"No, I meant since you reached puberty!" Kayla said crossly, avoiding his eyes as she continued to rock.

"Since I reached puberty . . . a few. Since I met you . . . no." He grinned.

"I bet it's disgusting how many women you've known in your sordid past," she mumbled grimly, jealousy nearly eating her alive at the thought of Nick with other women. All of the risqué stories she had heard about "Romeo" Trahern came closing in on her, raising her anger to a dangerous level.

Nick sighed and then walked over and knelt down beside her. "I don't know why in hell I'm going to bother trying to explain this to you, but for some reason I want to. You're right, I haven't always been an angel. When I was in college and for several years after, I led a pretty . . . carefree life. But never once did I make any promises, Kayla. When I went with a woman, she knew from the first that I wasn't interested in any long-term commitment. The ladies . . . um . . ." He cleared his throat, and Kayla could have sworn she saw a twinkle in his eye. "The ladies whom I associated with were usually in complete agreement with me on that score. At that time in my life I was out for a good time, nothing more."

"And I suppose you were accustomed to making a fool out of your . . . ladies," Kayla interrupted, "telling them things that weren't true. How many times were you 'Franklin,' Nick?"

Nick looked at her sternly. "Only once. And you're right again. At that time in my life I wouldn't have thought twice about using a ploy like Franklin to get a date with a lovely girl."

Kayla met his honest gaze. "And you wouldn't now?"

"They would have to cut my tongue out before I would ever play a trick like that again," he said with a grimace. "I've learned a painful lesson this time."

"It was rotten," she began.

"And conniving," he added.

"And miserable."

"And despicable, and all the other things you've hurled at me," he agreed. "But it's also in the past. I won't do it again. That's the only consolation I can offer you."

Kayla could feel the block of ice around her heart beginning slowly to melt as she gazed into his sincere gray eyes.

"Forgive me?" he asked carefully.

"Maybe." She grinned with intense relief.

"Okay." His eyes brightened. "How about the big question. Can you forget it?"

Could she forget it? That question had been on Kayla's mind constantly for the last few weeks. Would the lie Nick had told her always overshadow her feelings for him? "I . . . don't know," she admitted honestly. "I try, but there are times I feel so horribly resentful toward you. When I think of all the times you must have died laughing at the things I said and did. All the rotten things I used to say against Nicholas Trahern . . . all the things I called him." She blushed furiously.

"No, I didn't," he replied quickly, reaching out to touch her velvet cheekbone. "I only felt like a rotten heel."

"If you had only been truthful with me—"

"I know. But that's all water over the dam." What she said was true. Nicholas had said the same things to himself over and over again every long, sleepless night since he had met her. "Look at me, Kayla." He turned her face to meet his. "I've spent the last few months trying my damnedest to make you see that Nicholas Trahern, cad that he was, is deep down all the things you loved about Franklin. Can't you see, I'm the same man you were attracted to, the same man you willingly let share your bed and your life for that short time." His eyes grew solemn. "Those were the happiest days of my life, sweetheart. For thirty-six years I have looked for a woman who I wanted to love, and when I finally ran across her, I couldn't let her know how I felt because of one stupid indiscretion. Don't you think there might be some way we could start over, Kayla? Maybe if we began again . . . with no lies this time, we might be able to salvage what we once felt for each other."

"I don't know, Nicholas," Kayla broke in. It was so hard to deny him this request, but if they should fail to recapture what they once had, he would still be there to take her baby from her and with more vengeance than he felt now. She wanted to believe him so badly . . . but she couldn't rid herself of the persistent, nagging thought that he was trying to gain custody of his child

142

the only way he knew how: by wooing its mother into submission. And if she agreed to a marriage, should he ever ask again, it would only be one of convenience for Nicholas. A marriage he would eventually grow tired of and reject to go back to the life he had been accustomed to living. Kayla could not take that chance. She would be gambling with the only thing she had left in her life. Her baby. The stakes were simply too high.

Nicholas's hand dropped slowly away from her face, his eyes registering defeat. "All right. If that's the way you want to be, Kayla, I can't change it. I have my pride too, and I won't beg you. What you do with your life is up to you, but what you do with my baby's life involves me. You will never be completely free from me, so you might as well decide to make the best of the situation. I'll be around for a long time to come."

"I'm going to look for a man to marry who weighs two hundred and fifty pounds," she said grimly, "so he can come over and personally knock your block off, Nicholas Trahern!" Her temper finally exploded.

"As long as you're looking, you'd better up that weight by another fifty pounds. He's going to need it if he plans to take me on!"

"You don't scare me," she bluffed.

"Then maybe this will. I just *might* go out and find me a woman to marry who would be as mean as a snake to keep *you* under control. You think having to deal with me as a *father* will be tough, wait till you see what I'm going to turn lose on you as a *stepmother* to our baby."

Kayla shoved out of the chair and started toward him angrily. "You just try it, mister! You just try it!" The thought of having to share her baby with this maniac was bad enough without the added burden of another woman.

Nick grinned wickedly and rushed forward to pick her up in his arms, making her squeal with alarm. "Just a little reminder that I'm still bigger than you are, so you better start watching your step," he warned, walking out of the bedroom with her still clasped tightly in his arms. Kayla squirmed helplessly, achingly aware of the familiar smell and feel of him. It was all she could do to keep her anger alive and not wrap her arms snugly around his neck and let him carry her off to anywhere he desired.

"Put me down, you idiot!" she yelled as he strode through the house, ignoring her thrashing fists.

"No way. I'm going to take you down to the stables and lock you up with some of my horses," he threatened. "Maybe I can handle you better that way."

He opened the back door and walked outside with her. They were standing on a large covered patio facing a glistening oval-shaped swimming pool. The same kinds of late-summer flowers that Kayla had seen in the front of the house bloomed in large beds surrounding the pool. Overcome by her natural curiosity for the moment, she stopped her struggling.

"This whole place is gorgeous!" she observed reverently. "No wonder you fell in love with it!"

"Yeah. I'm bad about loving gorgeous things. Gorgeous little things that are starting to weigh as much as one of my horses." He winked, bringing her up closer to his chest.

"It's all your fault," she returned, a spark of combat still in her eyes. "And stop insulting me! If *your* baby wasn't getting to be such a little pig, I wouldn't be getting my appetite back so quickly."

"Remind me to have a talk with him when he gets here." Nick grinned.

Suddenly their laughter died as their gazes met, and they became acutely aware of each other. Nick's arms closed around her possessively.

"You feel good, did you know that, bossy?"

"As in cow? Or disposition?"

"Both."

"You're terrible." She smiled tenderly, hating the feeling of pleasure she was experiencing in his arms.

"No, I'm not. And if it takes me the rest of my life, I'm going to prove that to you," he said in a husky voice.

"Are you going to kiss me?" she asked expectantly, wishing fervently that he would.

Nick looked momentarily taken aback. "Do you want me to?"

"Yes . . . and no," she admitted softly, her pulse racing at the more than pleasant thought.

"Yes and no. Now, what kind of an answer is that? You either do or you don't."

Kayla lifted her shoulders impishly. "Hormones, I guess. At least that's what you always accuse me of." That was the only reason she could come up with for feeling so confused about him.

"Well, I'll tell you what." He brought her mouth close to his, barely brushing against the sweetness of her lips. "There's nothing in this world that I'd like better at the moment than to kiss you."

"So," Kayla teased, longing for him to complete the kiss, "what's stopping you?"

His breathing had become heavier as Kayla's arms crept up intimately around his neck.

"When I kiss you the next time, I want there to be no doubt whether you want it or not," he whispered. "When you're sure, you let me know."

Kayla froze, then dropped her arms irritably. "You're *not* going to kiss me?"

"Not today!" He started to walk down the path to the stables. "But I'll seriously consider it when you ask me again . . . Mommy." He grinned a lazy, self-assured grin.

"Don't hold your breath!" She reached out and punched him soundly on his broad shoulder.

Nick's delighted laughter rang out over the tranquil Arkansas hillside. Not that he wanted to, but he could wait because—he smiled smugly—he knew she would ask again.

The walk through the quiet stables was lovely. A serenity

145

came over Kayla and Nick as he led her to each stall and they peeked in at the horses. He kept his arm around her, explaining the various procedures for caring for the horses, showing her one of his favorites, who was about to give birth.

"When is the baby due?" Kayla asked in a hushed whisper as they stood at the door looking in at the expectant mother.

"Soon. Joseph said he expects it any day now."

"Is Joseph the man who takes care of the ranch for you?"

"Yes." Nick's hand came out to gently stroke the bay mare's bulging sides. "He's excellent with the horses, and I don't know what I would do without him. What's the matter, girl?" he crooned softly as the mare whinnied lowly. "Are you restless tonight?"

"Who takes care of your house?" Kayla asked.

"For the last few weeks I've been batching it. My housekeeper is away spending some time with her son and his family. Since I wanted to get the redecorating done, I told her to take some time off this summer. Besides, all I've done is sleep here since you've been so sick."

Kayla thoughtfully rubbed the mare's ears, commiserating with this animal who shared her condition. "You don't have to keep coming over every day," she told Nick. "I'm really beginning to feel like my old self."

Nick made no reply as he continued to stroke the horse's belly. He seemed to be lost in thought, to have completely forgotten her for the moment. "How would you like to name Sheba's foal?"

Kayla laughed quietly. "I wouldn't know how to name a racehorse. I'm having trouble coming up with a name for the baby!"

Nick turned to face her. "That shouldn't be too hard. I'll help you."

"Oh, no, you don't! I don't want our baby named something like Daddy's Bouncing Baby Boy," she teased, remembering one of the names she had read on her racing program.

146

"I couldn't even give a *horse* that name," Nick scoffed. "There's a rule about how many words and letters you can use when you name a horse. Does the same thing apply to naming babies?"

"I don't think so. Besides, I like the name Jared."

Nick thought for a moment. "Jared Nicholas Trahern. Not bad."

"I don't saying anything about *Nicholas Trahern,*" Kayla scowled.

"I'll make a deal with you. We'll name it Jared Nicholas Trahern if it's a boy, and Kayla Gayle Trahern if it's a girl. Gayle was my grandmother's name," he told her.

"Kayla Gayle? I don't know, Nick. I hadn't planned on naming it after me."

"Well, I had. I like your name," he said matter-of-factly.

"Kayla Gayle. Well, I'll think about it."

"I really don't care if it's a boy or a girl," Nick concluded, giving the mare one last pat, then shutting the half door to the stall. "I just hope it has its mother's good looks and its daddy's brilliant brains and winning personality."

"Your humility overwhelms me," Kayla observed with a laugh as he draped his arm around her and led her out of the stable.

"No humility involved. I'm simply an honest man."

"Ha!" Kayla grinned but snuggled closer to his side. Honest or devious? That was the question foremost in her mind as they walked casually back to the house under the star-studded sky. Why couldn't she make up her mind which one he was?

"Nick, were you serious when you said"—her voice grew smaller—"when you said you haven't been seeing anyone else . . . for a while?" For some reason that was very important to her tonight.

"No, I haven't been seeing anyone else. When would I have the time?"

"I don't mean to interfere with your personal life," she said

147

solemnly. "Now that I'm feeling better, you can . . . resume your own life."

"I plan on it," he said easily.

"Oh. You do?" Kayla frowned.

"Yeah." He sighed dramatically. "I'll have to start looking for a woman to live in my new house and help me take care of my new baby"—he paused—"on weekends and during the summer, of course . . . and protect me from the baby's two hundred and fifty pound stepfather, who's going to be after me for upsetting the baby's real mother all the time. That is, unless you've changed your mind and agreed to bypass all that fun and listen to reason."

"I haven't changed my mind. Besides, I haven't heard anyone asking me to change my mind." She held her breath, waiting for him to ask her to marry him again.

"You know the offer still stands," he said lazily. "Anytime you're ready, you just let me know."

"And in the meantime you'll be looking for that 'other woman'?" she prompted.

"You've got it. You're jealous, I hope?"

"Certainly not! Would you be jealous if *I* went out with someone else?"

"Certainly not!" he mocked. "Date anyone you choose. It will make you come to your senses sooner."

"Thank you, Mr. Trahern. I just might do that," she replied, wondering who in the world she could get to go out with her in this condition!

"Just be careful where you take my baby," he added, helping her into the Renegade once more. "And drink milk instead of beer, and be home, in bed, alone by nine o'clock every night. Other than that, you have my blessing to go out and have a good time."

Kayla looked at him in disbelief. "Have a good time? With those rules?"

Nick looked at her and shrugged. "That would be tough,

wouldn't it? Well"—he slid into the seat next to her and started the Renegade—"my advice is, stay home and forget the whole idea. If you're good, I'll bring my date by and keep you company for the evening."

"My, my. Jared or Gayle, Kayla, Nick, and 'the bouncer,' " she mused playfully. "Sounds like a lovely evening. I can hardly wait." She grimaced as he put the Renegade in gear and sped back down the road toward town.

CHAPTER NINE

The rented station wagon pulled into the Marriott Hotel the following Saturday and braked to a halt. Nick jumped out and went in, coming back a few minutes later with the keys to two rooms. Kayla couldn't help but be a little sorry that, true to his word, he had rented them separate rooms, but she managed to hide her disappointment.

"You *did* say two separate rooms, didn't you?" He grinned, swinging her door key in front of her face.

"That's right," she said calmly.

"Good! I did exactly as instructed," he pointed out. "Two rooms."

"Thank you," she responded coolly, ignoring his tormenting grin.

"Let's take our luggage to the rooms and then go on out to the racetrack," he suggested, opening her door and helping her out. Their plane had gotten in around ten A.M., and Nick had rented a car and driven straight to the hotel.

Within the hour they were turning off Mercy Road to the Ak-Sar-Ben field, a large complex located on three hundred acres in central Omaha.

"They have a coliseum, clubhouse, livestock building, and the finest barn area in Thoroughbred horse racing out here," Nick told her as they drove toward the racetrack. I want you to meet my trainer and groom and some of the jockeys who wear the Trahern colors."

"Do you mean the colors that are on their uniforms?" Kayla asked confusedly.

"Sure." Nick glanced at her. "The owner's silks."

"Of course," she replied dryly.

Nick reached over and patted her tummy. "Hang in there—you'll soon learn the lingo."

As the afternoon progressed she did indeed learn a lot of the lingo. Nick took her into the clubhouse and introduced her to a brilliant array of people, tossing out names and positions that flew right over her head. There was only one uncomfortable moment when Nick was introducing her to some of his friends. They had walked up to a distinguished group of gentlemen, and Nick had readily pulled her forward.

"Frank, Ron, I want you to meet Kayla Marshall, my"—he glanced at her swollen condition in consternation—"very good friend."

"How do you do," Frank said, reaching out to take Kayla's hand in his, his eyes running lightly over her slightly rounded stomach.

"Very well, thank you," Kayla responded, mentally kicking Nick's teeth out. Good friend indeed!

"Why did you tell that man we were friends?" she hissed under her breath as they continued through the clubhouse.

"I said we were *good* friends!" he said defensively. "Besides, what do you want me to do? Tell him the truth?"

"No. I just think we could think of a better word for me than *friend.*"

"How about *fiancée?*" he suggested helpfully.

She glared at him pointedly. "I *don't* think so."

"Mother? Sister, grandmother? You name it," he said agreeably, handing her a cold drink.

"How about *acquaintance* or *old friend of the family?*" she offered.

A few minutes later she was being politely introduced as a close acquaintance who was an old friend of the family.

The best part of the day for Kayla was when Nick took her to the training stables and introduced her to his trainer and groom. Both men patiently explained their roles and duties, adding considerably to Kayla's knowledge of what went on behind the scenes of Thoroughbred horse racing.

"How many times a day are the horses fed?" she asked, watching the groom ready one of the fillies to be taken to the paddock for saddling.

"While they're in training? Usually three times a day," the groom answered. "At four A.M., ten A.M., and four P.M."

"Your day must start pretty early," she said sympathetically.

"Yes, ma'am. Pretty early," he agreed with a flashing grin.

"How did My Pretty Baby do in her workout this morning?" Nick asked Sheldon, whom he had introduced earlier as his trainer.

"She's running beautifully today," he assured Nick. "No problems."

Post time was at two o'clock on Saturdays, and by the time Nick and Kayla had had a light lunch, it was time for the races to begin. There was a feeling of expectancy in the air as the race fans began making their bets.

"Here." Nick handed Kayla ten twenty-dollar bills. "Decide which horse you want to bet on, then get to the windows early."

Kayla glanced down at the wad of bills in her hand, her mouth gaping open. "Good heavens. What's all this for?"

"It's your mad money for today. Go have fun."

"You're crazy, Nicholas! I wouldn't bet that much money. Why, this would pay my rent and buy my groceries all month!"

He had already spent entirely too much on this trip anyway.

Her plane ticket, her motel room—always insisting on paying for all her meals. She sorted through the bills, then handed all of them back except one. "There. This is all I need."

"Twenty dollars?" he asked blankly.

"Sure. How many races are there?"

"With only twenty dollars, not very many for you," he observed dryly.

"I'll just bet two dollars until I run out," she reasoned contentedly.

"Wow, last of the big-time spenders," he marveled. "Have you figured out where your first two-dollar 'chunk' is going to go?"

"No," she mused worriedly, studying her program once more. "Will you help me?"

"I wouldn't miss this opportunity for the world. It's going to be one of the biggest challenges I've ever faced."

"What? Betting on a horse?"

"No, trying to stretch twenty lousy dollars over the next four hours!"

The afternoon turned out to be not only a challenge but one of the most enjoyable days of Kayla's life. They laughed, placed their two-dollar bets together, munched on hot dogs, drank Cokes and beer, and let their problems of the last few months disappear for the day.

Kayla's excitement grew to fever pitch as they approached the windows late in the afternoon to place their bets on a race that one of Nick's horses was running in.

"I think I'm going to bet four dollars on this one," Kayla announced grandly, in an effort to show her confidence in him.

"Four dollars!" Nick nearly choked on his drink. "Ms. Tightwad is going to blow four dollars on *my* horse!" he exclaimed disbelievingly.

"Cut the theatrics, Nicholas. I know my money's safe." She grinned, picking up her tickets. "I trust your horse."

"Aw," he sighed, putting his arm around her as they strolled back to their seats. "Lucky horse."

"He deserves my trust," she said pointedly. "Besides, look how much money he's made for you."

"Ha, ha, and double ha! If I were in this sport for the money, I'd be in bad shape."

"You don't win a lot of money?" she asked in surprise.

"Let's just say that I'm in it for the pleasure, excitement, and the love of the animals. Anything else is strictly speculation."

The roar of the crowd as the horses broke from the starting gate was deafening. Kayla's eyes became riveted on the horse wearing the Trahern colors of yellow and maroon and the number four. Nervously she watched as the horse ran in the middle of the pack, then slowly began to edge toward the inside rail.

"Oh, Nick, she's not going fast enough!" Kayla said with a groan, her hands restlessly toying with her tickets.

"Give her time," Nick said easily, displaying not the least bit of apprehension. "She breaks slow, but she'll make up for it in the last three eighths of a mile," he said confidently.

Kayla held her breath as Getha Leadout worked its way through the field, moving up slowly in position. The voice over the loudspeaker kept the crowd informed of the horses' positions, but Kayla noticed that Nick kept his eyes anxiously fixed on a monitor suspended from the ceiling.

Coming out of the final turn, the horses broke for the homestretch as the crowd surged to their feet in a deafening roar. Kayla and Nick both had to duck as one enthusiastic spectator threw his beer straight up in the air and jumped up and down as the horses streaked toward the finish wire.

Nick pulled Kayla over to his side and yelled, "Now watch your horse go!"

Sure enough, Getha Leadout seemed to find a new source of speed as the number-four jockey brought the horse neck to neck with the lead position. By this time Kayla was doing her own jumping up and down, trying to yell number four on to victory. She was unconsciously shredding her tickets into a million pieces, and they went fluttering wildly to the ground when she gave a triumphant shriek of joy as Getha Leadout streaked across the wire a good full length ahead of the second-place horse.

"She won! Getha Leadout won!" Kayla hurled herself into Nick's arms, hugging his neck with exuberance. "Aren't you excited? Your horse won!"

"I never doubted that she would." He smiled, closing his eyes as he pulled her closer to him, savoring the softness of her body pressing into his. "But I bet I'm not nearly as excited as you're going to be when you find out what you did to your winning tickets."

Kayla glanced down at her empty hand, then to the pile of rubble at her feet. "Oh, for heaven's sake! And that was four dollars' worth!" she said disgustedly.

Nick laughed and hugged her tighter. "I'll share my winnings with you!" he offered as he picked her up and whirled her around happily.

"Oh, Nicholas, I don't really even care! Your horse won, that's all that matters!" Suddenly she realized that she was in his arms. Her gaze came up to meet his, and the world around them faded into nonexistence. "Maybe you better put me down," she whispered a little breathlessly.

"Maybe I don't want to," he whispered back, bringing his mouth down to brush teasingly against hers.

A tiny whimper escaped her throat as his lips touched hers. It had been so long since he had kissed her, so long since she had been in his arms. "I thought you weren't going to kiss me until I asked," she admonished him as her hands came up around his neck and her fingers buried in the thickness of his tawny hair.

"You were getting ready to ask me," he said huskily, bringing his mouth down to touch hers again lightly. "I'm just trying to get back in shape. It's been a long time since I've had you in my arms. Too damn long, in fact."

"I don't know if I was going to ask you," she protested insincerely, growing weak at his touch.

"Well, you're going to now, or I'll end up asking you—"

"Nicholas!" A redheaded woman broke through the crowd, followed by a short, stocky man. Both of them were smiling, motioning to Nick. Nick swore quietly, burying his face defeatedly in Kayla's hair.

"I knew my luck was too good to be true," he murmured, refusing to release his hold on her.

"Nicholas Trahern! Where have you been lately?" The redhead breezed up and grasped Nick's arm as he stepped reluctantly away from Kayla.

"Janice. How are you?"

"Better since I've seen you," she breathed in a sexy voice. "I've been trying to reach you for the last six weeks! Why aren't you taking any calls lately?"

"Because he's a busy man," her stocky companion interjected, reaching out to shake Nick's hand. "How's it going, Trahern? Your horse just brought me in a bundle!"

"Hi, Pete. Glad it worked out for you. Pete, Janice, I want you to meet Kayla Marshall." Nick pulled Kayla to his side and placed a protective arm around her waist.

Janice surveyed Kayla's obvious pregnancy, then glanced up at Nicholas resentfully. "Glad to meet you, Kayla," Pete said and extended his hand to shake Kayla's.

"Where have you been lately, Nick?" Janice asked, ignoring Kayla's introduction.

"Busy. How are things with you?"

Janice's face took on a petulant look as Pete took over the conversation, quizzing Nick on the upcoming race. Janice stared at Kayla rudely, trying to ascertain her position in Nick's life.

"Let's all go out for a drink after the races," Janice broke in, interrupting the men's conversation. "Or maybe for dinner. It's been a long time, Nick," she pleaded, deciding simply to ignore the pretty pregnant woman by Nick's side.

"Sorry, Janice. Kayla's had a long day. I want to get her back

156

to the motel and let her rest. Maybe another time," Nick said politely.

Kayla was so grateful for Nick's refusal to have dinner with this odd couple that she nearly hugged him.

"We'll do that," Pete said, taking Janice's hand and steering her back in the direction they had come from. "Let's go, baby. The next race will be starting in a few minutes, and I haven't made my bet yet."

"You will call, won't you, Nicholas?" Janice persisted, unwillingly following Pete.

"We'll probably be seeing each other around," Nick said consolingly, pulling Kayla in the opposite direction.

"One of your 'lady' friends?" Kayla asked pointedly.

"She used to be," he said easily. "Say, how would you like for *her* to be the baby's new—"

"Forget it, Nicholas," Kayla warned in an ominous voice.

"Well, it was just a thought." He grinned wickedly.

"A stinking one, I might add!"

"I might add that too. I never did care much for Janice," he admitted.

That little observation made Kayla's day considerably happier.

It was late afternoon when they left for the motel. Kayla had spent a wonderful day, coming out of the racetrack with a lot more money than she had gone in with. She had insisted on paying back the original twenty dollars Nick had given her, despite his indignant protests.

"You're going to have to learn the value of a dollar," she scolded as they got into the car and started toward the motel. "If it hadn't been for me, you would have blown a lot of money today."

"Or made a lot," he grumbled. "But I had fun. What about you?" He smiled at her tenderly.

"I had a wonderful day. Thank you."

"Are you tired?"

"A little." She leaned her head against the back of the seat and closed her eyes.

"We're going back to the motel, and you're going to take a hot bath and rest before we go to dinner," he told her firmly.

"I won't argue with that." Her mind skipped back to the way he had playfully kissed her this afternoon, and her stomach fluttered. She had welcomed that kiss and was acutely disappointed when it was interrupted by Janice and Pete. When they reached the motel, Nick unlocked her door, then placed one arm between her and the doorjamb. "You need anything?"

"No." Her stomach filled with butterflies at the way his eyes were hungrily devouring her, yet he made no move to touch her.

"I'm in the next room. All you have to do is holler."

"What do you want me to holler?" she teased coyly, feeling none of the animosity toward him she usually did.

"I'd probably get arrested if I answered that question," he replied lazily. "But feel free to holler anything you want."

"Thank you, I will." She waited expectantly for him to kiss her, but he didn't.

"I'll let you rest for a while, and then I'll give you a ring on the phone. We'll decide where we want to eat. Okay?"

"Okay."

He reached out and absently brushed a lock of her hair away from her face. "I've been meaning to tell you how pretty you are lately. I've always heard that pregnant women had a special glow about them, but I must admit I had never noticed it. To me, they always looked pudgy and miserable."

"And I don't?"

"No." His finger slipped down the side of her face longingly. "You look very lovely and very desirable."

Her pulse leapt at the look in his eye. This was an entirely different man from the Nick *and* the Franklin she had known. And the look in his eye was the look of a man who was in need of a woman. Not just any woman, but the woman he loved.

"I think you'd better go take your bath," he said, letting his hand drop back to his side, "before I make a fool of myself."

Kayla felt such disappointment, it nearly took her breath away. For some strange, unexplained reason she had wanted him to come in with her, to take her in his arms and make love to her for the next week! She would not have uttered a single word of protest had he done just that. As she watched him walk to the room adjoining hers and slip the key into the lock, she wanted to call out and tell him how she felt, but somehow she couldn't push the words out of her restricted throat. Surely if he had loved and wanted her, he would have told her so. She would be a fool to push him. Still, how many times had she stubbornly told him she wanted nothing to do with him? Strange, but that was no longer true. Yes, he had made a mistake and lied to her. But she had made plenty of mistakes herself. She had to begin to put her trust in someone, sometime, and Nick was the only one she wanted to commit that trust to. If she did marry her baby's father, could that marriage withstand its shaky start and survive to become a happy, long-lasting one?

She lay soaking in the bathtub, mulling over all her puzzling thoughts for a long time. When she finally toweled herself off, her skin was rosy and pink, and she was completely relaxed after the long day's activities.

Liberally dusting herself with a fragrant powder, she surveyed her blossoming figure. Remembering Janice's sleek figure, she wondered fleetingly what chance she had of catching Nick's attention in her condition.

A soft tap on the door adjoining her bedroom interrupted her musings. Slipping into a soft, clinging robe, she unlocked the door and opened it.

"Hi." Nick lounged against the door, a towel wrapped loosely around his neck. "Did I wake you?" His eyes ran languidly over the blue robe, noting that the color almost perfectly matched her eyes.

159

"No. I just got out of the bathtub." She returned his look longingly.

"I didn't mean to bother you. I decided to clean up and then go down to the bar for a drink while you rested."

"Oh." She didn't know what to say. She wasn't tired now, but she didn't know if he would want her company at the bar.

"Did you happen to bring a *big* bar of soap? These tiny things they have at motels drive me crazy."

"Oh . . . yes, I brought one. Come on in." She turned and went into the bathroom, coming out a few minutes later with a bar of soap wrapped in a paper towel. "Here, you can keep it. I don't mind the small bars."

"You look refreshed and ready to go," he observed casually, taking the bar of soap from her.

"I feel great. Just a few sore muscles from jumping up and down all day." She smiled.

"Do you have a bottle of lotion?" he asked pleasantly as he sat down on the bed and looked at her.

"Lotion? I think so. Why?"

"I thought I'd offer my services as a masseur," he said nonchalantly.

"Oh . . . that's not necessary." She blushed.

"I know it's not. It would be my pleasure. Get the lotion and come here."

"Nick—"

"Get the lotion, Kayla." His voice was soft and persuasive in the quiet room.

A few seconds later she found herself handing him the lotion with trembling fingers.

"Stop looking at me like I'm the big bad wolf." He grinned, taking her hand and pulling her onto the bed with him. "You're going to enjoy this, I promise."

Kayla had no doubt she would!

"Slip your robe down," he urged, gently laying her down on her stomach. "Are you comfortable lying on your stomach?"

160

"I'm okay," she acknowledged, letting her robe slip down to her waist.

"I don't want our baby to have a pug nose," he quipped, uncapping the lotion and pouring a small amount into the palm of his hand.

"It won't," she assured him with a muffled giggle.

His large hands reached out and touched her bare skin, slowly smoothing the white lotion soothingly over her back. "Feel good?"

"It feels heavenly," she murmured as the tensions began to drain out of her body. The touch of his hands was not exactly soothing her, though. It was sending her pulse skyrocketing, and her body was responding in a scandalously shocking way.

"You tell me where it feels the best," he said quietly, massaging the small of her back where it seemed always to bother her the most.

"Right there," she murmured.

"Your skin's so soft," he marveled, running his fingers exploringly over the velvet moistness of her rosy flesh. "It's always amazed me how soft and sweet you feel and smell." Lean fingers slipped down the sides of her rib cage, barely touching the sides of her breasts. She moved uneasily, pulling away from him slightly.

"Don't get skittish," he said in a low, soothing voice, and his hand slid down to the backs of her legs and gently kneaded the tired spots. "Are you afraid of me?"

"No," she whispered, her breathing becoming more irregular. "I'm not afraid of *you.*" It was herself that she was concerned about.

"Do you think I'm going to try to make love to you?" Kayla was amazed at how calmly he said it.

"I . . . I don't know. . ."

"I told you once before, Kayla, I have my pride too. You won't hear me say the words."

161

Kayla's heart sank. Was she going to have to ask him?

Reaching for the bottle of lotion, he poured more out onto his palm and put the bottle back on the nightstand. With deliberate slowness he peeled away her robe, tossing it over onto the chair beside the bed.

"Nick," she protested, reaching for the sheet to draw it up over her bare bottom.

One large hand blocked her effort, gently placing her arm back down by her side. "Just relax and enjoy this, sweetheart. I'm not seeing anything I haven't seen before," he assured her, bringing his hands back to their task. In a few minutes he had covered every inch of her backside with the thick white lotion, gently massaging away the aches and pains.

Gradually, his motions become more lingering, his breathing more ragged; then he tenderly flipped her over onto her back and with a low groan buried his face in her soft, fragrant neck. "I hope I'm making you feel better, because you're making me ache all over, lady," he whispered.

"We shouldn't be doing this, Nick," she said gently, her arms holding him close to her.

For a moment he pulled away from her, his eyes running the length of her body. Then he placed both hands on her swollen abdomen and brought his mouth down to place tender kisses around her navel. "Hello, baby," he murmured softly. "This is your daddy talking to you now. I want you to know I'm here and I love you." His hands tightened possessively as he kissed his way back up her body, pausing to nuzzle the warmth of her breast. "Are you going to breast feed our baby?" he asked languidly.

"I've been thinking about it. Dr. Walters thinks it's a good idea."

"I think so too," he told her, his hands reaching for the lotion once more. "Even though these bring me great pleasure, I think the good Lord meant them to be more than decorative," he

162

murmured, lavishly spreading lotion on the objects of discussion.

Pausing for a moment, he suddenly leaned down, and they kissed deeply, the first real kiss they had shared in a very long time. He had kissed her teasingly this afternoon, but this was a kiss of passion and unconcealed desire. His tongue searched hungrily for hers as his hands closed around her breasts, and she willingly responded to his advances. Exchanging heated kiss after heated kiss, they lay pressed tightly against each other, both fearing to speak.

Kayla's hands reached out to work his shirt up his back, trying to remove the cloth barrier that was between them.

Understanding her need, he got up and stripped off his clothes, then stood for a moment, letting her drink in the once familiar sight of his aroused body. The look of desire that passed between them spoke more than any words they could say, and as he took her in his arms once more Kayla knew she loved Nicholas Trahern with all her heart.

Whatever had happened was in the past as far as she was concerned. If Nicholas didn't love her, only loved her baby, then so be it. She loved him, and in time maybe he could grow to love her in the same wild, impetuous way she loved him. She was going to work very hard at making sure he did!

With a low moan Nick released her, his breath coming in short spurts. "We're going to have to slow down some," he cautioned raggedly, stilling her wandering hands.

Kayla wanted nothing more than to lose herself in the sweetness of his love, but she still had to wonder where all this was leading. Nick had distinctly said she would *not* hear him ask her to make love. Was he waiting for *her* to make the suggestion? Not that she wouldn't . . . eventually, but it did hurt her feelings to think he would make her practically beg!

Slipping her hands into the blond hair that grew in lush thickness across his broad chest, she kissed him lovingly, her tongue teasingly searching out all the old familiar places that had driven him wild in the past. Playful kisses soon turned into ravishing ones as they tried to curb their passion but failed.

Nick shuddered and a moan escaped from his lips as he pulled away from her, and he reached for the bottle of lotion once more.

"Nick!" she gasped, every fiber of her body longing for him. "I don't *want* any more lotion rubbed on me, I want—"

His mouth cut off her impatient words. They kissed hotly as Nick laid her down gently. Then, taking a bit of lotion on his finger he began to write on her leg.

Kayla sat up and looked at her leg, and a smile began to form on her lips. Nick pointed to her leg, his silvery eyes aglow with passion. She read his words silently: "Hi, my name is Nicholas Franklin Trahern." Her eyes misted as she noticed that he had deliberately underlined *Franklin*. She reached down and wiped the lotion from her leg, then took the bottle from his hand and wrote, "Hi. I'm Kayla Marshall."

Again the lotion was erased, and Nick took the bottle. "I'm sorry I lied to you, Kayla Marshall," he wrote.

The bottle returned to Kayla.

"I know. You're forgiven" was the cleansing message this time.

Nick reached over and kissed her sweetly and lingeringly, then rubbed the lotion into her leg once more. This time his message would have melted the coldest of hearts. "I want you, Kayla."

"I want you, too, Nick," she wrote with shaky hand.

"Nick?"

He looked up from his scribbling, his eyes asking a silent question.

Kayla nodded, tears forming in her blue eyes. It was Nick she loved, not Franklin.

"Nick wants to make love to you" he wrote once more.

Again she nodded, the tears slipping down her cheeks. She wanted that too.

"We won't hurt the baby, will we?" he whispered hoarsely,

pulling her down into his arms. "I don't want to hurt you or the baby," he said, moaning as his mouth covered hers, no longer able to control his trembling need for her.

"No, we won't hurt me or the baby," she whispered through a veil of tears, impatient for his touch.

They came together in a hot surge of eagerness, reminiscent of the days when there had been nothing between them but love and the uncontrollable need to be with each other.

"I'm so sorry, Kayla. I'm sorry for everything that's come between us," he gasped, clasping her tighter as he drew her body close to his.

"I know you are," she whispered, sharing his agony and knowing that the road ahead of them would not be an easy one.

"I do want this baby, Kayla. Let's not fight about the baby again."

The baby. Was that all he wanted after all? It seemed to be uppermost in his mind at the moment.

"We'll work it out, Nick. Somehow we'll work it out," she promised.

"I'll never let you go, Kayla," he breathed against her mouth, his passion finally overriding his words.

Conversation ceased to exist as did the world as he joined his body with hers, both of them pouring out their love for each other in every movement, every murmur of endearment, every devouring kiss. It seemed so right to Kayla, this intense, fervid, poignant love she felt for Nicholas. Could a love so right be wrong? Long before they rushed toward the peak of that magical mountain, then tumbled swiftly over the top, she had answered her own question. No, her love was not wrong. Impractical maybe, but never wrong.

She honestly couldn't tell if Nick returned that love. Certainly he returned her desire. That was obvious as he held her tightly in his arms, his large frame shuddering with the intensity of the moment. He had said he needed her, wanted her. Wasn't that love? Maybe, but she needed to hear him *say* he loved her.

"Are you all right?" he rasped, relieving her of his weight as quickly as possible.

"Yes, I'm all right," she assured him, a trifle irritated. Secretly she wanted to pinch his head off for always worrying so much about the baby! She wanted to lie in his arms for hours like they used to do after they had made love, kissing and whispering love words to each other. Now all he seemed to want to do was make sure they hadn't hurt the child.

Nick pulled her face around to meet his. "What's the matter?"

"Nothing!"

"There is too. Did I hurt you? I'm sorry if I did, but damn, it's been so long—"

"You didn't hurt me!" she snapped, rolling away from him and going into the bathroom.

He was lying quietly, staring up at the ceiling, when she came back. He moved over and let her slide in beside him, reaching to pull her close to him.

"Are you sure you're all right?"

"I'm fine!"

Nick sighed and buried his face in the clean fragrance of her hair. "I'll be glad when you have this baby and things return to normal," he confided. "Those screwed up hormones of yours give me fits."

Kayla stiffened, offended by his words. Screwed up hormones indeed! Was it too much to expect some romantic pillow talk from the man you had just made love with?

"Are you hungry?" he asked, nuzzling her ear playfully.

"No, I'm just sleepy."

"Umm . . . me too. Let's forget dinner for the next few hours." He yawned and plumped his pillow up more comfortably. "Wake me up in a couple of hours."

"Wake yourself up," she said crossly. "I may want to sleep more than a couple of hours."

"I'll make it worth your while to give up a little sleep," he growled suggestively, kissing the graceful curve of her neck.

"Leave me alone, Nicholas." She shrugged away coldly.

Nick looked surprised, then resignedly covered them both back up again. "As I said, I'll certainly be glad to get the old Kayla back," he murmured.

"You may not get the 'old Kayla' back," she snapped.

"Yes, I will," he mumbled confidently, his large frame snuggling down next to hers.

"You just want *your baby*," she accused resentfully.

"And *my Kayla*. Now, stop looking for a fight and go to sleep. The baby needs its rest. Oof!" The air whooshed out of him as Kayla angrily punched him in the stomach with her elbow. "Good grief, why did you do that?" he exploded, crawling off the bed and reaching for his pants.

"Where are you going?" she demanded.

"To my *own* bed!" he said indignantly. "I have the feeling I'm not welcome here at the moment."

"Yes, you are! You get back in this bed this minute, Nicholas Trahern, you ratfink!" she screamed.

Nick dropped his pants and looked at her in exasperation. "All right! Don't get so upset!"

Tears welled up in her blue eyes as she threw herself back down on the pillows, unable herself to understand her swift changes of mood. Nick draped his trousers back over the chair and patiently crawled back into the bed, taking her tenderly in his arms. He didn't know what to say to her; he merely held her close and let her sob out her frustrations. He wasn't overly concerned with her moods. The baby book said there would be days like this one too. Personally he couldn't wait until the day came when he could take that damn little blue book and dump it in the nearest garbage can!

As much as he hated the thought, he knew he was going to have to give her some breathing room. He loved her, and he had done everything within his power to prove that lately, but she failed to realize just how deep his love was. Now he was going to have to force her into that realization.

"Kayla, listen to me." He turned her tear-streaked face up toward him. "I'm going to ask you one last time. Are you going to stop this nonsense and marry me, or not?"

This was the worst possible time Nick could have picked to ask for her hand in marriage. At the moment she was sure his only love was for the baby she was carrying.

"No! I won't marry you."

"Okay, then I don't see any point in going on like this." Nick put her trembling body away from his resolutely.

"What do you mean?" she said, sniffing.

Nick avoided her blue, limpid gaze, afraid he would never be able to go through with his plan. But if she *was* serious and really didn't have any intention of marrying him, then this was the time to make the painful break.

"I mean that if that's the way you want it, I'm tired of fighting with you." Nick slid out of bed and started dressing. "I'm taking you home first thing in the morning. Now that you're feeling better, I won't be coming around to bother you anymore. There'll be no need for us to see each other until the baby's born."

Kayla's heart leapt at his cold words. "You're walking out on me and the baby?"

"Not on the baby. When the baby's born, I still plan on doing all I've said I'd do. But if you stubbornly refuse to marry me, then I see no reason for me to make a fool of myself and grovel at your feet." His gaze met hers painfully. "When you're ready to come to me—"

"I'll never come to you," she said angrily, feeling betrayed once again. "I only wish you'd told me that I hadn't made an absolute fool of *myself* by sleeping with—"

"No one made a fool of themselves," he growled, picking up

his shirt and stalking toward the door. "And no one's been hurt," he added softly. "Be ready to leave early in the morning."

"Don't worry, I will!"

He slammed the door heatedly as Kayla fell back down into the tumbled blankets and sheets and pounded her fists against the pillow in abject frustration, wondering where it would all end.

CHAPTER TEN

"What color do you prefer? Apricot or mauve?" Paula asked, casually leafing through a book she had had her face buried in all evening.

Kayla glanced up, then back down at her own book. "Neither one. Why?"

"Oh, just wondering," Paula responded mysteriously. "What *is* your favorite color?"

Kayla sighed and laid her book aside, unable to concentrate on the story. If she had thought the first months of her pregnancy were bad, it was nothing compared to the last few months. Although all traces of sickness were now gone, the loneliness that had entered her life seven weeks ago was nearly unbearable. Nick had not phoned, come by, or tried to contact her in any way since he had angrily brought her back home from Nebraska. At first her anger had matched his, but as the days drifted methodically by, her rage had dimmed, then faded entirely. Now the feeling that dominated her was one of misery, loneliness, and the aching need to see Nicholas.

If it hadn't been for Paula these last two months, Kayla honestly didn't know what she would have done. Forgetting their differences, Kayla had crawled to Paula like a wounded animal, hoping that she could tell her what to do or where to turn. Paula, though, hadn't done that. Instead she had let Kayla pour out her heart, weighing the pros and cons of marriage to Nicholas Trahern, yet failing miserably to come up with an answer.

October was now here and Kayla's body was growing more cumbersome every day. The baby moved almost constantly now, and as she lay in bed at night, her hand on her stomach, feeling the strong, steady kicks, she would think of the radiant smile on Nick's face the first day he felt the baby move. He had been so proud . . .

"Well. What's your favorite color?" Paula persisted.

"Color? I don't know, Paula. Why? Is it so important for you to know my favorite color?"

"It's not important. I was just making conversation," she said lightly. "What about blue?"

"No, I don't particularly care for blue." Kayla pushed herself off the sofa with a strangled grunt. She walked to the kitchen and poured herself a glass of ice tea, then stood looking out the window of her kitchen as she sipped from the glass. The trees were beautiful this time of year. The one big maple in her backyard was vividly alive with the colors of fall. This had always been one of her favorite times of year—she loved it when the days were warm and the nights crisp and chilly. Unwillingly her mind drifted back to Nick, and she wondered where he was right now. He had been true to his word. He had told her he would not see her again until she came to him, and he had meant it. Kayla had debated about going to him several times, yet her pride had held her back. The baby was all Nicholas wanted. Not its mother.

Walking back to the living room, Kayla noticed Paula was putting her sweater on, making preparations to leave.

"Are you going home?" Kayla asked, a surge of disappointment racing through her at the thought of another long, empty night ahead of her.

"Yes. I promised Doug I would fix him a decent meal tonight." Paula couldn't help but note the look of longing on Kayla's face. "Why don't you come with me? Doug can drive you home later."

"No. I'm not very hungry tonight. I'll make myself a sandwich, then watch TV. Thanks anyway, Paula."

Paula walked across the room and hugged Kayla with fondness. "I wish I could make things better for you."

"I know. And I can't thank you enough for all you've done for me, Paula. In many ways you have made things better," Kayla assured her, returning the hug with affection.

"All you'd have to do is go to him," Paula said solemnly, her big, round eyes gazing at Kayla seriously. "That's all he wants. Some tiny sign that you're willing to bend a little."

"He wants some sign that I'm willing to give him the baby, Paula. And I'm *not* willing to do that."

"Not true." Paula shook her head stubbornly. "He loves you every bit as much as he loves and wants that baby. You're just too stubborn to see it."

"If he loved me, he would never have given me up," Kayla said childishly. "He would have stayed around until the baby was born and—"

"And what? Begged you to let him marry you? Really, Kayla. Up until Nick met you, he wouldn't have asked a woman for a *date* twice unless she was something pretty terrific. He has *never* gone out of his way to court a woman, let alone cater to her whims. You just don't realize how different the man is since he met you!"

"Has he . . . is he . . . seeing anyone lately?" Kayla knew Paula would know if anyone would.

"Would it matter to you?"

"Of course it would matter to me," Kayla blazed, then quickly regained control of her temper. "I want him to be happy."

"Then I would suggest you get your fanny in gear and marry the man!" Paula said decisively, picking up her car keys and walking to the door. "You're going to wait around until the last minute, and he'll have to marry you on your way into the delivery room. Remember that old Doris Day movie where she was being rolled into the delivery room and the minister was marrying her to the baby's father?" She laughed.

"I remember." Kayla grimaced. "But that's only in the movies, Paula. I think I could pick a better time to get married than five minutes before my baby was born."

"Well, you'd better hurry," she warned. "December isn't that far off. By the way, I like that dress you're wearing. What color is it?"

Kayla looked down at her dress, unaware that it was anything unusual. "Mint green, I think."

"It's nice. Do you like mint green?"

"Paula, what is this thing you've got about colors tonight?"

"Nothing! I simply asked if you liked mint green!"

"Yes!"

"*Fine!* I'll talk to you later." Paula blew her a kiss and went out the front door.

Another two weeks dragged by as Kayla continued to fight her feelings for Nick. The sound of the phone ringing one Thursday night was a welcome relief. After picking up the receiver on the third ring she was nearly floored when she heard the familiar man's voice at the other end of the line.

"Is this still the prettiest girl in town?"

"Tony?"

"That's right. Tony. Are you surprised?"

Surprised wasn't quite the word Kayla would have used. His voice was a reminder out of a past that she honestly hadn't thought about in months.

"Where are you?" she asked with a shaky laugh.

"Right here in town! I have business here in the morning, so I flew in tonight. Can you meet me for a drink?"

"Well, I don't know, Tony," she hedged, thinking of his wife, Maggie.

"I told Maggie that the first person I was going to call when I got here would be you. She agreed wholeheartedly, Kayla. I'd love to see you. How about it?"

"I guess I could, Tony. Where are you?"

"Some bar out here near the airport. Wait a minute." He put his hand over the receiver, and Kayla could hear him asking where he was. "Listen, maybe you'd better name a place for us to meet. I don't think this is any place for you to be."

Kayla laughed. "Okay." She gave him the name of a popular cocktail lounge and promised to meet him there in an hour. As she hung up the phone she couldn't help wondering why Tony had called. She hadn't heard from him since they had broken up, and as far as she knew, he didn't know where she was living at the moment. Obviously he had inquired about her and found out she had moved to Little Rock.

An hour later she pulled her car into the parking lot of the cocktail lounge and got out. Walking into the dimly lit lounge, she looked for Tony, hoping that he had arrived before her. He had, and as she spotted him he rushed forth, taking her in his arms for a large bear hug.

"Holy . . . " He stood back and surveyed her ballooning figure. "What is all this?"

Kayla grinned, then blushed prettily. "Kind of overwhelming, huh?"

"How many have you got there?" he teased, draping his arm around her and walking her to the table he had reserved earlier. Kayla didn't think a thing about Tony's affectionate ways. He had always been affectionate toward any woman he was around.

"I think only one, but it must be a very large one." She sighed, sitting in the chair he was holding out for her.

"Gosh, but you look good," he told her, his eyes sparkling sincerely. "It's been a long time!"

"Yes, it has. How are Maggie and the baby?"

"They're both fine. Just fine. Maggie gets prettier every day, and Tony, Jr. looks exactly like me!" he said proudly, fishing in his pocket for his wallet.

For the next five minutes they looked at baby pictures, both of them exclaiming about how cute Tony, Jr. was.

"Do you think I'm just prejudiced, or is that really the cutest baby you ever laid eyes on?" Tony asked seriously, his buttons about to pop of his shirt with pride.

"He's a beautiful baby, Tony. You sound very happy," she assured him.

"I am, Kayla. Happier than I deserve to be," he confessed solemnly.

Kayla reached across the table and took his hand. "I'm glad, Tony. I really am."

"That's why I wanted to see you, Kayla. I told Maggie I have never felt right about what happened between us . . . and I just had to see you again to be sure that your life was as happy as mine is. You don't know how relieved I am to see you all fat and sassy, carrying a baby of your own." He sounded tremendously relieved. "Who's the lucky guy?"

"The lucky guy—" Kayla's happy facade crumbled, and tears sprang to her eyes. She was mortified that she was going to break down in front of Tony, but she could sense it coming. "Excuse me, Tony," she mumbled, blindly fumbling in her purse for a tissue.

The tears started rolling down her cheeks unchecked as Tony hurriedly withdrew a snowy-white handkerchief from his pocket and handed it to her. "I gather I said something wrong?"

"No. I have these silly bouts of crying all the time," she snuffed, wiping ineffectually at the salty wetness. "I hope you don't think I'm crazy."

"Not at all. Maggie bawled for three fourths of her pregnancy! I was so happy when she finally had the baby, I could have shouted," he said sympathetically, trying to help her mop up the tears. "Here, let me get you a drink." Tony motioned for a waiter and gave him an order for a glass of white wine. "Now . . . you want to tell me about it? I know tears are just a sign of pregnancy, but there's usually something bothering the mommy to bring them on." He smiled at her tenderly, sensing that in this case there was indeed something bothering the mommy.

Tony had always been a good listener, and suddenly Kayla found herself pouring out the whole story of the past seven months. Amidst tears of recrimination and self-pity Kayla told Tony all about her love for Nick and the frustration it had brought her. Tony was still a good listener, and he let her spill her heart out to him, stopping her only occasionally to question her about some minor detail.

An hour later she was still sniffing but feeling that a tremendous weight had been lifted from her shoulders. It had been marvelous therapy to tell her problems to someone other than Paula. Paula had been a saint, but she was definitely biased in Nicholas's favor.

"So the question is, do you want to marry this guy and give the baby a name, or do you struggle through it all alone?" Tony summed up a few minutes later.

"Not exactly. The problem is Nick wants to marry me for the baby's sake, and I want him to marry me because—"

"Because he loves *you*. Right?"

"Right." Kayla blew her nose daintily on his handkerchief.

"Sounds to me like he loves you," Tony said reasonably. "Most men wouldn't have taken the time and gone to the trouble to see that you were taken care of when you were so sick."

"You would have," Kayla reminded him with a sniff. "As I recall, you said you didn't love Maggie when you married her. Like Nicholas, you felt a responsibility toward your baby."

Tony's fingers played restlessly with the napkin under his drink. "At the time I was very much in love with you, Kayla. I was torn between responsibility and love. But I have never regretted the decision I made. Maggie is one hell of a woman,

176

and I love her very deeply now. It has worked out beautifully for us. Our only regret was the way your life was torn up."

"I can't say that I didn't go through a pretty rough time, Tony, but now, since I met Nick—"

"You realize that love can find you in very strange ways?"

"Yes," she whispered softly.

"This Nicholas. He wouldn't happen to be around six one or two and have blond hair, would he?" Tony inquired abruptly.

Kayla glanced up at Tony in surprise. "Yes. Why?"

"Because unless I miss my bet, he walked in about ten minutes ago with a couple of other guys, and he's been sitting at the bar staring daggers at us ever since," Tony replied calmly, reaching for his drink and taking a casual sip.

Kayla's eyes flew over to the bar and encountered a frosty silver stare. "Oh, my gosh. It is Nick," Kayla mumbled, turning her head away quickly in embarrassment. "I hope he didn't see me!"

"Are you kidding? He hasn't taken his eyes off you since he walked through that door."

"I think I'll go to the ladies' room," Kayla said uneasily, hoping that by the time she returned, Nick would have gone.

Tony stood as Kayla slipped out of her chair and made her way hurriedly across the dimly lit room. The ladies' lounge was in the far rear of the building, safely away from the crowded bar.

Twenty minutes later she could think of no possible further reason to stay in the small room, having combed her hair and put on lipstick until she was sure the attendant thought she was a little weird. Stepping out cautiously, she peered around a potted palm, checking the bar area. A sigh of relief escaped her as she noted that the stool Nick had been perched on was now empty.

"Looking for someone?" an angry masculine voice asked from behind her. She whirled around.

"Nicholas! I thought you had left," she said irritably.

"Not on your life. Who's the man you're with?" he snapped curtly.

"None of your business," she snapped back and started to push resentfully by him. After all these weeks of leaving her alone to brood, he had nerve to suddenly reappear and demand to know who she was with!

"Oh, no, you don't." He reached out and grasped her arm, pulling her back into a dark alcove. Both arms came out to trap her between the wall and himself. "Now. Who is the guy?" he asked again tensely, that stubborn muscle on his jaw working tautly now.

"Tony," she spit out, trying to ignore how close his face was to hers and the smell of his familiar soap and aftershave.

"Tony?" Kayla could see the struggle on Nick's face to place the name. It took only a few seconds for grim recognition to replace the look of puzzlement. "Tony! The creep you used to be engaged to!"

"That's right. Now get out of my way!" Kayla pushed heatedly against the granite wall of his chest.

"What in hell are you doing with him?" Nick reached out and trapped both her flailing wrists in one hand.

"I don't owe you any explanation of who I see," she said, still seething but abandoning her struggles for the moment.

"You think not! Well, you're wrong, Kayla. What does that bum want? Surely he isn't wanting a reconciliation with you in your condition!" he fumed, gripping her wrists tighter.

"You're hurting me!" she said between clenched teeth. "Let me go!"

Nick fought to control his anger, loosening his grip on her very slowly. Kayla was surprised by his hot surge of temper. She had never seen him this angry. On the contrary, he was usually a pretty mild-tempered person.

"All right, I want you to march your little tush right over to that table and tell him to kiss off! Is that clear?"

"Kiss off! Are you mad? I'm not about to tell Tony—"

"Fine. Then I will." Nick whirled and started toward the table where Tony was sitting, his eyes blazing.

"No!" Kayla reached out and latched onto his tweed sports jacket, pulling him to an abrupt halt. "You're not going to go over there and make a scene!" she pleaded.

"Then you're going to tell him you're sorry, but *you* have to leave," he told her ominously. "And I don't mean later. I mean *right now!*"

"Where am *I* going?" she asked crossly.

"I want to talk to you," he replied sharply, straightening the cuffs of his shirt with short, aggravated jerks. "I'll wait for you outside. And, Kayla, don't try anything cute. I'm not in the mood for it tonight," he warned.

Making her hurried apologies to Tony, Kayla explained the situation and told him she would love to hear from him and Maggie soon. Tony assured her that she would and wished her the best of luck with Nick. Kayla laughed shakily, wondering what awaited her when she left the cocktail lounge. Nick had been in a nasty mood, and she anticipated a very unpleasant evening.

The night was chilly as she stepped out of the lounge and slipped her arms into the light jacket she had brought with her. Nick's red Ferrari squealed up to the curb, and he reached to sling the door open, motioning for her to get in.

"I have my car here," she protested as he pulled her into the car and peeled away from the curb.

"I'll send someone over to pick it up later," he barked.

They drove for several minutes without exchanging a word. The lights from the dash gave Nick's angry face an almost sinister look, making Kayla very uneasy.

Finally summoning up the courage to speak, she asked quietly, "What did you want to see me about?"

"Why were you with Tony tonight?"

Kayla sighed in exasperation. "Because he called earlier and wanted me to have a drink with him. How did you know I was at that lounge?"

"I didn't. I was there with a couple of business associates. I had no idea you would be there with your . . . boyfriend!"

"Good heavens. He's not my boyfriend, Nicholas. He's very happily married and has a child of his own now," Kayla said patiently, losing all desire to argue with him. She was suddenly just happy to be near him once more.

"He's got his nerve, asking you out for a drink," Nick stewed, shifting gears angrily. "If he's so damn happily married, where's his wife?"

"At home, I suppose. He's here on a business trip. And she knew he was going to call me. Where are we going?" she demanded as Nick cursed, then swerved to miss a car in front of him.

"I'm taking you home!"

"Thanks! But suppose I don't want to go home? Tony and I were talking—"

"I don't give a damn what you and *Tony* were talking about. What do you think I felt when I walked in there and saw you with that guy?"

"Nothing. I don't think you feel anything for me," she returned bluntly.

"Well, you're dead wrong! I felt plenty," he nearly shouted.

"You were probably worried about your baby, but you don't have to be. The baby is doing fine!"

"I know that. I talk to Dr. Walters every week," Nick barked curtly.

"You do?" Kayla looked at him suspiciously. "Why?"

"To see how you and the baby are doing. Why else?"

That *did* surprise Kayla. All these weeks she had supposed he couldn't care less how she was doing.

"And you're about five quarts of milk shy of what you should have drunk by now!" he said severely as he jerked the steering wheel to miss another car.

"Dr. Walters told you that? And slow down! You're going to kill us!" she yelled.

"No. Paula told me that!" he yelled back, ignoring her plea for sane driving.

"Paula . . . always Paula!" Kayla threw her hands up in the air disgustedly.

The sports car roared into Kayla's drive, and Nick slammed on his brakes with a screech. Turning the ignition off, he faced her defiantly. "Okay, Kayla, now I'm tired of fooling with you! I have patiently waited for seven long, unbearable weeks for you to come to your senses, and so far I've had no indication whatsoever that you have seen the light of day."

Kayla opened her mouth to respond, but one large hand clamped over it, preventing her words from escaping. "*No!* You're going to listen to me for a change," he said grimly. "I have *asked* you to marry me nicely. I have *pleaded* with you to marry me nicely. I have *waited* for you to marry me nicely. In fact, I am damn sick and tired of asking, pleading, waiting, *and* being nice! *You* are going to go into that house, pack a bag, then call a taxi, and come directly to my ranch. Now, I know you're wondering why I want you to come out in a taxi, but you have *got* to let me have one small shred of pride left, Kayla. At least I can always tell myself you *did* come to me, in a way. I'm not accustomed to getting down on my hands and knees and crawling to a woman, though in this case I'd crawl around the world if it would help. I know you don't believe I want you. I know you think it's only because of the baby that I want to marry you, but you're about as far out in left field as you can get. I want *you*. True, I want the baby, but I want *you* more. And I assure you I have *never* told another woman that in my life!" His gray gaze was solemn as he held her head, his hand clamped tightly over her mouth. "I want you to think back to the last night we spent together before all this fiasco began. I think you'll be able to come up with *the* most important thing I ever said to you. Not the lie. I want you to think of the truth I told you that night.

181

Think hard, Kayla. It's important. And when you remember, you call that taxi and come to me. I'll be waiting."

His free hand reached out and opened the door; then, releasing her mouth, he urged her out.

Kayla was standing out in the crisp night air, watching his red taillights disappear into the darkness before she realized that he was really gone. He had simply put her out in front of her house and driven off!

Slowly her mind ran over all he had just said to her. What *had* he told her that last night before she found out his true identity? She let herself into the dark apartment and without turning on the lights sat down on the sofa, her mind traveling back to six months ago. She had gone by Paula's office to have lunch with her, and they had discussed Kayla's love for Franklin. She had gone shopping that afternoon, wanting to look her best for Franklin that evening. He had taken her to dinner, and then they had made love. She remembered lying in his arms and his asking her to go away with him that coming Monday. She remembered the soft kisses, the hushed words they had shared. She could almost see his eyes, slumberous and solemn, as he had turned her face up to meet his and whispered . . . She blinked back the coming tears. He had whispered . . . A beautiful smile lit her face as she sprang from the sofa and ran toward the bedroom to pack her bag.

It was growing very late as the taxi pulled across the cattle guard and drove up to the ranch house. A bright harvest moon hung suspended in the sky, casting its silvery beams over the quiet, lush pastures.

Kayla paid the driver as he set her bag out on the drive. The house was dark except for one light burning in the back, where Kayla knew Nick would be waiting. As the cab pulled away she walked up to the door and knocked softly. When no one answered, she tried the knob and found it unlocked. Opening the door, she slid in silently, knowing deep in her heart that she would be welcome. After all, this was her home now.

She walked quietly through the darkened house, her way lit by the shafts of moonlight streaming through the windows. In the distance she could see the light coming from Nick's den. Love filled her as she pushed the door open and stood in the faint rays of the lamp.

Nick turned from the window he had been staring out of, a glass of scotch gripped tightly in his hand. His eyes ran lazily over her burgeoning figure as he stepped away from the window and held one large, comforting hand out to her. Stepping forward, she took it, placing her small one in its welcoming warmth.

"I've been waiting for you," he said softly, love radiating from his voice.

"Very long?" she asked, her voice becoming unsteady.

"All my life," he confirmed in a husky whisper.

"Well, I'm here now."

"It's where you should have been all along, you know."

"I know." Their eyes were hungrily devouring each other's features, only the crackling of the fire in the grate breaking the silence in the room.

"Did you remember what I told you that last night we spent together?" he asked urgently.

"Yes, I remembered." She smiled tenderly. "Though I *had* forgotten that night and what you told me," she admitted.

"I thought you had. Want to refresh my memory?"

"Have you forgotten?" she teased, her arms going up around his neck.

"Hardly. Since you're the only woman in the world I've ever said that to, I don't think I would forget a thing like that." He leaned down and feather-brushed her lips. "I want to hear you say it."

"You said . . . you loved me. You said that no matter what happened, you wanted me to remember that you loved me."

"Do you believe that? If you don't, step into that room down the hall that has that big old four-poster bed you wanted, and I'll be more than happy to prove how much I meant those

183

words," he offered huskily, his mouth touching hers again lightly.

"I plan on spending a lot of time in that big old four-poster bed," she assured him, "but I would kind of like to hear you say those wonderful words again."

"What? That I love you?"

"Yes," she returned shyly, her breathing quickening as his hand made its way up under her blouse and unsnapped her bra.

"You are really filling out," he teased, his hands closing over the voluptuous treasures he had uncovered. "Now, let's see, what were we talking about before you took my mind off our conversation?" He groaned as he kissed down the side of her neck, his hands roaming over her breasts lovingly. "Oh, yes, you want to hear me say, I love you."

"Do you mind?" she murmured happily.

"Not at all. I planned on telling you every day for the next fifty years anyway. I love you, Kayla," he said simply. "I will love you for the rest of our lives."

Kayla pulled away and surveyed his nose critically.

"What's the matter?"

"I was just checking to see if it grew any." She grinned, wrapping her arms around his neck once more.

"My nose hasn't grown, but I wouldn't make any bets about any other part of my body if I were you." He grinned back just before capturing her mouth with a smoldering kiss.

When they broke apart minutes later, Nick reached down and scooped her up in his arms hurriedly.

"One other thing I want to know before I start proving that everything I've tried to tell you for the last seven months was true," he said as he started carrying her toward the bedroom. "Are you *sure* we're going to have just *one* baby?"

"Positive," she replied happily, laying her head against his shoulder contentedly. "But maybe next time we won't be so lucky!"

"I want five or six, you know. Considering how mean and

184

cantankerous you get when you're pregnant, maybe it *would* be better to have them two at a time," he reasoned worriedly.

Kayla shrugged her shoulders, her mouth searching sweetly for his. "It's the hormones. Remember?"

Laying her down gently on the bed, he stood above her and began to slowly unbutton his shirt, the sight of the broad expanse of his hairy chest making her turn weak and trembly.

"There's one more thing I have to assure you of, and then I don't want it ever brought up again. I will always regret that we had to start our relationship with a lie, but I promise you there will never be another moment of deceit between us, Kayla. There's been a lot of long, lonely nights when I thought that one terrible mistake would destroy all the good things we had going for us. I know it will be hard for you not to remember that time in our life, but I'm going to work very hard to show you your trust in me will not be misplaced."

His shirt came off along with his trousers and then his briefs, and his smoldering gaze locked intimately with hers. Kayla ran her hands lovingly up his bare leg, marveling at how much love could fill her one small heart.

"I trust you," she replied with complete honesty. "Because if you *ever* lie to me again, I shall personally pinch your head off."

"Good. Now that we have that settled, come here, woman," he growled, crawling back onto the bed with her and enfolding her in his strong arms. "Oh, by the way." He stopped and propped himself up on his elbows and smiled angelically at her. "Did I mention we were getting married the day after tomorrow?"

Kayla smiled. "That's impossible. I couldn't plan a wedding that soon."

He cleared his throat nervously and picked up a lock of her hair to twirl around his finger absently. "Now, I don't want you to get upset, sweetheart, but I have something to tell you . . ."

Kayla's eyes narrowed. "What?"

"Well . . . now, look . . . you know I've always known you would eventually marry me . . . and time *is* running out. I didn't want to take the chance we'd have to hire a baby-sitter while we were on our honeymoon," he explained sheepishly, "so . . ."

"So?" Kayla sat up and glared at him distrustfully.

"So . . . Paula and I . . . well, now, honey, you can change *anything* you want except the color of the bridesmaids' dresses. They've already been ordered. The cake and the flowers have been ordered, and the church is reserved, but you can still select the music if you want to. Paula doesn't have to make a final selection on that until ten tomorrow morning."

Kayla gaped at him, her mouth dropping open wide. "You planned *our* wedding without even consulting me . . . without knowing whether I would accept . . ."

"Now, don't get upset, sweetheart. I *knew* I was going to get you to marry me one way or another. You had exactly thirty-eight more hours to make up your mind, or I would have personally come over and hauled you to the church in that ridiculous circus tent you're hell-bent on wearing!" he said firmly. "Doug and Paula were going to help me."

"But what about a wedding dress?" she protested, amazed that he would go to such lengths to arrange their wedding.

"It's lovely. You're going to be crazy about it," he assured her quietly, kissing her into submission. "Don't fight it, Kayla. I love you, and we're getting married Saturday afternoon at two o'clock . . . period."

"You . . . I can't believe you!" she sputtered lovingly.

"What's to believe? I told you, I can be pretty damn stubborn when it comes to something I want. And I've never wanted anything as badly as I wanted you," he whispered in a low, husky voice vibrating with emotion. "You're not really mad, are you?"

It took very little convincing to make Kayla agree to the forthcoming wedding, and minutes later Nick reached out and switched off the bedroom lamp, their passion overriding all else for the moment.

"Nick," she murmured against his plundering mouth. "Are those bridesmaids' dresses by any chance . . . a mint green?"

"I think so," he breathed raggedly. "Why?"

"No reason," she muttered a trifle irritably, returning her attention to the exciting man who lay in her arms.

But at the back of her mind a tiny, little voice sang out at the top of its lungs, "Paula, you wonderful, glorious, marvelous . . . *ratfink!*"

HISTORICAL ROMANCE
BITTERSWEET PROMISES
By Trana Mae Simmons

Cody Garret likes everything in its place: his horse in its stable, his six-gun in its holster, his money in the bank. But the rugged cowpoke's life is turned head over heels when a robbery throws Shanna Van Alystyne into his arms. With a spirit as fiery as the blazing sun, and a temper to match, Shanna is the most downright thrilling woman ever to set foot in Liberty, Missouri. No matter what it takes, Cody will besiege Shanna's hesitant heart and claim her heavenly love.

_51934-8 $4.99 US/$5.99 CAN

CONTEMPORARY ROMANCE
SNOWBOUND WEEKEND/GAMBLER'S LOVE
By Amii Lorin

In *Snowbound Weekend,* romance is the last thing on Jennifer Lengle's mind when she sets off for a ski trip. But trapped by a blizzard in a roadside inn, Jen finds herself drawn to sophisticated Adam Banner, with his seductive words and his outrageous promises...promises that can be broken as easily as her innocent heart.

And in *Gambler's Love,* Vichy Sweigart's heart soars when she meets handsome Ben Larkin in Atlantic City. But Ben is a gambler, and Vichy knows from experience that such a man can hurt her badly. She is willing to risk everything she has for love, but the odds are high—and her heart is at stake.

_51935-6   (two unforgettable romances in one volume) Only $4.99

HISTORICAL ROMANCE
HUNTERS OF THE ICE AGE: YESTERDAY'S DAWN
By Theresa Scott

Named for the massive beast sacred to his people, Mamut has proven his strength and courage time and again. But when it comes to subduing one helpless captive female, he finds himself at a distinct disadvantage. Never has he realized the power of beguiling brown eyes, soft curves and berry-red lips to weaken a man's resolve. He has claimed he will make the stolen woman his slave, but he soon learns he will never enjoy her alluring body unless he can first win her elusive heart.

_51920-8 $4.99 US/$5.99 CAN

A CONTEMPORARY ROMANCE
HIGH VOLTAGE
By Lori Copeland

Laurel Henderson hadn't expected the burden of inheriting her father's farm to fall squarely on her shoulders. And if Sheriff Clay Kerwin can't catch the culprits who are sabotaging her best efforts, her hopes of selling it are dim. Struggling with this new responsibility, Laurel has no time to pursue anything, especially not love. The best she can hope for is an affair with no strings attached. And the virile law officer is the perfect man for the job—until Laurel's scheme backfires. Blind to Clay's feelings and her own, she never dreams their amorous arrangement will lead to the passion she wants to last for a lifetime.

_51923-2 $4.99 US/$5.99 CAN

LOVE SPELL
ATTN: Order Department
Dorchester Publishing Co., Inc.
276 5th Avenue, New York, NY 10001

Please add $1.50 for shipping and handling for the first book and $.35 for each book thereafter. PA., N.Y.S. and N.Y.C. residents, please add appropriate sales tax. No cash, stamps, or C.O.D.s. All orders shipped within 6 weeks via postal service book rate. Canadian orders require $2.00 extra postage and must be paid in U.S. dollars through a U.S. banking facility.

Name _____

Address _____

City _____ State _____ Zip _____

I have enclosed $_____ in payment for the checked book(s).
Payment <u>must</u> accompany all orders.☐ Please send a free catalog.

FROM LOVE SPELL
HISTORICAL ROMANCE
THE PASSIONATE REBEL
Helene Lehr

A beautiful American patriot, Gillian Winthrop is horrified to learn that her grandmother means her to wed a traitor to the American Revolution. Her body yearns for Philip Meredith's masterful touch, but she is determined not to give her hand—or any other part of herself—to the handsome Tory, until he convinces her that he too is a passionate rebel.

_51918-6 $4.99 US/$5.99 CAN

CONTEMPORARY ROMANCE
THE TAWNY GOLD MAN
Amii Lorin

Bestselling Author Of More Than 5 Million Books In Print!

Long ago, in a moment of wild, rioting ecstasy, Jud Cammeron vowed to love her always. Now, as Anne Moore looks at her stepbrother, she sees a total stranger, a man who plans to take control of his father's estate and everyone on it. Anne knows things are different—she is a grown woman with a fiance—but something tells her she still belongs to the tawny gold man.

_51919-4 $4.99 US/$5.99 CAN

LOVE SPELL
ATTN: Order Department
Dorchester Publishing Company, Inc.
276 5th Avenue, New York, NY 10001

Please add $1.50 for shipping and handling for the first book and $.35 for each book thereafter. PA., N.Y.S. and N.Y.C. residents, please add appropriate sales tax. No cash, stamps, or C.O.D.s. All orders shipped within 6 weeks via postal service book rate. Canadian orders require $2.00 extra postage and must be paid in U.S. dollars through a U.S. banking facility.

Name_____
Address_____
City _____ State _____ Zip _____
I have enclosed $_____ in payment for the checked book(s).
Payment <u>must</u> accompany all orders.☐ Please send a free catalog.